the folded lie

jeremy cooper

the folded lie

●●●ellipsis

First published 1998 by
●●●ellipsis
2 Rufus Street
London N1 6PE
http://www.ellipsis.com
@ellipsis.co.uk

Edited by Rosa Ainley
Designed by
Jonathan Moberly
Printed and bound in
Great Britain by
Butler & Tanner Ltd at
Selwood Printing,
Burgess Hill

BRITISH LIBRARY
CATALOGUING IN
PUBLICATION
A CIP record for this
book is available from
the British Library

ISBN 1 899858 54 7

●●●ellipsis is a
registered trade mark of
Ellipsis London Limited

To Martin Knottenbelt,
in admiration

All I have is a voice
To undo the folded lie

W H Auden
1 September 1939

prologue

i

It was mystifying for the hundred or so Japanese lawyers engaged on the trial. And irritating.

Anger may have been the concealed feeling of many. Anger at the language of western law, adversarial, underhand. Anger at the pomp of the clerks in the antechambers and lobbies and interview rooms. Anger at the angled rules of admissible evidence. Anger at demands for the country's leaders to defend themselves, instead of laying flowers of shame on the grave of defeat. Anger at the immateriality of truth.

Kenzo Takayanagi watched almost all of it. Beginning on 3 May 1946 beneath the sodium heat of newsreel lights; ending in November 1948 in public humiliation. He watched and heard the twenty-eight accused men – five of whom were ex-prime ministers – indicted for crimes if found guilty of which the punishment was death. Saw seven of the nine judges present on the opening day put on sunglasses against the glare. Although there was no sun. Indeed no window in the walnut-panelled court, a few months earlier operations centre of the Ministry of War, several months before that the main lecture theatre of the Imperial Military Academy. Buildings in Tokyo were rationed. Food, it should in fairness be affirmed, was plentiful. American food freely dispensed, at the price of passivity.

Defence attorney Takayanagi was paid to watch, and occasionally to speak. Paid by the same hands which purged parliament and the civil service, on the personal orders of SCAP:

Supreme Commander Allied Powers, General Douglas Mac-Arthur, a man in a battered braid cap. The most experienced of all the Japanese in European law, a graduate of Harvard and Northwestern Universities and a member of London's Middle Temple, Takayanagi spoke English fluently enough for the Australian President of the International Military Tribunal to allow him a word or two in court.

Now and then. Reluctantly.

Yellow scum, His Honour Mr Justice Webb, the President, was overheard by the ranks of interpreters in their glass cubicles to say, barely beneath his breath.

Takayanagi declined to be affected by Webb's barbarism. He was used to legal crudity, knew the trade's tricks: the cut of wig to eschew smoothness; repetition of conjecture as fact. Although he tolerated life in the law, it would be a mistake to think Takayanagi did not care about the state of things. He did. He cared a lot. And showed it in ways people found strange, misinterpreting his meaning. The practice, for example, of wearing odd socks beneath his workaday tail coat and herringbone morning trousers, the mismatch seldom violent, two different shades of grey, maybe, or dark blue and black. A habit that annoyed his wife, perplexed his colleagues in the Tokyo partnership to which he had returned after the years abroad, and amused his secretary.

'Why do you do it?'

'Oh ... I don't know.'

'You must know.'

'Must I?'

His secretary blushed at her impudence. 'Forgive me, Takayanagi-san. Before the war things were ...' Her hands fluttered in the air in front of her chest. She was not young, the mother of four grown children, two of whom had died in the fighting in the Philippines. Her hands came to rest at her side, and she stared out of the window of the reinforced-concrete office block at their devastated city. 'Nothing will ever be the same.'

'I hope not!'

She stared at him. Then giggled, girlishly, when she saw the smile in his eyes.

'I'm serious. Didn't my socks warn you? I've always wanted things to be different. Now they'll have to be. We've no choice.'

In giving voice to such a thought Takayanagi did not wish to imply that he and his fellow elite were bound to do what the occupying army ordered, but that systematic change, one way or another, was irresistible. Far from being depressed by military defeat, Takayanagi sensed impending release, felt the weight of restraint which had built up inside him shift, inch towards the exit. The trickle of past hopes might – it was reasonable now to believe – become a stream, one day a river. He anticipated the achievement of something of distinction, was wary of telling even himself precisely what.

In conventional terms Kenzo Takayanagi had already achieved everything it was safe to desire: money, public prestige, a fine familial home. At fifty-nine years-old he appeared content with his place in an oriental world much improved, in his judgement, since the Emperor's new year confession that he was not, in actual fact, divine.

Fumi, Kenzo's wife, was less supportive of change, felt comfortable with the charade of male omnipotence.

'Has our Emperor gone crazy?'

'There's more.'

'Worse?'

'His Highness has declared false the Shinto doctrine of Japanese racial superiority.'

A sniff from Fumi. 'That was always a daft idea.'

'And Hirohito the infallible makes sense? How come we lost the war?'

'Criminal advisers. Bribes, factions, feuds.'

'Mightn't a god have noticed?'

'He's never been bright, has he?' Fumi replied. They laughed, in loving accord.

The Takayangis' house in the wooded hills above Zushi Station, in a southern suburb of Tokyo, had survived the war unharmed. Apart from decapitation of a terracotta finial at the entrance gate by flying shrapnel from the bomb which reduced to rubble the Ichikawas' home a hundred yards down the lane. Their house was large – larger than a childless couple needed, with a quaint walled vegetable and fruit garden behind the kitchen wing. In England in the early 1920s Takayanagi had lived in Surrey, off the Hogs Back, in a flat in a mock-Tudor mansion. The house butchered by the subdivision leaving its gardens intact, formal and at the same time – with the expansive control typical of Anglo-Saxons – both luxurious and homely. In his kitchen garden, one of its high walls flanking the lane, Takayanagi had transplanted a corner of the home counties to out-of-town Tokyo. Pride of place he gave to an asparagus bed, wildly prolific in the fertile soil of Honshu. Their kitchen was also semi-European, with gas hobs, twin sinks and a refrigerator, an expensive rarity in post-war Japan.

In every other respect no. 16 Ogawa-machi Dori was a traditional single-storey house, with overhanging eaves to the wide verandahs. Laid out symmetrically, the rectangular rooms opened onto contemplative views, the style – of life and space – serene. In the evenings husband and wife sat alone in their individual studies, she usually reading, he often practicing calligraphy. At night's close they retired together to the room furthest from the kitchen, where the trees of the forest – birch, spruce and mountain oak – encroached closest to their property. They listened to the wind in the branches while falling asleep.

At home Takayanagi's oriental mode of dress was immaculate. No odd socks. No socks at all. In winter, *tabi* and woollen leggings beneath full-length robe. In summer, bare feet – slim and long, in the creep of old age his veins beginning to swell blue across the bleached-beech colour of his insteps, his skin moist and smooth from the steam baths he took in the wooden hut at the centre of the larger of the two stone gardens. He wore his hair differently at home, aromatically oiled and combed straight back from his bald forehead. He looked himself: engaged and engaging, restlessly compassionate, a man who saw in the circumstances of each generation the need to improve on the past, not, in nostalgic self-deceit, to repeat the same old absurdities. To Takayanagi, being contemporary was fact, not polemical act.

The Takayanagis had continued to entertain guests at home every second weekend throughout the war, despite the irregularity of public transport and a government ban on recreational use of motor cars. Friends made their way on foot or pedal cycle up the winding lanes from Zushi Station, sure of a feast of fresh garden vegetables and, in season, steamed crayfish from the pools in the forest streams Kenzo baited and trapped. On those afternoons when the mists closed in early, guests from a distance were made welcome for the night, setting out next morning at break of day. Aware of the presence everywhere of tale-tellers, Kenzo prepared in advance his and his friends' defence against accusation of pacifist subversion – by ensuring that women and children were central to these weekend gatherings, and by committing not a word of discussion to paper.

Given the range of contradictory views expressed and the conflicting political mix of the guests it would have been difficult to identify the host's line of belief.

'On the other hand …' Kenzo said incessantly.

In reply to the question: 'What do you really think?' he became famous – amongst the regulars – for saying: 'I don't think, I dream.'

Those whom this remark irritated revenged themselves on his steamed crayfish.

Attendance at the Takayangis' weekend parties continued to demand discretion under the occupation. With senior responsibility in the defence of compatriots accused, amongst other things, of crimes against humanity, Kenzo had been allotted a car and chauffeur – black, from Lynchburg, Tennessee. Few of his friends were as fortunate. Many found themselves without work, dismissed by US Military Intelligence from positions of presumed responsibility for the war.

These were confusing times.

As the trial progressed Kenzo came to respect one of the judges above the others, Mr Justice Pal, a Brahmin from Calcutta, the last of the eleven to arrive in Tokyo. Kenzo decided to invite Pal to join them for lunch in Zushi.

'Your Honour?' he said, interrupting Pal's preoccupied passage up and down the courtyard, like a polar bear, during an adjournment.

The judge halted. 'Dr Takayanagi?'

'My apologies. You were in thought.'

Pal smiled. 'Yes.'

Kenzo stepped back. 'Please, conclude it.'

'I can't, I'm afraid. Too many unknowns.'

From Pal's interventions in court Kenzo assumed he knew to what the judge referred. 'Law in the making. It isn't easy,' he said.

'Nor just, I fear,' Pal said, plainly unhappy with the Tribunal's conduct.

'We do our best.'

'You do very well. Your defence of Foreign Minister Shigemitsu is intriguing. I look forward to hearing more.'

'On the conspiracy issue?'

'Certainly.'

'In Japanese political culture there's no such concept. I maintain that ...'

An imposing figure, his grey-flecked hair cut short, western style, Pal broke in: 'Keep it for the court, my friend. The court.'

'Forgive me, I ...'

'No harm. You wished to ask me something?'

'I'm embarrassed now. You'll suspect my motives.'

'Concerning?'

'An invitation to lunch on Sunday.'

'I'd be delighted.'

'Would you?' Kenzo made no play to conceal his pleasure. 'The air is fresher in the hills. There'll be a few friends. Family, more-or-less. Very informal.'

'By Japanese standards?'

Kenzo laughed. 'I'm such a mixture I can no longer tell. You'll be made welcome, that I know.'

The following Sunday was sunny, and humid – not unlike Calcutta, Pal informed Fumi. The guests gathered at a crossing point between two wings of the house, where a room-sized void offered through-views to the second stone garden and, in the other direction, to a sheltered plantation of flowering shrubs and trees, leading up into the naturally wooded slopes of the hillside behind. It was the one place, apart from the kitchen, where western habits were permitted to intrude, with its cushioned rattan chairs and drinks tables set out beneath the open beams of the steeply-arched black-tiled roof. Two hammocks hung from the forks of supporting pillars on the forest side of the verandah. In these children played, knocking the pillows onto the slatted boards, inch gaps in which meant that pieces of party food fell to the ground several feet below. In the shade of this space beneath the house lived a family of racoons.

'You're very secluded,' Pal remarked.

'We're lucky. The temple grounds extend almost to ours. There's no road in between. So no buildings,' Kenzo explained.

'An old temple? Should I visit?'

'Not old. Beautifully new. Yes, well worth seeing. I can take you later.'

'I'd like that. Thank you.'

Fifteen people stood on the through-verandah, with room for more. In the centre Fumi and another women were involved in conversation. Sharp-tongued, it sounded.

Pal's patriarchal eyebrows arched. 'What are they saying?' he murmured.

Kenzo put his hand on the judge's elbow and drew him a few paces from the other guests. 'My wife is riding her hobby horse. She's violently opposed to the Americans' plans to give the vote to women. I'm not sure she'd mind quite so much if I wasn't involved with drawing up the legislation!'

Pal chuckled. 'I sympathize.'

'With her or me?'

'Her, actually!'

Fumi's voice rose higher.

'And now?' Pal enquired.

'Our national decline is epitomised, she avows, by the appointment of a female tutor to the Crown Prince. A Quaker, Fumi's heard.'

'To whom is she talking?'

Kenzo glanced back over his shoulder. 'A niece of mine. Isuzu. Married to a Hungarian. He's lived in Kobe for twenty-five years. Selling coal-mining equipment. Would you like to meet him?'

Pal coughed, as if clearing his throat. 'Er ... not really.'

'No? He's fine. Isuzu's the one to avoid.'

Isuzu was dangerous – in Kenzo's terms – because she spoke her mind indiscriminately, to whomever she happened to be talking. Were she not the wife of a foreigner, her indiscretions would long ago have landed her in trouble. Instead it was others who suffered, people who allowed themselves to be influenced by her ideas without learning to anticipate the consequences. People, it has to be said, who were easily led, who declined to think for themselves and whose lives were bound, therefore, to be blighted. So Kenzo believed. He did not blame Isuzu for the views she held, but for neglecting to harvest their fruit. Of rotten apples they had plenty in Japan.

Fumi found it difficult to resist over-reacting to Isuzu's provocation, in a language of excess which Kenzo hated hearing.

He shook his head. When would she learn?

'Why do you shake your head?' Pal asked.

'At the waste.'

'Of energy?'

'Of potential. My wife could be a help to Isuzu. And Isuzu to her. Unity in difference. Where, to my mind, lies all the moral and most of the practical power to civilize society.'

Pal ran a finger along his upper lip, removing a runnel of sweat. 'Tell me, Dr Takayanagi. Why did you agree to join the defence team? According to files we've been given, you opposed the alliance with Germany.'

'My father was against our joining the League of Nations. His father, a century ago, against opening trade with the west. We're a family of dissenters! Personally, I care only for the very small and the very large. The individual and the world. I agreed to be attorney to my political opponents because against the state everyone deserves a defence. Especially against punishment by foreign states.'

'There is, I agree, revenge in the Tokyo air.'

'Why, may I then ask, did you allow yourself to be co-opted onto the bench?'

'Because I hope in my work for this Tribunal to see decisive steps taken towards what I call enforceable world law.'

'Meaning?'

Pal grimaced. And for a moment Kenzo saw the awkwardly intense, isolatingly clever child the judge must once have been, in despair of anybody paying him serious attention.

'I mean ... things like the dismantling of national armaments systems. A universal penal code. Criminalization of defensive as well as offensive war. Multilateral police forces. The classic utopian's dream.'

Kenzo's next opportunity to talk confidentially to Pal presented itself on Armistice Day, 14 August 1946, celebrated by the allies with rabid glee in the conquered capital of Japan.

The day began with a service of remembrance on a mound of soil beside the burnt-out stump of a tree, all that remained of the church and cemetery of St Andrews. Three-quarters of central Tokyo had been destroyed by American bombing. In a single March night of the previous year two hundred and fifty B-29s had flown in to drop two thousand tons of incendiary bombs on the city. Fires fuelled by a freak wind had raged unabated for four days, incinerating sixteen square miles of the eastern section either side of the Sumida River – into which thousands plunged to escape the flames, and were boiled to death. Eighty-four thousand people were killed in the raid of 10 March 1945. It took the municipal authorities twenty-three days to collect the charred corpses for ritual cremation.

Kenzo watched the British and Commonwealth contingent of trial lawyers and secretaries file past the tree stump to place wreaths for the Christian dead. The eccentric Comyns Carr was there, wearing a long linen jacket, straw hat, silk cravat, army issue desert trousers and on his large feet a pair of plimsolls. Kenzo admired the Kings Counsel's juridical mind. For his junior, Christmas Humphreys, who wore an opium poppy in the lapel of his pinstripe suit, Kenzo held no professional respect at all.

A platoon of Cameron Highlanders marched off around the streets, rolling their drums and blowing their bagpipes. Leaflets were distributed to Japanese survivors of the war, inviting them to free screenings at Hibiya Hall of Olivier's *Henry the Fifth*.

High point of the celebrations was the Medical Corps' production of Gilbert and Sullivan's comic opera *The Mikado*, staged in Kokyo Gaien, the vast outer court of the Emperor's palace. Half the population of Tokyo turned out to feast on hamburgers and Coca-Cola, and to watch a cast of thousands sing and dance their way through this elaborate insult. On stage 'The Ruler of Japan' was escorted by a troop of US marines in samurai armour, followed by a mincing chorus of eighty kimonoed hostesses recruited from the Ginza. At a sideshow a doctor in drag revived Marie Lloyd's Hoxton hit of the eighteen nineties:

> Ev'ry little Jappy chappie's gone upon the Geisha.
> Trickiest little Geisha ever seen in Asia!
> I've made things hum a bit, you know,
> Since I became a Geisha,
> Japanesey, free and easy Tea house girl!

Fumi had refused to attend.

'You go, if that's the sort of thing you enjoy,' she had said at breakfast.

'Your absence will be noted,' Kenzo had warned.

'So?'

'Is it necessary to court displeasure?'

'In this case, yes.'

'You know my response.'

'Fine. You go on your own. I don't mind. Honestly.'

Pal, Kenzo learnt, had also declined to take official part in the proceedings. He ran into him at the open market which had formed on the bombsite behind General MacArthur's headquarters, serving the crowds of foreigners drawn into the centre of the city. Kenzo followed Pal unobserved for several minutes, watching the judge trail his fingers across rolls of silk, then pause to examine a stall of tin toys.

'Can I help?' Kenzo offered.

'Ah, Dr Takayanagi. Could you?'

'What do you need to know?'

'They're beautiful. I just wonder if the toys are safe to play with. I have grandchildren. I'd hate them to be harmed.'

Kenzo was puzzled. 'How could they be?'

'Boys put soldiers into their mouths. If the paint is enamel, and toxic, they can be poisoned.'

'I'll ask.'

The stallholder spoke rapidly. To demonstrate a point he rummaged in his woven-reed trunk, from which he produced a jam jar of bright yellow paint, and brushed a stripe across his tongue. Pal looked on, in astonishment.

'He says they're home market toys. That of course they're safe!'

'I'd better buy some.'

Pal selected a dozen tin figures, paying for them in cash – US dollars, the only currency the toymaker would accept.

'Some tea? At my hotel?' Pal held up his brown paper bags. 'I need to return these to my room. Would you join me?'

Kenzo happily agreed.

On their way back to the Imperial Hotel they spoke of their

eastern unease with western materialism. Pal criticized the British for failing to value the spirituality of the peoples of India and declared himself, despite his anglophile education, a supporter of the popular surge for independence. Kenzo complained of the Americans' systematic undermining of Japanese self-confidence, the racist propaganda which labelled their ancient way of being evil. He blamed this flight from reason on the pain and ugliness of the war.

'Not the war, all wars,' Pal insisted. 'I beg your pardon,' he apologized to a man with whom he collided in the crowd. 'I've come to appreciate the sense inside Ghandi's ill-argued ideas. Violence is a criminally inefficient means of dealing with disputes. I mean, the ...' They were again separated in the throng – two men, aged either side of sixty, as eager to talk as teenagers. '... the endless repetition. Victor and vanquished changing places across the centuries.'

An image surfaced from Kenzo's memory of the honeymoon trip he and Fumi made to Europe in the autumn of 1932. On holiday in Paris they visited one Sunday morning, as it opened, the Rodin Museum. Instead of following the other tourists into the grand house in which the artist lived out the fame of his dying years, Kenzo and Fumi were drawn – by the golden play of morning light slanting through the chestnut trees – down towards the bottom of the garden, past the orangery stuffed with sculpture, to sit together on a bench beside the round pond, entirely alone. The bronze mouth of a sea serpent began, as if at their command, to spout water. To their left the burnished dome over the tomb of Napoleon rose above the garden wall. The peace of this man-made sanctuary brought tears to their eyes, Kenzo recalled, before his mind raced ahead to fix on the memory behind this for which he was reaching. Of a picture.

In an upstairs room in the museum?

Painted – Kenzo knew this for certain – in 1887, the year of his birth. By Vincent van Gogh. A picture purchased by Rodin at a show in which the two of them were exhibiting. The front-on portrait of a bearded man, hands clasped in his lap, wearing a straw hat with upturned brim, yellow scarf and blue jerkin. Pinned to the wall were Japanese prints: of actors from the Kabuki, a cherry tree in blossom beside a river and, as if balanced on the old man's head, Mount Fuji at sunset. The colourful woodcuts overlapped, filling the background to the portrait.

What had happened since then to alienate the West? Kenzo planned, one day, to find the answer.

At the Imperial Hotel Pal and he settled into a pair of square armchairs and ordered tea. Which the waiter placed on the glass-topped table between them.

'Anything else, Sir?' he asked. Pal looked at Kenzo, who shook his head. 'That'll be all, thank you,' Pal replied.

The waiter, an American-Asian, clicked his heels and retired. Kenzo poured the fresh-smelling green tea. It was his choice to sit and talk in the open, beneath the gaze of the hand-picked staff, imported for the duration of the Tribunal. The Imperial was a club these days not an hotel, the private domain of senior officials and officers of the occupying forces. Kenzo wished it to seem he had nothing to hide in his friendship with Mr Justice Pal, a powerful player on the Tokyo stage.

'How's your wife? Not in town for the festivities?' Pal enquired.

'At home. Sulking!'

Pal tut-tutted. And began to speak of his own wife, back in Calcutta. 'Mine hasn't left the house for ... oh ... eight years? A recluse, to some. To us she's at the centre of things. Every day, all day long, arranging the family's life.'

'Your children live with you still?'

'The four boys. With their wives and their children. Two are lawyers.'

'Like father like son.'

'Like their mother, actually.' The whites of Pal's ageing eyes were a bruised yellow. They flowed with tenderness. 'To their good fortune.'

At a table to their right, by the wall, an army officer knocked over his bottle of scotch.

'Goddamn!' he exclaimed.

In grabbing the bottle as it fell he sent a plume of whisky shooting into the air, drenching the chest of his companion, a young Japanese woman. The officer leaned over the woman, pawing at the buttons of her tailored jacket.

'Take it off! It's wet!'

She tried to push him aside, her eyes darting nervously around, aware of the stares. 'It doesn't matter,' she said, in Japanese.

'Off with it! That's an order!' he bawled.

With brisk efficiency, two military policemen lifted the woman bodily from the settee and escorted her to the door. A third calmed the colonel. In the lobby conversation resumed.

Pal snorted his disgust.

'Please,' Kenzo cautioned. 'We are watched.'

The judge put a hand to his face. A brown finger, the nail sharply curved, tapped his brow. He sighed. 'There are limits to my patience.'

'What good would it do to give way?'

'They're not rid of me yet,' Pal reassured.

Kenzo bowed in his chair. 'We rely on you. The rest of the bench has predetermined our guilt,' he risked saying.

They fell silent. Kenzo pushed his spectacles back onto the bridge of his nose. His admiration for Pal had swelled to affection, a private feeling which conflicted with his public need to make use of him. He sought in his mind for a lead, a line to follow towards the expression of his loyalty to Pal the person. He could think, right then, of nothing helpful.

We'll see, we'll see, Kenzo said to himself.

'We'll see, we'll see,' he repeated, out loud.

The trial proceeded slowly, in part due to wrangles over the daily transcripts in English and Japanese. To those – like Kenzo – who could read both, critical differences in the legal meaning of words mattered.

'Of the hundreds of specialists flown in to assist the military, doesn't one of them understand the language?'

'Of course they do!'

Translations of Japanese defence statements were designed to mislead the ten English-speaking judges, Kenzo had concluded. He dreaded to think what garbage the eleventh, a Russian, Zaryanov, was fed by the Western allies.

Early on during the occupation Kenzo had decided the main hope for progress in Japan's internal affairs lay with SCAP himself, General MacArthur, the Supreme Commander Allied Powers. Kenzo looked to MacArthur because he judged him to be in many ways a remarkable man. A man, moreover, whose character appealed to the people of Japan. The Japanese, high and low, loved men in love with power. General Douglas MacArthur was good at power. He worked at it. Seven days a week, three hundred and sixty-five days a year, Christmas day no exception, arriving at his office in the Dai Ichi building at seven o'clock every morning, returning home at one for lunch, after which he undressed to take a nap, before driving back for the late afternoon round of meetings from five until eight. When alone in his room he paced from end to end, several miles a day, chewing a long-stemmed corn-cob pipe. Though he followed – fanatically

– the West Point football results, MacArthur had never been known to play games, was rumoured to be faithful to his young second wife. As the months of the occupation lengthened the citizens of Tokyo had come to depend on SCAP more confidently than on the Emperor.

The other key figure in Kenzo and his colleagues' plan was Kijuro Shidehara, enticed by MacArthur from political retirement to be Prime Minister. In the old days, in Saitama Prefecture, where the Shidehara family lands were located, generations of Takayanagis had served as treasurer to the ruling family. The ties remained secure, despite Showa disavowal of feudal structures. Kenzo still referred to Shidehara as Baron. Shidehara playfully addressed the country's leading Professor of International Law as ex-Treasurer Takayanagi.

At the beginning of November 1945 Kenzo had arranged a confidential meeting at the Prime Minister's home. The two men had talked alone, their contact, though formal, warm. Shidehara had listened attentively, ruffling his two-tone moustache and taking periodic sips of sake, poured into his celadon cup from a warmed flask standing on a lacquer dish. Kenzo had spoken with confidence in the logic of his argument: that for ministers of the realm to be threatened by an International Tribunal with death, for losing a war fought in self-defence made further maintenance of military capability a waste of money and manpower. Safety by force of arms had proved an illusion. They should cease, by law, to recognise the right to belligerency. After what had happened to innocent civilians in Nagasaki and Hiroshima there could be no point, ever again, engaging in war.

'My dear ex-Treasurer, are you seriously suggesting I tell MacArthur this?' the Prime Minister had caviled.

'Yes.'

Shidehara had sat motionless for many minutes, his eyes

closed, head lowered. 'How do you imagine he will react?'

'With enthusiasm.'

The old man had laughed, heartily. 'No, no ...' His laughter had rumbled on. 'It's a wonderful principle, your commitment to the resolution of interstate disputes by supra-national arbitration. To expect a general to agree ... isn't that casting a net at the stars?'

Kenzo had shrugged his shoulders. 'I'm not so sure.'

'He'll grasp the moment, you're saying? To write history?'

'Wouldn't you, Baron, in his position?'

At a private meeting between Douglas MacArthur and Kijuro Shidehara at the Dai Ichi building on 24 January 1946 the die had been cast. Its permanence guaranteed by SCAP's speech to the Allied Council for Japan on 5 April:

> Members of the Allied Council for Japan.
>
> I welcome you with utmost cordiality in the ernest anticipation that, in keeping with the friendship which has long existed among the several peoples represented here, your deliberations throughout shall be governed by goodwill, mutual understanding and broad tolerance. The purposes of the occupation are now well advanced. Japanese forces on the home islands have been disarmed, demobilized, and returned to their homes, and in other respects the Japanese war machine neutralized. Dispositions have been taken to eliminate for all time the authority and influence of those who misled the people of Japan into embarking on world conquest, and to establish in Japan a new order of peace, security, and justice; to secure for the Japanese people freedom of speech, religion and thought, and respect for the fundamental human rights; to remove all obstacles to the strengthening of democratic tendencies among the Japanese people; and to readjust the Japanese industrial economy to produce for the Japanese people after reparations an

equitable standard of life. All of these dispositions in implementation of principles outlined in the Potsdam Declaration have already been taken. My policy in the Administration of Japan for the Allied Powers has been to act as far as possible through existing instrumentalities of the Japanese government.

The soundness of this policy has been unmistakably reflected in the progress of the occupation. I have sought, while destroying Japan's war potential and exacting just penalties for past wrongs, to build a future for the people of Japan based upon considerations of realism and justice. Without yielding firmness, it has been my purpose to avoid oppressive or arbitrary action, and to infuse into the hearts and minds of the Japanese people principles of liberty and right heretofore unknown to them. As success of the Allied occupational purposes is dependent upon leadership as well as upon direction – as only through the firm application of those very principles which we ourselves defended on the battlefield may we, as victors, become architects of a new Japan, a Japan reorientated to peace, security and justice – this policy shall continue to be the aim of my administration and should serve to guide the Council throughout its deliberations.

A new constitution has been evolved, patterned along liberal and democratic lines, which the Japanese government intends to submit for consideration to the next incoming National Diet. While all provisions of this proposed new constitution are of importance, and lead individually and collectively to the desired end as expressed at Potsdam, I desire especially to mention that provision dealing with the renunciation of war.

Such renunciation, while in some respects a logical sequence to the destruction of Japan's war-making potential, goes yet further in its surrender of the sovereign right of resort to arms in the international sphere. Japan thereby proclaims her faith in a society of nations governed by just, tolerant and effective rules of universal social and political morality and entrusts its national integrity thereto. The cynic may view such action as demonstrating childlike faith in a visionary ideal but the realist will see in it far deeper significance. He will understand that in the evolution of society it became necessary for man to surrender certain rights theretofore inherent in himself in order that states might be created vested with sovereign power over the individuals who collectively formed them; and that foremost of these inherent rights thus surrendered to the body politic was man's right to force in the settlement of disputes with his neighbour. With the advance of society, groups or states federated together through the identical process of surrendering inherent rights and submitting to a sovereign power representing the collective will. In such manner was formed the United States of America, through the renunciation of rights inherent in the individualstates in order to compose the national sovereignty; the State first recognized and stood guarantor for the integrity of the individual, and thereafter the nation recognized and stood guarantor for the integrity of the State.

The proposal of the Japanese government – a government over people who now have reason to know the complete failure of war as an instrument of national policy – in effect but recognizes one step further in the evolution of mankind, under which nations develop, for mutual protection against war, a yet higher law of international social and political morality.

Whether the world is yet ready for so forward a step in the relations between nations, or whether another and totally destructive war – a war involving almost mass extermination – must first be waged, is the great issue which now confronts all people.

There can be no doubt that both the progress and survival of civilization is dependent upon the timely recognition of the imperative need for some forward step. Is dependent upon the realization by all nations of the utter futility of force as an arbiter of international issues. Is dependent upon elimination from international relations of the suspicion, distrust and hatred which inevitably result from power threats, boundary violations, secret manoeuvring, and violence to public morality. Is dependent on a world leadership which does not lack the moral courage to implement the will of the masses who abhor war and upon whom falls the main weight of war's frightful carnage. And finally is dependent upon the development of a world order which will permit a nation such as Japan safely to entrust its national integrity to just such a higher law to which all peoples on earth shall have rendered themselves subservient. Therein lies the road to lasting peace.

I therefore commend Japan's proposal for the renunciation of war to the thoughtful consideration of the peoples of the world. It points the way – the only way. The United Nations Organization, admirable as is its purpose, great and noble as are its aims, can only survive to achieve that purpose and those aims if it accomplishes as to all nations what Japan proposes to accomplish through this constitution: abolish war as a sovereign right. Such a renunciation must be simultaneous and universal. It must be all or none. It must be effected by action – not words alone – and open, undisguised action which invites the confidence of all men who would serve the cause of peace. The present instrumentality to enforce its will – the pooled armed might of its component nations – can at best be but a temporary expedient so long as nations still recognize as coexistent the sovereign right of belligerency.

No thoughtful man will fail to recognize that with the development of modern science another war may blast mankind to perdition. But still we hesitate. Still we cannot, despite the yawning abyss at our very feet, unshackle ourselves from the past. Therein lies the childlike faith in the future. A faith that, as in the past, the world can somehow manage to survive yet another universal conflict. In that irresponsible faith lies civilization's gravest peril.

We sit here in council, representatives of the military might and moral strength of the modern world. It is our responsibility and our purpose to consolidate and strengthen the peace won at the staggering cost of war. As we thus deal in the international sphere with some of the decisive problems I have briefly outlined, it is incumbent upon us to proceed on so high a level of universal service that we may do our full part toward restoring the rule of reason to international thought and action. Thereby may we further universal adherence to that higher law in the preservation of peace which finds full and unqualified approval in the enlightened conscience of all the peoples of the earth.

ii

In the weeks immediately after his Armistice Day tea with Pal Kenzo was too busy with work for the Diet to have time to follow up their conversation. Parliamentary sanction for constitutional change was proving tougher to secure than Shidehara and MacArthur had envisaged. The Secret Service tightened control, urged by SCAP to hurry the process along. Disappearances multiplied – some voluntary, opportune escapes to safety in the countryside. Kenzo kept extra vigilant. The summons to SCAP Headquarters for a meeting with Major General Willoughby, on previous occasions taken in his stride, this time troubled him. He shared his worries with Fumi.

'Which one is Willoughby? Tennis player or pseudo-Buddhist?' she asked.

It was night. They were in the room by the forest, their necks resting on twin ceramic tiger pillows. The racoons could be heard at their business beneath the house.

'He's the US Army's ex-tennis champion. Doubles. He plays every day.'

'Hope he has a heart attack!'

'Before Tuesday? Unlikely. Wouldn't make any difference. He's replaceable.'

'You're not. Not only to me. To them also. They need you.'

Kenzo sighed. 'I know they do. That's how I thought I

wanted it to be. Now I'm not so sure.'

Nice of her not to crow, Kenzo thought, as he listened to a gust of wind rustle the leaves of the trees.

'You've been correct all along. I should stick to what I know. The law. I'm an advocate, not a political agent.'

'You're a good person, Kenzo. With nothing major to regret.'

'Not yet.'

'Need there be?'

'If I'm careful. No.'

'Be careful.'

'I will.'

To brush clean his mind for sleep Kenzo picked upon a memory from his year in England. Of the softness of the rain on his bare head during a walk he made the Sussex Downs, with a colleague from the Middle Temple.

What was his name? That's right, Evelyn, he whispered to himself, and fell asleep.

On the morning of his appointment with Willoughby Kenzo awoke within the shadow of a dream. 'Ah! The joy tokens!' a slim red-haired woman cried out, leaning back into her seat in a railway carriage, selecting a dark oval chocolate from a tray.

The headquarters of the occupying forces faced the nursery wing of the Imperial Palace. Built of iron and cement, in the classical style, shortly before the invasion of Manchuria in the Great Asian War of Liberation, the Dai Ichi had survived the bombing intact. Kenzo's chauffeur dropped him at the foot of the steps on which dozens of women daily prostrated themselves in the path of MacArthur. Tall for his race, Kenzo extracted a salute from the armed pair of military police guarding the swing door.

At the marble desk a receptionist inspected his identity papers.

'General Willoughby, you say?' she asked, with her blue-eyed stare of disbelief.

'At eleven.'

She consulted a clipboard. 'Nothing on the list.'

'Then telephone his office, please.'

'If you insist.'

Kenzo nodded.

'Your name again?'

'Dr Ta-ka-ya-na-gi,' he said.

The receptionist scowled at the voice at the other end of the phone. She pointed at the row of sparkling brass and bevelled-glass elevators. 'Fifth floor.'

Major General Willoughby stood at the doors of the lift as they sprang open, and bowed, twice, in a perfectly executed greeting. Kenzo returned the compliment. Stepping free of the closing concertina gates, he followed the tubby American down a windowless passage.

Willoughby's private office was thick with photographs, hanging corner to corner across the walls and standing in mono-grammed silver frames along the tops of the fitted bookcases. Mostly of him: receiving tennis trophies; meeting dignitaries at airports; smiling at the open turret of a tank. Also of his family. Of his son, as vice-captain of the high school water polo squad.

The US Chief of Military Intelligence was conservative, iras-cible, and exceptionally sympathetic to the oriental sense of decorum. He liked, he was fond of saying, their loyalty. With the Japanese you knew where you stood: at the far side of the mountain.

'Coffee? Cigar?' he offered.

'Tea, if that's not too difficult,' Kenzo requested.

'Sure. Mandy!' he shouted into a trumpet-shaped mouth-piece which he unhooked from the wall. 'Bring us a pot of tea, will you? And a box of cigars.'

'That's awfully kind, but …' he caught the Major General's beady eye. 'I don't smoke.'

'Give them to Yoshida. He smokes in the latrines,' Willoughby growled.

It was the best tea Kenzo had tasted since before the war. 'Beautiful tea, thank you.'

'Okay! Take a case of tea! Christ! Are you hard to please!' This was said with a smile. 'So. Tell me. What's the news at the gym?'

'We're advancing. Slowly. The anti-war article demands delicacy.'

Willoughby looked puzzled. 'What article? Which paper?'

'Article Nine, of the Constitution.'

'Not my pigeon. I'm talking about the Trial. Nuremberg was wrapped up in six months, start to finish. You people have been at it for as long, and have gotten … where? Nowhere. Why?' He did not wait for a reply. 'I'll tell you why. Because the defence counsel … I don't mean you. Don't get me wrong. I mean those imbeciles they sent from New York. They're screwing it up.' His tone changed, to cool control. 'Screwing it up for us all. For you, I reckon, the worst.'

'Me? In what way?'

Major General Willoughby gazed down at his desk, at the photograph of a youngish woman in a ball gown, inscribed: To Charles, from your affectionate Mother. He transferred his gaze to Kenzo.

'Left to yourselves, what would have happened? Defeated leaders shamed into killing themselves. Leaving the rest of you free to make … ? Yes, money!'

'The Allies have laid unprecedented charges. Which deserve a full hearing.'

'No problem with that, Doctor. Place the evidence on the table. And accept judgement according to the law. Why all the wheeling and dealing? That's what I want to know. Now listen, I'll square our people.' He emphasized the point with a clenched fist. 'There's just ... what's the Indian up to? Tell me. I'm curious.'

This tack took Kenzo by surprise. What, he tried to decide, was Willoughby's private view, his personal agenda? Kenzo sensed behind the bluster a passion for fair play, a naive faith in the triumph of the West's version of truth.

'In what context?' he asked.

'In the "context" of your buddy-buddy act.'

'Mr Justice Pal and I've spent a large part of our lives study-ing international law. We have common interests.'

'With the opposing team?'

'No, we ...' Kenzo paused, unsettled by the sharpness in his own voice, the highish pitch of which he had never liked. He steadied himself. 'I doubt if Pal sees himself on any particular side. Other than that of justice.'

'You've learnt nothing from your cosy chats?'

'Plenty.'

'What?'

'He's attached to his wife.'

'So are you. So am I for Christ sake! That's news?'

'There is one slightly disturbing development,' Kenzo responded, judging it wise to pass on something of value. 'Pal will not put his signature to a majority judgement should he, at the conclusion of the trial, disagree with it.'

'Sounds reasonable. Will that create legal problems?'

'No. The terms of the Tribunal's Charter permit execution of its sentences on a simple majority.'

'You're uneasy,' Willoughby observed. 'Why?'

'Not on legal grounds.'

'On moral?'

'I'm a pragmatist. Pal, on the other hand, has a vision.'

Silence.

Willoughby stared again at the tall, broad-shouldered woman in the photograph. He smiled. So did Kenzo. The interview was over.

'Thanks for calling, Dr Takayanagi. Need I say? There's no record of our having met today.'

The snail's pace of the Tokyo Trial quickened during the remaining months of 1946. Without warning, early in the new year Pal was absent from the bench. A phone call to Willoughby revealed to Kenzo no sinister circumstances – the reason, it seemed, was familial: his sister's death, gently, from old-enough age.

Kenzo persevered with the defence of Mamoru Shigemitsu, Foreign Minister from 1943 to 1945. While Ambassador to China Shigemitsu had lost his left leg, in a Korean assassination attempt, by a home-made bomb hurled at the podium during a commemorative address in Hongkew Park, Shanghai. With the help of the US attorneys Kenzo gathered affidavits attesting to Shigemitsu's consistent anti-militarism: from Lord Killearn, a contemporary at the British Embassy in Peking; from Lord Hankey, at the Foreign Office in Whitehall; from the US Ambassador to China, Nelson Trusler Johnson; and from Joseph Kennedy, America's Ambassador at the Court of St James, a close friend of Shigemitsu's in London in the early war years, before Japan's entry into hostilities with the attack on Pearl Harbour of 7 December 1941. To no avail. Webb ruled the testaments inadmissible evidence. Kenzo maintained that Shigemitsu entered the Cabinet explicitly to bring about a peaceful conclusion to the war. And in fact did so. By signing his country's unconditional surrender to General MacArthur on board the battleship *Missouri*, moored in Tokyo Bay on a drizzly morning at the beginning of September 1945.

Each of the twenty-five defendants – reduced from the original twenty-eight by two deaths in the cells and the slide of a third into insanity – were granted the right to make a personal statement in court, without challenge by cross-examination. Prime Minister Tojo's took two days to deliver. The logic of his argument was irrefutable. At his desk in the War Office in Tokyo, he had neither authorized nor committed any greater crimes against humanity than Winston Churchill, pacing the subterranean passages of his bunker in King Charles Street. Hideki Tojo flourished in his hand a copy of the official rules of military conduct ordered by him to be read out to troops in the field, insisting that they behave decently towards the enemy population and treat prisoners of war fairly.

'I believe firmly and will contend to the last that it was a war of self-defence and in no manner a violation of presently acknowledged international law,' he said, in a crisp tone to the judges, in the formal Japanese reserved for addressing servants.

Was Churchill in person to blame for dropping at 10.58 a.m. on Friday 9 August 1945 on the women and children of Nagasaki a plutonium triggered atomic bomb christened, in his honour, Fat Man?

The only response to this question which made moral sense to Takayanagi was Article Nine of the revised Showa Constitution, ratified by the Diet on 3 May 1947:

> Aspiring sincerely to an international peace based on justice and order, the Japanese people forever renounce war as a sovereign right of the nation and the threat or use of force as a means of settling international disputes.
>
> In order to accomplish the aim of the preceding paragraph, land, sea and air forces, as well as other war potential, will never be maintained. The right of belligerency of the state will not be recognised.

Kenzo wept in telling Fumi that his cherished Article Nine had finally become the law of their land. His wife stood in silent empathy at his side, her head lowered.

'It's not finished. It's not over,' Kenzo moaned.

'What, my love? What isn't?'

Kenzo took several deep breaths, and sat down in one of the rattan chairs, drawing Fumi by the hand to sit in the chair next to him.

'I'm sorry. I never quite convinced myself it was going to happen. Now it has. And ... I'm happy. Of course. Except it's just a beginning. What's a law? The start, that's all. We won't live to see the world change.' Kenzo paused. 'I'm tired. Getting old. I don't know I've the strength to go on. I must. I will.' He squeezed his wife's hand. 'We will.'

'You've Pal's support,' Fumi reminded him.

In the moonlight they looked, to each other, young again. They were smiling.

'So? What're you complaining about?'

Kenzo threw back his head and laughed. 'Tojo! His clinical sacrifice of our people in war. I can't bear the thought of him going unpunished!'

Although Pal in due course returned to Tokyo, Kenzo was concerned about his friend's increasingly frequent absences from the courtroom. He was afraid the judge had lost interest in the case. It was important to talk to him.

An opportunity to do so arose one evening at the Shichi-go-san, a hall of family entertainment. Kenzo was surprised to find Pal there, seated beside Bert Röling, the Dutch judge on the Tribunal, at a table occupied by several of the Japanese legal support staff, minor officials with whom he had no idea Pal was on familiar terms.

'Good heavens! Pal!'

'Where?'

'Two pillars to the left, three in.'

Fumi counted off the carved supports to the roof of the smoke-filled hall. 'So it is. Why not go over and say hello?'

'Later, maybe.'

Kenzo took off his spectacles and polished them on the sleeve of his kimono. He was embarrassed to be seen in such a place.

'They've reopened the Shichi-go-san. Shall we try? What else is there to do in town these days?' Isuzu had proposed on the latest of her visits from Kobe.

'I adore all that stuff. Magicians and jugglers. Rude comedians,' Paul, her husband, had added, in his fluent Japanese.

'Why not?' Fumi had agreed.

They sat on cushions at long scarlet lacquer tables, three or four hundred at a time, drinking and eating. A band played on a stage in the centre, with gusto, on traditional instruments, competing against the din of the crowd's chatter.

'Great place. Reminds me of a dive in Constantinople I used to patronize. Down by the bazaar,' Paul de Guyarmathy shouted.

Kenzo cupped a hand to his ear. 'Can't hear!'

'Miss the belly dancing!'

'Nice atmosphere,' Fumi remarked.

'Could you pass the soy?'.

'Rice?'

Kenzo shook his head, and pointed at a stoneware bottle.

'Oh, the soy. Here you are,' their neighbour at the communal table responded. A farmer from Yamagata, Kenzo gathered from his accent.

The noise level in the hall dropped when the band gave way to solo entertainers. A Korean migrant, on trousered stilts, kept five flaming torches spiralling through the air, and was applauded for his skill and courage. After a while Kenzo excused himself, slipping outside for a breath of air.

And there was Pal, seated on a low stone wall, stroking his nose.

'Good evening, my friend. How are you?'

'Extremely well, thank you,' Kenzo replied. 'And you?'

Pal hesitated. 'Honestly? Up and down. Right now I'm fine. Glad of the break.'

'From the noise?'

'From work.' Pal squeezed his nostrils. 'Actually, I've a favour to ask.'

'Please.'

'In court the other day you quoted Francis Sayer on Criminal Conspiracy.'

'*Harvard Law Review*. 1922.'

'I couldn't borrow it?' Pal requested.

'Of course. You're welcome to any books you need.'

'Are you sure? I'd be very grateful. Thank you.'

In their many conversations over the following months, when Pal dropped in at Ogawa-machi Dori to borrow and return various legal works, Kenzo learnt in detail of the Indian's plans. From the start, it transpired, Pal had felt duty-bound – as a man both of the law and of the East – to produce an independent judgement. He had set himself a giant task. The hostility of the American staff, on whom he relied, had sapped dry his energy. In fulfilment of a sense of duty of his own, Kenzo came to see himself as guardian of Justice Pal's intellectual wellbeing. They became, to their mutual gratification, co-conspirators in the fight to lay the foundations of enforceable world law.

Against the sovereign powers of conquering nations, armed to the teeth with state treaties and international charters, Pal chose carefully the legal territory on which to do battle. Reaffirmation of the Pact of Paris, signed in the Salle d'Horloge of the

Quai d'Orsay on 27 August 1928, was the key to legal release into a new world order, Pal believed.

Kenzo needed convincing.

'Are you sure? I know it says they renounce war. But that's not what the signatories meant. Look.' He lifted down a book from his study shelves. 'From a letter sent by the British Foreign Minister to the Soviet Ambassador in London, written a couple of weeks after ratification of the Pact. "The language of Article One as to the renunciation of war as an instrument of national policy renders it desirable that I should remind Your Excellency that there are certain regions of the world the welfare and integrity of which constitute a special and vital interest for our peace and safety. His Majesty's Government has been at pains to make it clear in the past that interference with these regions cannot be suffered. Their protection against attack is to the British Empire a measure of self-defence. It must be clearly understood that His Majesty's Government in Great Britain accepts the new treaty on the distinct understanding that it does not prejudice their freedom of action in this respect. The Government of the United States have comparable interests any disregard of which by a foreign power they have declared that they too would regard as an unfriendly act".' Kenzo gestured with the open palm of his free hand. 'No disguise. The British and Americans intend to go to war whenever they wish, wherever they wish. Exactly as they've always done.'

'You misunderstand me,' Pal said. 'I agree. No state has ever abrogated its right to self-defence. No!' He silenced Kenzo's protest. 'Let me finish. The prime question is this. Who decides when an individual nation's security is threatened?'

'Quite!'

'Well? Who does? At law?'

'Until now, nobody. That is: every nation decides for herself. All wars are claimed to be defensive. And therefore legal. "Only a lost war is a crime", Field Marshal Montgomery complained. After Nuremberg. Distressed by the execution of ordinary generals. Of men like himself.'

Pal smiled. 'You wanted to interrupt earlier. I know why. To preach Article Nine. Answer me this. What's the use without prior inter-state agreement to arbitration of disputes by non-military means?'

'None.'

'Now that's the nut my Dissentient Judgement must be fashioned to crack,' Pal concluded, in his sometimes awkward English.

Kenzo cast around in his mind for someone to support their cause. 'What about young Röling? Seems to have on his shoulders a head?' he said, on occasion equally uncomfortable in his second language.

'Obsessed with retribution. Like most Christians. Frightening fault in a judge.'

'Is it true Röling climbed Fujiyama on his first free weekend in Tokyo?'

Pal chuckled. 'Don't ask me, I'm deaf to gossip. Though I happened to hear that he and his wife — she visited, you know, for three months — went camping on Sado. To sketch crested ibis.'

'How Dutch of them.'

Pal pulled a watch from his waistcoat pocket. 'Must rush. Is your driver about the place? I'm late.'

'Moses!' Kenzo shouted, in the direction of the kitchen. 'Judge Pal's ready for the station.'

'I'm having trouble with crimes of omission,' Pal confessed on another afternoon, seated at Kenzo's side on a limestone bench amongst the trees, looking down onto the back of the house, testing the cut of his ideas. 'I'm keen that the powerful be held responsible for any failure to act humanely. All the same, society must tell its leaders in advance what it expects of them. Retrospective law is unjust. I'll have none of it.'

'You could view it as progress,' Kenzo advocated. 'At Nuremberg a new capital crime, against "humanity", was invented. Now at Tokyo another hangable offence, the crime of "omission" is to be defined. Good, sensible, preventative legislation. Leading my logical old friend Shidehara to declare the war system illegal. Thus insuring he will never be put on trial for not having stopped our army defending vital Japanese interests against Western imperialism. Instead, we refuse to have any army at all!'

'You sound angry. Has something happened?' Pal wondered.

Kenzo put his hand, for a second, on the Indian's knee. 'I was quoting Fumi. I'm too spineless to fight she tells me!'

The judge appeared to find this intensely amusing. Kenzo had never seen him laugh so freely.

Pal shook out the cream silk handkerchief from the top pocket of his grey suit jacket to dry the tears from his eyes.

'Women! I do love them.' He sniffed the forest air. 'Mother nature, mother courage, mother country, mother … what else?'

'Mother tongue.'

'Mother church. Regrettably.'

'I recollect an English friend, with whom I used to hike, telling me that motherwort heals diseases of the womb. Odd. Such a neglected, dirty-looking plant.'

'We Calcuttans treasure mother-of-pearl. Inlaid, on bedheads.'

'My mother's father was a fisherman. Our family's reciter of stories.'

'I'm partial to William Blake. Are you?'

Kenzo frowned. 'Not really. A blind spot, I'm afraid.'

'Pity. Wonderful stuff.

> Struggling in my father's hands
> Stirring against swaddling bands
> Bound and weary, I thought best
> To sulk upon my mother's breast.'

'The crime of omission. You were saying?' Kenzo prompted.

'Yes, my problem. How to lend support to the making of new laws of which I approve. Without judging Tojo and the rest guilty of offences which were not criminal at the time they were committed.'

'How?'

'By insisting that the significance of the majority's determination to condemn Japan's leaders be made crystal clear. I don't want lawyers to argue in future International Tribunals that the judges in Tokyo didn't know what they were doing. Which is why I intend to warn my colleagues before they sign. That a time may come when American troops are on the losing side. And will be seen by the world to have committed atrocious war crimes. When, if they judge Tojo guilty now, the President of the United States will then, without doubt, also be indictable.'

Pal paused.

'When this trial ends, a decent law will exist. What people do with it is up to them.'

iii

After the court hearings were completed in May 1948, the International Military Tribunal for the Far East took a further seven months to produce its written conclusion. The text of the four separate judgements was read out in open court between 4 November and 12 November 1948 by the Tribunal's President, then Mr Justice, later Sir William Flood Webb. Hideki Tojo, victor over the British in Singapore and the Americans at Pearl Harbour, declined to put on his headphones to listen to the interpreter's simultaneous translation into Japanese of the Tokyo Trial Judgement. In two sentences from his original address to the court he had already made his position clear: 'As to the question of responsibility for defeat, I feel that it devolves upon myself as Prime Minister. The responsibility in this sense I am not only willing but sincerely desire to accept.'

The majority judgement found the twenty-five defendants guilty. Tojo and six of his companions were sentenced to death by hanging, General Iwane Matsui on the single charge of the crime of omission – for his failure to prevent troops a thousand miles away in Nanking from raping women and killing children, against his specific orders.

Sixteen of the twenty-five were to be imprisoned for the rest of their lives. The last two, Shigemori Togo and Mamoru Shigemitsu, both of whom were career diplomats not generals or politicians, were sentenced, respectively, to twenty and to seven years in jail.

Three of the eleven judges had refused to sign the 1445 page majority judgement and instead filed dissenting opinions of their own. In his modest twenty-two pages the Frenchman, Mr Justice H Bernard, dismissed the legitimacy of the Tribunal on which he had been sitting since the spring of 1946, without mention of the defendants themselves or of their supposed crimes. In his 249 pages the Dutchman, Mr Justice B V A Röling, judged Koki Hirota, one of the ex-Prime Ministers condemned by the majority to death, innocent of all charges, as were, in his opinion, Togo and Shigemitsu. In the magisterial

1235 pages of his Dissentient Judgement the Indian, Mr Justice Radhabinod Pal, found all twenty-five defendants innocent of all the Allies' charges. Pal's expert analysis of the Pact of Paris – otherwise known as the Kellogg-Briand Pact, after its principal negotiators – forced Webb into this unequivocal statement in the majority judgement: 'Under the most liberal interpretation of the Kellogg-Briand Pact, the right of self-defence does not confer on the State resorting to war the authority to make a final determination upon the justification for its action. Any other interpretation would nullify the Pact; and the Tribunal does not believe that the Powers in concluding the Pact intended to make an empty gesture.' The decision of the majority of judges to uphold the Pact of Paris and impose death penalties on the leaders of Japan confirmed Webb's declaration in court on the opening day: 'There has been no more important criminal trial in all history.'

The Tribunal's Charter reserved ten days for the delivery of appeals for clemency to the Supreme Commander Allied Powers, General Douglas MacArthur, whose sole responsibility it was to authorize execution of the sentences passed by majority verdict of the judges, in three cases dependent on the casting vote of the Court President. On 18 November 1948 Mamoru Shigemitsu's defence attorneys, George Furness, Kenzo Takayanagi and Hiroshi Yanai, handed in their petition at MacArthur's private office in the Dai Ichi building. The appeal incorporated accounts, sworn on oath, by a number of Western dignitaries of their personal knowledge of Shigemitsu's opposition to his country's militarism. Lord Hankey described, in detail, confidential Foreign Office meetings with Ambassador Shigemitsu at the Savoy Hotel in London early in 1941, at which the Japanese diplomat expressed anger at his country's signing, in October 1940, of a non-aggression treaty with Germany. At a later meeting, at General Piggott's house at Ewhurst in Surrey, close to

Shigemitsu's country residence, the Ambassador urged Lord Hankey to arrange high-level diplomatic visits to Tokyo to counteract the increasingly influential presence there of Nazi politicians and agents. If Shigemitsu's guilt was to be established in international law this – in Hankey's opinion – would condemn as criminal anybody entering politics in the future to promote a minority position while, by democratic custom, accepting the principle of collective cabinet loyalty. As Furness phrased it in his clemency submission to MacArthur: 'To enter a Cabinet, and to assume an office through which one obtains the power necessary to be able to work for peace, is a duty rather than a crime.'

Worried about political unrest in occupied Japan in the aftermath of the Tokyo Trial, General MacArthur, with his celebrated decisiveness, dismissed the appeal within a couple of days. On 24 November he publicly confirmed all the verdicts, including the seven death sentences. The gravity of the language in MacArthur's address that day to the Allied Council for Japan allowed no room for doubt about his motives:

> No duty I have ever been called upon to perform in a long public service replete with many bitter, lonely, and forlorn assignments and responsibilities is so utterly repugnant to me as that of reviewing the sentences by the International Military Tribunal for the Far East. It is not my purpose, nor indeed would I have that transcendent wisdom which would be necessary, to assay the universal fundamentals involved in these epochal proceedings designed to formulate and codify standards of international morality by those charged with a nation's conduct. The problem indeed is basically one which man has struggled to solve since the beginning of time and which may well wait complete solution till the end of time. No human decision is infallible but I can conceive of no judicial process where greater safeguard was made to evolve justice. I therefore direct the Commanding Officer of the Eighth Army to execute

sentences as pronounced by the Tribunal. In doing so I pray that an Omnipotent Providence may use this tragic expiation as a symbol to summon all persons of good will to realization of the utter futility of war – the most malignant scourge and greatest sin of mankind – and eventually to its renunciation by all nations.

In desperation, Koki Hirota's and Kenji Dohihara's lawyers sought stay of execution through the US Supreme Court in Washington, arguing that, as the Tribunal had been conducted under American court rules, for justice to be seen to be done the defendants must be granted judicial right of appeal.

'If not,' their attorney said, 'it leaves the powers of these Tribunals absolute. Prisoners held under its mandate have a right to appeal to the conscience or mercy of an executive, in this case General MacArthur alone. But they apparently have no appeal to law.'

MacArthur received notice on 20 December that the Washington Supreme Court appeal had been turned down. He summoned to his office Ambassador William Sebald, Chairman of the Allied Council for Japan, and Lieutenant General Walker, Commander of the Eighth Army, and instructed them to make immediate arrangements for the death sentences to be carried out at Sugamo prison. There was to be no photographic record of the event, he ordered, no non-military presence except the four members of the Allied Council, and no prior announcement of the date or time of execution. The next day Sebald called on his three colleagues on the Council – a Russian, an Australian and a Chinese – to tell them of their assignment, fixed by Walker for the early morning hours of 24 December, Christmas Eve 1948.

Hideki Tojo recorded in his prison diary his relief at news that the time had come to die. On the day of his original arrest he had tried to kill himself, but the bullet aimed at his heart had missed,

and American medical expertize had restored him to sufficient
health to stand trial. At Sugamo, after the 12 November sen-
tencing to death, the guards had confiscated his dentures and
spectacles, fearing their prize criminal might again attempt to
take his own life. Prompting the entry in Tojo's diary: 'It only
shows that they do not understand our Japanese mentality. We
want to be executed with honour and, until then, we only wish
to maintain our health.' Tojo refused his defence counsel's request to appeal against the Tribunal's judgement. While awaiting the result of his colleagues' hearing in Washington he spent
much of his time with the prison priest, Hanayama. 'My health
is good, and I feel refreshed,' he wrote. 'I am spending the days
with Buddha, hoping that the execution will be carried out as
soon as possible. I am calm.' At the final meeting with his wife
and daughters Tojo was manacled to an American army officer
who sat at his side, with an armed military policeman standing
behind. Noticing his youngest daughter's distress at this indignity, he smiled, saying: 'They can bind my hands and my feet. But
no one has ever bound my heart.' On the night of his death Tojo
wrote a parting haiku to his wife, Katsuko.

> A lonely goose
> In the sky
> My heart aches

That same evening William Sebald and his wife were at a black-
tie dinner party in downtown Tokyo. They left early, at ten,
making the excuse to their disappointed host that Marilyn was
tired, and did not wish to risk falling ill for Christmas. Back
home Sebald changed from dinner dress into a dark blue suit.
He had agreed with the three other council members that they
would call – casually, as it were – for a drink at his residence,
and share two unmarked cars on the trip across town to Sugamo prison.

It was a cold night. The streets were empty. They reached Sugamo, a modern concrete jail, shortly after midnight and were ushered into the brightly-lit reception hall. The four diplomats did not have long to wait before Lieutenant General Walker led them, in single file, the darkness silent but for the crunch of their shoes on the frozen gravel, on a walk of four minutes through the prison grounds to the death house. In the small high-ceilinged room they stood against the bare back wall, facing a raised dais. Five ropes hung above closed trap doors.

From the yard outside they heard overlapping shouts of 'Banzai!', the condemned men's final 'Hurrah!' of loyalty to their Emperor. In marched Dohihara, Muto, Matsui and Tojo, passing close enough for the diplomats to feel the chill in their stare and to hear their muttered Buddhist prayers. The Japanese leaders, dressed in too-large US army fatigues, mounted the customary thirteen steps to the platform and stood in line beside the numbered ropes. Black hoods were drawn over their heads and the nooses tightened.

'Proceed!' the executioner yelled.

The four traps sprang open precisely in time, with a sound like a single rifle shot.

Pronounced dead, the bodies were lowered into plain wooden coffins, and the ritual repeated for Koki Hirota, aged seventy, and his younger compatriots, General Heitaro Kimura and General Seishiro Itagaki.

On MacArthur's instructions the ashes of the hanged men were scattered in the sky above Tokyo Bay, poured from the bomb hatch of an American fighter plane.

In April 1955, when the occupation ended, Japanese workers at the crematorium announced that they had managed to hide some of their leaders' remains.

By 1960 a granite memorial had been built on the top of San-
ganesan Hill at Hazu, inscribed: *Schichinin no Junshokusha no
Haka* – Tomb of the Seven Martyrs.

one

Willem Boymans stumbled on Justice Pal's Dissentient Judgement in Auckland University Library one afternoon in the summer of 1958. Sanyal of Calcutta, Pal's hometown publishers, had produced in 1953 an English edition of this measured indictment of the Tokyo Trial, banned by Major General Willoughby from publication in Japan, Europe and America in the interests of post-war political stability. At his desk in a single-window bay on the third floor, looking out over the oceanic expanse of Manukau Harbour, his neck red, running with sweat in the sun, Willem was shocked by this chance discovery. Shocked by the fact that, until now, he had been ignorant of judicial dissent against the decision to hang Japan's war criminals.

The hanging itself troubled him. It hurt to think that the wartime leaders of Japan had been denied the dignity of death by firing squad, dressed in military uniform, medals blazing.

Out in the harbour, between sky and water, Willem saw through the library window, several times on certain days, himself. Lying flat on his back in the long grass at the edge of a copse. At night, the moon exceptionally bright. Hearing their roar before seeing the formations of transport planes high overhead, on route to drop supplies at prearranged points behind the enemy's lines in occupied Holland. Supplies vital to his own and to his troop of commandos' survival.

Why do you do it?

Why do I?

Why do we go on?, he recalled shouting silently inside, tears pouring from his eyes, aware from the barrage of anti-aircraft fire ahead that the pilots and crew knew they flew – some of them, maybe many – to their deaths. Why don't you turn aside from this suicidal mission and head back across the North Sea?

Why don't I run from the certainty of one thing only? That as day breaks and we move in towards the bridge I must kill or be killed.

Are there no alternatives?

No, I have to, he had answered then. I couldn't live with the guilt of letting down the side. Of admitting it was meaningless, that comrades needn't have given their lives.

Yes, there is another way: he was hunting the reason for that answer now. There has to be.

Willem Boymans was one of those fortunate people with the money, and therefore the time, to look for reasons. At the end of the war he had found he was rich, the heir – with his elder brother – to his father's sugar fortune, made in Indonesia after the First World War, before the family settled in London. Willem was free to travel wherever in the world he wished. That he chose, on resigning late in 1946 his commission in the Dutch Commandos, after a brief flirtation with commerce in Jakarta, to escape to New Zealand was an indication of how badly he needed to stop and take stock. Journeying at leisure around this primeval land, a country without snakes or foxes, Willem had renewed his reserves. Ending up in Auckland, on North Island, a sprawling city, small by European standards although much the largest in New Zealand, he had there sat down to work out how to fill the void of war.

In search of a purpose, Willem was drawn to the Far East. At Cambridge, before cutting short his history degree to volunteer, he had been intrigued by Japan's turn-around from centuries of self-willed isolation to world power in the relatively few years since Admiral Perry sailed into Tokyo Bay in 1853. On resuming his studies Willem found that he carried at the back of his mind the word-perfect memory of a quote from the London *Times* of August 1863, justifying obliteration of the port of Kagoshima by a British battleship:

A nation like the Japanese has no right to shut themselves up

from intercourse with human kind in selfish exclusion. It is an
act of gross barbarism and inhumanity, and the other members of the human family have the right, and even the duty, to
enforce mutual discourse.

Ahah!: he had said to himself. Three Oscars in one! For arrogance, inaccuracy and inter-GALACTIC hypocrisy!

It was also, Willem had less pugnaciously observed, an attitude still held by many in the West. By Admiral Bill Halsey, in his
comments to the press on US Navy reprisals for Pearl Harbour:
'We are drowning and burning the bestial apes all over the
Pacific, and it is as much pleasure to burn them as to drown
them. I hate Japs. I'm telling you, man, if I met a pregnant Japanese woman, I'd kick her in the belly.'

'I don't understand,' Willem had said to one of the friends he
made in Auckland, Michael Dwyer, a semi-retired lecturer at the
university. 'I found them so civilized. Such a sense of order. I've
never had any trouble with the Japanese.'

'In Burma?'

'Mopping up after the surrender. I respected them.'

'Terribly cruel.'

'Were they? I doubt it. I think it's a myth.'

Dwyer had laughed, good-naturedly. 'Don't say that too
loud. Not in these parts.'

For several years Willem read everything he could find on the
history of oriental interaction with the West. In so doing he
learnt of personal responsibilities nobody had told him about.
He was at first annoyed at the denial – by teachers, by members
of his family – of information he had a right to know; then grat-
ified by a growing sense of connectedness. He read of ancestors
on his mother's side – Catholic refugees from the march of
Calvinism – setting up licensed trading posts in Japan. Distant
relatives, he concluded, were among the thousands of foreign

residents of Urakamimura atomised by Fat Man's detonation in the sky above their cathedral, fatally close to a Mitsubishi weapons factory in the north-western suburbs of Nagasaki city. To service his need for understanding Willem collected more and more books on Japan, bought by post through a dealer near the British Museum, Mr Probsteyn, a Lithuanian Jew.

In due course Willem discovered Article Nine of the new Showa Constitution. And fell upon it in passionate recognition of its significance. To him.

After living for eighteen months in rented accommodation at Mount Eden, with a free view of the cricket, Willem had bought a dilapidated house an hour and a half's drive east from Auckland, near Thames, at the neck of the Coromandel Peninsula, two miles up a shingle road shadowing the Kauaeranga River. In the three years he had lived there Willem had done not a thing to repair his disintegrating house. Which he loved. Especially at night, when he sat out on a wide deck overlooking the valley, sharp volcanic hills unfolding towards the horizon. The stars on a cloudless night appeared more attainable than from any other spot he knew on earth. With a reference library now of his own, Willem spent less time in Auckland. Patterns emerged, a way of being with which he declared himself content.

His day started early, with a tumbler of orange juice crushed from the fruit of his own trees. Willem took better care of the sixty fruit trees than he did of the man-made fabric of his property. While the municipality maintained in excellent repair the old bushman's road leading up to the head of the Kauaeranga Valley, the driveway to Caldera had become so deeply rutted it was impassable to motor vehicles. Willem's fourth task of the day – first the glass of orange juice, second a cold shower and vigorous brushing of the teeth, third a tour of the orchards to gather, in a pair of wicker baskets slung from his shoulders, fruit at the moment of ripening – was to collect his mail from the tin box by the roadside. This Willem read and thought about on the walk back up to the house to make himself a decent English breakfast of eggs, kidneys, mushrooms, tinned tomatoes, toast and tea. H drank gallons of tea all day, wandering out through the open library windows onto the deck every couple of hours to piss through the balustrade onto a quartz-streaked rock twenty feet below. At lunch, timed to coincide with the news on the BBC's World Service, he ate a plate of cold meat and salad, followed by a swim in a deep pool at a bend in the Kauaeranga, fifteen minutes walk down an idyllic path through the tropical undergrowth. Willem swam naked. And swallow-dived, twice, from the iron girders of a disused railway bridge. He was not yet forty, tall, upright in stance, with a big head and slender legs. His legs, he felt, were his best feature. In the afternoon he again read. Or wrote – letters, and pieces intended one day for publication. On most evenings, after eating the meal cooked for him by a Maori girl who bicycled up from Parawai, he sat in candlelight. On the deck in summer. In a chair drawn close to the window when it grew too cold to be outside. Listening to the radio, drinking rough red wine and staring into the dark. He knew he drank more than was good for clarity. But if he did not drink he could not sleep, and that he found intolerable.

Willem reserved the weekends for what he termed, in military manner, logistics: shopping in Thames; the purchase of postage stamps; an occasional check-up with his GP. Every second Saturday, before driving home with his groceries, he called in at a tavern on the main street, where Michael Dwyer was usually to be found.

These days they talked as often as not about Dwyer's son and daughter-in-law, with whom he spent the weekends in Thames.

'Down the hatch,' Dwyer drawled, sinking a small glass of

liquer, pouring himself another from the unmarked green bottle. 'Bad, isn't it? How the coarse things repeat themselves. Never the pure.' He drove a hand through untidy hair. 'My son, he's worthless.'

'Doesn't think. Not like you. You think too much,' Willem responded.

'He's the spit image of my father. God, how I hated that man. Sick with pity for him and beside myself with rage. That's how I was. That's how I was,' he repeated, drawing out the words.

'And now?'

'No change. And he's been dead twenty years! You? Your father alive?'

Willem shook his head.

'Mother?'

'Very much. In a flat in Highgate.'

'I knew Highgate. Near the Heath?'

'Right by,' Willem confirmed. 'Round the corner from where we lived when I was a child. My brother's not far away. He keeps an eye on her.'

'Hey! Cindy!' Dwyer called down the long *kauri* bar to a woman ordering a drink at the other end. 'Bring it over here!'

The landlord of the Brian Boru, Ken Twohill, raised his tangerine eyebrows at the noise. A blonde in her mid-thirties, curly hair tied into a mushroom on top of her head, strolled across with her glass of lager.

'Hi, Mike. How're you doing?'

'Good. Cindy, this is Bill Boymans. Lives up the Kauaeranga. Bill, Cindy Callcott. One of our leading potters. How did it go? Been in a special show, down at the Museum in Otago.'

'That was last year. Moved on since.'

'What sort of stuff do you do?' Willem enquired.

Cindy Callcott cast him a questioning glance. The rising pitch of her response implied – to Willem's not-insensitive ear –

suspicion, edging towards disapproval. 'Know anything about ceramics?'

'Not much,' he admitted.

'No point in my trying to explain.' She turned back to Dwyer, a smile playing at the corners of her unmade-up lips. 'Hot little marriage guidance counsellor, I hear.'

Dwyer chuckled. 'Do what I can. Rosannah should kick him out.'

'Seriously,' Cindy said. 'Oughtn't she be getting help? Your weekend visits keep the peace. Doesn't resolve anything, does it?'

'How go the oyster beds?' he asked, changing the subject. 'Cindy farms oysters in her spare time. Worth a call. Keen on fish, aren't you Bill?'

Willem nodded, but did not speak.

He loved fish, in fact. Swimming in the sea with them, catching them, eating them. Though he had never tried farming them, he felt sure he would enjoy that too. Water was his element, a master at prising sea urchins from Cornish rocks and extracting their flesh without a prick to his own. He liked rain. And the steam which rose from the earth in tropical storms, through which he from time to time pranced naked, in the privacy of Caldera's orchards.

'What brings you to New Zealand?' Cindy asked. 'The landscape?'

'The distance from Europe,' Willem replied.

She smiled. 'Mike here, isn't he a chip off the Wicklow Hills? Me too, I'm Irish. Can't escape. Cut off your roots and you fall over. Rot to death in the undergrowth.'

'It's what I'm running towards which matters. Not what I've left behind.'

'Which is?'

'Failure. At School House I was the most beaten boy in my

year. Why? Because I scowled at the prefects warming their priv-
ileged bloody bums against the radiators. When I complained
about the lunch Matron scolded me. "Why is it always you who
makes difficulties?" Awkward! Without a second of regret!'

'What're you aiming at now?'

'Wouldn't that be telling!'

'Please yourself, man. I'm off.' At the swing doors of the
Brian Boru Cindy turned and gave a single salute-like wave. 'See
you guys,' she said, and was gone.

'Did you have to do that?' Dwyer complained.

'What?'

'Behave like an idiot.'

'She's nice. I liked her.'

Dwyer glowered into his brandy glass. 'She liked you too,' he
muttered.

Later, Willem struggled to see his friend home. When Dwyer
folded himself across the front fence of his daughter-in-law's
corrugated iron bungalow, refusing to go a step further, Willem
left him there, walked up the path and knocked at the kitchen
window. A child was screaming inside the house. He knocked
again, straining to block his ears against the sound.

'Hello, Rosannah. He's back.' Willem pointed to the figure
hanging over the fence. 'Got to rush. 'Bye.'

The pale girl nodded, and closed the door, returning to her
troubled son. Willem retreated down the path. He patted Dwyer
on the cheeks of his bottom. 'Easy does it,' he said, and passed
on along the street.

His pace slowed. A bittern kaw-kawed on the Thames mud-
flats, and he beamed in relief at again hearing the calls of nature.
Drunks he did not mind. Even as a boy Willem had sympathized
with drunks, at school, at Oundle, flanking the playing fields of
which was a poor house, where homeless alcoholics gathered at
dusk to be fed. He used to empty his pockets of boiled sweets

and the change from his father's generous allowance. The chatter of drunks was fine; children crying he could not bear.

On detailed study of Pal's seven hundred-page Dissentient Judgement, two copies of which he had ordered through Mr Probsteyn, Willem developed a passionate admiration for the balance and humanity of the Indian's minority opinion. Puzzled by the other judges' decision to ignore Pal's argument, Willem tried to find out from the New Zealand representative on the bench, Harvey Northcroft, what had happened behind the scenes.

Nothing: Mr Justice Northcroft maintained. Pal was, quite simply, wrong: he assured Willem over lunch at his retreat on the River Wilkin, where he devoted his retirement to trout fishing.

False! Pal is a paragon, a knight errant, brave crusader against manipulation of massed humanity by the global political elite!

In his campaign to proclaim the justice of Pal to the world, Willem threw himself into the writing of a pamphlet: *The Pacific Path to Peace*. He liked titles, enjoyed the roll of words capitalized across the head of a page. Incensed by the evasions of Northcroft and the rest, Willem indulged himself:

On 12 December 1948, the London *Times* injudiciously permitted a breeze briefly to lift her protective petticoat. On that day she reported that the United Nations General Assembly had unanimously proclaimed genocide to be a criminal offence. The sport of exterminating supernumerary persons, whether subjects or objects, and whether by bomb, bullet, gas-chamber, or blockade, was no longer to be permitted. Thenceforth governmental flunkeys could be held personally liable. "However," the Thunderess said, "the convention was not drafted without weeks of debate in the Assembly's legal committee, in which eight countries, including Britain, abstained from voting. The British attitude has been, broadly, that genocide is essentially a crime committed by states, which can be brought to judgement only by war, and that any convention must remain vague and idealistic."

So: at the western end of the world the Brits had one posse of gents doggedly maintaining that the most widespread, hideous crime can never be punished except by war. While at the eastern end, walking their customary tightrope of chicanery, other Brits were intent on protecting the capitalist state of Japan while hanging, illegally, seven yellow men.

This being the general situation, it is hardly a cause for wonder that the Tokyo Trial and its vile Majority Judgement were so prudently soft-pedalled by the Brits' peerless changeless Bicycle Bitch. By, specifically, the London *Times* – spinster in disaster; liar of Printing House Square; daily fare coloured childrens' livers sauced with white adult corpuscles; her fangs stained by the unrequited pangs of, at one time or another, almost all the English-speaking union race and of *all* other races. Which being the case it merits mention that at the time when she was impelled to permit a glimpse of what suppurates beneath her squalid slips, men condemned for having followed policies in which she takes such pride had just ten days before they died.

'And who is listening? No one! Precisely? Nobody!' Willem lamented to Michael Dwyer on a hot Saturday afternoon in the Brian Boru.

Dwyer jabbed a finger at the wad of hand-written manuscript sheets on the bar.

'Calm down. When you speak I hear, when you write I'm deafened. Do you give a single thought to me? To your reader? Who am I, do you imagine? A masochist?'

Willem threw back his large head and roared with laughter. 'Oh! Oh! Oh!' he chanted, in a descending scale. 'What a funny little fellow I am. You're right. Of course you're right. It's unreadable. Back of the class, Boymans! Detention for you, my child. A hundred lines. "I must not meddle with the affairs of men. I must not meddle with the affairs of men. I must not meddle …" Okay. I give up. Wave the white hankie.'

'Bill, please, this is important stuff.'

'Who cares?'

'Give it time. They'll come round. Got to, haven't they? It's in their interests.'

'"The right of belligerency of the state will not be recognised". Finis. End of story.'

They were silent for a moment, enclosed in their separate dreams.

'Yup, A9's the answer,' Willem said.

'One of the answers.'

'Name another.'

'Cindy,' Dwyer proposed.

Willem again laughed, less ferociously. 'Could be.'

'I should try her, if I was you.'

'I will,' Willem promised.

And he did. The next day he drove the ten miles up the coast of the Coromandel Peninsula to the fishing hamlet of Colville, and dropped in unannounced on Cindy Callcott.

The peace of the headland at Colville, in the lea of which Cindy lived, was even deeper than at home in the Kauaeranga. Standing by the bank of *harakeke* at the gate to her cottage, its tall stems of budding flax reaching for the sun's heat, Willem was caught undefended by an attack of terrifying aloneness. The severity of the pain quite took his breath away.

Come on now, chin up. You'll be alright. Forget about it.

He found Cindy on the porch of her studio, at the sea-end of the vegetable patch, reclining in a hammock, a sketchbook balanced on her tummy. She seemed not a bit surprised to see him.

'Hi, stranger. How is it?'

'Not bad. You?'

'Good. Fancy a stroll? It's beautiful up the back there.' Cindy pointed at the headland. 'You know it?'

'No, I've never been this far.' Willem spread the palms of his hands, hanging at the end of long arms against his denim thighs. 'Want to show me?'

'Come on then.'

She slid from the hammock, jumped – in one – down the four wooden steps of the studio and led the way along a path through the shrub up towards a field of sheep. They walked to the tip of Te Whau Point, where Willem began to pick the wild daisies which grew there in windblown profusion.

'I'd rather you didn't,' she said.

Willem looked down at the heavy-headed flowers scattered among the spiky green grasses, and raised his eyes to gaze up across the bay, over the humpbacks of a shoal of islands to the massive forest-covered ridge of Mount Moehau surfing the haze. He tried, with all his might, to push aside the rebuke. Told himself any distractive tale he could think of to curb the impulse to hit back. Tried and tried and … for once succeeded.

'Stupid of me,' he said. 'Why take? What's this mania for possession? I'm not normally like this.' He blushed. 'I did it for you.'

'That's extra-stupid.'

They wandered across the sheep-clipped grass at the top of the cliffs, hands in pockets, bumping elbows.

'Are you totally self-absorbed?' she asked.

'No, I don't consider I matter at all. I want to erase myself from the story. Article Nine. Pal. The Pact of Paris. Supranational justice. All I care for is to coax all this into the forum of open appraisal. Worldwide.'

'Why?'

Willem knew that what instantly entered his mind to say was childlike, crazy. He said it all the same. 'To save the planet.' Cindy kicked a pebble of jasper ahead of her. It flew in a sparkling arch out over the void, and skittered down the cliff to the seashore. 'Fair enough,' she said.

Willem was tempted to take the woman in his arms and kiss her, bury his nose in her hair. He resisted. And when they had made their way back down to the cottage and she invited him to stay for supper, he refused.

'Thanks. Another time.'

'Another life?'

They smiled, self-mockingly.

Later, alone on the deck, listening for helicopters, expecting any second to see the beam of a searchlight rake the forest, he drank a little less wine than usual.

One of the things Willem also thought about that night, influenced by passing earlier in the day on the road to Colville numerous small-holdings, with their chicken runs and pigs foraging in apricot orchards, was an incident near the close of the war. After victory at the battle for Arnhem, in which Willem's commando unit had parachuted behind the German defences, during two days' rest from front line fighting he had borrowed a motorbike and ridden off into the heart of the Veluwe to check on an aunt of his father's. He found Great Aunt Marijke and her equally old companion housed in a hen coop, in which they had been forced to spend most of the war, unaware that the Germans had vacated their country mansion a few days previously. They were filthy, too bewildered at first to speak. He helped them venture the few hundred yards from the hens' shed by a stream back into their home. Where within hours they recovered, and the again-proud Jonkheer berated Willem for incorrect etiquette in the pouring of a glass of burgundy from the German officers' well-stocked cellar.

Willem was regularly visited in the Kauaeranga by another war memory. From the time he spent training in north Wales. Literally. On his days off from military exercises he had volunteered for work in a narrow-gauge steamtrain, shovelling coal on the journey up from Porthmadog to the slate quarries at Blaenau Ffestiniog. Fifteen years ago. Since when so little, it seemed to him, had changed. He was the same person, doing many of the same things, in much the same kind of place. He had travelled to the other side of the world, as far as he could go before starting to come home again, to hide himself away in a wooded valley not unlike dozens of places he knew in Europe. It made no sense. On vacant afternoons he hiked into the New Zealand hills in search of unexplored mineshafts exactly as he had on the slopes of Y Garn, up behind Dolmelynllyn Hall. With a torch, a gold-miner's pick, a ball of heavy-duty twine and a whistle, carried in the haversack he had bought before the war – for what was then a fortune – at the climbing shop in St James' Arcade.

Where's the progress? What's the use? If there's never going to be a different me.

As Cindy had predicted, tragedy did strike Dwyer's daughter-in-law. At the end of a miserable week, at Friday midnight, Rosannah pressed a pillow over the face of her sleeping son, an incurable sclerotic. Having decided it was better for everybody if he did not grow up. Better for her, for sure. Better for the boy too, with a father like his, she reckoned. Rosannah made no attempt to evade arrest, and left to serve sentence in Moretons Penitentiary with a spring in her step.

'She's perfectly happy,' Cindy said, after a visit. 'Everything routine. No surprises.'

'No sex!' her friend Jane said. 'Bliss!'

'Wouldn't be certain about that.'

'With men, I meant.'

The women giggled. And checked to make sure Willem had heard, lying on his back in the sand a few feet away. All three wore no clothes, their bodies bronzed, drops of sea-water and grains of mica glittering on their skin in the sun. They were near the cliffs of an almost deserted beach which stretched for a mile to their right, fine old *pohotukawa* trees in ruby flower clinging at irregular intervals to a high-tide shelf of rock, their roots exposed. Jane Watson, like Cindy, was of Irish descent – from hill farming stock in the Slieve Bloom Mountains. Neither woman was married.

'"With all my heart I believe that the world's present system of sovereign nations can lead only to barbarism, war, and inhumanity, and that only world law can assure progress towards civilized peace",' Willem pronounced.

'What are you talking about?'

'Not my idea. Albert Einstein's. In a radio talk of May 1947. He, surely, is worth listening to?'

'At the beach?'

'Anywhere.'

Cindy clapped a hand to her forehead. 'For fuck's sake, Billy Boymans! Spare us! We're supposed to be having fun!'

Willem enjoyed his day at the beach. Jane was a gourmet camp-fire cook, and as darkness fell produced a delicious meal which they ate on their knees at the high-tide mark, the sea lapping at their feet. He felt exceptionally peaceful, sipping peach juice, chatting about the silliest things. About the songs their mothers crooned when they were young – many of which coincided. About the divergent images they each saw in the constellation of the stars. About the best way to keep skin moist, soft to the touch.

Jane was an only child, Willem learnt. A no-nonsense

woman with a passion for sheep.

'You're joking!'

'Far from it. I'd like to breed them. Odd old pedigree sheep, fit for the bush.'

'Really? What do you do in the meantime?' Willem asked, finding himself – on a personal level – uncustomarily curious.

'You being polite? I was wondering what's wrong with me. Or with you. That you show no interest in what I do. Where I work. Good to hear you're human.'

Willem's face – like hers – was a silhouette in the dark. He shut his eyes. Tight, like he used to as a child. Closed the castle drawbridge against adult entry. Through long disuse, the chains had rusted.

'The war messed things up for my generation,' he managed to say. 'Cut into that special time. At Cambridge. Many of the best are dead. Most of the rest of us morally maimed. Which is why it's vital, when we find the way, to fight for it. A thousand times harder than to win at war.'

'I understand,' Jane whispered.

Do you? No woman can.

Can she?

Nobody ever understands anything. I don't.

'There is one marvellous man around,' he decided to say. 'Emery Reves. Author of a book called *The Anatomy of Peace*. Which Einstein, Thomas Mann, General MacArthur swear by. In it he states fundamental truths. Peace, he says, is order based on law. There's no better definition. Any other concept of peace is sheer utopia. Peace is a method. A method of dealing with human affairs, a method of adapting institutions to the flow of change created by the inexorable dynamics of life. War is the alternative method, foisted on us by the sovereign state. Nationalism, according to Reves, is our collective inferiority complex. He's critical of Christianity too. Says it's manufactured a veneer of ethical conduct, a crust, only, of civilization. The tragedy is that we're neither heading nor thinking in a new direction. Those in power haven't the time or incentive to think. And those who think have no power.'

'What's happened? You're making sense,' Cindy teased.

He sighed. 'Luck. Talk enough, and once in a while the words fall into place. The law of averages.'

Breaking the silence which followed, Jane responded to Willem's earlier enquiry. 'I'm a city vet. I dock the tails of boxer puppies. Neuter tomcats for a living.'

'Are you happy?' Willem was amazed to hear himself ask.

'Are you?' she replied.

Willem was masterful at dismissing from his mind issues which, if he gave them space, might force him to deviate from a chosen path. His remedy for most internal troubles was to take off on an arduous hike. There were two things he was particularly keen to forget: Rosannah's murder of her child; and the question of whether or not he was happy. This latter issue triggered a third subject about which Willem was also anxious to avoid thinking: his growing fondness of Jane.

On the short drive to the top of the Kauaeranga Valley, from which he planned to take one of the trails looping through the forest, Willem turned over in his head key phrases from *The Anatomy of Peace*, comparing them with General MacArthur's speeches, with which he was equally familiar. The language, he had begun to suspect, was too close for coincidence.

Take MacArthur's barn-storming address at a presidential election rally three years before in Los Angeles. Did Emery Reves write it for him?, Willem wondered.

The leaders are the laggards. The disease of power seems to confuse and befuddle them. They have not approached the basic problem, much less evolved a working formula to implement public demand. They bring us to the verge of despair or raise our hopes to Utopian heights over misunderstandings that stem from the threat of war. But never in the chancelleries of the world or in the halls of the United Nations is the real problem raised. Never do they dare to state the bald truth, that the next great advance in the evolution of civilization cannot take place until war is abolished. Science has outmoded war as a feasible arbiter. The great question is: does this mean that war can now be outlawed? Sooner or later the world, if it is to survive, must reach this decision. When?

Well, now! What about that! And from a five-star US general!

Refreshed by thoughts of MacArthur, Willem set out energetically up the least travelled of the paths towards Table Mountain, not caring where it took him, content merely to be on the move.

An hour into the forest he stopped by a fallen tree blocking the overgrown track and ate a chunk of cheese, stored in a side pocket of his patched haversack. Willem refused to carry an ounce more weight than necessary. He had a particular aversion to wearing waterproofs in an equatorial climate, maintaining that vigorous walkers dried out on the hoof from the occasional storms of warm rain. Another of his foibles focused on the water bottle, which he refrained from filling at the start of a hike, arguing that he would cross hundreds of sweet-tasting steams at which to quench his thirst. The cheese parched his throat, and he got up from his seat on the tree-trunk to push through the undergrowth towards the sound of cascading water. The mountain torrent was further away than he expected, hidden behind a grove of giant *kiokio* ferns, their ribbed leaves bending over him. Like the fan-vault of a medieval cathedral. Having filled and drunk from his water bottle he tried to retrace his steps to the path, but found it impossible to do so. The primeval forest had closed in around him. He panicked, and stampeded in a straight line to where he believed the fallen tree – and his haversack – lay. Within a couple of yards Willem was hauled to a halt, his limbs gripped by a tangle of flying tendrils. He took several deep breaths, and extracted himself from the imprisoning foliage.

Willem was forced to accept he was lost.

Every year the Kauaeranga claimed half a dozen lives, often of experienced hikers, men whom Willem had previously assumed must – in some part of themselves – have wished for death. Because of ill-health, or sadness, a feeling that all the good things were in the past, the future a desolate decline.

Willem found himself unable to banish from his mind's eye an image of Rosannah, pale and purposeful, striding into her son's bedroom, with a pillow under her arm. He saw the boy cease to struggle for breath without emitting a sound, his limbs limp beneath the sheet. He sighed in relief at not hearing his cry echo through the forest.

Willem had two alternatives. To relocate the stream and follow it down until – within a few hours, a day at the most – it led him to a sea-bound tributary of the river, and safety. Or beat a patient track back up to the ridge along the top of which the original path passed. He chose the latter. And after thirty minutes' steady progress came across the narrow path. This he walked along for quite a while until recognizing he must be heading further into the forest, away from his abandoned haversack.

On eventually reaching his car Willem read the Manaia Maori inscription on a Forestry Commission noticeboard:

Our lands and our waters give us our turangawaewae, the place where we belong, the place to stand tall, the place to be ourselves.

Willem had decided, he discovered, to ask Jane to marry him. She accepted. How eagerly, Willem could not tell. It was hard enough to know how pleased he felt himself.

Willem certainly liked her father, Elliott Watson, a wholesale butcher. He was nearer in age to the father than to the daughter, who at twenty eight when they married – in the summer of 1959 – was eleven years his junior. In every other respect Jane appeared the maturer of the two. Of all three. Strengthened by the experience of nursing her father through devastation at the death of her mother – when she was twelve, in a swimming accident.

Willem treated Jane to a four-week honeymoon in Hawaii. Shortly before returning to Caldera – which was being repainted, its roof and decks repaired while they were away – Jane was reduced to tears of fury on receipt of a telegram from Auckland, announcing that her widowed father had married his secretary, Belle.

'How dare he!' She stomped through the bridal suite, beating her fist into the palm of her hand. 'Without asking me!'

'You might've said no,' Willem said, half-jokingly.

'You stay out of this!' Jane shouted. 'You don't understand the tiniest thing. It's a disaster!'

She began to blubber, her capable mouth falling open, lips slack and unappetising. Willem patted her back, his eyes averted. His sympathies lay with Elliott, released by his daughter's marriage to please himself.

No, that's not fair. Jane's a brick. It's a shock, that's all. She doesn't normally make a fuss.

'Look. Would you mind leaving me alone for a bit?' she asked, after he had supplied a handkerchief. 'I'll have to ring them. I can't sit here, like a nincompoop. It's embarrassing. What'll Belle think?'

Willem was delighted to be off-duty. 'Not at all.'

'How long will you be gone?' she asked.

'Three hours?' he suggested.

'Great. Thanks.'

It was early evening, warm. Willem strolled down to the port, out along the harbour wall – worried that he had not yet managed to say 'I love you' to Jane. The phrase would break his teeth, he feared. He had told her, plenty of times, how beautiful she was. That he adored her breasts. Willem knew he was exceedingly fond of Jane, admired and respected her. He felt more comfortable with the idea of loving her father than he did his wife.

On the spur of the moment, in the dark near the end of the concrete jetty, he stripped off and slid into the water. Swam the width and back of Pearl Harbour and returned exhausted to the hotel.

two

Willem had always known that to progress with his work he would have to spend time in Japan. Marriage was a diversion, an attempt to redraw the emotional map. Regularly though he harangued anybody with the patience to listen to his critique of the Christian evil of predestination, Willem was himself a fatalist. He saw it as his destiny to discover Pal and devote his life to the cause of enforceable world law. All he hoped was that marrying Jane might ameliorate the inner sense of helplessness. The contracted presence in his home of a Mrs Boymans encouraged him to believe in the possibility of fulfilment.

It was good too to be forced to think of someone other than himself. Difficult, he found. Worth the effort though, most of the time.

He was particularly pleased with her impact on the orchards at Caldera. Jane's introduction of sheep kept down the grass between the trees. And she tended the trees themselves, taught herself how and when to prune, learnt to recognise signs of pests in time to prevent harm to the fruit.

'You're so impractical,' she complained. 'Thousands of books, and not one on looking after fruit trees. On something you genuinely love.'

'Do I? What makes you say that?'

'Before we were married you spoke endlessly of your orchards. Talked of little else, as far as I can remember.'

'To you, maybe.'

'To others?'

'What do you think?'

'Article Nine. Your other topic.'

'My only, actually. Work which my dear young wife considers worthless!'

Jane's indifference to his quest hurt more than Willem cared to admit. In an act of typical perversity, he had ceased contact with Elliott Watson.

'What's Dad done wrong?' Jane asked, when she heard of Willem's crude cutting-off from her father.

'Nothing,' Willem replied.

'Then why won't you speak to him?'

'Because I haven't anything to say.'

'You used to.'

'So?'

'What happened?' she pursued.

'Nothing,' he repeated.

'It must have. Some mistake. You can't simply go silent, without an explanation. It's unfair.'

Willem was standing with both hands gripping the creosoted balustrade of the deck, staring into the distance, towards the fort-like hulk of Table Mountain, bright in the mid-morning sun. He turned to Jane, seated in the shade beneath their new orange awning.

'Fair? What's fair about your family's unconcern for the greatest fraud perpetuated on mankind this century? Yes! Fraud! Fraud! Fraud! I talk and nobody listens. What's the point?' He shook his head. 'I haven't the time to waste.' He rubbed the back of his hand against the ball of his right eye, vigorously, over and over again – and went on, in a calmer voice: 'It's become necessary for me to go to Japan. There're records I need to study. People to meet.'

'How long will you be away?'

'I'm not sure. Several months. Don't worry. Everything's in order. It's all yours.' He gestured at the house, extending an arm to take in the orchards, and the land beyond the river which he had bought for Jane to breed her sheep. 'Do anything you wish with the place. I won't mind.'

'I'll be all right,' Jane said. 'Don't fret.'

Although Willem knew about Japan in his head he was not at all sure what to expect in physical experience of the place.

His first surprise was the size of Tokyo, the vibrancy of its teeming metropolitan life, incomparably more sophisticated and cosmopolitan than Jakarta, the only other Asian capital with which he was acquainted. To a mind saturated with images of Japan's wartime devastation, his delight at finding himself immersed in a helter-skelter of development was intense. Tokyo in the autumn of 1960, five years after the withdrawal of an occupying army, was alive in ways Willem had never imagined possible. He felt liberated.

In Willem's personal almanac of do's and don'ts, to decide not to fix on a strategy was the one option guaranteed to be wrong. Incapable of sitting back and letting things – anything – happen, within two days of touching ground he had rented an apartment, hired a maid, located a pool for his daily swim, and registered as an extra-mural researcher at Tokyo University, with unrestricted access to its libraries, canteens and cinema clubs. The apartment he chose was in an ultra-modern block of business flats in Shoto-cho, a twenty-minute walk from Yoyogi Park in one direction and the bar-life of Shibuya in the other. It was hard to believe that almost everything he saw, from back-alley shack to boulevard villa, *shirataki* stall to department store, was new. Willem walked and walked the city streets, marvelling at the oriental will for renewal.

One of the advantages of believing in snap decisions was the speed with which Willem felt able, without a speck of guilt, to change his mind. Within a week of hiring the local tobacconist's daughter to clean his flat he had fired her.

'No hard feelings,' he explained to the tobacconist's English-speaking son. 'I made a mistake. I can keep the place clean myself. No complaints about Tatsu. Please. Take this.'

He sought to press a wad of notes beneath the Perspex window of the street booth.

The boy pushed the money back. 'No work, no pay. We do not accept.'

'You must, I'm at fault,' Willem insisted.

'Too much, sir. It is not correct.'

Willem wavered. He appreciated the point of family pride. Thought of asking them to consider the money as a gift, of suggesting they treat Tatsu to a beautiful new kimono. Her mother too. But feared this might be taken as an insult. With quaintly appropriate grace, Willem saluted. 'Major Boymans at your father's service. He may summon me at any hour, in any cause, and I will spring unhesitatingly to the good tobacconist's defence. *Au revoir.*'

Willem wanted to live disconnected from emotional attachment, free to come and go as he pleased. There was also, with regard to a maid, the threat of misunderstanding about his socks. Willem had travelled from New Zealand to Japan with three indestructable socks. Three identical socks were all any able-bodied man required, two on and one in the wash. Left foot to right foot to wash. Left foot to right foot to wash … observing this ceremony every morning he kept his elegant feet in excellent condition and insured, with similar home-laundry disciplines for his underwear and brushed cotton shirts, that he need depend on no one. Willem enjoyed being able to carry all he possessed on his back, all he valued in his head, blessed with a splendid memory.

It took Willem eight weeks to discover that the man he most needed to meet in Tokyo was Dr Kenzo Takayanagi, whom the records showed straddled the twin rivers of his crusade: the Tokyo Trial, in which Takayanagi had performed a leading role; and Article Nine, the crux of the attorney's current concerns as chairman of the Commission on the Constitution. Willem reconnoitred the territory of Takayanagi's past. Encouraged by the impression formed of a liberal intellectual and committed internationalist, Willem traced his office address. Following his usual practice, he dropped in one morning without an appointment.

In January 1957 Dr Takayanagi had been charged by Prime Minister Ishibashi with the duty of producing a full legal review of the Showa Constitution, considered by many influential Japanese an imposition by MacArthur. Chairmanship of this Commission placed Takayanagi in a position of some delicacy. Willem appreciated his predicament. He understood that the lawyer's professional experience in the West made the nationalists suspicious of him. Their aim, in an alliance of overlapping elites in government, private finance and the military was simple: ditch the idealism of Article Nine and rearm.

Was the judiciary strong enough to resist?, Willem wondered. In order to find the answer to this crucial question Willem was prepared, if necessary, to be awkward.

The location of Takayanagi's office, on Kasumigaseki, running from Hibiya Park up to the National Diet Building, placed him among the men of power. Willem adjusted his knitted woollen tie, and mounted the granite steps. According to a board in the lobby, the secretariat of the Commission on the Constitution occupied floors two and three.

Accustomed to rejection, the alacrity with which declaration of his interests to the receptionist secured an interview with Dr Takayanagi left Willem open-mouthed, momentarily wordless. He was shocked too by the attorney's age. In his mind he had seen a man in vigorous mid-life. The figure who rose to greet him from behind a large mahogany desk appeared ancient, with wrinkled smile and wispy grey hair. Takayanagi pointed to a G-plan suite by the window. They sat down. The receptionist filled two glass cups with tea, and left, backwards, bowing. Takayanagi was wearing an expertly tailored double-breasted suit and stiff-collared shirt. He crossed his legs. Willem noticed he was wearing odd socks, blue and black.

'You were there,' Willem said, sitting on the edge of the low square chair, leaning forward. 'What was it like? How did you contain your fury?'

Takayanagi smiled, and recrossed his legs. 'Professionally,' he replied. 'I learnt restraint in England. To speak with effect, not for the sake of producing a sound, of announcing that you exist. A half-filled bottle makes a noise, we say in Japanese.'

Willem guffawed, his big sweaty features and loud voice contrasting with the tranquillity of his companion. 'How true! So basic, the Brits. When I went up to Trinity I became an oarsman. Being half-blind, it was about all a fellow could do. As it happens, I was pretty good. It's not difficult, is it?' He laughed again, anxious to draw Takayanagi into his life's narrative. 'Rowed all season for Cambridge. Until a week before winning a blue they chucked me. I know why. Because I made it clear I didn't share their assumptions. There we are. What's that got to do with the Tokyo Trial? Absolutely nothing!' He wiped his face on a Dutch bargee's handkerchief, bright red with white palmettes, and shoved it back into the top pocket of his jacket. 'I'm sorry,' he apologised. 'I'm just so pleased to meet you. To talk to someone who knows how much it all matters. Justice Pal. Tell me about Pal. He must be a wonderful chap.'

Takayanagi nodded. 'I stayed with him in Calcutta not long ago. To hear him give the Tagore Memorial Lecture. You know the poetry of Rabindranath Tagore?' he enquired.

'Not well.'

'No? You should.

> You are the evening cloud,
> floating on the sky of my dreams.
> I paint you and fashion you ever

with my longings.
You are my own,
dweller in my deathless dreams.

Pal taught me these lines. In the library at home in Zushi. Working together on his judgement. Terrific times,' he said, in the
silted tones of a man grown physically old, whose tongue no
longer controlled the foreign words fresh in his young-feeling
mind.

'You did help him.'

'Not much, not with the arguments. With food and friendship. The text was his.'

'Is it remembered in Tokyo?'

'For the wrong reasons. By the militants, to discredit the
post-war settlement.'

'They have a point. Victor's justice, to put it mildly!' Willem
blustered.

'Not Pal's point,' Takayanagi insisted, lighting a sweet-
smelling cigar. 'Dialogue. Engagement with live law. This is the
path. Pal seeks to broaden the issue. It's the greedy nationalism
of the west which poisons world affairs, from which our fanatics take their cue.' In a puff of conciliatory smoke, Takayanagi
murmured: 'Why else is it taking me so long to guide the commission to endorse the Peace Constitution?'

'Will you succeed?'

'We'll see, we'll see.'

They talked for an hour, each eager to explain to the other
the significance – moral and political – of Japan's decision to
make war illegal. Impatient to tell his own version of history,
Willem listened inadequately.

'Remarkable,' Takayanagi commented.

'What?'

'How much you know about it all.'

Puzzlement washed across Willem's features. 'Of course I do. It's vital.'

'I know.'

'Glad to hear it!'

They stared at each other, Willem's aggression threatening to flare.

Then they laughed, quietly, peacefully.

'It's happened before. I refer my students to Nakae's *Three Drunks Talk About Japanese Politics*, published in the 1880s. Which tells of the necessity of abolishing armaments, to demonstrate to the citizens of neighbouring countries we have no intention of killing them. There's a phrase of Nakae's I'm fond of. "Remove the walls around the castle". Excellent advice. Not heeded then.'

'If not now, when?'

'One day those in power around the world will wish to make the change. I won't see it. You might, Mr Boymans. If your work is published.'

'You think?'

Takayanagi stood up. 'We must meet again. For luncheon? I'm in Rome next week. When I return, we'll get together. Thank you so much for calling.'

In need of unobtrusive company, of a place in which to sit and think, Willem walked back along Kasumigaseki towards the Ginza district, on the southern side of the railway tracks. He quickly found what he was looking for. One of the daytime bars where they played, unendingly, records of classical music, frequented mostly by younger people, reading books beneath bottle-green lampshades. Students, Willem presumed.

'What's this delightful establishment called?' he asked the plump waitress.

'Ambre, Sir,' it sounded as though she replied.

Willem nodded. 'Thank you,' he said – and meant it.

He sipped his beer and gazed about, picking out the other customers, many, like him, on their own, nestling in the high upholstered seats of the concert-bar. At a nearby table an older man waved his arms to the music. An amateur conductor, turning the pages of the score laid out on the circular wooden table in front of him. Everyone there was Japanese, all – except the waitresses – in Western dress.

Willem needed a quiet moment to think, not about the Takayanagi meeting, but about Jane. With Takayanagi he felt secure, connected by ideas. Jane was a different matter. He hated having difficulties with women. In the physical sense there were few with Jane. The mechanics of their relationship worked efficiently; apart, that is, from the periods of enforced abstinence – unnecessarily extended, he felt – after a couple of miscarriages. Circumstances never to be repeated: after the last drama, when Jane almost died, a surgeon had removed her womb. The problem lay elsewhere. With him, he acknowledged. Without wishing to examine why, Willem was aware that the intimacies he unreservedly enjoyed were those he knew, before they began, were fixed term, predestined to terminate. Jane he had made the mistake of marrying.

In the bar they were playing a pre-war recording of Verdi's *Requiem*, a performance of which the Tokyo Symphony Orchestra had given the week before in the restored open-air theatre in Hibaya Park – with a choir of Japanese schoolboys, trained to perfection. Judging himself tuneless, unmusical, Willem had gone for the social spectacle. At this repeat hearing it occurred to him that maybe music had failed to move him for the lack of his attention. The old man closed his eyes at favoured phrases, conducting only with his fingers.

Willem shut his ears and concentrated on Jane. The time had arrived to make a decision.

As in previous experience of facing up to choice, Willem realized he had already crossed beyond the point of no return. Was it clear to Jane when he left for Japan that their marriage was over? Did she already know of something he was at the time not consciously aware? That he was never going back to Caldera?

So be it.

Once my home alone, now hers.

The best way: Willem affirmed – happy he had not reproduced himself, that there were no children to bind him to an unwanted wife.

Nor you to me, Jane dear. Try your friend Roddy. You'll be happier within a week with him than I could make you in a million years.

Although Willem was pleased to feel liberated from the debilitating unreality of marriage, he sensed injustice. Not specific. General. Crushing him.

Women! Huh!!

He was thinking, at that moment, of a particular FANNY. Or was she a WAF?

Willem could not remember exactly what had happened sixteen years ago in seaside Eastbourne, where the Dutch Commandos were stationed for the final countdown to the Battle of Arnhem.

Probably a FANNY. More the mentality, proud behind the wheel of their official limousines.

'What do you think I am?' she hissed.

And spat at me. Full on my cheek.

Willem shook his head.

He simply did not understand women. An ordinary proposition, nothing untoward, no hint at perversity. Dinner in exchange for sex. He had done it before, dozens of times.

Well, no, not dozens. For others had also refused, found some kind of excuse. The weather, mostly. Nobody else spat in my face.

Bitch!

Willem said such things to himself all the time, felt under permanent feminine threat. Not that this stopped him seeking the company of women, wanting to be with them, to feel their flesh next to his, touch skins.

In Tokyo Willem explored the different types of bar life, from Ueno to Shinjuku to Akasaka and back – repeatedly – to the Ginza. Where he made friends with Moichi Tanabe, a bookseller, author of an autobiographical guide to the rituals of professional seduction. Beneath the polluted skies of the Japanese capital Willem made it his business to lay bare the secret of oriental ease with love. A ridiculous idea, pursued with unassailable conviction.

His favourite hostess worked in a bar with no name, in the main night street of Shibuya, a stroll from his apartment. Not until his twentieth visit – after endless instruction from Mr Tanabe – did he manage to entice Chieko home with him.

Chieko was a lovely woman, steady, patient, her centre of emotional gravity close to the ground. What first attracted Willem was the feeling she imparted, as he watched her in the bar, of being herself. The woman he saw serving drinks, sitting listening to alcoholic anecdotes was, he was convinced, the same person who shopped for vegetables in the market and collected her child from school, rocked him to sleep before leaving for work. Chieko was whom she seemed.

'Don't they drive you mad? With their complaining.' Willem frowned at the other customers, scattered among the tables in the narrow room, with a balcony opening through latticed shutters on to one of the city's once-numerous canals. 'They do me. If it wasn't for you, I wouldn't come. I like the place,' he reassured. 'It's people I can't stand.'

Chieko stared directly into his eyes, without pretence to comprehend the words – while conveying, nonetheless, the impression of sympathy.

'Do you know what I'm saying?' he asked with a smile.

She smiled back, shaking her coiffured head.

'You don't understand, yet you answer correctly!'

Chieko stroked the back of Willem's hand.

The drill at this type of bar – as expounded by Mr Tanabe – was for the favoured customer to wait a discreet distance down the street at closing time. It puzzled Willem that Chieko took so long to appear after the last customers were ejected. One evening, his patience strained, he peeked through a window and saw the hostesses standing in a circle around the manager, a middle-aged woman, discussing the night's business. Chieko was rewarded in her wage packet, Willem discovered, for suggestions to improve client satisfaction and boost the bar's profits. She displayed the same conscientiousness in their lovemaking.

Willem adored the attention Chieko gave to his feet. While she kissed and massaged his toes he used to talk to himself, out loud, in tones of rare gentleness.

'Can I tell you about my mother? I'd like to. You see, my mother was never happy in England. She never complained. Still there, thirty-five years later. Stuck on Highgate Hill. A little Dutch girl. When all she's ever wanted is a flat in the Denneweg, a whisper away from the coffee shops of The Hague. What made my father insist on settling in London? Arrogance? Rich he was. As I am. Why deny it? It's a privilege. Did he not see how Mother pined for Holland? I know I didn't. Then I never notice anything, Jane says.'

He paused.

'None of us belonged in England. Billy Boymans!'

Willem laughed. Chieko laughed too, in intimate harmony.

'What chance has a fellow at prep school with a name like that?

'None! My mother too, she found it impossible to make

friends. She worried all the time what she might be doing wrong. What I might. She felt we were always on the point of making a social gaffe. That our neighbours were laughing at us behind the privet. After the war and everything. With her son a hero. Did you know I'm the Dutch equivalent of a VC? Your Billy of the beautiful toes? Oh yes. Every bit a hero as Japan's cherry blossoms. Undying love for their mothers, they proclaimed. Shouted "Mother! Mother!" as they plunged to glorious extinction. Call that love?'

Another pause.

'Is it love to enshrine wives in mansions on the lip of Hampstead Heath? It's important to think about these things. So we can change them.'

Willem gave Chieko a key to his front door, freeing her to come and go as she pleased, leaving the choice to her when they spent the night together. An early riser, Willem left for the library before Chieko awoke. When he returned to his apartment the remnants of her presence moved him, on occasion, to tears. The refolding of his few clothes in the cupboard drawers. The placing of a bucket of water beside the lavatory pan, with which to wash his behind. Loo paper, Chieko explained one night, in a hysterical display of slapstick mime, was for savages.

Not all her actions pleased him. He was furious when she cut up one of his torn cotton vests to make a dishcloth.

Other touches he did not spot for weeks. Her cleaning of the windows, for example.

He noticed, instantly, when Chieko removed from his ivory-backed pair of brushes years of accumulated hair. They confronted him on the bathroom shelf as new as on his eighteenth birthday. A present from his godfather, Felix Golding – Uncle Felix, a Suffolk architect, whose Dutch wife was his mother's cousin.

The monogrammed hairbrushes were a source of pride,

guarantor of his surrogate Englishness, more valuable to Willem
than any medal.

three

At the end of the war one of the few buildings of stature to stand intact was the Military Academy at Ichigaya, on a hill overlooking central Tokyo. Occupied in the final months of battle by Prime Minister Tojo and the war cabinet, it was left in error, the Americans directing their bombs by mistake at the similarly monolithic Waseda University on an adjacent hill. The brutish square tower at Ichigaya still dominated the skyline during Willem's year and a half in Tokyo, by which time the city was already launched on cycles of perpetual regeneration. He often took the tram to the top of the hill; and stood at the gates, trying to imagine the feelings of Dr Takayanagi, driven there each day to attend the Tokyo Trial, the devastation of war all around, rubble as far then as the eye could penetrate the clouds of dust raised in the wind.

In the course of his research Willem came across the file copy of a petition signed by Mamoru Shigemitsu and four other defendants at the trial, addressed to Mr Justice Webb, President of the International Military Tribunal for the Far East. From the date of the petition it was clear to Willem this must have been a final plea for reason – after judgement, before imposition of sentence. Enclosed with the petition was a questionnaire drawn up by Dr Takayanagi for distribution by Webb to specified world authorities, polling their opinion on the legality of the trial. Included on the list of names were Karl Barth, H G Wells, Aldous Huxley, Mahatma Gandhi and Roscoe Pound, Takayanagi's tutor at Harvard. Among other arguments, the petition pointed Webb towards a book published by H G Wells in 1930, entitled *The Open Conspiracy*. A copy of which Willem promptly obtained. To read, on page four, a text he would like to have written himself.

It seemed to me that all over the world intelligent people were waking up to the indignity and absurdity of being endangered, restrained and impoverished by a mere uncritical adhesion to traditional governments, traditional ideas of economic life and traditional forms of behaviour, and that these awakening intelligent people must constitute first a protest and then a creative resistance to the inertia that was stifling and threatening us. These people I imagined would say first, "We are drifting. We are doing nothing worthwhile with our lives. Our lives are dull and stupid and not good enough."

And then they would say, "What are we to do with our lives?" And then, "Let us get together with other people of our sort and make over the globe into a great world-civilization that will enable us to realize the promises and avoid the dangers of this new time."

It seemed to me that as, one after another, we woke up, that is what we would be saying. It amounted to a protest, first mental and then practical; it amounted to a sort of unpremeditated and unorganized conspiracy against the fragmentary and insufficient governments and the widespread greed, appropriation, clumsiness and waste that are now going on. But unlike conspiracies in general this widening protest and conspiracy against established things would, by its very nature, go on in the daylight, and it would be willing to accept participation and help from every quarter. It would, in fact, become an "Open Conspiracy", a necessary, naturally evolved conspiracy to adjust our dislocated world.

Willem chuckled at his by now regular desk in the main university library on reading, in a later chapter, the invention by Wells of the 'Parable of the Whole Hog' to illustrate his pet federalist theories.

Willem recalled the story over lunch with Dr Takayanagi.

'Ahah! Yes, I almost forgot,' he chortled, sauce dribbling

from his busy mouth. 'Most amused by your H G Wells reference. The sailors and the cabin boy. Remember? Hams and loins
chops and chitterlings. Pig traps on Provinder Island! Marvellous stuff!'

'I met him. In east Sussex.' Takayanagi gesticulated with his
chopsticks, flinging food onto the restaurant floor. 'An ignorant
parent, that's the trouble. The older I grow the less forgiving I
am of clever people who crucify their children.'

'Not my field.'

'Children? Or crucifixion?'

'Neither. I'm an atheist.'

'I am decidedly not!'

Willem was surprised by this response of Takayanagi's.
Their conversation had grown increasingly intimate during the
long lunch, yet no previous mention had been made of religion.
He felt dismayed. Betrayed.

'You're a Christian? You can't be! I don't believe it!' Willem
more or less shouted.

'Don't take exception. There's no need. I'm a Buddhist.'

'Apologies. My soft spot. I do apologize. Did Wells reply to
your questionnaire?' Willem asked, returning to the safety of
his obsession.

'Webb refused to send it.'

Takayanagi adjusted his spectacles, and peered over his
guest's shoulder. Willem swivelled to see what he was staring at.
The restaurant was full of young people, a high-ceilinged room
hung with *ikat* banners, the modern metal tables pressed close
together. Takayanagi patronized the place, he had told Willem
earlier, not merely for the excellence of the food, but also for the
company, for vicarious contact with the zest of youth.

'Webb was opposed to the death penalty,' Takayanagi continued. 'Judged Japan's generals undeserving of death while our
Emperor, the supreme authority, walked free. I've never under-

stood how Webb squared his conscience. How he brought himself to sign the warrant for their execution.'

'Doesn't have a conscience,' Willem murmured.

Takayanagi again gazed at the tables gay with chatter. He bowed his head, half rose from his chair. A man in a baseball cap clapped a hand on his shoulder, pushing him back down into his seat. They talked rapidly, in Japanese, before Takayanagi turned to Willem.

'My nephew. Jojo, his fans call him. Mr Boymans. An admirer of our constitution.'

'Your constitution, Uncle, we all admire,' the young man said, grinning broadly, his English strongly accented.

'The family tease me,' Takayanagi explained. 'Because I boast how fit I used to be. Proclaim my skill at school on *tetsubo*. In America I challenged a colleague to an endurance test. He passed out, unconscious!'

'And what does your nephew do?'

'Plays with his guitar,' Masayuki Takayanagi replied. 'Makes a noise.'

'A beautiful sound?'

'Not if I can help it! Come and hear.' He handed Willem a Roneoed leaflet. 'Cheers, Uncle. Excuse me. I'm with friends,' he said, these last phrases again in Japanese.

Willem followed the musician's bouncing step back across the restaurant to join companions in a smoke-filled corner. He looked down at the leaflet in his hands, admiring the visual urgency of the script, unable to extract a drop of sense from what he saw. 'What does it mean?' he asked. Takayanagi translated. Willem took note in his diary of the time and place of the concert.

They stayed talking for another hour.

'No children, our only sorrow,' Takayanagi revealed. 'Substituted over the years by closeness to my students. Whose sons and daughters I play with when they call on Sundays. You must come too. To see us in Zushi. Do. Any weekend.'

One of the things Willem felt comforted by in Tokyo was its formality, the refinement of social exchange. The casual cameraderie of New Zealanders had made him anxious. Although he dropped in on people whenever he chose, he hated anybody doing the same to him. With the Japanese he felt safe. Except now, with Takayanagi. Willem disliked open invitations.

I'm a polemicist. An irritant: he told himself. If I'm welcome, I can't be getting anywhere.

Takayanagi also talked, at length, about politics. Willem listened hard to this. Pressed him for details of Pal's concern that America's desire for revenge threatened the fall of Asia to communism.

'Look what's happened,' Takayanagi elaborated. 'Maoist revolution in China. Russian duplicity in Korea. Pal's right. Asia for the Asians. Make Japan into an economic clone of America and all our freedoms are at risk. He's a brilliant man. And powerful. Pal persuaded the Indian government not to attend the 1951 San Francisco Conference, where the Peace Treaty with Japan was signed. He knew what it meant. Gromyko too. That's why Russia abstained. Because the treaty amounted, in effect, to the arming of Japan as a Western satellite. Have you come across the work of Theodore Sternberg? No? A German Jew. Lived here from 1913, until his death five years ago. Professor of Law at Tokyo University. I introduced him to Pal, and the two of them got on. Sternberg contributed to the Dissentient Judgement. He was of the opinion that ...'

Information flowed. Willem learnt that Takayanagi had been responsible, as President of the Japan Cultural Forum, for publication of the first issue of *Jiyu* (Freedom, in English). That it was he who guided the magazine towards opposition to the proliferation of American military bases on Japanese territory.

He who criticized the investment of millions of aid dollars in reconstruction of the Mitsubishi armaments empire.

'Did Sternberg publish anything on the Tokyo Trial?' Willem asked.

'Not specifically.'

'The other day the librarian recommended *Buddhism and Culture*. In which there's a piece by Röling.' Willem peered into a notebook. 'Here it is. "It was the Tokyo Judgements which made the crime against peace enter positive law. The judgements stand in history as indelible fact. They form a precedent. They have the power of the beaten path." Pal's Dissentient Judgement also. It's all international law. In ten years, twenty years. Forty years time, the path will remain open.'

'Röling acquitted Shigemitsu.'

'I know.'

'I know you know. Worth repeating,' Takayanagi insisted.

Soon afterwards they left the restaurant. Takayanagi shook hands with Willem, placed a beret on his head and walked briskly off out of the Ginza, towards his office. It was four o'clock in the afternoon, a mediterranean time to return to work. Takayanagi considered conventional timekeeping an irrelevance. All his life he had slept and eaten whenever he felt the need, at any time of day or night. Willem was equally non-conformist. He judged each day on individual merit, on what it happened to bring. In this instance rather too much, he felt. Willem made off in the opposite direction to Dr Takayanagi, and walked for as far as he could go. To the shore of Tokyo Bay. Where he sat on a rock and sought to forget – and, at the same time, never to forget.

On the night of Masayuki Takayanagi's concert at the *Gin-Pari* Willem realized his emotions were exhausted, burdened with the self-assumed responsibility to save the world. All day long, sitting in the library, the desire for personal peace had been so strong he was afraid he may have called out. May have cried: 'Away! Go! Leave me!'

Meaning?

Willem clenched his fist inside his trouser pocket as he strode down the street.

If I – in truth – don't want to know what I mean, how can others be expected to understand?

Although not at all what Willem had imagined, the music which squeezed up the steps of the *Gin-Pari* brought a smile to his face. His mood switched, instantaneously. Willem listened with innocent ardour to the coolest of jazz, to Jojo's virtuosic solo improvization on electric guitar.

Willem checked to see if Dr Takayanagi had changed his mind and decided to come – 'It's not the jazz I know. Off the beat. Formless,' the cosmopolitan had criticized – but he was not there. The small room was full enough, the atmosphere relaxed, appreciative. Willem ordered a beer and sat down at a table in the centre of the room, unafraid of prominence.

At the end of the session Jojo laid his guitar on the floor and walked across to Willem's table, at each step bouncing up on the tip of the toes of his Greenflash tennis shoes. He drank straight from the neck of the bottle in his hand, and sat down. Willem beamed his approval. Jojo smiled back.

'Well?' he wondered.

'Thought you were into noise,' Willem responded.

'Later.'

'Is your uncle coming?'

'Never.'

A man wearing his thick black hair long, on to his shoulders, like a samurai helmet, selected a disc at the jukebox. Bubbles of coloured oil circled through the machine's tubes.

'Tell me. How did Dr Takayanagi remove his name from the

list of ruling elite purged at the end of the war?' Willem decided to enquire.

'Ask him.'

'I have.'

'What did he say?'

'He said the Americans made a mistake. Which they corrected.'

'Yes?'

'There's more to it. Isn't there? There must be.'

'I expect so,' Jojo agreed.

'What?' Willem asked.

'What're you implying? Has feeling been bred out of you westerners? You're so predictable. With your scatter-shot insults. Uncle's fought for fifty years for law between nations. Won't you try and comprehend?'

Jojo delivered this diatribe without emphasis, as if a statement of ordinary fact.

'I'll try harder.'

'I'm serious.'

'So am I. I'm the most serious person on earth,' Willem half-joked.

'No you're not. I am!'

Willem ordered a second beer.

'You speak English like a professor. Where did you learn?'

'From my uncle. I've never been abroad. I'm closer to old Kenzo than to my father. Much. He believes in me.'

'Do you?'

'When playing guitar. When the sounds inside find a way out, through my fingers into the air. When I don't apologize.'

Willem shook his head. Not in disagreement. More in mystification. At why anybody might want to say such things, put public shape to such sentiments.

He failed to think of a response.

Jojo continued to talk, between bursts of silence.

'I demand a lot of the bands I play in. Essentially that we have something worth saying, beyond self-exposure ... The New Century Music Laboratory we call ourselves. We have a manifesto. With three pledges. To pursue the quality of real art. To engage audiences in the creative process, so listeners will learn to enjoy not only the surface but the core of music. To provide young musicians a place to play and, by being mutually inspired, to grow as human beings ... Solo improvisation is different. In that I do examine myself. Explore memories. See what I might be able to hear.'

Willem felt drawn in and down, down into the stream of himself by the conflict of sound Jojo improvised in his second session. Unlike regular music, which imposed order onto the chaos of nature, Jojo's abjured resolution. Willem could scarcely believe his ears.

'Amazing.'

'You liked it?'

'Loved it.'

'I'm glad. Thank you.'

Throughout the remainder of his stay in Tokyo Willem followed Jojo and his friends from the New Music Laboratory to wherever they played. He became known in most of the city's *jazukissas*, welcomed on daytime visits for his insistence on buying everybody there a cup of coffee. At two hundred and fifty yen a cup – one US dollar, roughly – the cost was minimal, to him. With it he purchased the willingness of young people to talk. And to translate for him the anarchic comments scrawled in notebooks scattered about the cafes' shelves, amidst piles of corner-curled Manga comics and racks of black American jazz records. Most *jazukissas* were tiny, with huge speakers and few chairs. Willem knew he had found a home in this community when he was able to participate in the jokes they serially told each other about the approaching Tokyo Olympics, with which the politicians promised to turn defeat at war into victory at peace.

'Japanese legs are too short.'

'For what?'

'To hop, step and jump.'

'Then pole vault.' Willem learnt to respond.

'I'm practicing!' Jojo promised.

Friendships in the jazz cafés made up, to some degree, for the loss of Chieko.

Willem rejected any idea that he might have been to blame for what happened. In his view, the request to meet Chieko's parents and the two aunts with whom she lived was unexceptional. Her refusal elevated the issue, in his misguided mind, to a matter of principle.

'It's the natural right of man to look his lover's mother in the eye over a glass of wine. I insist. I will not be insulted.' He wagged a finger at Chieko, her usually pliant features a lacquered mask. 'Are you ashamed of me? You'll take from the ugly long-nose his pretty money. Not fit, though, to sit at table with your father. Is that what you're saying? Have I read the message right? You're the same as every other madam. A betrayer of trust. I'm an idiot to have dreamed it might, this once, be different.' A frown rucked the taut skin of Chieko's forehead. 'All right, all right. I'll ask one last time. Will you permit me the pleasure of inviting your mother and your father and aunts Tomoko and Tamie to dine with me at the Imperial Hotel?'

Poor Chieko bowed from the waist in acquiescence. Willem gave her shoulder a companionable pat, and sat down at his writing table by the window. He handed her a note, confirming the agreed arrangements. 'Here, give this to Aunt Tamie. She'll tell you what you've promised me. Don't worry, I forgive you. It's all over. Everything's better again.'

At the end of the occupation the Imperial had returned to being an extraordinary hotel, the diasporan masterpiece of a modern American genius, Frank Lloyd Wright. On breaks from his mission to universalize Article Nine, Willem took a critical interest in architecture. Frank Lloyd Wright was a hero of his.

'You see, he wasn't British,' Willem explained to Aunt Tamie, seeking, through the folds of her best kimono, to take an arm and guide her across the marble floor of the Imperial's lobby. 'To his great good fortune, he was an American. Being so, he escaped the stain of orientalism. Frank Lloyd Wright came to your country and looked at what he saw, not at what he thought. An obvious ploy? To you far-sighted Japanese, yes, of course. To a prairie-bred American also. Not, I'm ashamed to confess, to those whose dear papas paid a prince's ransom for them to be educated by the blinkered Brits. Swot, my son, at the conventions of history. And the world will be yours. Because it was theirs, if you follow my meaning. They knew about the orient. How to manage it. What to bring home to hang on the wall. Now Frank Lloyd Wright, he suffered none of these disadvantages, he ...' Willem stopped in mid-sentence, transfixed by a pool of golden light at his feet. 'He's dead. Were you aware of that, *ma petite Tante Tamie*? Fell off his perch last June. Never mind, eh? Happens to us all.'

Although Aunt Tamie had learnt in the post-war years to make limited sense of Arabic lettering, the spoken word defeated her. Unable to say anything to Willem at the dinner table, laden with accoutrements, the family said nothing to each other either. Nor to the brigade of waiters attentive to their uncertain moves. Chieko's mother, seated – at Willem's decree –

in pride of place at the head of the table, nodded and blushed and barely ate.

'Lobster Thermidor for six. No, no argument,' Willem insisted, at the top of his voice. 'A family celebration. We'll have the lot. Eat our way through the menu. Why not?' He gestured at the staff in their high-collared white tunics, British-India style, bearing trays from the kitchen at a ceremonial pace, backs stiff and straight. 'It's what they're here for. To render Chieko's hard-working old mum a decent service.' He raised above his head a long-stemmed glass of Chardonnay. 'A toast. Come on now. Chop chop,' he cajoled, forcing them to imitate his action. 'First a word of thanks. Don't want to spoil the festive spirit. It's just that ... How shall I put it? ... your daughter, madam,' Willem said, bending his head to within an inch of the mother's frightened face, 'is an angel! One of the chosen. A paragon of paramours. It is to her we owe this happy occasion. To Chieko, ladies and gentlemen.'

Willem attempted to clink Tiffany glasses. Aunt Tamie pulled hers away to evade catastrophe, causing Willem to slop wine onto the embroidered table cloth.

'Please, don't apologize. It matters not a jot. Waiter!' he called. 'Clean cloth, pronto. There's a good lad.'

Willem applauded the bustle and scurry around their table. When the lobster arrived he tucked a napkin into the collar of his shirt and attacked with relish, cracking and sucking the beast's claws.

'Excellent!'

'Excellent!' he repeated.

'Frank Lloyd Wright was a fish fanatic. Several major buildings conform to the lobster plan. Shellfish, Froebel kindergarten toys and Japanese garden temples, they were his inspiration. He played the viola. Badly. His home was destroyed three times by fire. The first burnt his second wife to death. He rebuilt the house. And remarried. You must never give up, you see, Chieko. My cardinal rule.'

Before the sweet Willem ran out of information to impart to his mute audience. He clapped his hands. 'I know! Music! We'll have someone sing to us!'

A waiter summoned the restaurant manager, the restaurant manager summoned the Imperial's Chief of Staff and he – reluctantly – sent out to the Ginza for a geisha girl. Willem enjoyed his evening.

'Taxi!' he bawled at the door – and bundled Chieko and her family in. '*Bon nuit*. I'm walking home. It was awfully good to meet you. We must do it again. Often.'

Willem banged his hand down on the roof of the cab, and waved them away. Setting off at a strenuous pace in their wake, Willem was several streets from the hotel before he pulled out the envelope slipped by Chieko into his pocket as they left the dining room. He stopped by a confectioner's illuminated window and prised open with his thumbnail the seal. Inside was Chieko's set of keys to his apartment.

However many times Willem revisited the bar in Shibuya where Chieko continued to work, she declined – with inscrutable grace – to be intimate.

Jojo, when he heard the story, forgave Willem his heroic stupidity. Mr Tanabe took his protégé's rejection to heart, and was mortified by his failure to effect a reconciliation.

four

On the return journey to New Zealand Willem mislaid his conviction of eighteen months earlier that his marriage to Jane was worthless. He found her at home at Caldera. Jane's enjoyment of the house and the land confirmed to Willem that what he felt there was pleasure too. In the complex way of relationships, Willem was happier with Jane's pride in Caldera than he had been with his own.

'It's a slice of paradise,' he said on completing, in Jane's footsteps, a tour of the orchards. 'Rescued by you.'

Jane had cut her hair while he was away, short up the back, exposing the elegance of her neck. She half-turned to present Willem a smile freed from restraint. 'You discovered Caldera. And me.'

At that moment it seemed possible to Willem he might one day dare to love his wife.

They settled to a mutually agreeable routine. In Willem's absence Jane had devoted most of her attention to the sheep. She continued to do so, expanding her knowledge and reputation through secretaryship of the Thames District Sheep Breeders Association. Jane was ambitious, organized and hard-headed. With the advantage over local farmers of a wealthy husband, she was already winning prizes at North Country agricultural shows. Willem was impressed. Instead of working through into the evening till too tired to think, fit for little else than drink, he packed up his papers at five o'clock sharp and walked the fields with Jane on her end of day round of the flock. Willem cut them each a hazel staff and sealed the knots with linseed oil.

'It's in your blood. From the Slieve Bloom Mountains,' he declared.

'Nonsense. I've no idea what they look like.'

'Quite a bit like this.' Willem pointed at the rain-clouded sky and emerald pastures of the Kauaeranga. 'Wouldn't it amuse you to see?'

'One day I do want to visit Europe. Not on my own. With you.'

'When?'

'When the flock's established. In a year or two.'

'You'll meet Mother. If she isn't dead by then.'

'Why should she be?'

'No reason. To live or die. As far as I've ever been able to tell.'

'You're horrid to your mother.'

'About her. Not to her.'

'No?' Jane tried to take his hand as they walked up the drive of Caldera, but he pulled away. 'Were you a good son?' she asked.

Willem snorted. 'Too right!' He rubbed the the usual eye with his fist, as if it itched. 'Never good enough to make a difference.'

'What do you mean?'

'I mean that Mother gained nothing from having me.' He jabbed his stick into the earth. 'The last time I saw her she was almost emotional. On the night I left for Jakarta, Mother told me she knew she didn't need to worry about me. Knew I was going to be all right. Since jumping off the table.'

'You jumped off the kitchen table and didn't hurt yourself? When you were tiny?'

'No, no. She did. Pushing for a miscarriage.'

Willem put on weight in Jane's care. At her instigation, he filled with a gold replica the gap left by a tooth knocked out in a practice parachute jump. Spurred by the experience of Japan, by his admiration of the integrity of its people, Willem put order into his thoughts. He commissioned a printer in Auckland for the letterpress inscription – in Basle Roman – of two favourite quotations. These he framed and hung above his desk in the library at Caldera. The first from Thunberg, an eighteenth century traveller, reporting on the visit he made to Nagasaki in 1773; the second by Albert Camus, a response – dated 8 January 1955 – to critical misreading of *The Outsider*.

Above the library door, on the hall side, Willem stencilled the motto another of his heroes, Dr Christopher Dresser, had displayed in an identical place in his home in Holland Park: KNOWLEDGE IS POWER. He was furious when his researches had unearthed, too late for him to visit, that this Victorian Japanophile's great grandson Stanley was born, brought up and still lived in Kobe. On Dr Dresser's trip to Japan in 1876 he had been honoured by an audience with Emperor Meiji. And he had left behind, in charge of the family's burgeoning export business, his second son Christopher, who married a Japanese weaver. Neither the son nor his heirs had dreamt of returning to London.

'Don't blame them,' Willem commented, filling in Jane on his day's work, as they wandered through their river-meadows, checking the health of winter lambs.

'Do you regret coming home?' she asked.

'Part of me, yes,' he said. 'No offence. No reflection on you, my dear.'

'Should hope not!'

'They have the answer. Talk. Always talk. Never fight. It's the only way.'

By the summer of 1963 Jane decided she was ready for a long holiday. They flew to London – their first port of call – and booked in to the principal suite of a small hotel in Bloomsbury.

Willem had not warned his mother of the plans to introduce his wife to Europe – he was not entirely sure he had told her he was married. Neither did he telephone on immediate arrival, but approached tangentially, making his way up to Highgate on his own. On foot. With the intention, first of all, of dropping by the old family home.

The early June afternoon was warm and sunny, and Willem felt in buoyant mood, despite disorientation at the disappearance of the doric opulence of the Euston Arch, sold to a shipping magnate from Thessalonika.

He cut left towards Regents Park.

'Ahah! Now there's a sign of life!' he said, to nobody in particular – to himself, in fact. 'Shades of the master.'

He was referring to a brand new building, the Royal College of Physicians, standing white and cubic at the south-eastern end of the Outer Circle, which put him in mind of Frank Lloyd Wright. Accustomed to Tokyo's embrace of the contemporary, Willem felt a certain irritation at the number of prime plots of unused land. The only other recently erected building which he passed, a tectonic aviary at the zoo, he despised, its angularity anathema to the nature curves of birds in flight. It was a longer walk than he remembered, through the backstreets of Kentish Town and Gospel Oak, in which children played mischief, up onto Highgate Road. He stopped for tea and scones in Parliament Hill Fields, and watched the bowls for a bit before tackling the final climb.

It angered Willem to find he was unable to resist an overflow of memory. Too much had happened in these streets to be suppressed. Years ago Willem had promised never to dwell on the past, never to make excuses to himself, never to accept that anything was unachievable now because of some hidden, impossible thing he had failed to do then. And yet, when he came to the wall over which he used daily to scramble, squeezing beneath the sooty branches of an overhanging yew, he did so again, automatically, even as he told himself not to be such a fool.

Willem dropped to the ground at the other side of the wall,

making scarcely a sound, and stood in shadow against the trunk of the tree to survey the scene. His eyes widened. The wilderness of his youth was gone, cleared away. What had once been a jungle of soaring brambles and festooned ivy, threaded by beaten-earth paths between secret dens and houses in the trees, was now ... his hands flapped uselessly at his thighs ... what had once been Willem's private playground was now someone else's garden. Water ran down over artfully placed bolders, the Edwardian design of what had seemed to him, in the late 1920s, a buried civilization, now restored to its flawed grandeur. The stinking marshland of his childhood, from which he used to harvest bulrushes – lances for galloping knights, javelins for Roman cohorts – was again a goldfish pond. He raised his eyes to gaze up the slope, expecting to see the mansion's charred ruins, sealed from entry by a tall mesh fence and attenuated rolls of barbed wire. In its place? A luxury block of flats. Willem turned his head in the other direction and looked down, over the wall, to the far side of the road. There his family's home stood unaltered. Except the windows and front door were newly painted Tuscan green.

He stepped from beneath the branches of the yew tree, walked up a meandering yorkstone path, across the courtyard and out through the condominium's beaconed entrance. Fifty yards down the road Willem was forced to turn around, persuaded by the numbered gateways of the location of his mother's retirement flat, known to him in New Zealand only by its address. He walked back between the brash brick piers, and pressed the bell marked Boymans.

'Oh, it's you! I didn't catch the name,' his mother said, on opening the fifth-floor door of her apartment. 'You'd better come in.'

'You never told me it was here you lived!' He marched to the picture window and stared down onto the territory of his childhood laid out below. An open book, flat, featureless. 'It's not fair.'

'What did you say, dear?' his mother enquired, slipping without visible effort into familiarity. 'It's rude to mumble.'

Willem kissed the shapeless old woman on both cheeks and squeezed her arm, a little too hard. 'Good to see you, Mother. Looking pretty pecker. How're the waterworks?'

'When did you arrive? I was expecting you next week.'

'Is that what I told brother Dirck? Sorry to hear he's been pensioned off by his own nephew. Or is he pleased to be shot of the responsibility? I'm in the dark. Never much of a communicator, our Dirck.'

'Don't be difficult, dear. If you'd wanted to keep in touch, you wouldn't have gone so far away. Now tell me about yourself. How's the research going?'

The best thing about his mother was her disdain for the inanity of chatter. She talked if she had something to say, otherwise remained silent. Of what was said to her she remembered only the material points. Who but his mother – and Mike Dwyer, when sober – cared a fig for his work?

'Nearly ready to publish. Not sure what. I've a suspicion the historical approach will pay dividends. It's radical stuff, you know. Leads inexorably to world unity.'

'Now that you're here you should speak to Gerald Gardiner.'

'Papa's legal eagle? Isn't he a Quaker?'

'I've no idea. He's chairman of the National Campaign for the Abolition of Capital Punishment. That I can vouch for.'

'Good for him.'

Willem's mother glanced at the ormolu cartel clock on the wall by the door to her bedroom. It was five forty-five. She trotted across to the sideboard at the dining end of the large room, overfull of reproduction furniture.

'Sherry, dear?' she offered. 'There's nothing else.'

'A touch early, isn't it?'

'I think we can make an exception today, don't you? It's later in Australia.'

'New Zealand.'

'Why New Zealand?'

'Because that's where I live.'

'You don't. You live in Australia.'

Willem roared his delight. 'Really, Mother. Credit me with knowing the name of the country I reside in.'

'Very peculiar. I've told everybody it's Australia.'

They sipped their sherry. From the familiar gilt-rimmed glasses, which Willem felt an urge to hurl through the picture window. Instead, he told his mother about his wife.

'Don't mistake Jane for an Australian. And make sure you don't call her Beatrix, she's not my sister.'

His mother frowned. 'You know I'm bad at names. Warn her. I'm sure she'll understand.'

'Probably. She's very forgiving. I'm lucky.'

'Landed on your feet? I'm glad.'

'Jane keeps things in proportion. A fixture at my side, by which I calibrate the size of my ideas. Not small, by any means. Gargantuan!'

'You've never lacked courage. I'll grant you that.'

'Foolishness not courage.'

'You survived,' his mother pointed out. 'Isn't that a talent?'

Willem shook his head from side to side. In painful agreement. How did she do it? This ceaseless contradiction: insensitivity one minute and then, from nowhere, wisdom. It maddened him.

'Don't mess up your marriage,' she added. 'It'll be the end of you.'

He again shook his head.

No, there's no use. No point in arguing.

'Do you have Gardiner's phone number?' Willem asked.

'I expect so.' His mother flipped the pages of her address book, open beside the telephone, on the table by the upright chair in which she always sat. 'Home or chambers?'

'Both.'

She read out the numbers, which Willem noted in the London section of his pocket diary.

'I remember his hatred of blood sports.'

'The only topic on which Gerald and your father failed to see eye to eye.'

'Was Papa keen on hunting?'

'Don't you remember? On Boxing Day? Driving out … to Beaconsfield. Chesham. Somewhere. Frantic map-reading, trying to find the appointed village square. Or public house. "The Meet' he called it. It bewildered me. Another of those things people did. By the time I understood, you children were grown up, your father dead. And people had stopped doing it. Stopped traipsing about in motor cars on a day when any sensible person wants to be at home. I'm in Gerald's camp on this one. Hunting should be banned. It's barbaric.'

'Bold words.'

'Give the Gardiners my regards when you see them. He's influential. Make use of him. How else do you expect to get your work published?'

Willem held back from needless dispute, and half an hour later departed peaceably.

Gerald and Lesley Gardiner lived in Victoria Tower. Closer to Westminster Abbey than the station, Willem was instructed on the telephone.

'Hello, Willem. Haven't seen you for ages,' Lesley Gardiner greeted him at the door of their high-rise flat. 'Since the funeral. You're looking fit.'

The instant he saw her shrewd face, caught the force of the challenge in the corner of her eye, Willem recalled how much he distrusted his father's QC's wife. And she him. Their dislike was mutual. The sight of Gerald Gardiner, tall and thin-lipped, standing on the tribal rug in front of the unlit gas fire, was a relief. A relief to Willem to be reminded of his genuine respect for this austere figure. He declined the drink he was offered, and the two of them sat down immediately to talk – while Lesley Gardiner worked at correspondence at the secretaire near the door, the sheen on her lacquered curls refracting the light from an Anglepoise lamp.

Their conversation opened on generalities. The state of his mother's health. The prospects for a Labour victory at next year's general election. The menace to New Zealand's prosperity of Britain's desertion to the European Economic Community. Of which Gardiner declared himself wholly in favour. As a bulwark, he said, against the rising tide of fanatic nationalism. Distressed by Gardiner's clichéd representation of these issues, Willem invoked Albert Einstein, the least ordinary thinker of the century: "World Government is not a protection against tyranny; it is protection against the threat of destruction, and existence, after all, must have priority." Willem rose from his chair and paced back and forth in front of the fireplace, his voice rising in pitch as he ticked off on his fingers the stages of his argument, passionate and eloquent and impossible fully to comprehend. He tripped on the tasselled edge of the kelim and fell headlong. A bowl of cashew nuts crashed to the floor. Lesley Gardiner screamed. Picking himself up from among the bits of broken china, Willem held his bargee's hankie to a cut on his cheek. He glanced at Gardiner. And the two men began to giggle, like a couple of schoolboys.

They laughed, helplessly.

'I'm terribly sorry,' Willem managed, in the end, to say.

'Couldn't matter less,' Gardiner assured him, righting the coffee table and brushing the debris into an enamelled tin dustpan. 'You all right?' he asked.

'Of course he's not,' his wife answered. 'He's pouring blood. Onto the carpet!'

'It's nothing. Honestly. A scratch.' Willem held up his handkerchief to prove it – bright red, the bloodstains invisible. His cheek, nicked by a flying shard, had stopped bleeding. 'Where was I?' He recounted the points on his fingers. 'That's right. Kellogg-Briand. The Pact of Paris. Henry L Stimson, the US Secretary of State for War at the time of the signing, he was clear. War had been declared illegal. And it was on this foundation that the trials at Nuremberg and Tokyo administered international justice. A truth incorporated by the Japanese in their Peace Constitution. Universalized ... that's what I try to explain to you people ... universalized when the nations of the world promulgated, at San Francisco in 1951, their treaty with Japan. War's illegal. It just is.'

Gardiner crossed his long legs. He was wearing a dinner jacket, with double stripes of black silk running up the outside of his trousers.

'Who stops opposing sides fighting?'

'You legal eagles. By setting up an effective international court of justice. With the means at its disposal to enforce world law. Come on! What're you waiting for?'

'Easier said than done.'

'Saying it gets us nowhere. Twice now, after both the last world wars, every nation said it. The Japanese, they did it. Why? Simple. Because they know what it's like to be the victims of nuclear holocaust. They know everybody loses at war. The dead their lives, the alive their consciences. There's nothing worth doing with survival until we've removed war from our world.'

'Impossible,' Lesley Gardiner pronounced.

Willem, who had felt himself to be talking alone to her husband, flinched.

'Don Quixote leaves me cold.' She pointed to the window. 'My concern is for window cleaners. Landlords in these modern blocks exploit them dreadfully. We should legislate. Gerald will, won't you darling? When we win the election. Please, do let's be practical.'

'Lesley's right,' Gardiner said. 'It's difficult enough to stop people killing themselves by cutting commercial corners. Trying to earn a better living. How can the law prohibit a nation's defence of its interests?' He shot the starched cuff of his dress shirt, to consult his wristwatch. 'Time to go. Can I offer you a lift?'

In the back of the chauffeur-driven Rover Willem warned Gardiner he intended sending him, when completed, a copy of his manuscript.

'I've hit on a title. *The Pacific Path to Peace*. What do you think?'

The older man smiled. 'Clever.'

'Too clever?'

'Perhaps.'

'Tell me the truth, won't you? If it's wrong-headed I'd rather know.'

'I'll give you my opinion.'

'Thank you.'

His GLC chauffeur delivered Gardiner to the Inner Temple, where he was due to address the annual dinner of the Society of Labour Lawyers, attendance swelled this year by the prospect of a socialist government and pickings from power. Willem was dropped off at a pub in Clerkenwell, in an upper room of which the Evan Parker Trio was billed to perform free jazz.

When Willem and Jane met up at the hotel after their separate evenings out they both began to talk at once. Then both fell silent. Instead of laughing aside the silly misunderstanding, Willem took offence. Which annoyed Jane. And they ended up saying things neither quite believed. With the result that Willem declared implacable opposition to accompanying Jane on her visit to relations in Ireland.

'This is my break. Gerald Gardiner knows publishers. Lunches twice a month with Victor Gollancz. I haven't the days to fritter away on family gossip.'

'Can't you see how much this matters to me?' Jane complained, on the verge of tears.

Willem let out an ugly little laugh. 'My dear woman, it's a question of priority.'

'A week. Is that so much to ask?'

'It's not "a" week. It's next week. When I happen, I'm afraid, to be busy.'

'Then I'll go on my own.'

'Do.'

And she did.

Feeling – by the weekend – unacceptably alone, Willem invited himself up to Suffolk to stay with Uncle Felix.

Set of hairbrushes, cricket ball, Arthur Ransome books, loose-leaved stamp album, microscope ... Willem listed in his head the Christmas and birthday presents received from his godfather. Though not always something he had known he wanted, Uncle Felix's parcels had never failed to please.

I expect he's lonely in his old age. When did Aunt Willemien pass away? I imagine she's dead. Isn't she? I'd like to see him anyway.

The Goldings lived in Leiston, three miles along the coast and slightly inland from Aldeburgh – the two sons, their wives and children in the main house, Felix in a smaller home in the spinney. Both buildings were designed by him, the spinney house first, for his bachelor self: a merry essay in proto-modernism. When he married Willemien, shortly before the First World War, he built for her a triple-gabled mansion in the Dutch style, with black and white stone entrance porch, shuttered windows and roof of Flanders-red tiles. Willem was put up for the weekend in the big house, leaving Uncle Felix and his latest lover, the retired headmistress of a local primary school, undisturbed. Aunt Willemien, Willem concluded, had indeed died.

It was a revelatory weekend. The glory of the Golding brothers, upheld to Willem by his mother as ideal, their passage from school through university to glittering careers and on into ecstatic marriages he discovered to be an invention. Not of theirs. They, it was clear, had never pretended to be more than ordinary. Uncle Felix was the culprit, the creator of a myth around his sons.

'You took all that seriously?' Rupert – the eldest, a country estate agent with limited imagination and impeccable taste – patted the top of his bald head. 'Dad's batty idea I'd be the saviour of British tennis?'

'You did play at Wimbledon,' Willem grunted, in involuntary defence of a life-long illusion.

'When I was ten. In a charity event. To raise money for the demilitarization of East Anglian beaches.'

'You were good at it.'

'I was adequate.'

'Better than me.'

Rupert was three years Willem's senior. He laughed, in cousinly good humour. 'You're half blind. How the hell can you expect to hit a tennis ball? Those spectacles you used to wear. Poached your eyes! God knows how the world appeared from behind them.'

Willem thought about this.

A virescent green tendril from the elderly wisteria had

pushed its way, he noticed, between the sash windows into the sitting room.

'It looked odd,' Willem answered. 'Quite early on I worked out that what I saw wasn't the same as what you and Ferdinand were seeing. The gap has widened with time. Not narrowed, as I hoped it might. Take this leaf.' He broke the tender stem of wisteria. 'Such a simple thing. You'd think there could be no misconnection between you, me and a leaf.'

Rupert scratched his armpit. 'Fear you've lost me there, old chap.'

Willem smiled. 'You see? Never mind. I'm used to it. Aunt Willemien, how did she cope with his fantasies? She and Uncle Felix seemed terribly happy.'

'They were. Mother encouraged him to dream. He's a jolly good painter, after all. And a reasonable architect. They really loved each other.'

Willem had stopped listening, his attention drawn to a framed set of narrative postcards on the wall between the windows, partly obscured by the bunched fall of velvet curtain. 'What Did You Do In The Great War, Daddy?' the postcards were titled. Hand-tinted photographs of a boy in a blue serge sailor suit, in one of which he perched on the knee of his father, seated in a button-upholstered chair in a richly decorated library. The father's face pale, his hair brushed smooth and flat, neatly parted, wearing a stiff white collar and wide-lapelled three-piece flannel suit. Willem pulled a magnifying glass from his inside jacket pocket and read the verses printed below the three scenes.

"What did you do in the great war, Daddy?"
A boy asked his father one day;
The fighting was done, the vict'ry was won,
And peace reigned in place of the sword and the gun.

"Tell me what you did," the boy once more cried,
Then proudly the father replied:-

·"What did I do in the great war, laddie? – what did
                    I, do you want to know?
When they called for men, I was ready then, to go
                    and fight the foe;
I did my best for King and Country, laddie, just to
                    keep old Britain free,
But when I'm old and grey, for what I've done today
                    what will Britain do for me?"

"What is that medal you're wearing, Daddy?
Why is your sleeve empty there?"
A pause and a sigh – then came this reply;
"I gave that for Britain, no need to ask why,
And if my country were calling for me,
Why! I'd do the same, lad, again!"

On hearing athletic steps along the gravel path outside, Willem turned away from the postcards. It was David, Rupert's second son, a sixteen-year-old, home from boarding school for the weekend. He slid in over the sill of one of the open windows. Willem liked David. The night before, after everybody else had gone to bed, the two of them had sat talking over a pot of tea in the communal kitchen. About all sorts of things. Nothing personal. Ideas. Information. Images of the world as it seemed to Willem to be changing into. David was solid, in mind, body and temperament, self-labelled – while yet a schoolboy – a person who could be depended upon. Willem felt for him. Feared for him.

'You've never told me what you did in the war, Uncle Willem,' the boy said.

Willem muzzled his sudden fury. 'That's fine. I just don't talk about it. All right?' He risked a glance in David's direction. The boy was standing on one leg with the other doubled back against his bottom, stretching the thigh muscle, wearing tight white tennis shorts. 'All right?' Willem repeated.

'I noticed you looking at Grandad's postcards.'

'It's the past. Not important.'

'If you say so.' David stuck out his chin at his father, who lay with his feet up on the chesterfield, fondling the head of a spaniel. 'Fancy a game? The grass is dry.'

'Thought you were playing Sam?'

'He couldn't wait. Had promised to mend his bicycle. Or something. His sister's bike, I think. I'm not sure. If you don't want to, don't worry.'

'No, it'd do me good. I'll go and change.'

'Great. Meet you on court.'

Left alone, Willem took the framed postcards down from the wall and held them out into a beam of sunlight for closer examination. The scenes, and the sentimentality of the doggerel, were horribly real. Twisting the frame he found the postcards had been mounted to show the writing on the back. A message beginning on the first in the series, carried across to the second, ending with the flourish of a signature on the third:

18 May 1916,
Melbourne

Dear Heart,

Let me open with the positive: you are safe in Suffolk. I too am unlikely to be killed. With luck we will live to go on loving.

Thus the body. What about the spirit? Here in this

glorious place I am detailed to enlist young colonials to fight
in Europe. Dispatched by their mothers and wives, they
flock in their hundreds. Boys from the outback, fit and
handsome. Such a relaxed sense of time, and of themselves,
of their place in the order of things. Impressive.

On signing them up I have been ordered to distribute to
each recruit twenty of these Bamforth postcards. I have
never been party to anyhing so ugly in my entire life!
Is the civilized world worth saving?

Your affectionate,
Marmoset

(Below this was the pen and ink drawing of a cat-like monkey,
building a house with children's bricks.)

In the Tuesday morning mail at his Bloomsbury hotel Willem
received a postcard from Jane: a mystical view of the Round
Tower in Glendalough, County Wicklow. Her handwriting was
curled and regular, simple to read.

Willem

I'm really sorry you're not here. You'd adore the
countryside. Different from home. But similar all the same.
You know this, though. You've been to Ireland.

Lots to tell you. Back in London on Tuesday night as
promised.

Love,
Jane XXX

Willem was eager to see his wife, the details of their quarrel forgotten. He listened with undivided attention to the story of her
visit, interrupting from time to time only to press for deeper definition of the picture which formed in his mind as she spoke.

The places he found easier to make out than the people. He clearly saw the schoolmaster's house in Abbeyleix, where Jane stayed a couple of nights with Maud, her grandfather's youngest sister – only a child when her brother had emigrated to New Zealand, at the beginning of the century. A stone building in the market square, with hints of gothic in the mullioned windows and diagonally latticed glass. Abbeyleix was typical of small towns in central Ireland: one long wide street linking open country to open country. Jane's family were Protestants: 'As rich and thick as their cream', a man in a bar had said to her, scoffing pickled eggs between pints, his eyes unsmiling. Maud's daughter and son, a nurse and a civil engineer, drove down from Dublin to meet their relation from the other side of the world. They took her on a tour of the locality, up into the Slieve Bloom Mountains. Which Jane would have called hills at home. She loved the name, and was happy to be acquainted with the land of her origins. Shenagh, the nurse, guided them to the gate of the actual farm on which her grandmother – Jane's great-grandmother – was born and raised. A low cottage, with a room either side of the recessed front door and a large cobbled yard at the rear, the walls loam-sealed and painted white. Many times more space, in the sheds and barns, for animals and crops than for people.

They drove Jane down into the valley, following the route the family had taken to prosperity, and called at Knochfin, the house in which their mother – Maud, the thirteenth of thirteen – had spent her childhood, and where the two unmarried children – Albert and Dinah – lived still. The fields were fertile, sustaining a herd of Aberdeen Angus beef cattle and a show flock of Suffolk Down sheep, with black faces and feet, the wool on their backs cut flat to enhance their stature. Shenagh told Jane that her mother remembered, when very young, riding the sheep in off the fields for the late summer cull. And being beaten for her playfulness by her mother, with a cane of split bamboo, hurting her so badly she was unable to sit down for a week. The roof of the verandah had fallen away from the house, and the ground floor windows to the formal front were shuttered. Albert and Dinah drew the water they required from a hand pump in the scullery. When not milking cows, making butter or feeding the hens, Dinah lived out her life in the large kitchen, seated in her Windsor chair against a wall covered with faded rosettes, won years ago by the sheep. Dinah listened a lot to the radio, for though she knew how to sign her name she had never learnt to read. None of the family chose to explain to Jane what had gone wrong for Dinah. Jane was told that Albert refused to spend a penny on repairs to the house, convinced it would keep out the weather until he and Dinah were dead. They moved bedrooms rather than mend the roof. According to Maud, her brother was wealthy enough to pull the old house down, put Dinah into a home where she could be cared for, and build himself a beautiful bungalow in the walled garden. That – Maud felt – would be the sensible thing to do.

The farm buildings he kept in perfect order. New yellow ploughs and harrows, a beat lorry, a hay cutter and bailer, a muck spreader and other pieces of machinery were drawn up beneath the trees in the drive. In the coach house the leather upholstery of two pony traps was protected by a dust-laden coat of pig fat.

'It's true. Ireland is incredibly green,' Jane said to Willem. 'The green of the moss on the front door steps of Knochfin's an amazing colour. Different from the green of the goose pond. And from the grass in the paddock. Albert doesn't look well. His face is ill-red, not weather-beaten-red. I asked Maud how he managed to keep going. "God willing, he'll be found dead in the fields one of these days," she said, in her funny Irish brogue. *Ahavoe*. Isn't that a beautiful word? The name of the family graveyard. Up beyond Borris-in-Ossary. I felt I was in a movie!

Great black thunder clouds. And this ruined abbey on its own in the middle of the countryside. Me and Shenagh unable to think of a prayer to recite.'

'*Ahavvah* in Hebrew means love,' Willem said.

Jane handed Willem a book, with the letters J W stamped in gold at the base of the Moroccan leather spine.

'It's mine. Maud gave it to me. Open it.'

The pages, Willem found, were filled with extracts from literature – poems and prose – taken down in a round flowing hand.

'The eighth of October 1835. That's the year my namesake, another Jane Watson, began this commonplace book. Look properly. Please. Read the first entry. Out loud.'

'"The Broken Heart",' Willem read. '"It is common practice with those who have outlived the susceptibility of early feeling, or have been brought up in the gay heartlessness of a dissipated life, to laugh at love stories, and to treat the tales of romantic passion as mere fictions of novelists and poets. My observations on human nature have induced me to think otherwise. They have convinced me that however the surface of the character may be chilled and frozen by the cares of the world, or cultivated into mere smiles by the arts of society, still there are dormant fires lurking in the coldest bosom, which when once kindled become impetuous, and are sometimes desolating in their effects. Indeed, I am a true believer in the blind deity, and go to the full extent of his doctrines. Shall I confess it? I believe in broken hearts and the possibility of dying of disappointed love."'

'Do you?' Jane asked.

'No, I don't, I'm afraid.'

'Nor do I.'

Although Willem rejected the fantasy of death from a broken heart, he did not deny the acuteness of his dismay, on visiting

Calcutta on the journey home, to learn that Justice Pal was away
for a month, at an international law conference in Geneva.

five

Two days after returning to New Zealand Willem despatched to Pal a large manilla envelope of material, the pick of his research. Mindful of the judge's age – he would be eighty in two years' time – and the possibility, therefore, that they might never meet, Willem enclosed a list of questions about the inner workings of the Tokyo Trial. Together with his antagonistic analysis of a recent article by B V A Röling, Pal's colleague on the bench. What, he asked, did Pal make of the Röling thesis?

A reply found its way surprisingly quickly into the tin mail box at the end of the drive at Caldera.

Hotel International et Terminus
Geneva
23 September 1963

Dear Mr Boymans,

I have received your letter dated the 11th inst. with its enclosures, and also your review of the article.

I admire your collection and I must thank you for vastly adding to my information.

As regards your queries, I must say I do not know anything about items 1 to 7, 9, 11, 12 and 18. Items 13 to 16 are matters of expert legal advice, and I am afraid I cannot pronounce any opinion on any of the questions therein raised. As regards queries 8 and 10, I do not remember anything about them. I believe the record of the proceedings and the judgements would throw some light on them. As regards 17, it would be proper for you to approach the secretary, Law Commission, direct with the query and request. As regards the last two, 19 and 20, as far as I remember those were the reasons given and so far as I am concerned, I had no reason to doubt the reality of the same.

Your notes are highly illuminating and deeply
penetrating. But I must refrain from saying anything about
the merits of the contents thereof.

Your review again is on a topic which, in my view,
disentitles me to express an opinion on its merits. It seems
that you refuse to be deceived as to the true purpose and
nature of those trials. I would add that I found your article
enlightening in many respects.

I am really sorry I cannot be of any help to you in your
searching effort. Indeed I am ignorant of any of the alleged
designful processes of long-range politics. I must permit my
Dissentient Judgement to speak for itself.

I wish you every success with your effort to make
known the unknown. Only in order to explore the unknown
you should avoid assuming it is already known.

Yours sincerely,
Radhabinod Pal

The signature was shaky. Willem read the letter several times,
without making much sense of it. Pal said nothing. Nothing that
Willem needed to hear. He drank, in a single swig, a tumbler of
crushed orange juice. When he picked up Pal's letter again, after
marching up and down the deck, Willem felt the hoped-for swell
of encouragement. Pal meant him to continue. It was his duty.

And on recommencing work on his manuscript after the trip
abroad, Willem was relieved to find it further advanced than he
had feared. In a fit of optimism, he completed a first draft of *The
Pacific Path to Peace*, rewrote certain sections, paid for this version to be typed up, and sent off a batch of copies in time for
Christmas.

Three months later, the first response Willem received was
from Gerald Gardiner.

Willem Boymans   12 King's Bench Walk
Caldera   Temple EC4
Kauaeranga Valley   18 March 1964
Thames, New Zealand

Dear Willem,

I am sorry to say that the manuscript has come back from Gollancz. The reviewer's report seems to me unnecessarily discourteous (I had told Gollancz who you were, but he obviously didn't tell the reviewer), but I am enclosing it as you had particularly asked to have any comments.

I am sending you the manuscript insured etc. but this may take a little time to reach you.

Meanwhile, may I say how very sorry I am not to have been of more help.

We are still hoping to get to Australia and New Zealand in 1965, and if so we very much hope to see you then.

With all good wishes,

Yours ever,

Gerald

Gerald Gardiner, Esq., QC   Victor Gollancz Ltd
12, King's Bench Walk   14 Henrietta Street
Temple, London EC4   Covent Garden, WC2
12 March 1964   London

My dear Gerald,

I am awfully sorry, but it doesn't look as if *The Pacific Path to Peace* will do. I enclose my chief (and very careful) reader's report.

Yours ever,

V

The Pacific Path to Peace
By Willem Boymans
Approximate length 104,000 words

Mr Boymans begins, very reasonably, with the complaint that
A J P Taylor's *The Origins of the Second World War* 'grandly
overlooks' the origins of the Pacific War. 'He does concede
that the warfare preceding Pearl Harbour could hardly be
called world-wide. But he devotes not one single page to
reviewing the origins of Japan's break with Anglo-Saxon-
dom.' Mr Boymans apparently sets out to repair the omission.
But even on his first page his approach seems curious: he
begins not be directly criticising A J P Taylor but by attacking
a Mr F G Stambrook for failing, in his review of Taylor's book
in the *New Zealand Quarterly*, to mention the omission. Mr
Boymans is, one gathers, himself a New Zealander, and he is
quickly involving us in the intricacies of Australasian academic controversy. The main part of his book is cast as an open
letter to a Professor Julius Stone ('enclosing for the Professor's
consideration, a rough draft of the manifesto entitled "Article
9 of the 1947 Japanese Constitution and its bearing on the
Future of Mankind"'). A great deal of crabbed, cranky argument follows, on the significance of Article 9. Then Mr. Boymans wanders off into a rambling discussion of Chinese and
Japanese history. But it is impossible to follow his 'Path to
Peace' for more than a page or two at a time without losing
one's way; and even when the path seems clear, Mr. Boymans's
prose is an encompassing thicket through which one can
hardly hack one's way.

Willem settled down within an hour of receiving the post to
write back.

Caldera
Kauaeranga Valley
Thames, New Zealand
26 March 1964

Dear Gerald and Lesley,

There is something odd about me which I just cannot
explain, nor do I suppose that you can, but which now I
want to mention. The afternoon after Papa died I several
times had my hand on the phone, to ring you and tell you
the news. But I never did. The day before Papa's cremation
and my leaving England, I wrote to thank you for all the
sympathy you had shown. The letter stayed in my pocket.
And returning also from this last visit I had you very much
in mind when I bought several copies of a most attractive
postcard. Of the elephants Lutyens put into a wall of the
government buildings in New Delhi. But in the event I sent
them to others. This is oddness, I would say, carried to
absurdity.

Thank you, Gerald, for your letter. I am nowise
surprised by the thing being rejected. It was abysmally
stupid and even rude of me to ask your assistance with a
manuscript I knew to be unpublishable as it stands. But all
the same, the commentary proffered by the fastidious
gentleman whom Gollancz employs as a chief (and very
careful) reader is a bit grotesque. His commentary provides
his boss with not an inkling as to the basic theme, and yet
this is surely stated with stark simplicity on more than one
occasion. For your entertainment I am enclosing my
brushed-up version of what he might have said. But please
don't think I want to draw you into correspondence on this
subject. I am extremely grateful for the interest which you
have shown and the help you have given, and now it is up to

me to write something which at least in its form of presentation is readily publishable.

Kind regards,

Willem

The Pacific Path to Peace
By W J Boymans
Length approx. 104,000 words

The theme: asserts the emergence of Rule of Law to be mankind's primary requirement, and the principal obstacle to this to lie in the supine slavishness of the plebs of the English Speaking Union (ESU) coupled with the ruthless lawlessness of the ESU elite. The title of the book derives from the potential which lies embodied in Article 9 of the Showa Constitution. A9 introduced a crucial limitation into the concept of National Sovereignty. In the hands of a capable people like the Japanese, it carries economic implications which can shatter the system of world disorder which gave rise to the Pacific War and is breeding World War Three. Thanks to the dogged resistance of the Japanese people, it continues to stand on the statute book unaltered in a single word. This politically-conscious race are evidently aware that their A9 embodies the potential for a devastating counter-attack on the part of the overplundered peoples of the world against the heart which wrought the A-bomb – namely Christian-capitalism, with the ESU elite at its core. The puppets in charge of Japan have, it is true, nullified Article 9 since the time, in 1950, when the ESU elite first realised its fearful implications. But this nullification is possible only for so long as the world remains ignorant of the real significance of the issue. For in terms of world history, in terms of releasing mankind from the serpents 'overpopulation' and 'underdevelopment' which lurk in the bog of Conventional National Sovereignty, this nullification of A9 at the behest of the ESU elite constitutes a mammoth act of genocide, an all-time high in crimes against humanity.

The criticism: Unfortunately or fortunately – depending on whether one would welcome this curious interpretation of the contemporary scene to be openly discussed, or would prefer discussion to continue to be blocked – a great deal of the argument is crabbed in form. His often cranky association of ideas is hard to follow. And even when the path seems clear, his prose is an encompassing thicket through which one can hardly hack one's way. These excellent reasons for summarily rejecting the ms render it unnecessary to look around for any others.

Not long afterwards, a mottled grey envelope arrived from Japan.

Commission on the Constitution
3-2 Kasumigaseki
Chiyoda-ku, Tokyo
Japan
31 March 1964

Dear Mr Boymans,
    This is to acknowledge with many thanks the receipt of your excellent book *The Pacific Path to Peace*, which I have already read with keen interest.
    Enclosed is an excerpt from the statement I made at the opening session on 24 February of the sixth conference of the Afro-Asian Legal Consultative Committee, which I hope you will find interesting.

With best regards,
Sincerely yours,
Kenzo Takayanagi

Mr Chairman, Excellencies, Ladies and Gentlemen,

Article Nine of the present Japanese Constitution is unique and unprecedented in that it renounces not only an aggressive but a defensive war as well, accompanied by the banning of all armed forces. Realists might say that its author is a lunatic. Yet, since in this atomic age, even defensive war conducted by hydro-nuclear weapons means annihilation of the victor as well as of the vanquished, the principle set out in Article Nine may after all be highly realistic. Not an unattainable dream; on the contrary, potential world law.

As to the origin of Article Nine there has so far been a widespread misunderstanding both in Japan and in the United States that it was put into the constitution by order of General MacArthur, the Supreme Commander of the Allied Powers, to perpetuate the total disarmament of the defeated nation. Recent investigations, however, have made it clear that its proponent was not MacArthur but Baron Kijuro Shidehara, the Japanese Prime Minister. It was a home-made not an imported article.

On 24 January 1946, Shidehara met for secret talks with MacArthur. The Prime Minister seems at first to have been hesitant to lay his idea before MacArthur, for the latter was a professional soldier. MacArthur says in a letter to me that he was astonished by Shidehara's proposal. He was deeply moved, and finally gave his consent. "The world will laugh and mock us as impractical visionaries," Baron Shidehara said. "But a hundred years from now we will be called prophets."

Again Willem responded promptly – fuelled by drink.

> Caldera
> Kauaeranga Valley
> Thames, NZ
> 10 April 1964
>
> Dear Dr Takayanagi,
>   Yesterday I received your letter of 31 March with which
> I am truly delighted. It conveys the first word of
> encouragement received for years. Apart from it, only blank
> silence, or pretended incomprehension, or summary
> rejection, has greeted the distribution some sixteen weeks
> ago of thirty copies of my ms. to publishers in many and
> commentators in several countries.
>   In August, on my flight back to Kiwiland from a grim
> sojourn in Europe, I called upon your admired friend Mr
> Justice Pal in Calcutta. Unfortunately, he was abroad. The
> letter I wrote to him (photocopy enclosed) secured a
> courteous yet not specifically informative response
> (photocopy also enclosed). Could you enlighten me on any
> of these points, which I neglected to raise at our enjoyable
> meetings in Tokyo? At the same time, detailed comment on
> the thrust of the argument in my manuscript would be
> judiciously appreciated.
>   Truly, your few words have given me great
> encouragement. With respect, and kind regards.
>   Yours sincerely,
>   W J Boymans

In the wake of another heavy night's drinking, Willem allowed
his longing for a meaningful exchange of ideas with Takayanagi

to surface in a petulant follow-up letter. Which he sent as soon
as he pulled it from the typewriter, dismissive of Jane's advice to
sleep on such things. She hated – Jane had several times told
Willem – his conviction that whatever concerned him mattered
equally to everybody else.

Caldera
Kauaeranga Valley
Thames, NZ
24 April 1964

Dear Dr Takayanagi,
     I confirm my letter of 10 April. I'll admit I was a bit
disappointed when I cleared my tin mailbox this morning to
again find no word from you. But I quite well realise that,
for a man in your position, it may be impractical to enter
into correspondence with a man in mine.
     And yet you did declare my little effort to be 'excellent'.
And from your public statement of 24 Feb it is evident that
you underwrite the crucial importance of this issue. From
which I trust I may draw the conclusion that you will not
deny me the critical comment which is urgently required in
order to put a cut-throat edge to *The Pacific Path to Peace*.
But – as said – you may not feel able to do this yourself.
Perhaps you might then consider passing the ms. to
someone who approaches you in competence, and who is
not tied by the discretion imposed by public office.
     I was much interested to see in your statement that
hitherto there has been widespread misapprehension as to the
source of Article 9, and that it is only recent research which
has disclosed this to have been not MacArthur but Shidehara.
This point is of course fundamental to the whole issue.

Now the only clue which I had when writing this ms. was the observation made by MacA. before the Congressional Committee, and quoted by Sissons as per my ref. note no. 41.

Subsequently I have found that this account is fully confirmed by our ferocious friend Maj. Gen. Courtney Witney, on pp. 249, and 257–262 of his *MacArthur – His Rendevous with History* (Knopf, NY, 1956).

And no less interestingly it is confirmed – albeit only by cautious implication – in the penetrating study 'The Origins of the Present Japanese Constitution', by R E Ward (*Am. Pol. Sc. Rev* Dec. 1956). Ward takes great care to refrain from admitting that it was Shidehara who proposed Article 9. Instead, he writes (p. 1008) that: 'the effective support for the quixotic Article 9 ... derived solely from General MacArthur. No other branch of the US Government ... is known to have considered such a clause prior to 13 February 1946.' Then, after a very guarded indication of Article 9's potential in calling a halt to ESU tyranny, Ward bitterly affirms: 'the responsibility for this would seem ... to rest squarely on the Supreme Commander's shoulders.'

Ward candidly affirms it to be inconceivable that prior consultation of the State Department could have failed to prevent MacA. from committing this disastrous blunder. And in this he is, of course, quite right. Any third-rate diplomat possessed of a passing knowledge of political science and law could have pointed out to MacA. that the implementation of Article 9 must inevitably spell the end of national armament. But such advice was never sought. MacA. took the bait proffered by Shidehara, hoping thereby to stand in history as a top-notch Man of Peace. With the publication on 13 Feb. of the MacArthur Draft the die was cast. Nothing that the State Dept then said or did could prevent Article 9 from passing into law.

But the US has since then of course prevented it from becoming effective law. And the Cold War has been the principal means to this end. It is my belief that the ESU elite's felt need to erase A9 as an effective force lies at the bottom of almost every important development in world history since 1946.

I very much hope you can find a moment to give me a comment – either directly or indirectly – on this analysis. To which I may add that if you do, then I rather expect that you will disclose that you have long been aware of its substantial truth. From my encounters with you three years ago I was at first puzzled to find so obviously reasonable and moral a man as you apparently presiding over the despicable attempt to formally erase A9. And then it occurred to me that your appointment to the post is merely another instance of Japanese political ingenuity. That, in other words, Ishibashi appointed to the task the man best calculated to ensure that no headway would be made in accomplishing it. If you find it necessary to tell me that this construction is erroneous then – evidently enough – I shall again be deeply puzzled.

With best wishes and kind regards,

W J Boymans

The silence pained Willem. He waited and waited, unable to begin his writing day until the mail van had passed each morning. He cursed himself for his weakness, and embarked on a radical revision of the entire text of *The Pacific Path to Peace*.

In his increasingly isolated evenings at Caldera, Willem often ruminated on the individuals and institutions who declined to reply to his letters. Publishers who denied his existence – it felt –

by refusing to acknowledge receipt of his manuscript. International legal bodies with their formulaic rebuttals, identical in phrase and lack of feeling around the world. They had their reasons. Willem was not insensitive to the personal agendas, private and public, which made his passion awkward for others to embrace. In October Harold Wilson led the Labour Party to victory in the British election, and appointed Gerald Gardiner Lord Chancellor. They had their priorities. A sharper edge to Gardiner's declared ambition to abolish peerages. Enactment of his promise to reduce the voting age to eighteen. Support of the Abortion Bill. When the Rhodesians announced their Unilateral Declaration of Independence, Lord Gardiner warned his chums around the table in Wilson's kitchen cabinet that the United Kingdom was about to be made a fool of in the eyes of the world.

Nineteen sixty-four was a year of public acclaim also for Kenzo Takayanagi. The Emperor honoured him with the Order of the Sacred Treasure. And the pieces he had from time to time contributed to *Eigo Seinen*, a Japanese journal of English literature, were collected for publication in a limited edition. Takayanagi also drew towards a conclusion his commission's deliberations on the constitution, Article Nine safely enshrined. He was planning, when the commission disbanded the following year, to resume his internationalist campaigns through the foundation – funded by an organic tea-grower's association – of the Asian Centre for Democratic Institutions.

For Willem it was a difficult time. Everything he touched disintegrated in his hand, each step assumed to be forward proving to be in a mistaken direction. He felt at best confused. While tinkering with the manuscript he continued his research into crimes against peace and against humanity. He followed – as closely as he could from so far away – the war crimes trial which had opened in Frankfurt the previous year, its charter limited to the pursuit and punishment of individuals who had practiced day-to-day savagery at Auschwitz. Willem was not alone in his distress at the crude hypocrisies of international law. Hannah Arendt, herself a survivor of the Holocaust, objected to the court's treatment of Dr Franz Lucas, one of the Nazi medical officers detailed for work in the death camp. Friends of Arendt's testified to the tenderness and integrity of Dr Lucas. 'He was the only doctor at Auschwitz who treated us humanely,' they said. 'Who did not look upon us as unacceptable people.' 'We were quite desperate when Dr Lucas was gone.' This man risked his life to help. His person to their person. Fought with skill, wit and love to alleviate the misery of designated enemies of his nation. There was no glory in what Dr Lucas did. On balance, no crime either. Tried – as at Nuremberg and Tokyo – under the Anglo-Saxon system of jurisprudence, the ex-prisoners who appeared for the defence of Dr Lucas looked on in dismay as opposing lawyers battled for victory not truth. This legal system gave the judges no choice, the prosecutors claimed, but find kind Dr Lucas guilty. Because documents recorded that the Auschwitz commander had ordered Lucas, on suspicion of sympathizing with the inmates, to stand on the ramp while Jews were herded from cattle trucks and to pick out the able bodied, committing the rest direct to the gas chambers. This he neither denied nor excused. And was sentenced to spend his old age in jail, twenty years after doing more than the entire British War Cabinet to help the prisoners in Auschwitz.

Nothing rang true. The trials were theatre. A play at life. Diplomatic acts of appeasement. Before affairs of state returned to the normal game of power. Until more wars became necessary. Outside Europe, preferably.

What a farce!

A tragedy: in Willem's experience.

What did any of it mean?

Japan's wartime Foreign Minister Mamoru Shigemitsu, condemned in 1948 to seven years' imprisonment on being found guilty of crimes against peace, was released in 1950, and again served his country as Foreign Minister, from 1954 to 1956, the crucial years of Japan's re-establishment on the international stage.

Shumei Okawa, the principal propagandist of militarism in Japan, sole civilian among the twenty-eight original defendants at the Tokyo Trial, had been ruled insane on the first day of the court's proceedings. The day after the trial ended the Americans released Okawa from asylum, his evidence of western collusion in anti-Soviet indoctrination unheard in court, saved from the public record. Even Röling expressed his unease: 'Okawa was so clever he could play the fool.'

Who's fooling whom? The leaders their people? The generals their troops?

And why? To retain control of the world's resources?

These were the lines along which Willem's thoughts travelled.

Conversations in Tokyo had persuaded Willem that the majority of Japanese blamed their leaders for undertaking a policy which, after losing them the war, left the people hungry and poor. Pragmatic consensus among Asian intellectuals suggested that, after the face-saving execution of Prime Minister Tojo and his colleagues, the international community was at liberty to minimize the danger of another world war through commercial interdependence, global regulation of finance, and cross-racial integration. Willem had been advised to study a TV film of 1958, Shinobu Hashimoto's *I Want To Be A Shellfish*, which had aroused widespread sympathy for the families of the nine hundred and twenty- three ordinary Japanese citizens executed in the plague of post-war show trials. The important thing was for individuals to bear witness to their experiences of war, to explain to each other why they were drawn to do whatever they did. For people to listen not accuse. Willem read, in the report of a conference sent to him in New Zealand by his Bloomsbury bookdealer, of the sociologist Shunsuke Tsurumi's humble confession: 'I managed to get through the war without killing anyone, but that was due in a large part to chance. That feeling remains with me today, and I cannot bring myself to condemn those who did kill people. I think this feeling exists among the mass of Japanese today.'

Willem was affected that same year by the death of General Douglas MacArthur, at whose state funeral President Johnson shed newsreel tears. MacArthur's way had become Willem's. He had felt personally the pain of his hero's betrayal in April 1951, dismissed as Supreme Commander in the Far East for purported insubordination in conduct of the Korean War. Summoned to Washington to appear before the US Senate Joint Committee, MacArthur swore on oath that a life spent in military service had convinced him that abolition of war was crucial to the world's future.

Willem's obsession with Article Nine was cited by Jane as principal reason for his being impossible to communicate with. Nothing else, she said, touched his heart. Unable to pretend otherwise, the following spring Willem packed a trunk of clothes and essential papers and removed himself to a rented apartment in Auckland. From where he launched a campaign of international correspondence, merciless in its tenacity.

P.O. Box 17
Auckland, NZ
9 March 1965

Dear Gerald,

Your commission to the unreceptive Rhodesians must
have been frustrating, and if this is indeed the way it has
struck you then I must tender you my sympathy.

Although it was not of course comparable in
complexity, about a year ago I also undertook an abortive
mission to the unreceptive Anglo-Saxons, in the form of an
ms. which I submitted to some thirty leading publishers
belonging to this species. The ms. was, I admit with shame,
replete with errors and atrociously typed. But I do believe
that it made a substantial point, and that this has nowise
eroded over the intervening year. However, in every case the
response was either nil or negative. But from other quarters
I did receive the odd word of casual encouragement. As
from Dr Takayanagi, who is I suppose about as influential
as nowadays it is possible for a Japanese to be on the world
stage. This means, of course, incomparably less influential
than, for instance, you. His reaction is indicated in the
accompanying enclosures.

I do not know what was your reaction to this ms., nor
even whether you had time to glance through it. If you
didn't then, then you will be unlikely to have time now.
Anyhow I have been vegetating and just recently have
started to recast my notions, and this time less polemically.
On this count, I wonder whether I might be overstepping
the mark in changing the close of para. 2 on p. 49 to:

... and then a voice whispered in Her Majesty's ear, that if only
she would foreswear this Doctrine of Predestination, then she

might freely surface, in order to scuttle her Polaris submarine,
and to cause thereby to ring aloft the well-nigh worldwide cry:

> Please god, good god, dear god do try,
> When she stands trial, as is foreseen,
> To cast your kinder eye upon
> This lately unpugnacious Queen.

This preoccupation has prompted the thought that the
present administration of which you are a member, if indeed
it be keen to embark on some measure both far-reaching
and beneficial and calculated to earn widespread approval,
might perhaps give consideration to the formal recognition
of Japan's Article 9, and/or the formal elimination from the
thirty-nine articles of the Doctrine of Predestination. This
thought is offered to you in all seriousness and in all
humility.

 With kind regards, and not forgetting Lesley,
 Willem

House of Lords
London SW1
17 March 1965

Dear Willem,
 Thank you for your letter and interesting enclosures. As
you know, I fully appreciate your point of view.
 We are going to the Commonwealth Law Conference at
Sydney in August, with three or four days in Auckland and
it would be nice if we have the chance of meeting you there.
 Yours ever,
 Gerald

P.O. Box 17
Auckland, NZ
March 12 1965

Dear Dr. Takayanagi,

For many months following our telephone conversation last year I felt bitter on account of it. But over recent weeks I have come to see that this sentiment is false. So the primary purpose of this letter is to thank you for the courtesy of having spoken to me.

Secondly, it may interest you to know that my ms. is no nearer publication now than it was a year ago. From the publication aspect it has in fact got nowhere. In our free occidental world the freedom of the written word is nowadays not taken so very seriously. And in that sphere no change seems probable.

So, thirdly, I merely inform you of the fact that a copy of this ms. has for over a year been in the possession of Lord Gardiner, who is now Lord Chancellor of UK. I happen to know him personally, and in June '63 discussed with him my previous draft. Although he was then extremely cautious, I can assure you he is thoroughly familiar with the theme and its implications.

Thus, a few days ago, I wrote to him suggesting that the administration of which he is an important member might consider embarking on the simple step advocated in my ms. Of course, I do not expect him to reply to this. Nor do I expect him to do anything about it unassisted. For to one so familiar with its implications it must be a terribly hard decision. But nevertheless he is a very moral man. So I leave it to you to consider carefully whether there be any way in which you might assist him to deal rightly with this terribly hard problem. If any way occurs to you, then surely the rapidly deteriorating world situation provides a sufficient reason for you to make use of it.

    With kind regards and great respect,
    W J Boymans

(No. 1)
Auckland 15 March 1965

Dear Justice Pal,

    Some thirteen months ago I took the liberty of sending you both in Calcutta and in Geneva copies of my manifesto.

    Let it be granted that my work is full of errors and omissions. And at times I am less than kind to those I deem unkind. Let all these deficiencies be granted, and doubled if you like, and even then does not the point and purpose of my text emerge with reasonable clarity? And is not my point pertinent to the pursuit of that nimble phantom, reasonable peace?

    Or let me put it this way. In your home city countless thousands live and die in fantastic squalor. Beyond doubt you disapprove of this state of affairs. Of course you desire to see it terminated. But how? Interested parties who need not be named here assert that there is no feasible solution to this problem, and certainly no reasonably quick solution. Well, my manifesto denies this point of view, it warmly asserts the contrary, and if at times my style is a bit unmannerly then this might be attributed to the urgency of the situation.

    For I am rational enough to suppose that Polaris submarines have been built with some useful purpose in prospect. I assert that the creators of this weaponry are well aware that the so-called overpopulation problem is

essentially their problem, created by themselves and calling
in turn for that weaponry to enable them to 'control' it, and
prospectively 'solve' it: through victory in the next
'defensive' war. When this final solution is eventually
attempted, I sincerely hope that you may survive the ensuing
holocaust. But then I must also wish you the best of
strength to endure the thought that it might well have been
prevented if in later days there had been made articulate just
a small further dose of the moral punch delivered by Justice
Pal in 1948.

So: please help me, sir, by giving me advice on the query:
'How can I, a loyal – though ever absent, and merely male –
subject of Queen Juliana of The Netherlands, bring legal
action against her government on the score of its continued
sabotage of Japan's Article 9?' For your advice on this I
shall be deeply grateful, and would gladly pay. With a view
to economy of effort, I am taking the liberty to send copies
of this letter to Dr Takayanagi, Lord Gardiner, and
Professor Röling. Come, sir! Come gentlemen! Peace I know
is a sultry theme, and the copious tomes penned on progress
have merely landed us with the P-submarine. But surely
you'll lend a hand to help defend the dignity of man!

 Yours truly,

 W J Boymans

(No. 2)
Auckland 23 March 1965

Dear Justice Pal,

 My letter of the 15th was sent to you c/o the
International Law Commission, Geneva. This present letter
will go to your Calcutta address, and registered. Its main

purpose is to confirm my previous writing; but also to invite
your help on a few points which are not quite clear to me.

I have asked you to advise me how I can initiate against
the Netherlands government due process of law with the
aim of obliging it to terminate its involvement in the
criminal conspiracy to suppress Japan's Article 9. When you
favour me with a reply I apprehend that it may tend to
dismiss my project as unfeasible. But let me remind you then
that in your Dissentient Judgement you declared: 'I believe
with Professor Lauterpracht that it is high time that
international law should recognise the individual as its
ultimate subject and maintenance of his rights as its ultimate
aim. The individual human being – his welfare and the
freedom of his personality in its manifold manifestations – is
the ultimate subject of all law.'

Well now, whatever be the terms in which others may
describe me, I declare myself to be an individual. As such, I
declare my welfare to be gravely prejudiced by the continued
sabotage of A9. And if already in 1948 you considered it
'high time' that one such as I have access to the means of
obtaining legal redress, then surely you'll agree that it is by
now hardly too soon for this high noon to be sounded from
some appropriate steeple?

So that is my most cherished project. But if perchance
you persist in the view that that avenue continues to be
blocked by your fellow lawyers, and blocked so cunningly
that I can make no headway through it, then I must adapt
my approach accordingly.

To save your time, and mine, let me assume that the
individual is not yet permitted to bring suit against his very
own government. All right. But surely the individual is
permitted to sue another Individual? This has, after all, been
going on all over the place, and since time immemorial.

Who, then, shall I sue, and what will be my charge?

The person my preference tends to is the editor of the London *Times*. To wrap him up tidily we have at hand the charge of criminal omission. For, ever since the tribulations of generals Yamashita and Matsui a man may be hanged not only for what he has deliberately done, but also for having failed to do what he ought to have done. The said-editor, I contend, is gravely at fault in having failed to point out to the ESU elite that it is by now high time for it to desist from its sabotage of A9. This same omission might lead to the subsidiary charge of having failed to revere the memory of General MacArthur, who had fondled the hope that Japan's set course 'may well become the Asian way, leading to the ultimate goal of all men – individual liberty and personal dignity – and history finally point to the Japanese constitution as the Magna Carta of free Asia.' The christian 'boys' currently engaged on freely dousing Asian villages with napalm are probably for the most part unaware of how personally they share in this atrocity. Has said-editor ever pointed out to them how relevant to such actions are the corrections inserted in 1943 in the chapter Superior Orders in their Guide to Correct Behaviour? For instance: 'Obedience to the order of a government or of a superior, whether military or civil, or to a national law or regulation, affords no defence to a charge of committing a war crime?' Of course he hasn't! So there we have yet another peg from which to suspend the charge of criminal omission.

Perhaps you can suggest some way to cut even closer to the bone? Or has the day not yet dawned when lawyers may stand condemned for having failed to give the advice which they ought to have given?

As with my previous letter, and again with a view to economy of effort, I am taking the liberty to send copies of this letter, and registered, to Dr Takayanagi, Lord Gardiner, and Professor Röling.

Yours truly,

W J Boymans

(No. 3)

Auckland 24 March 1965

Dear Professor Röling,

You will have received copies of my two recent letters to Justice Pal. The purpose of these multiple epistles is, permit me to assure you, to evoke replies. Yet, I am aware that latterly eminent men of law have become rather cautious. Delighted as I would be to receive a response, I would also be surprised. So, it has occurred to me to build these letters into a series, addressed to each of my four legal friends as the whim moves me. For this reason, although it is years since I last wrote to you, this letter carries the number 3. This serial monologue may then in due course occupy an appendix to *The Pacific Path to Peace* when, as of course is bound to happen sooner or later, in one form or another, it gets published.

In your published backward glance at the Tokyo Trial you, while acknowledging that overall it was a pretty ghastly fraud, took the line that nevertheless mankind stands to reap stupendous profit from it. But only, naturally, if it be not ignored. The judgements then delivered, you declared, 'stand in history as indelible facts.'

Are you perhaps a rather shaky student of philosophy? Or is it that you never studied the UK empiricists Berkeley, Locke and Hume? These gentlemen declared, and the ESU elite has in no other sphere followed them more loyally, that a thing can be said to exist only inasmuch as one sees it. Ergo: if a thing is inconvenient, one merely refrains from looking at it, so that then one cannot see it, so that then it does not exist. Ergo: the only 'indelible facts of history' are those which suit the ESU elite to see. And when such a 'fact' ceases to be convenient, then the pimps of the Oxford-Harvard axis display sufficient prudence with regard to their dinner pail to refrain from remembering it. Thus a duster is softly wiped across the board of history, providing the ESU elite with carte-blanche to undertake its next exercise in villainy.

This all-embracing process is so startlingly obvious, and the Tokyo Trial provides so obvious a case in point, that I blush at the impertinence of reminding you of yet another illustration. Glance if you please at the para. connecting pp. 18 and 19 of your cherished copy of my ms. What has become of that 'inherent and inalienable right of man' to Migration Freedom, asserted by solemn treaty between the US and China? It was convenient at the time it was signed in order to provide cheap and often kidnapped labour for the building of the Pacific railroads. A shift in circumstances then rendered this subsidiary to the convenience of denying the right of migration freedom. Simultaneous with this shift, this indelible clause in the 1868 Treaty started to evaporate. Like the morning dew, it has ceased to be. So that nowadays even to recall that it once existed marks one to be a rude and untutored fellow.

So much for my steadfast belief that the ESU elite is, in very deed, the arch-villain in this present century's disgraceful story. But the widow's mite contributed by lesser Europeans has lately looked like becoming an important secondary source of villainy. 'It is my considered view,' you wrote to me on 18 March 1961, 'that there exists a

'conspiracy of silence' on the Tokyo Judgements, and not
only on the dissentient opinions.' Very good. Very good, too,
that in your article you emphasised sundry streaks of
fraudulence in the UN. Very good, too, that at the end of
that article, after again pointing to the main benefit to be
derived from the Tokyo precedent, you wrote in heavy type
'...to arrive at a stage of legal development in which this
individual criminal responsibility is but the logical
consequence of the international juridical situation, may be
the precondition of the survival of civilization.'

That, I submit, is very good. And so what? What, may I
ask, is the point of a man of your status penning such an
incisive critique in a book published in, of all places, Japan,
and which becomes virtually unobtainable the moment it is
printed? What have you done to popularize this notion? Or
what, precisely, have you done to crack the conspiracy of
silence? I would welcome details on what you have done.
And whatever you have done, let me observe that it has been
hopelessly ineffective. My reading of such Dutch
newspapers as I see amply confirms that there is not one
scrap of moral notion proffered in the present day to your
porcine plebs.

For myself, a few years ago I did deliver a puny punch at
the conspiracy in silence, which was smoothly smothered by
his excellency the Minister of Foreign Affairs in The Hague.
In my next letter to you I shall seek your assistance to
breathe fresh life into the squabble I have with this dignitary.
And if space then permits, I shall also try to point out to you
how frantically reactionary was your Tokyo discourse on
the status of the soldier in society.

Yours truly,

W J Boymans

c.c. RP, GG, KT

(No 4)
Auckland
25 March 1965

Dear Dr. Takayanagi,

I was deeply grateful for your response to my ms. But
why has this response remained so thin and scanty? After
all, my reply was to deluge you with letters, and then to put
through a very expensive phone call. All this would seem to
have been a waste of time. Why? For this there may be many
explanations, but there is one that I cannot accept: that you
are not interested.

The contemporary Japanese elite suffers substantially
from the Christian-capitalist regime of bribery and coercion.
That is so freely stated – in between the sheets of public
commentary – that one blushes to expend four lines upon it.
And yet I hesitate to believe that you have accepted bribery.
Tell me, please: how have they coerced you? Following your
discourse last year to the Afro-Asians, were you perhaps
subjected to a fortnight's deprivation from hearing your
favourite geisha sing your favourite song? Was that the
penalty imposed on you by Uncles Sam and Bullybeef? Do
please tell me your tale of woe. And don't omit to make
three extra copies of it.

Next time you have lunch with your Prime Minister,
why not suggest to him that he publicly affirm that same
afternoon Japan's determination to abide most strictly
henceforth by her A9? If he agrees to do so, then I suggest
you skip nimbly onto a train, and betake yourself post-haste
to your country retreat, and stay there until the dust has
settled. The dust, I mean, of Tokyo. For such a public
affirmation would of course be (correctly) interpreted in
Washington as an ultimatum; as an outrageous hostile act

aimed at the very heart of the ESU elite's vital interest. And
it need not be doubted that the atrocious weaponry sited in
Okinawa can quite readily be resited. Away, for the
moment, that is to say, from Peking, Canton and Shanghai,
and on to Tokyo and Osaka. And send a wire, if you would
be so kind, to Justice Pal in Calcutta, advising him to spend
the next few weeks in Darjeeling. And remind him please to
take with him a copy of his Dissentient Judgement, and to
bury it under some stone, so as to provide our cave-man
posterity with some inkling as to what it was all about. For
certainly no copies will be likely to survive in Christian-
capitalist libraries.

Re the Tokyo Judgements, can you explain to me why
not one mention was made of A9? Of course one would not
expect any reference to be made to it by Stalin's comrade
judge, nor by his ESU comrades. And Chang-kai-shek's
nominee was, I understand, so preoccupied with his black
market affairs that he would have had no time to think of it.
And Manila's Jaranilla, apart from being an ardent
Christian, displayed in his published report such staggering
immorality as to make this omission on his part self-
explanatory. But what about Bernard, Pal and Röling? This
omission on their part I find extraordinary.

Please do not misunderstand me. All reasonable men
must feel grateful to Justice Pal for the intellectual and moral
tour de force which he delivered then. Nevertheless, the
overplundered peoples of the world might perhaps have
gained more immediate benefit from it if he had written in
shorthand. If he had said: 'All right, the events antecedent to
this unpacific episode are too complex, our prejudices too
much tied up in them, to render reasonable evaluation
feasible. Anyhow, the accused has now turned over a new
leaf. Beyond dispute this event merits celebration. Some of

the more primitive fellows who occupy this bench with me insist that it would be nice to mark this party with some human sacrifice. I would prefer to refrain from this. Yet I shall not resist beyond stating this desire. Let us then unanimously condemn to the noose the twenty-five men who stand here before us. But on one condition. That, namely, on the very day they die every one of our eleven governments publicly proclaim Japan's A9 to be absolutely lawful and absolutely admirable.'

Nobody can speak with certainty about an 'if' of history. But it may be asserted with assurance that the judgement which Pal in fact delivered has had nil influence on the conditions since then suffered by the world's war-exposed peoples. The shortened version just now suggested could not have had less influence.

Why did you not make any suggestion along these lines in your otherwise admirable book published in the course of this trial? I greatly cherish the copy which you gave me, and I shall likewise cherish your advice as to whether it is conceivable that Shidehara was the only man in Japan who fully understood the economic implications of A9. I find it hard to believe this; yet the evidence does tend to point that way. And by the way: I am aware that he was a very old man, and that the health of Japanese citizens did not on the whole loom very high in the occupation's order of priority, but all the same I would be grateful if you would instruct one of your clerks to summarize for me the circumstances in which Shidehara died.

Yours truly,

W J Boymans

c.c. GG, R., BR.

(No 5)
Auckland 27 March 1965

Dear Lord Gardiner,
    Permit me to exercise my humble right to address to
you, in your official capacity, a modest twin entreaty. In
contrast to the second, the basis for my first entreaty is
extremely flimsy. This flimsiness proceeds from the fact that
one cannot say with certainty that one ought to have
received the letters which one hasn't received. This because
usually it is only the receipt of the letter which gives one
the certainty that it has been sent. Yet I must confess to
having a hunch that, in so far as it relates to me, the sanctity
of H.M. mail has not over the past year been respected.
Would you mind dropping a line to your appropriate satrap
in Wellington, inviting him if indeed he has been pinching
my mail to desist, and to let me have whatever he may
have stolen?
    My second entreaty proceeds from an incomparably
more substantial basis than does the first. Yet, in a
rudimentary sense, they are intimately connected. I feel
myself to be blockaded. I feel extremely lonely. This I do not
like. I desire to air my ideas in company with others. So I
look to you to provide me with that company. That is what I
request of you.
    On p. 66 of my ms I reminded you that Mr Adam Smith
has reminded us that consumption is 'the sole end and
purpose of all production, and the interest of the producer
ought to be attended to only so far as it may be necessary to
promoting that of the consumer.' This maxim is so perfectly
self-evident, this mister then archly added, 'that it would be
absurd to attempt to prove it.'
    Fine and dandy. Please now join with me in giving brief

consideration to global law and order in terms of it being a commodity. Who are the producers of this commodity? What is the condition of the article which they place on the global counter? What do its consumers think of it?

One hundred? Twenty? Twelve? Three? How many are the men who in effect preside over this global corporation, Law and Order Inc.? Let us not waste time in finickity precision. Whether it be three or ten times three, the coterie of co-presidents is obviously compact, to put it mildly, compared with the total of their workers and maintenance-men. And the total of these producers is, when compared with the three billion odd consumers of their product, hardly less startlingly tiny.

Now it is beyond dispute that you are at this moment one of the very top co-presidents of this incorporation. On behalf of the three billion-odd consumers of your product, permit me to suggest to you that it is not entirely satisfactory. Personally, as you know, I declare the product to be bloody awful.

So what do you, Milord, propose to do about it? Do you propose to countenance the indefinite continuation of your product being geared solely to the mistakenly asserted interest of a minority of its producers? Or are you prepared to help throw this fraud overboard? Are you prepared to hurl your weight behind the project to subject your product to a radical redesign?

There it is. The choice lies in your hands. I would rejoice exceedingly if after your coming Sydney Conference you could find a few hours to spare for me. I would like very much to barbecue for you a juicy T-bone steak. But there are more important things, and these you will want to deal with first. I shall, meanwhile, continue to take reasonable care of myself. Thus, if I find myself ailing and in need of a

penicillin injection, I shall take precautions to ensure that
the medico who gives it to me is not over-imbued with the
ESU elitist attitude.

Yours truly,

W J Boymans

c.c. KT, RP, BR.

(No. 6)

Auckland

28 March 1965

Dear Justice Pal,

Tell me, if you please, what do you propose to do about
all this. Now let it be said right away that you, for all I
know, may in fact be dead. Were you alive, then assuredly
the issue would interest you. But, as said, you may be dead.
If perchance this is not so, then you can readily efface my
doubt by writing to tell me. In the absence of such notice,
permit me to be fancy-free, and to outline what the late
Justice Pal might have done to ameliorate the situation.

Now Mr. Radhakrishnan, Pal's President, happens to
be a man of outstanding morality and insight. This is
made amply clear in his *Eastern Religions and Western
Thought* published many years ago (viz. 'Nations, like
individuals, are made not only by what they acquire, but
also by what they resign.'). Since when he has of course
grown older. Old men often lose their punch. Nevertheless,
it is hardly conceivable that he, alive, could ever reach the
stage no-punch.

Reasoning thus, the late Justice Pal might quite
conceivably now toss this issue into his president's lap.
President, he would say, please take a look at it. President,

please take thought on it. President, please do something about it. For after all, my dear President, he might quite reasonably add, this surely is the crux of the so-called 'problem' which confronts this planet's overplundered peoples.

Yours truly,

W.J.Boymans

c.c. GG, BR, KT.

(No 7)

Auckland 30 March 1965

Dear Professor Röling,

Do please let me know if you happen to be dead, so that I may cease to irritate you with my epistles. In that event, would you consider passing this request for aid to some other latter-day Grotius?

In your Tokyo verdict on Hata you wrote: 'No soldier who merely executed government policy should be regarded as a criminal ... The duty of an army is to be loyal ... In this case, the danger of a situation where military men influence the policy of a country has been clear for all time. The army should be the power ... which executes the policy decided upon by the government. It should not make, or influence, that policy.'

Now I must admit I find this just a bit extraordinary. To begin with, this dictum repudiates the whole gist to the amendments on Superior Orders introduced in 1943 into the Christian-capitalist manuals of military law, which say in effect that everybody from head of state to drummer boy is personally responsible for his acts.

In the law as it now stands the individual conscience

takes clear-cut precedence over institutionalized loyalty. Just
as during the last war care was taken to ensure that the
soldiery remained ignorant of those crucial 1943
amendments, so likewise now those amendments are so
thoroughly soft pedaled that the vast majority of serving
men have never heard of them. Nor, apparently, had
Professor Röling in 1948.

You assert in effect that the soldier must be a political
moron; that he must be a moral eunuch. As a one-time
soldier, permit me to reply: 'Thank you very much indeed!'.
This cabbage mind is, it may be supposed, shared by all,
from cabin boy to commander in chief. Which then leads
straight into a totalitarian society like the US or USSR,
where the c-in-c happens to be the no.1 politico.

The most exquisite whimsy of this notion of yours is
that it is precisely this asserted primacy of loyalty which lies
so close to the core of our latterday occidental immorality.
In 'feudalistic' society by contrast, and in Japan especially,
unconditional loyalty had never been accepted. There had
always been the reservation of the primacy of human
conscience. There, loyalty had been deemed to be owing
only to those deserving loyalty. There must be a reasonable
quid pro quo.

We could argue about this deep into the night. That is
not the present purpose. All that I wanted to point out was
that in terms of the law as it stood from 1943 onward, your
Tokyo discourse on the status of the soldier in society was
curiously reactionary.

Yours truly,

W J Boymans

c.c. RP, KT, GG.

(No 8)
Auckland 31 March 1965

Dear Dr. Takayanagi,

Yesterday we were engaged in stoning, with a few
candid thoughts, our friend the legal quack. Today it is
Takayanagi's turn to earn his pay. Being a true-blue
Japanese elitist, you are shot through with feudalistic
sentiment. Permit us then to pause to peer into that which
in this democratic age is a curious anomaly.

'No allegiance without protection; no protection
without allegiance'. Would you agree, Dr T., that this
adage constitutes the basis of the feudal ethos when its
condition is reasonably healthy? You do? Thank you.

And who in this present day, please tell me, protects
me? Does Mistress Elizabeth, Headgirl of the
Commonwealth in which I reside? Does Juliana Regina,
my national Majordomo? Does your old Hirohito?

You can name every single one of this planet's
contemporary potentates, lump the whole lot together, and
the answer remains the same. I rejoice in nil protection.
My fate, like every other earth dweller, lies in the hands of
imbeciles whose mental state may lie dormant or may at
any moment shake itself awake into applied imbecility.

Ergo: neither I nor anybody else owe allegiance to any
earthly entity. If he so chooses, anybody may tender his
allegiance to anything. Or, if he prefers, to nothing.
Whatever his choice, he is completely free to make it as he
wishes. To owe allegiance to some specific entity was at
one time usual, and that time may come again. Today it is
the inherent logic of the nuclear situation that no
allegiance can be owed to anyone because no protection
can be provided by anyone. The truth of this maxim is so

perfectly self-evident, as our friend Mr. Smith would conceive, that it would be absurd to mess around with proving it.

And yet this situation is, I suggest, disturbing. The plain fact, as I see it, is that this thing called national sovereignty has now run into a dead end. Every moment that we linger in this dead end alley we stand to be obliterated by catastrophe. Suicide being of course a serious offence, to act lawfully we must either retrace our steps, or we must skip nimbly over the wall. To help us make a prudent choice, let us reflect upon just one of the core flaws in this thing 'national sovereignty'.

Caveat emptor, did I hear you say? Let the buyer beware, is that what you said? Yes? Very good. Top marks to you, my boy, my excellent Dr T. For it is this hideously hoary maxim which holds in its fond embrace our producer-inclined society. From the moment it be accepted that the producer has no real responsibility for his product, society stands doomed to become an ever more awful snake-pit. With due apology to serpents, which are, by comparison, really rather friendly creatures.

This poisonous social recipe of producerdom posits pressure to be the dominant flavour of life. Under this maxim's regime, the only way in which the lonely little consumer can achieve a modicum of protection from that seducer, the producer, is by frantically trying to carry 'the war' into the enemy's camp.

Might it not be better to say that the time has now come to refrain from making again the same mistake? The mistake of not perceiving that it is a basic cause of our occidental immorality that we are producer-inclined. That it is only by reverting to essentially oriental (or Smith-sonian, if you like) consumer-orientation that we can

extract ourselves from our dead-end alley.
Yours truly,
W J Boymans
c.c. BR, GG, RP.

Cheap-rate Telegram. Reply paid for 3 text words.
5 April 1965
Lord Gardiner
The Lords
London

Number 8 despatched. Have you received them all? Have
you replied? Do you surrender unconditionally? Three
question marks. Reply paid three words.
Sender: WJ Boymans P.O. Box 17, Auckland, NZ

(No 9)
Auckland 6 March 1965

Dear Lady Gardiner,
Is it not unscrupulous of me to affix a vulgar number to
this letter? And to send copies of it to three men to whom I
have not been introduced? Of course it is, and extremely so.
Utterly unscrupulous is what I am, diligently tracking the
trail of the ESU elite. As I trot my way through life I simply
devise whatever 'rules' may seem to suit me best, and revise
them as needs whenever and in whatever way fits, and at all
times affirm that whatever seems best for me constitutes the
rules. Never let it be said that my expensive UK upbringing
has been lost upon me.
Over recent weeks your GG has been sustaining a few

prods from the antipodes. Do tell me, please, have these
prods troubled him? If they haven't, then he isn't the man I
judged him to be.

In the telegram sent to him yesterday I used a word
which he might deem to be uncouth. This is the word
'unconditionally'. If perchance he be annoyed, then please
suggest to him that maybe I was obsessed, when I used that
word so ill-advisedly, by my annoyance with recent history.
From which, as you know, this word in the manner used has
derived a high-hell reek of infamous attitude, and ought for
that reason be meticulously avoided. So I withdraw it,
unconditionally, and offer in its place the word
'honourably'. In the given context the two words boil down
to pretty well identical meaning. But what is the use of
having the Japanese share this planet with us if we cannot
learn from them a modicum of politesse?

Anyhow, Milord being so preoccupied with the more
important affairs of his weighty state, why not invite him to
invite you to put your hand to this affair? Look you into it,
reflect on what is happening all around you, and then maybe
you'll turn upon him in your most persuasive manner and
tell him that, as gee-gees go, he is of course excellent, but
that now you do desire him to qualify as very best, to which
end he must refrain from stalling at this hurdle, but take it
rather boldly in his stride, thus putting himself bang on-side
in the eye of posterity and enabling our contemporary racing
community to rejoice in substantially enhanced self-respect
and legitimate pride.

Or is it your experience that he is less susceptible to the
sporting than to the feminine touch? If so, then you might
say a few crisp words on behalf of the innumerable madams
and wenches who already have been fried in napalm, and on
behalf of the millions, or indeed likely tens of millions, who,

as things now stand, await a similar fate. Surely it is quite
unnecessary to mess around through another half-century
before someone says enough is enough? Is it conceivable
that a project of such urgency can stall and atrophy merely
for lack, at the right time and in the right place, of a small
intermediary? And who, I ask you, could be a better broker
than Lesley, Lady Gardiner?

Fondly yours,
Willem Boymans
c.c. KT, BR, RP.

(No 10]
Auckland
7 April 1965

Lord Chancellor, Sir,

Do you linger in the pallid cast of thought? Do you
hesitate to do?

Brushing aside the obvious impertinence on the part of a
trivial individual (for the last word my typewriter, I regret,
has no smaller type) to suggest to you what you ought to do,
permit me to suggest precisely that.

Having persuaded your Prime Minister and his most
Privy Council that the time is now superbly ripe to refrain
from further natter and instead to act, act.

At a certain time on a certain day this week – and there
is no earthly reason why this need not be today – to summon
the envoys of USSR, of China, and of France, and to request
them collectively to advise their respectful governments by
means of their most intricate codes that: Her Majesty your
Queen is due to make, in one hour's time, a world-wide TV
broadcast of the most radically reorientated peace

proclamation of all time. Her royal message need not in itself occupy more than one minute of her royal time. Very simply, she may say that she has already affirmed to Tenno Hirohito, that Japan's Article Nine is now fully acccepted by UK law, and in-copied her PM to his PM. And that the ambition is, by popular referendum, for A9 to be adopted as part of the new British constitution.

That, I suggest to you in all humility, is approximately all that her Majesty need say in order to halt, and probably forever, the present seeming predestined atrocious turn of the wheel of history. There would, of course, be a few other details to be attended to. But my impertinence would run to quite unnecessary excess if I tried to detail them to you.

Yours etc.

W J Boymans

c.c. RP, BR, KT.

Personal and Airmail

House of Lords

London SW1

15 April 1965

Dear Willem,

I am afraid that your letters and telegram have defeated me.

I do appreciate the strength of your views on the subject matter of your letters, but as you will appreciate a member of a government is not at liberty to express personal opinion in conflict with his government's views, particularly on a subject which is the province of one of his colleagues.

All he can do at the same time would be to express his

own views to his own colleagues and he would then have to abide by their joint opinion.

I am afraid therefore that I cannot give any opinion to you, in reply to your letters, but as I wrote to you on 17 March we hope to be in Auckland for three or four days in August and it would be good if we were able to meet then.

Yours sincerely,

Gerald Gardiner

Willem was unable to make up his mind which he preferred: swimming in the sea, or bathing in the rock pools and gullies of the Kauaeranga River.

The salt buoyancy of the sea sustained the desire to venture forever, to swim on and on around the Coromandel Coast. The effortless rhythm of his overarm stroke, the perfect summer temperature of the water and the lack of any other human presence gave Willem on his early morning swims a sense of the absolute and of belonging. His thoughts as he swam through the sea were uniformly constructive.

In the Kauaeranga, by contrast, nothing was certain, an inattentive swimmer liable to be knocked unconscious by a hurtling log. The fresh water, stained brown from the seams of copper in the hills through which it ran, was always cold. All the same, Willem had adored the unpredictability of after-lunch swims in his home river, where pools changed shape daily, the flow of water dependent on falls of thunderous rain miles up into the forest. He had felt envigorated, even inspired by the Kauaeranga. While loving the sea, he missed the river.

On return to his apartment in Auckland one morning, later than usual, after a particularly long swim and large fisherman's breakfast on the quayside, Willem received an anxious phone call from an ex-neighbour, warning him of the overnight shift in direction of a forest fire. Caldera was now in its path. Jane and the neighbour's husband were herding the sheep to safety. There was nobody left to guard the house.

Willem telephoned for a taxi. Calm in the centre of the back seat of the dusty Mercedes, out of reach of the sun, Willem let his thoughts wander where they wished.

He was not afraid of losing Caldera. Nor the collection of orientalist rarities which stood unattended on the library shelves, two years now after the separation. Reading had become too painfully slow. He knew – he felt – enough already.

Nothing seemed to frighten Willem. A fact of feelinglessness he was aware horrified those who came close to him.

Except Mother and Jane.

They're as tough as I am. Tougher. Because they're women. Less prone to self-abuse, more tolerant of their own and the world's imperfections.

There'll never again be anybody in my life like Jane.

Forest fires were a regular summer hazard in the Kauaeranga, and it was unusual for houses as close to the trees as Caldera to survive for fifty years. Willem had kept himself on red-alert for something like this. He saw before they came the flames leap from oak to oak on the steep hillside behind Caldera, down towards the upper orchard, its old apple trees released by Jane to run wild, cherished for the enchantment of their shape in blossom, the fruit mean, uneatable, left to rot on the ground. He heard – in the back of the car, fanned by the wind of his imagination – the fire crack and crescendo, roaring its destruction in his ears. Willem's arms twitched, the whole force of his will engaged in suppressing a desire to press his hands to his eyes and bury his head in the sweet-smelling grass.

You have to look. If you don't look you'll never know what happened. Never know what you did. That's the worst.

By the time the taxi reached Caldera a second fire engine was negotiating the drive, the sky black with smoke, the noise dreadful. Willem walked towards the house, his open jacket flapping in the hot wind, trousers flattened against his slim legs. People – strangers – shouted at him. He took no notice, and made his way up to the yard, where firemen stood spraying water onto the burning roof. He pushed past them towards the steps to the front door.

'You can't go in there. It's suicide.'

'I certainly can.' His arm was held. 'Let go. It's my home.'

Willem shook himself free and dashed for the open front

door. The smoke in the hall did not trouble him unduly, and he marched through to the library. Where he gazed around the familiar room, at a sudden loss to know why he was there. A corner of burning ceiling fell to the floor, the flames licking yellow tongues up the shelves of books. Willem stepped towards the blaze, then away from it.

Frantically though his mind raced, Willem could think of nothing he needed to rescue. No single object he was sure he wanted to keep.

There must be something. I must be here for a reason. A moment ago it was urgent.

Why? What have I forgotten?

Willem stood rubbing the ball of his right eye with the thumb-knuckle of his left hand.

No, no memories missing. All present and correct.

I won't forget. I'll never forget.

He opened his eyes and caught sight of his cork model of the Wren Library at Trinity College Cambridge, on top of the bureau bookcase, its glass dome cracked in the heat. Willem smiled.

That'll do.

He grabbed the model, leaving the damaged dome behind, and ran out onto the deck.

Willem had chosen to save Uncle Felix's twenty-first birthday present, the duties of godfatherhood completed. It was the architectural modelmaker's label which had pleased him most about this gift. In gothic script and cast-brass frame, praising the library's benefactor, Dr Isaac Barrow, Newton's tutor, who in 1669 resigned as Professor of Mathematics in favour of his twenty-six-year-old pupil. The pinkish stone of the Wren Library was quarried at Ketton, on the border between Northamptonshire and Rutland, the label informed.

'Willem!' Jane screamed.

The deck collapsed in a spray of sparks. Willem fell with it, rolled down the side of the quartz-streaked rock and came to rest by the fence to the kitchen garden. The bottoms of his trousers were on fire. He jumped up, and took them off.

'Are you all right?' Jane ran across to ask.

'I dropped it.' Willem was laughing. 'After all that trouble. I dumped it in the flames!'

The firemen lent Willem a crimson blanket, which he wrapped around his lower body like a skirt. Jane and Willem left the professionals to it, and walked up the road to their neighbour's new brick bungalow, where they sat together in the garden, beneath the shade of a dark-leaved rata tree.

The muscles in Jane's face were taut. 'Could've been worse. The foundations are still sound. We'll rebuild. It'll be fine. Don't worry.'

Willem looked the more relaxed. 'The years of effort. All those rare words. Gone. Up in smoke. Have you any idea how much time I spent in pursuit of my books on Japan? How desperately I felt the need to own each one of them? What a ludicrous mistake!'

'Was your library valuable?'

'What have I been saying?'

'In money?'

'Yes, as a matter of fact. It cost a fortune.'

'Why didn't you tell me? We could have put the books in store. What if they'd been stolen while I was out on the farm?'

They fell silent, seated side by side on the wooden bench encircling the trunk of the tree. The play cries of children rose from the front patio, where the neighbour's kids were engaged in a tricycle joust, with brooms for lances. Willem and Jane had been left alone with their mugs of tea and a plate of buttered raisin bread.

'Shall we try again? I can't recreate Caldera on my own.'

Willem stiffened. 'No?'

'Is that a question? Or your answer?'

'Both, I'm afraid.'

The tension in Jane's face eased. 'Thank you. I needed to be sure. This isn't the way I want it. But what's the use, if I make you miserable? None. Our marriage doesn't work. Let's get on with separate lives.'

'I'm not miserable.'

'Good.' She patted his blanketed thigh. 'Keep it up!'

Without wife or library there was nothing to tie Willem to New Zealand. He felt it was time to root himself, to see his ideas bear fruit. Time – he decided – to live in Holland, the land of his fore-fathers.

Within a couple of months of the fire at Caldera Willem had tidied up his affairs in Auckland, shipped off his research files and the few belongings about which he cared, and was standing holding Jane's hand at passport control.

'Without me, you'll be a motherless calf,' she said. And turned away.

Willem pushed aside the chrome barrier. A uniformed offi-cial beckoned him through. He was determined not to look back.

Had she?, he wondered.

Was Jane among the crowd gazing down from the public observation roof when he crossed the tarmac to the plane?

Did she wave?

He did. At the scratched plastic of the cabin window as the jet became airborne.

Willem took a year's lease on the first apartment he was shown, a block away from the *Leidsegracht*, in a bohemian district of Amsterdam. His studio flat was on the fourth floor, at the top of a narrow flight of stairs, with a view over the roofs of houses a few feet across the street. Where people had created for themselves lives as varied and vibrant as any in the street cafés and tethered psychedelic barges below. He shared a bathroom on the half-landing with a friendly painter.

'Conceptual artist. I don't paint,' she said.

'That's a cheek,' Willem replied. 'I could be one too. I devote my life to a concept so far removed, as yet, from practicable reality it might as well be art.'

'Fine.'

'What's your speciality?'

'The artist.'

'The conceptual art of being an artist?'

'Why not?'

'How's it done?'

'I've cloned myself. Made me into "me". It's great. All the rubbish, all the self-centredness, all the boring bits I've given to the artist. Leaves me the person miles better off.'

'Simple in theory. Difficult in practice.'

'Other way round. The theory's incredibly complicated. Idealist exchange mechanisms. Syncretic systems of multitudinous conviction. The struggle for modernism, basically. A guide for the perplexed.'

'Ah, I see … and in practice?'

'I enjoy myself. Cut the crap and get on with it.'

Willem spoke Dutch with an English accent, branding him a foreigner in his native country. He exploited the freedom this gave to question things other people accepted without thought. Such as his compatriots' habit of talking in cosy diminutives. Willem hated overhearing grown women arrange their days around 'little' cups – *kopjes* – of coffee, at 'little' Heleen's on Thursday, 'little' Joanna's on Friday, with time built in to the hectic schedule for several 'little' games of bridge.

'Doesn't it madden you?' he demanded of his artist friend, over a 'little' beer – *biertje* – in the bar next door (which was, in fact, tiny, with no room for tables, the regulars perched on stools at shelves running down both side walls and across the maroon, green and amber leaded-glass window to the street).

'Never noticed.'

'Now that I've pointed it out?'

'It'll probably irritate me. Which'll make me annoyed with you. Because everybody does it. And nothing's going to stop them.'

Willem opened his mouth to speak. Then closed it. She had jumped a stage of the conversation, to the core of his argument. 'The same with armies?' he asked, leaping further ahead.

'I don't understand.'

'Every country has an army? Which nobody can prevent being used in self-defence?'

'Yeah, right.'

'No, wrong. "Army" isn't a figure of speech. It's you and me. Used to be me, is now you. Your boyfriend. Your brother. They've done national service. Why didn't they refuse?' Willem silenced her with the touch of his fingers to her wrist. 'Soldiers are trained to win at war. For whom? Not for themselves. Look at me, I "won". Who did I do it for? For the nation? The people are the nation. I am the nation. You are. The sovereign power of every nation, under all forms of political organization, resides with the individual citizens. Back again with you and me. We are our own sovereigns. Not the Queen. Not the Politburo. Not the Senate. It's the truth and it's the law. And it's time your brothers-in-art conceived of the means of enforcing an international state of peace.'

From his new base in Amsterdam, Willem resumed the battle of letters. He received the occasional supportive reply.

Department of Foreign Literatures and Linguistics
Massachusetts Institute of Technology
Cambridge, Massachusetts 02139
Nov. 1968

Dear Mr Boymans,

    I am disappointed, but not surprised, that you haven't
had much success with your excellent pamphlet. Such is the
state of the world. I'm glad to hear that you are intending to
pursue the matter further. As to supervision of a thesis, I am
not sure whom to suggest. To my knowledge, the few people
who deal specifically with the topics you mention are rather
'establishment-oriented' – one of the reasons there is so little
decent or informative work. I would suggest that you write
to John Dower, c/o Committee of Concerned Asian
Scholars, 1737 Cambridge Street, Cambridge, Mass. 02138.
Dower is getting his PhD degree now, and is doing very
good work on wartime and early post-war Japan. He might
be able to give you some good suggestions. You can mention
that I recommended that you write him, if you like.
Your conclusion that – in the paranoid eyes of our leaders –
our mysterious and dangerous enemy is Asian economic
competition is not far from my own. The British economist
Joan Robinson once characterised the American crusade
against communism as being, in reality, a campaign against
development. This seems to me entirely accurate.
    Best of luck,
    Noam Chomsky

The main target of the Boymans offensive in Holland was
Professor Röling, entrenched in his Polemologish Instituut,
at the *Rijksuniversiteit* of Groningen. An effective campaign

against the man whom Willem considered the most dangerous of his adversaries required troop reinforcements. The peace movement, he reckoned, was the first place to look for recruits to his cause.

Willem gained an introduction to the protest scene through Saskia, the girl with whom he shared a bathroom. He accompanied her to several meetings, and handed out at an anti-Vietnam march copies of his *Tribute to a Trial* pamphlet, emblazoned with Chomsky's quote of praise. At a local street fair, centred around the *Leidseplein*, Willem agreed – on the principle that one good turn deserves another – to play in a band of radical improvizers.

Noise Abuse, they christened themselves for the day. Willem enjoyed himself intensely – improvising with percussive abandon on an array of children's toys laid out on a trestle table: growling bears, squeaking pigs, a clockwork monkey clashing cymbals, a humming top, numerous whistles, whizzers, rattles and buzzers, a toy telephone, a primary-coloured plastic radio, several talking books, a doll which cried 'Ma-Ma', a police car with siren, a model xylophone and a laughing jackass. The organisers booked Noise Abuse to perform two fifty-minute gigs during the twelve hours of the event. Willem wished to experience it all. There was time to get drunk, sober up, play his second gig, and attend again to the endlessly inventive exchange between performer and audience, art and life.

Behind the stall next to Saskia's pitch sat two immaculately pale young men dressed in sleeveless embroidered coats, the banner above their heads reading: Advice About Absolutely Anything – One Guilder. Impertinent questioners queued to break the artists' deadpan commitment, never the chink of a smile. Crowds formed to gape and listen, giggling at the gentle humour of the responses. Willem took his place in the line of seekers of advice.

'How can we stop going to war?' he asked when his turn came.

'Go to bed late, sleep in, and miss the troop ship,' one of the young men replied.

'Get up early and feed the poor,' his companion advised. 'Your problem, sir, is personal. Your use, if you'll pardon me for saying so, of 'we' is misleading. It posits the universal. In the limited amount of time available to devote to the case, I am unable to ascertain if your intention is to guide me up the garden path. Or have you deceived yourself into belief in the sanctity of mass movement? Which indeed is the path to war. How can I stop going to war? Now that is an interesting question. Which you failed to ask.'

Saskia's game for the day – with the assistance of her friend Tom, a printer – was rodent roulette.

Around a central wooden turn-table she had chalked on the street a roulette board. 'Every player wins a prize!' she chanted – dressed as a picture-book major general. 'Roll up! Roll up! Rodent roulette. Pistol provided.'

Fixed to the turntable was a chair, on which the volunteer sat, a rat mask pulled over his head. Round and round Tom whirled the table, until Saskia held a cap pistol to the rodent's nose. Bang! Bang! The giddy rat rose to his feet and staggered about the chalked board, coming to rest on one of the numbered black and red squares, according to which rewards were distributed. Saskia had made all the prizes, from worthless bits and pieces scavenged in derelict buildings around the city, cleaned up and transformed into objects of delight. A cache of wooden clothes pegs, thrown out from a flood damaged hardware shop, onto which Saskia stuck painted paper ears. By the end of the day dozens of winners wore the symbolic rats on the lapels of their jackets. And from the same source, actual traps, set with wedges of pink plaster cheese. Another prize: dark brown shoelaces clipped to handwritten recipes for rat-tail soup.

Tineke, a friend of Saskia's, chose the afternoon of the fair to launch her latest exhibition. In an emptied document store on the *Lijnbaansgracht*, warm and windowless, she set herself to live without external contact for a week, naked. With a comprehensive supply of art material to experiment on, and a stack of records to listen and dance to. Passers-by watched through four three-inch-square panels of glass cut at waist height in the warehouse doors. The glass was mirrored, to prevent Tineke seeing those seeing her. She became cocooned in her own elected rhythm, sunless and moonless, unaware of the voyeurs bent to the peepholes. Mismatched rows of them. Awkward, ugly, separated from the world of art. From the art inside themselves, Tineke sought to convey.

The trouble with the crowd which Willem met through Saskia was – as he saw it – their lack of focus. He judged the peaceniks woolly in their way of thinking, foolish to campaign for nuclear disarmament separately from abolition of the entire war system.

'Candlelit vigils. Flower power. The love-ins. It's all so irrelevant,' he complained to Saskia.

'So's your A9. Since Japan is armed to the teeth.'

'Illegally.'

'So what?'

'A lot. If the man in the street makes a noise, the government has to listen,' Willem maintained. 'Last year the Japan Socialist Party gained enough votes to force the removal of bomb sights from the Defence Force's F-4 Phantom Jets. And blocked the in-flight fuelling systems, preventing use for offensive purposes.'

'Big deal! So they let the Yanks do their dirty work. Who allows hundreds of thousands of US Marines to be stationed in Okinawa? Who repairs helicopter gunships and sends them back to Vietnam? The bloody Japs!'

Willem winced. 'I do wish you wouldn't use that word. It's the language of Hiroshima.'

The publicity which surrounded the court martial of Lieutenant Calley, following initial attempts by the Pentagon to suppress news of the massacre at Mai Lai, strengthened Willem's case. Lawyers opposed to the American presence in Vietnam had for some time argued that the policy of patterned B-52 bombing raids of undefended villages was an indictable war crime. The rape and murder of five hundred civilians in the Mai Lai no. 4 hamlet of Son My village by Calley and his cohorts on 16 March 1968 was no less criminal. Why, though, was it considered more so? Why were the generals who ordered napalm to be poured from the skies onto the heads of women and children not also court martialled? And what about instructors at boot camps, dedicated to the dehumanization of teenage recruits? The mother of David Paul Medlo, another of the Mai Lai soldiers, had given this last question some thought. 'I sent them a good boy, and they made him a murderer,' she said.

The military were themselves confused. A letter Captain William Miller wrote to his parents was published in the Bridgport Post of 17 February 1970: 'It is not the Lt Calleys that are at fault. It's our people. Our own people. They send us to fight a war, and when we fight it, they criticize us for the way we fight that war. Now I ask, if you people of the United States did not want us to do what we did, why did you provide us with weapons of mass destruction? Logically it follows that you want us to kill, slaughter, brutalize and mutilate.'

Faithful to his obsession, Willem insisted that an Asian resolution to the problem was readily available.

'It's staring us in the face,' he lectured Saskia. 'MacArthur knew when he hanged General Yamashita in Manila he was signing the death warrant of a future US chief of staff. His resolution? Article 9. What better authority than MacArthur do we need, the man on the spot? In the context of this global issue, it may seem trivial of me to mention that Yamashita demonstrably was a finer general than most. That he lived and died a better man than many. It may seem trivial. But it isn't.'

Around this time Willem visited London, to attend David Golding's wedding. He travelled by day-boat from Hoek van Holland to Harwich, spending most of the trip on deck, keen on the feel of the wind pulling at what remained of his hair, desperate for a sense of distance journeyed.

His godfather's grandson was marrying a Bostonian. They had met and fallen in love during David's first long vacation from Cambridge, part of which he spent at a summer camp in up-state New York, teaching tennis to Jewish kids from Yonkers. Susan – on the way to becoming on of the cleverest Harvard Law School graduates of the post-war generation – was a councillor at the sister camp across the lake. She was two years older than David, peach-blossom beautiful, and passionately disenchanted with all things American. When the camps closed Susan invited David to spend a week at her family's home in the other Cambridge, where her academic parents astonished him with the range of their concerns. Though puzzled – and hurt – by Susan's insistence that he adhere to his original plan and travel on his own around the States for the remainder of the summer, David refused to be diverted. He wrote to her every Sunday night, until they were married four years later.

'She's so sensible,' he had told Willem, on a walk along the beach at Aldeburgh – on his previous trip to England, for Uncle Felix's funeral. 'I trust her. Completely.'

'What's wrong, in that case?' Willem had asked, with concern for the young man's unspoken anxiety.

'There's always something wrong. Just wish I knew what it was!'

'Would knowing make any difference?'

'Oh no, not at all. I'll be with Susan for the rest of my life. Whatever happens.'

'You do that, young fellow. Stick to her. For both your sakes.'

'Thanks, Willem. I will.'

It was Susan's wish to marry in England. She too rejected a traditional church wedding, in favour of a combined concert and reception at Dulwich College Picture Gallery, where her father had connections. Willem knew Sir John Soane's house in Lincoln's Inn Fields, but had never visited his Picture Gallery. Nor had he met Susan. He set out on the thirteen minute train journey south to north Dulwich from London Bridge prepared to celebrate.

My God!, he said to himself at sight of Susan, standing beneath the dome at the end of Soane's chain of spaces, flanked by a pair of Gainsboroughs.

What am I thinking? Jesus! I mean ...

He was silenced, reduced to the inner invocation of idols in which he disbelieved. She was both magnificent and modest. And neither of these. A slim, tall, unnaturally blonde woman with the sharpest green eyes Willem's had ever seen. This shocked reaction to seeing Susan was caused by her being unlike the person he had pictured from David's description.

Willem's mother was already at the reception, dressed to kill, in matching everything.

'Hello, dear,' she greeted him. 'You could've borrowed your father's tails. I'd no idea you didn't have any.'

Willem was baffled. 'No, I ...' He then noticed other men were wearing morning dress, bearing in their hands grey toppers and gloves. 'The ridiculous Brits!' he exclaimed. 'On a Thursday afternoon in the suburbs!'

'It's right and proper.'

Willem held up his hands. 'Okay, Mother. KO. I surrender.'

'Don't be silly. How are you, anyway?'

'Flourishing. How're you? Haven't seen you since Uncle Felix's funeral.'

'We're none of us getting younger.'

'Probably not,' Willem was able to agree.

'You've heard how Felix really died?'

'No?'

'In bed.'

'Ah.'

'Well, not exactly in his bed. On the rug in front of the drawing room fire, as a matter of fact.'

'Ahah!'

'What's the joke?' Dirck butted in to ask.

'One of Mother's dirty stories. How's the head of the family?' Willem scowled at his elder brother, irritated by his hangdog stoop. 'Cares of the world on your poor old shoulders?'

'You're the soldier, not me.'

Willem exchanged glances with his mother. Dirck's words were slurred. He was already tipsy.

'Thieves broke in and stole the Rembrandt, I seem to remember,' their mother remarked.

'Got it back.'

'Apparently.'

'How's Jane?' Dirck enquired.

'We're divorced.'

'I know. How is she? Don't you hear from her?'

Willem closed his eyes for a moment. Then stared sideways at the trees in a picture on the wall. 'Of course I do. She's remarried. An excellent man. With grown-up children. Caldera is … well, it's twice the size it was, totally changed. I'm not involved. It's not my life.'

The information Willem gave was basically correct. He lied,

though, in claiming to have heard from Jane. At Auckland Airport he had extracted from her a promise never again under any circumstances to make direct contact with him. He had sworn identical forbearance.

'You weren't suited. We knew it wouldn't last,' his mother said.

Willem feared he might explode. Detonate. Blow himself, the wedding guests and most of Dulwich Village into fragments in the sky.

'How did "we" know?' he asked.

'She made you nervous. Unhappy.'

'Mother, you're wrong. I wasn't happy long before meeting Jane. Let's not blame my wife, please.'

'I never liked the woman,' Dirck stated. 'After your money.'

'Dirck, you …' Willem controlled himself. 'I'm sorry, I … I'll get some fresh air.'

He rushed out of the Gallery, across the road and in through the gates of Dulwich Park. Willem marched towards a great bank of rhododendrons, shedding faded petals, and sat down hard on a bench.

He rubbed his eye, rhythmically.

He hated his feelings so much that he refused to admit he had any. He wanted to think, not feel. Keep his head clean for the crusade.

A brisk walk, that's what I need.

At the far side of the boating lake Willem met a course of crazy golf. He hired a ball and putter, and set off on his virgin round. The game suited him, poor eyesight and an unconventional image of the world allowing him to accept without blinking the odd trajectories. Flushed with success and refreshed by an ice cream, Willem returned to the wedding in time for the concert.

seven

In the autumn of 1970 Willem reached his fiftieth birthday. He spent the day on a train travelling from Amsterdam to Paris. On his own, looking out of the window, dreaming a future for the towns and villages of Flanders and the Somme through which he passed, their names lent through the centuries to battles for power over the peoples of Europe.

How had the notion taken root in Western culture: that it was right to sacrifice your life because some new ruler wished to control the tax you would have paid, the land you might have rented, the air-space above your head had you not been killed?

Willem did not see this as the only puzzle facing the human race. No other, though, in his opinion, more urgently demanded universal resolution.

Thirty years to the next millennium.

Willem neither expected nor wanted to make it. His hopes were limited to continuing to feel, year by year, for as long as he was allowed to live, a decreasing sense of bewilderment. The only method he could think of for achieving this internal aim was by external dedication to a laudable cause. Anything worth doing was worth doing well. Was worth doing badly, Willem needed to reassure himself when forced to admit he was getting nowhere. Birthdays were a particularly challenging time, he found – although becoming fifty in itself meant nothing but an advance on forty-nine, a chance to again make things a little bit better.

Shouldn't be difficult. Considering where I started.

Why would I want to celebrate the day of my birth? Fifty years ago today I was born into a family resigned to my presence. There was no welcome, as far as I've been told. Or can remember. And we do remember, I believe.

Everything.

Willem continued to stare from the train window. At washing hanging on a concertina clothesline fixed to the kitchen sill of a flat in a row of terrace houses tight against the railway track.

Could be anywhere in Europe. Vienna. Paris. Breda … name your treaty.

Westphalia.

Maastricht. Seriously.

No, we must've left Holland by now. Though I didn't notice a border. Are these the outskirts of Antwerp? Brussels already?

I could travel to Moscow. Or Peking. With nothing more than this shoulder bag of necessities. Without once setting foot outside railway stations and their hotels. Most of which were built by the British.

It's true: by adventurers like Josiah Conder. The architect who emigrated from Birmingham to Japan, where he built in the only style familiar to him. In "the screeching, sensational poetry, or Daily Telegraphese of the Gothic Revival." According to the *Furniture Gazette*, 4 July 1874.

I remember reading about him. This Brit designed Tokyo's first railway station. In gratitude for which the Emperor awarded him an ORS – Order of the Rising Sun, fourth class, being a foreigner.

With nobody around to whom he wished to talk, Willem enjoyed these silent conversations with himself. Reaching Paris in the late afternoon, he settled to a glorious meal at his favourite restaurant, the *Train Bleu* at *Gare de L'Est*.

The fiftieth anniversary of a day his mother had failed to avert passed without mishap, the train returning him in the early morning hours to Amsterdam.

Willem reacted with uncharacteristic immobility to the news that Pal and Takayanagi had both died in 1967. Without his hearing at the time of their loss, without feeling their absence. Now he knew they were gone – from reading their obituaries in the back copy of an international law journal – he missed them terribly. For the first time in his life Willem did not get up when he awoke. The morning after the discovery, he opened his eyes to see no point in the day. He could find no reason to move an inch, and continued to lie flat on his back, on his futon, on the painted floorboards, arms at his side, not conscious of breathing.

He was aware of thinking: about the sadness of lost opportunities to talk to the two men he admired most in the world. Willem was angry with himself for the imbecilic letters he had sent Pal and Takayanagi in their dying years, instead of flying to see them. What did he imagine there might have been more pleasurable to do than sit at the feet of these great old men and hear their stories? Their experience flowing into his own, swelling the river of sense. Willem felt weak and stupid, felt he deserved to be alone.

Death is final. It reduces us to what we were. To nothing.

When Pal and Takayanagi died their achievements remained undiscovered by the world for years. They ceased to exist. Were, quite simply, no longer there. Or here. Or anywhere. They live now only in the images we friends and admirers recreate of them in our minds. A plea, therefore, for accuracy. For each individual's truthfulness to his personal experience of Judge Pal and Defence Counsel Takayanagi. Privately. And public memory of the Tokyo Trial will be prevented from descent into oblivion.

Willem repeated in his head the facts.

Pal went first. On 10 January 1967, in Calcutta General Hospital, of a heart attack. Aged eighty-one. Survived by eleven children, thirty-eight grandchildren and thirteen great grand-children. Colleagues at the Bar commissioned a bronze bust of the judge, and placed it in a niche on the main staircase of the Central Courts of Justice.

Takayanagi was a year younger than Pal when he died, on 11 June 1967. In bed at the Mirama Hotel in Hong Kong, of a stroke. On the way home from an international peace conference his brain ceased to function. His widow, Fumi, fifteen years his junior, flew out to collect the body. The ashes she lodged in the family shrine in Kumagaya. Takayanagi's library of twenty thousand volumes was presented to Seikei University, of which he had been the founding chancellor in 1949. His students remembered him as a man of the Meiji spirit, devoted to what he believed to be for the wider public good.

Emery Reves? Is he dead too?

Willem caught his breath, in shock at the thought of another death unmourned. The possibility, indeed the likelihood that the author of his favourite book was no longer alive, drove Willem from his bed. To reach down *The Anatomy of Peace* from his shelves and reread, for the hundredth time, the London publisher's postscript of January 1947, which contained:

An Appeal to the students of England

We, Student Federalists, representing groups of students in sixty American universities and colleges, among them Yale, Smith, Vassar, Wellesley, Chicago and Stanford, urge you, students of England, to read, study and discuss Emery Reves' book *The Anatomy of Peace*. Most of us were soldiers in the last war and have just been demobilized. We are young enough to be soldiers in the next war. We feel certain you will agree with us that we must do everything in our power to prevent another world war, which this time, with the atomic bomb, may destroy our whole civilization.

We have been studying this problem very carefully and have come to the conclusion that no treaty, no alliance, no league such as the United Nations, can protect us from another catastrophe. Only law can bring peace.

We know of no book which deals with more clarity and

conviction with the need for worldwide legal order than *The Anatomy of Peace*. That is why we ask you to read it and urge your friends to do so.

If you agree that this book points the only road to survival, then organize your fellow students into an active movement in all universities and colleges as we have done in the United States. If you succeed, then we hope to hear from you so that within a very short time we can join forces and create a powerful worldwide movement of youth which will impose on our governments our will to live and our demand for the unification of the conflicting sovereign nation states into a worldwide legal order, which alone can make it possible for us to do our share to promote human progress.

News of the death of two key observers of the Tokyo Trial left Willem feeling precariously reliant on Professor Röling for corroborative support. Youngest of the eleven judges on the International Military Tribunal for the Far East, Röling was also the least antagonistic – apart from Pal, of course – to Asian culture. An agnostic, on the political left of the Dutch judiciary, Röling travelled extensively through Japan during the twenty months he spent there for the trial. He made friends with native Japanese, with three of whom he formed a string quartet, meeting regularly in each other's homes to play. He studied under the Buddhist philosopher Daisetz Teitaro Suzuki, a fluent Enlish speaker – a skill acquired at the pillow of his American wife. Röling considered Suzuki the most impressive person he had ever encountered, a man of genuine wisdom. In his separate judgement, and in subsequent work at his peace research institute in Groningen, Röling argued that Japan's build-up of economic and military power in Asia during the 1930s was defensive action, wholly legal, indeed the only peaceable means open to them to reverse centuries of violent Aryan exploitation.

Imagine – Röling instructed his postgraduate students – if the boot had been on the other foot. Picture the Chinese, after creation of the compass (two hundred years before the West), getting together with the Cambodians, the Mongolians and other racial equals to discover Europe, leaving only the island of Britain uncivilized, reckoned too small and insignificant to be bothered with. If then, in the middle of the nineteenth century, the Chinese and their allies had compelled the British to trade with the rest of the world, who would have blamed their grand old Queen Victoria for saying: 'Loyal subjects, national pride obliges us to become supreme in these matters, thus to protect the integrity of our cultural heritage.' Come the 1930s, think of Britain finding itself grown powerful enough, through trade and treaty with its seaboard neighbours, to expel the foreigners from mainland Europe. Would the French and us Dutch have regarded this as a crime against peace? Good riddance, we'd have said. Go back to where you came from centuries ago. Leave quietly and there need be no bloodshed. And do take that fat old Buddha with you, won't you? We're terminally attracted, you see, to the wracked agony of our dear Lord, Jesus Christ.

Although Röling's language lacked Willem's vivacity – he was, after all, a lawyer – their themes were identical.

'The trials in Nuremberg and Tokyo advanced the legal position that the launching of war is a criminal act,' Röling said at a symposium. 'Individual accountability for acts of state helped crystalize the conviction that war is by nature criminal.'

Röling called for ex-Presidents Nixon and Johnson to appear before the International Court of Justice in The Hague, on the charge of negative criminality. Their responsibility for atrocities committed in Vietnam was greater, Röling argued, than ex-Prime Minister Hirota's for Japanese conduct of the Second World War. In Röling's Dissentient Judgement, Hirota, who had retired from public life in 1938, was pronounced innocent of all the crimes for which he was indicted. Hirota's execution – in 1948, in his seventieth year – was a gross injustice, Röling held. His shame at being refused permission by General MacArthur to attend the hangings in Sugamo Prison, thus to bear personal witness to the old man's murder, never left him.

Willem's antipathy to Röling was a matter more of style than of content.

'International law is in a miserable state,' Röling had said at one of their meetings. 'The world lacks centralized organs for producing and enforcing supra-national order. That's the situation we live in. You're tilting at windmills, Mr Boymans. If you think any government is ready to pay the price of peace.'

'Which is?'

'The pooling of sovereignty.'

'Defeatist! Lackey of the elite!' Willem had stormed.

Willem wished he could leave war behind him and paint, make a fortune, learn to ski. There were occasions when he so loathed the sounds he heard emerging from his mouth that he vowed never again to speak. He sustained these periods of silence for a week at the most, until the tedium of contributing on a notepad his half of conversations with Saskia in the bar next door tried his patience beyond its limit.

'I give up! What you're saying, Saskia my poppet, is bunkum. Balderdash. A can of soup. The population of this funny flatland is not divided into the good on your side, devils on the other. Life isn't a game of ice hockey. "The police are such pigs." Nonsense. The only thing wrong about the Dutch police is their lack of power. They can't trot off to Brussels and arrest Dr Luns in his NATO lair. Can't impound tanks. Can't telephone their pals in Washington and say: What's happening in the Far East is uncivilized. A survival from the Dark Ages. What's more, it's illegal. Chapter and verse to follow, policeperson's oath. Clap the handcuffs on your besmirched President and restore justice to earth. Finito. Fin. End.'

Throughout these embattled years Willem regularly visited London, to study in the Reading Room of the Imperial War Museum, keepers of the only public copy in Europe of the original transcript of the Tokyo Trial. On these trips he often stayed a few nights with David Golding – in his and Susan's flat off the Kingsland Road, subsequently in the house they bought in Bethnal Green, overlooking Victoria Park. Willem fell into the habit of sending David file-copies of the articles he submitted for publication. The tone of his typed accompanying notes was warm:

A'dam
22 April 1977

Mon cher,

Many thanks for your letter, and bearing in mind what that drip the editor of the *Observer* may deem to be (probably not) publishable, today I have toiled at memo 'Philosopher Fou's View', copy of which I shall send you tomorrow when it has been duplicated. Together with items specified in my letter no. 104, copy encl.

It now being the basic statement of my case, I also enclose copy of the Tokyo Judgement, d. 16 December 1976, with attached thereto three relevant letters received.

Then for full measure, and for no better reason than I am rather fond of it, copy of 'The Röling Gang', d. 22 December 1976.

After all, for quite some time I have been telling plenty of people, both here and at the Imperial War Museum, where a dossier of my correspondence has been building up, how bloody-minded all editors are, including that of the bloody London *Observer*, with regard to the A9 issue.

Never again shall I waste time on trying to tailor-make anything for any of those bastards. I offer them all the info that I can, including of course hard viewpoints interlaced with the hard and not-so-hard facts – and there it is. And if they don't care for the way I serve it up, why, so kind am I that I even welcome their making of it whatever they wish; and don't even ask to be shown a copy of the trashy mess which as like as not their miserable scribes will make of my mostly rather simple and straightforward exposition.

If you or anyone else seriously interested cares to try to state the issue more clearly than does memo TTJ, in 3,000 or for that matter 30,000 words, then good luck to you. You have my blessing.

I meanwhile have fallen back on focusing briefly on fragments of this vastly complex issue; on building it up in the way small beasties do coral.

Willem

On the morning of New Year's Eve 1977/8, Willem hired a car and driver and set out to call on Professor Röling in Groningen, two hours drive north of Amsterdam, across the *Afsluitdijk* enclosing the *Ijsselmeer* from the sea. His purpose was double-edged: reconciliation of perceived differences; and the placing of a cautionary marker to publication promised for the coming year of the Tokyo Judgements, under editorial supervision of the Professor. Willem halted his journey at a café half way across the Zuiderzee and dialled Röling's office number from a telephone kiosk.

Röling refused to make, at such short notice, an afternoon appointment with his ill-tempered critic.

'I'm afraid I have to insist, *Zeer Geachte Heer Directeur*. It's time we talked peace.'

'I never talk anything else.'

'Time I did, then. When it comes to the crunch we are, I realize, on the same side.'

'If you say so.'

'I do.'

'I'm sorry, I'm busy. Write, if you wish. Whether or not you and I agree is of no concern. There's work to be done.'

'Precisely my contention. Tomorrow another year opens. The sheet must be clean. You will find me an altered man, Professor Röling. I surprise even myself.'

A sigh passed down the line. 'Very well. At four?'

'My thanks. Till later.'

Willem had never visited the Province of Friesland. The land through which he travelled looked fertile, the small rectangular fields around the home farms crowded with dairy cattle, fat and peaceful, their hides shining in the winter sun. In the vicinity of Leeuwarden Willem was impressed by farm buildings of a design he had seen nowhere else, the living quarters constructed of brick, on two floors, connected by neck-like covered passages to vast wooden barns at the rear, creosoted dark brown, with chamfered roofs of verdigris tiles. They looked like aberrant beetles. Like ancient spacecraft, abandoned to man. Willem and his driver Piet stopped to make architectural enquiries at the Princesshof Municipal Museum, where the tearoom served excellent omelettes. Reaching Groningen with time still to spare, Willem and Piet together inspected the Niemayer Tobacco Factory and Information Centre. The Gift Shop – incredibly – was closed.

Röling was in generous spirits, and shared with Willem personal memories of the Tokyo Trial. He told him about the presence in the public gallery for all the interminable hearings of Mrs Togo, a neat German woman, whom Shigenori Togo had married when a young diplomat in Berlin – to where he returned with her in 1937, as Japanese Ambassador. Second of the three acquitted by Röling of all charges, Togo was committed by the majority verdict to serve twenty years in jail, a sentence death prohibited his completing. Röling described an emotional meeting with Mrs Togo – years later, at her request – in the West German Embassy in The Hague, at which she presented him with her husband's dress set of Imperial medals.

'Unlike the Nazis at Nuremberg, not one of the Japanese defendants gave a shred of evidence against another. I admired them. The way they spoke. The way they moved. Adult. Dignified.'

Willem's close-of-year reconciliation ended with the story of Röling's last meeting in Tokyo with Major General Willoughby. The two men had formed an unlikely friendship, Willem heard, playing tennis regularly on the restored courts at the Imperial Hotel, where they both lodged. A staunch Republican, a product through and through of his military education and experience, Willoughby allowed himself to admit to Röling, over a farewell drink on termination of the trial, that he considered it the worst wartime hypocrisy of the century. In response to which he forbade his elder son to join the US Army, breaking a family tradition of professional military service intact since the Civil War.

At the door to Röling's office Willem warned of his determination to check every semi-colon of Radhabinod Pal's two hundred thousand-word Dissentient Judgement in the forthcoming publication.

In the event he found one solitary error, in transcription of the final sentence: 'When time shall have softened passion and prejudice, when reason shall have stripped the mask from misrepresentation, then justice, holding evenly her scales, will require much of past censure and praise to change places.' In the Calcutta printing of 1955, reason was underlined.

Was it reasonable for Röling, while acquitting three defendants whom the majority condemned to hang, to have judged deserving of capital punishment an additional three? Was Professor Röling's recommendation of judicial death any different in essence from President Truman's order to Major Charles W Sweeney, his B-29 bomber pilot, to drop Fat Man on Nagasaki?

Alongside the rigours of his war with the global elite, Willem found time for milder interests: swimming, fine buildings and friendship, principally. Willem loved to be diverted by sharing in his friends' pursuits. He became a familiar figure in Victoria – Victory, he called it – Park, a staunch storm trooper in the campaign to save its open-air swimming pool, five hundred yards from the Goldings' home in Gore Road. He was always game for a picnic, and generally amenable to pushing his namesake, baby William, around the deerpark in his pram, while Susan drove the older two – Carol, born in 1973, and Daniel, Boxing Day 1975 – to some other appointment.

Willem drew the line at becoming a godfather. God did not exist, and the idea of even surrogate fatherhood pained him.

Hard though he tried, Willem failed to understand Susan. She eluded him – on purpose, he suspected. He liked her integrity. Very much. Susan did not disguise, from herself nor from those she numbered friends, the struggle inherent in truthful living. Daily life in the Golding household appeared simple and straightforward and, at the same time, rich and complex. To Susan it seemed obvious that this was so. David found ordinary things much more difficult to deal with, making a convoluted mess of social arrangements, which his wife ironed out while he was away on business – forging a career for himself at Warburgs, the merchant bankers.

David spent the 1970s in flight back and forth from the Middle East. First Tehran, arranging finance for the construction, equipment and staffing of hospitals. Then, after the fall of the Shah, in the United Arab Emirates, advising sheiks on the international investment of petrodollars. He talked to Willem about his experiences, shared his private horror at the sight of white rats racing to supply arms – fighter planes, tanks, chemical weapons' factories – to anybody with the black money to pay for them. David's interest in Article Nine was genuine, William felt.

'I'm not sure how long I can keep it up. If I wasn't so fantastically well paid, I'd pack it in tomorrow.'

'And do what?' Willem wondered.

'Same sort of thing. For different ends. Work for the World Bank.'

'Worse! Murder by debt!'

David laughed. 'Then I'll look after the children. Free Susan to sort out the world. She's better at it than I am.'

At the end of the decade Willem's mother died, suddenly, of a perforated ulcer. Dirck telephoned with the news after she was already dead, denying Willem the chance to see her alive one last time.

He left it at that, and declined to attend her funeral. Until then he had made an effort on his mother's territory to – as she used to put it – behave. There was no need now for pretence.

Willem's sole regret at staying away from his mother's funeral was the lost opportunity of bumping into Gerald Gardiner. After Labour's defeat in the 1970 election, Baron Gardiner of Kittisford – the grotesque form of words by which this Quaker socialist deigned to be addressed – became chancellor of the Open University. Half of Willem longed to knock the dapper hypocrite from his pedestal; the other half knew it would be wasted energy.

While Susan pledged open support, David was unable to hide his disapproval.

'She'll be so upset.'

'Mother can't be anything. She's dead.'

'What harm will it do to pay your respects?'

'A lot.'

'Tell me. I don't understand.'

They stood on the concrete summit of the mountain range in the children's playground in Victoria Park, applauding Carol's dexterity and daring. Willem felt for his young friend's puzzlement. Yet he could not answer him. Could not tell the truth, it would not be believed.

'You'll understand. In time,' Willem said. 'When memories conflict, something has to give.'

'It won't be the same for me.'

'Why not?'

'Because I haven't fought for my country. I would, willingly. But I'll never be asked. Your kind of war is out of date.'

'Done it! I'm the King of the Castle!' David's daughter crowed. 'I'm the King of the Castle!'

News of the death on 25 June 1980 of a bodyguard of President Assad of Syria, blown to pieces when he threw himself onto a hand grenade tossed from the crowd by an assassin in the pay of President Saddam Hussein of Iraq, troubled Willem more than the passing away in old age of his never-happy mother. He saw on the film screened inside his head bits of the man's flesh spread around the podium. Felt the heat in the spots of this obedient young soldier's blood spattered across Assad's cheeks.

'There's more than enough war around,' Willem responded.

'I'm the King of the Castle!' Carol continued to chant.

'No reason not to go to your mother's funeral,' David repeated.

eight

In times of difficulty Willem's prime diversionary tactic was to take himself off, on the spur of the moment, to visit a place or a person from the past. The two frequently merged. As happened on a trip he made to Porthmadog – the nearest town to his Dutch army training camp in Snowdonia – on which Willem bumped into a man to whom he used to feel attached, a survivor of the specialist unit under his command. Jan-Otto Jonkman was the soldier's name. After the fighting ended Jonkman had made his way back to the Lleyn Peninsula to marry his freckled sweetheart, the Welsh-speaking daughter of a cornershop owner. Drawn by a distant sense of familiarity, Willem entered the shop to buy an ice-cream. Not until glancing into the man's eyes to thank him for the change did Willem recognise his old comrade, then the woman standing in steadfast misery at his side. They recognized him too. And let him leave without a word.

When Willem returned one spring morning to his great-aunt's house on the Veluwe – on a bicycle, this time – he was sure of meeting nobody known to him.

The new proprietor had created an idyllic retreat of *De Drie Eiken*. Less antiquated than in Aunt Marijke's day, while preserving the casual eighteenth-century elegance. A place still of privilege, named after the Rembrandt etching – though there were by now many more than three oaks on the crest of the knoll rising behind the house.

Willem reconnoitred, keen to acquire an undercover feel for the property before ascending the curved flight of stone steps to knock on the front door and introduce himself. The stream greatly pleased him, with miniature rapids created by the exposure of tree roots, below which clear pools formed, as deep and swimmable – in Willem's swollen imagination – as the Kauaeranga. The hen coop had been converted into a year-round garden room, its verandah facing a spinney of larch and birch, the ground just now covered with bluebells. He saw through the window a wood-burning stove, cane chairs, a writing table and shelves empty of books. Beyond the spinney the landscape opened into rolling heath typical of the district. An avenue of horse chestnuts in the middle-distance began and ended nowhere.

Leaning against the shadowside of one of the pineapple-topped piers which supported open wrought-iron gates, the house's personal appeal to Willem cooled. Architectural characteristics he had first judged languid began to look self-satisfied; the decorative smiles of the curled volutes above the windows turned to sneers. It was, he acknowledged, a valuable relic from the age of proclaimed enlightenment. The trouble with this being Willem's conviction that everything he loathed about structures of power in the modern world stemmed from ideas then established as common currency in the European psyche. The house stood for rules of social, racial and moral authority he was dedicated to uprooting.

Despite this disapproval, Willem could not help liking the sound which accompanied his pull to the recessed iron knob on the wall beside the front door, causing a brass bell to toll brightly through back passages of the house.

'Don't worry, I'll go,' he heard someone call.

Nor was Willem inclined to feel anything other than warmth towards the woman who opened the door, her grey head bent forward, blue eyes smiling up at him.

'Good afternoon,' she said, her voice rising inquisitively on the final syllable.

'Hello. I didn't phone because I don't know your name,' Willem responded, in his usual excessiveness at first meetings. 'The truth is I probably wouldn't have anyway. I seldom do, I'm afraid. Badly brought up. Blame the British public school.'

'I'd rather not. My grandson goes to Rugby. Maybe things've improved since your time?'

'Are the Dutch still traipsing off to England to educate their brats? Pity. The system here's superior.'

'I agree. My Diedrich's Herbert-Jan is the dullest of boys. Not a thing to say for himself. Cup of coffee?' She waved Willem into the flagged hall. 'Who are you, incidentally?'

They introduced themselves. And walked through to an untidy breakfast room, its panelled walls painted duck-egg blue, a basset hound asleep on a chintz-covered armchair, one ear trailing on the floor. Madam La Baroness – as Willem internally named her – came out with the statement that he looked liverish.

'Nothing a dose of country air can't cure,' she added.

Again Willem was disinclined to find fault. She expressed what he was feeling: jaded; under-exercised; fed up with his increasingly isolated city life. In twelve years in Amsterdam Willem had managed to alienate most potential allies. Even the humanists had stopped trying to understand him. Activists in the Campaign for Nuclear Disarmament, Lawyers Against War, Pugwash, International Physicians for Nuclear Responsibility, the World Federalist Movement, the International Peace Research Association, the Albert Einstein Institution, *Soka Gakkai*, the Global Citizens' Association, the *Dag Hammarskjold* Information Centre on the Study of Violence and Peace, and the World Constitution and Parliament Association had all ended up – in his eyes, not theirs – the enemy. Because when pressed to stake their faith in Article Nine they directed Willem to their own better-supported methods of progressing towards the shared goal of supra-national sovereignty.

A pox on them!

Only Garry Davis – founder in 1953 of the World Service Authority, which issued citizen of the world passports recognized as legitimate travel documents by Burkino Faso, Ecuador, Mauritania, Togo and Zambia – continued to offer Willem unequivocal encouragement. 'Brilliant work! *Tribute to a Trial* is precisely what I need at the moment,' Davis had written in his Christmas 1980 letter. 'My candidacy for World President, while crazy to most, will serve to give me a political platform necessary to challenge both politicians and movement leaders not to mention the vast voting public. But funds for mailing and printing are desperately needed. Help! I can't draw from World Service Authority revenue. It is barely enough to cover WSA expenses. (When Beirut airport closes, we lose upwards of $2,500 per week such is the volume of passport applications from that stricken land.).' Towards the end of this long letter Davis had informed Willem of his appointment as co-ordinator of the World Mediation Commission of the World Government of World Citizens. 'Your commitment, persistence and honesty in this field over the years aptly qualifies you for the position within the framework of the only global sovereign government with the sanction of common world law. You may of course refuse the appointment but until you do, I shall consider you co-ordinator of this Commission whose other members you may nominate at your discretion. As a World Government Commission co-ordinator, you join Yehudi Menuhin, Badi Lenz, Isaac Asimov, Carol Sue Rosin (deputy), Admiral Ted Welles and William Perk, cultural, forestry, space, ocean and design science commissions respectively. We will add commissions as the competent co-ordinators come upon the world scene.' By return post, while enclosing his customary cheque, Willem had declined the appointment. Garry Davis was a crank, in Willem's opinion. Likeable enough, but a crank all the same.

'Will you join me for lunch?' Baroness van den Hoorn invited.

'Happily.'

Luncheon was served by the housekeeper, in the dining room, the table laid with blue and white export porcelain and crested silver. The Baroness proposed that he stay for the summer, a paying guest, with exclusive use of the garden room in which to work.

'It's a perfect place for writing. You'll be inspired to greater heights.'

She was in her late seventies, she told him. For eight years now a widow: of a diplomat and poet.

'You haven't said no,' she noted as he climbed on his bicycle.

'Does not-no mean yes?' Willem asked.

'Usually.'

'Then I'll see you again. Next week sometime? I'll drop you a line.'

'I look forward to it.'

'So do I,' he said, and pedalled back to the local railway station.

The move to the Veluwe provided Willem with another opportunity to sift his possessions. He was disgusted with himself for having sanctioned the acquisition of so much superfluous baggage since his departure, lean and keen, from New Zealand. Toasters, water filters, expresso machines, knife sharpeners, food mixers, coffee grinders, waffle makers ... Willem gave the lot to Saskia, who sold most of it – at knockdown prices – to immigrant Surinam labourers, the regulars at her Sunday stall at the *Anti-Antiek Markt*.

Willem threw out reams of paperwork: file copies of the letters which rolled obsessively from his typewriter; folders of dreamed-to-be-useful cuttings from newspapers; and stacks of the relentlessly inadequate manifestos, reports and magazines which organizations he had at one time cultivated despatched around the gilded west. The two or three pieces of furniture he wished to keep went into store, before closing up his flat and handing the keys to an agent commissioned to sell the remainder of his lease. Life in Amsterdam had begun to make Willem ill with anger, sick in the stomach. He needed to lie low for a couple of years and re-equip his ideas, define the millennial resolution.

'There's expectation in the air. An intensity of public focus I haven't seen since the months after the war ended. Do you feel it? Or am I whistling in the wind?' Willem asked Madam La Baroness.

'It'll come. You're ahead of your time,' she replied.

They were taking their morning constitutional, along a public path across the heath, armed with pointed sticks with which to spike trippers' litter. Abelard, the basset hound, ambled in their wake.

'Where were you on D-day?' he enquired.

'Washington. You?'

'Number 2 Troop, the Green Berets.'

'Forgive me Pekelvlees.'(In the spirit of their friendship, Baroness van den Hoorn had nicknamed Willem Pekelvlees – salted meat – a reference to his complexion when heated in argument.) 'I am aware you're a distinguished commando. What you've never told me is what you did.'

'Nor will I.' Willem drove the steel spike through a spent carton of fruit juice. 'It's irrelevant.'

Willem valued the regularity of life at *De Drie Eiken*. The framework of their day secure, they could risk disagreement. Behind everything the Baroness said Willem felt her belief in him. Which made pleasurable the household responsibilities he one by one assumed. Removal of ticks from the folds of Abelard's skin, braving the dog's bloodshot gaze of disdain. Donation of Baron van den Hoorn's legion of dead shoes to the hostel for alcoholics in Arnhem.

Rejuvenated, Willem set about the complete reappraisal of his battle plan, a map of the world pinned to the pitchpine wall of his campaign headquarters beside the stream. Out of respect for Madam La Baroness's aversion to alcohol, he took to

tobacco and black Bolivian coffee for stimuli, equipping himself
with a MacArthuresque pipe, which he smoked ferociously as
he paced up and down the garden room, battering his thoughts
into publishable order. He wanted what mattered to him to
mean as much to somebody else. And through this other to
friends of theirs, on and on, till a multitude of sympathizers
forced democratic governments to take notice.

His new strategy required gaining the semi-offical status of
expert – specialist, at least – on the international conference circuit. To this end he booked to attend the Southern Region Conference of the Association for Asian Studies in Lexington,
Kentucky, eager to observe how the system worked. Determined
not to repeat the old errors, whenever he felt his anger boil he
thought of Madam La Baroness, and of how disappointed she
would be to learn he had let himself down. With the result that
everything went extraordinarily well.

The elite were less efficiently defended than he had supposed, their linked chains of exclusion made of paper, not steel.
To his amazement the organisers welcomed the single-side sum-
mary of his argument and included a copy of it in the package
handed to delegates on registration at the Blue Grass Country
Conference Centre (BGCCC for short, the Cs formed of horse-
shoes). Professor Theodore McNelly, a traditionalist from the
Department of Politics at the University of Maryland, referred
to *Tribute to a Trial* in his speech:

Mr Willem Boymans asserts that the effect of the Tokyo
Judgement was to deprive the state of the authority to decide
for itself whether or not defense was a legitimate justification
for going to war. Because forty-eight countries (all of them
members of the United Nations) accepted the Tokyo Judgement by signing the Japanese Peace Treaty (San Francisco
1951), all of these countries lost their sovereign right to judge

the legitimacy of defensive warfare, in line with the Kellogg-Briand Pact (Paris 1928). The ultimate result, according to Boymans, was to unversalize the principle of Article Nine of the Japanese Constitution – the renunciation of defensive as well as offensive wars. The validity of Mr Boymans' ingenious argument depends heavily on the interpretation that one places on the somewhat ambiguous texts that he cites. The argument, however, is important for us because it suggests that the Tokyo Trial, the Peace Treaty and Article Nine, taken together and as a whole have a greater significance than they would have if viewed as quite separate historical events.

For an opponent of Japan's Peace Constitution to describe, on the printed record of an accredited conference, the documentation of his thesis 'ambiguous' amounted – Madam La Baroness agreed – to a ringing endorsement.

'That's not all. Look what I dug up in the MacArthur Archives.'

At the close of the conference Willem had taken a Greyhound bus-ride into the next state, to Norfolk, Virginia, home of the MacArthur Memorial Foundation. Where he had spent a congenial week making a nuisance of himself.

'Will they allow historical fact to discolour their war-hero image of Generalissimo MacArthur? You bet they won't. Sweep his championship of A9 under the carpet, let the dust settle, and deny all knowledge of the affair.'

'What's this about?' Madam La Baroness waved the Xeroxed sheets of paper Willem had given her. '"Supreme Allied Commander South East Asia". Signed "Dickie Mountbatten". We met him once. A vain nonentity.'

'Read it.'

The letter, dated 16 August 1945, delivered by hand to MacArthur in the Philippines, written in Malaysia by Lord

Mountbatten, had been marked by the Norfolk archivist with a ruled red line beside the pregnant passage:

I am sure that your views coincide with mine, namely that it will be the greatest mistake to be soft with the Japanese. The fact that you have been prevented from inflicting the crushing victory which operations OLYMPIC and CORONET would undoubtedly have produced and that I have been prevented from carrying out ZIPPER and MAILFIST will, I fear, enable the Japanese leaders to delude their people into thinking they were defeated only by the scientists and not in battle, unless we can so humble them that the completeness of the defeat is brought home to them.

  Normally I am not a vindictive person, but I cannot help feeling that unless we really are tough with all the Japanese leaders they will be able to rebuild themselves eventually for another war.

'Idiot,' the Baroness growled. 'Games of toy soldiers, with other people's lives. What I respect in you, Pekelvlees, is your seriousness. Don't let's leave the world in the hands of boys like Mountbatten.' The old woman made a naughty-girl face. 'Please.'

  'I'm doing my best.'

  'Never give up.'

  'I won't. The powerful aren't about to hand over their globe without a fight.'

  'Who would you like to hold onto it when you're gone?'

  'Difficult. Someone I trust,' Willem replied, rubbing his eye.

Willem's hopes for the future began to centre on David Golding. He took to making two carbon copies of every letter he wrote and sending one of them to David for retention in his London file. When writing to lawyers and politicians in Britain Willem noted, in postscripts, that additional material was available for study at David's address in Bethnal Green. Although nobody bothered to explore, the potential for them to do so helped Willem feel supported, the leader of a could-be movement.

On Susan's initiative, moved by the Women's Peace Camp at Greenham Common, the Goldings had registered family membership of CND. David occasionally wore the deluxe lapel badge in to work – to provoke his colleagues, never neglecting to remove it before an appointment with clients. Willem persuaded David to challenge CND's director – a priest, on loan from the Vatican – to make productive use of *Tribute to a Trial*. David's persuasive letter was the first of many he wrote on Willem's behalf. It elicited a response. Prompting Willem to comment: 'Perhaps your letter of the 9th to CND dwells overmuch on the "remarkability", such as it is, of WJB. The urgency of promoting A9 hardly allows for a personality cult, which in this case offered Monsignor BK the opportunity, happily snapped up by him, naturally, to focus his reply on the problem of how to "plug in" your patently unsuccessful friend, your wayward bedraggled broken-legged kangaroo.' During this period of comparative well-being, at home with himself in the garden room of *De Drie Eiken*, Willem developed a taste for third person self-deprecation. In a letter – to take another example – to the Peace Studies Association of Japan: 'UNESCO is entitled, I suppose, to regard the Article Nine Syllogism as the worthless figment of some scarecrow's troubled mind, and ignore it accordingly. But how about A9 itself? Assuredly the Showa Constitution does actually exist?'

In the spring of 1982, on learning of a symposium – The Occupation of Japan: The International Context – to be held in October at the MacArthur Foundation, Willem threw himself into the task of making an impact. Memorandums and papers poured forth, the majority addressed to the Foundation's director in Norfolk, aimed at securing an invitation to address the conference. Willem pounced on the idea of issuing a series of statements, to each of which he penned the question: What are your views on this?, abbreviated half way down the first page to WAYVOT? An initial ten cardinal points extended to thirty-eight, lengthening from a crisp sentence into dense paragraphs of contentious Willemisms. By the end of the summer this ever-adjustable draft had expanded to thirty pages, heading towards a century of unanswerable questions.

A month before the conference was due to convene, Lyman H. Hammond, Director of the MacArthur Memorial Foundation, acknowledged his mystification – 'Many times I have not answered your letters, mainly because I did not know what you desired' – and offered to cancel Willem's reservation, refunding his deposit.

'Got them on the run!' Willem telephoned, in glee, to tell David. 'It's the chance I've been waiting for. They can't duck this one!'

'You're still going?'

'My dear boy! Listen to this. "19.45 Dinner – Addressed by Ambassador Akira Matsui – The San Francisco Peace Treaty: A Day that Changed the Fate of Japan and the World." Well!'

'Sounds promising.'

'Th-i-r-t-y ye-a-r-s I've worked for this opening. Look, the questionnaire thing isn't feasible. They've sniffed danger and upped the drawbridge. What I need is an account in plain-English of background and argument. Printed up for distribution to the assembled dignitaries. You must have some chum who could do this for me? All the material's in your file. Some clever fellow in the bank's research department? I'll pay. A ransom.'

'That won't be necessary. I'll do it myself.'

'Have you the time? Marvellous.'

After dinner that evening with the Baroness, Willem let himself back out to the garden room and drank, before going to bed, a bottle of vodka.

Tired to death of always being right, Willem wanted, once and for all, to be proved wrong. He wanted the dark, slithering fear that David did not really understand him to be a delusion. He wanted to fly in to Norfolk, take a cab to the Omni International Hotel, collect his room key and airmail package of pamphlets and find the text perfect. Willem so much wanted to be wrong not to trust David that he left early for America, before the typescript was ready for him to check.

In those weeks of frenzied preparation for battle, Willem had become conscious of a need to hold in his hands the original copy of the Judgement of the International Military Tribunal for the Far East. Study of Röling's published text and of the microfiche in the Imperial War Museum in London had failed to reveal the fact of crucial significance he was convinced lay hidden there. Something so obvious once seen that the due process of international law in crimes of war, paralysed since Nuremberg and Tokyo, would be reawakened and civilization saved from self-destruction. Obedient to instinct, Willem flew first to Washington, to the Modern Military Branch of the National Archives, to see with his own half-blind eyes what he could find.

At Baroness van den Hoorn's suggestion, Willem lodged with friends of hers in Georgetown – a retired senator and his wife, Robert and Mary-Ellen Fraser, the owners of a pair of brindle Pekinese. The well-being of the dogs – neutered male cousins, in prime of life – ordered the entire household. Every afternoon at two-fifteen Mr Fraser collected the convertible from its lock-up garage a block away and parked it outside their house, ready for Mrs Fraser to drive the Pekes up to Dumbarton Oaks for daily exercise. With time always spare for agreeable distractions, Willem asked if he might accompany her.

'What do you say, boys?'

The dogs acquiesced.

'Would you mind holding these?' She handed him two draw-tied velvet bags, one plum the other navy, and two identical roller-tape leads. 'It's not far.'

The controlled contours of Dumbarton Oaks looked depressingly British to Willem, with its giant beech, scattered oak trees and designer-tumble of boxwood. The autumn display in the chrysanthemum beds impressed him, however. As did the skill with which Mrs Fraser evaded the entanglement of her Pekes, with themselves or with other dogs, tugging and plucking, reefing and releasing their long leashes with the precision of a kite-flyer on Yokohama Pier.

'Hi there Humperdink. How are you today?'

A black poodle waddled across the grass, slavering at the mouth. Mrs Fraser hauled in her two, ruthlessly.

'Sit!'

She placed their leads on the ground, covering them with the sole of her Wellington boot, and fished in her pocket for the navy bag of vitamin E dog biscuits, a gloved handful of which she fed to Humperdink.

'Keep you on your toes.'

Mrs Fraser patted the poodle's curly head, nodded unsmilingly at its owner and continued on her way. After a second rendezvous, with an Irish setter, to whom she chattered about the weather and offered a titbit from the plum bag, they returned to the car.

'Did you also know Mountbatten?' it occurred to Willem to ask.

'Sure, everyone knew Dickie. Shame they let the IRA get him.'

'Had a good innings,' he heard himself say.

Next morning at the National Archives Willem made a discovery: the signature page of the Judgement was missing. He at first assumed there must be some technical explanation. That it was kept elsewhere, on public display. That it was away being photographed. That ... but, no, the staff were as mystified. And worried.

'I know it exists. There's a copy in London,' Willem said.

'Yes, there's a copy with our copy. No original. I don't understand.'

Nor did Willem. Did the real page say something different? Had the truth been mislaid? To whose advantage? Nobody gained by denying the illegality of war. By pretence at justice. No one gained by pretence at anything.

Of what are the powerful afraid? What impells them to lie, to spy, to cheat? To amass underground stores of lethal armaments? To plot the destruction of nations, of races, of creeds?

Better dead than red.

For God, King and country.

Just war. Holy war. Jihad.

Come on, come clean. You're frightened of death, aren't you? You monarchs and ministers and managing directors. That's what motivates you. Terror of dying. You're incapable of being honest with yourselves. Unable to accept your own frailty. Afraid to be human. Afraid of day-by-day life, in effect.

And we poor fools have let you get away with it. Have indulged you players of games, you inventors of strategies, you creators of theory, you writers and readers of books.

There, there, don't fret: we've comforted, over the centuries. We'll fight the demon death for you. We'll defend your illusions. Sorry to trouble you, guv. Time's up. Can't say we didn't give you a chance. It's getting serious now. You'll do yourself an injury. Can't have that, can we? Come another war and you'll blow yourselves sky high. Won't just be us who'll be dead. You will too. End of the world stakes, mate.

Willem put off writing the necessary letter to David until he arrived in Norfolk.

Omni International Hotel
777 Waterfront Drive
Norfolk, Virginia 23510
21 Oct 1982
Early in the morning

Dear David,

Thanks for your letter of the 17th with 3 copies of ON A9, and I confirm my yesterday's card from Washington. Awaiting me here was also the parcel containing 150 copies, which I do not propose to open.

Today I shall attend the Symposium in the hope of picking up some useful info, and more especially to get the feel of it. So then to draft and duplicate a one-page statement. Your ON A9 is I regret not merely useless for my purpose, but would if used be grist-to-the-mill for the antis. Its p.1 provides them opportunity to brick me fairly hard three times, and to shoot me down in flames twice. And so it goes on.

Please add the enclosures to the file you are holding. You are to distribute no further copies of ON A9, and if I get around to constructing a correction sheet I'll send you a copy.

See you in Nov. Greets to Susan.

Yours,
Willem

He sent a follow-up letter from Stanstead in Quebec, to where he had moved on after the conference, to discuss tactics with

Duncan Graham, founder-president of the Global Citizens' Association.

Canada
2 November 1982

Dear David,

Thank you for your letter of 25 October awaiting me when yesterday I arrived here. And I confirm having acknowledged your letter of 17 October in the note I scribed early a.m. 21 Oct from the Omni Hotel. Which by the way is a well appointed hostelry, patronized for instance by a sheikh (or so he was described to me) who drives around in an armoured limousine not much shorter than a London bus, and with his own Virginia State Police motorcycle escort.

Looking back on it I am glad I refrained from using the 150 copies of the fifteen-page brochure ON A9. That unopened parcel is now with Garry Davis at the World Service Authority in Washington, to be kept there for a couple of months just in case I can think up some way to employ its contents usefully. In the absence of any such inspiration it is to be pulped.

Without overlooking my very own and very obviously pathetically wrong decisions that have contributed to this disaster – for such, in terms of 'might have been', assuredly it was – let me say that jobbing backwards or indulging in recrimination, which for preference are to be avoided anyhow, seem to me permissible only when so doing enhances the prospect of achieving success in the future.

So naturally I prefer to waste no more time – nor, for that matter, adrenalin – on it.

Onwards.

W

After a number of increasingly confused exchanges, by letter and on the telephone, Willem terminated contact with David in a memorandum dated 24 January 1983, written in his garden room back on the Veluwe, in the fog of winter.

DG

This memo is typed in a mood of cool fury. This because WJB is aware that it is up to him, and to no one else, to awaken in time awareness of A9. Meaning that positive thinking, positive posture, positive application are what at age sixty-two is required of him. Whereas utterly negative is the drag thrust on him by the sickening pigs-breakfast dished up by DG, at age thirty-five.

In your letter of 21 Jan you question my mental balance and in one respect at least you are quite right. Obsessively polite being what I am inclined to be, my indignation at the (insolent?) idiocy of your text was not made clear in my comment of 21 October 1982. Pure wishful thinking led me to suppose it was. Quite nuts – you are quite right. Anyhow, that is a spill for posterity to sponge around in.

On the one hand I continue to be perplexed – while noting with wry amusement that never does anyone devote even a moment to explaining it to me – as to what precisely is the reason for the CND gentry's venomous hostility to A9. On the other hand my perplexity does not prevent me from recognising that this peculiar stance does indeed exist. Bringing it about that I admit to fulsome admiration for the damaging ('devastating' seemed on consideration to be overstating it) undermining of A9 that you have accomplished on behalf of your Monsignor BK.

This memo simply serves notice within a reasonable lapse of time from when you accomplished your brilliant stroke, that I am aware of having been defrauded, and intend in due course to seek redress.

WJB

Willem's strategy for survival obliged him to move on from distressing events as though they had never occurred, as if the people involved no longer existed. David Golding was no exception. The only noticeable effect of the quarrel was to make him extra-appreciative of Madam La Baroness and the sanctuary they shared. While he continued to pay rent only for the three rooms he exclusively occupied, Willem was encouraged to treat the whole property as his own. For as long as it proved useful, the Baroness insisted. Until the old lady died, Willem had more or less decided, aware of how much she, in her different way, had come to depend on him.

At no time in his adult life had Willem gone for long without intimacy. The regular touch of another's body felt a natural human right. He did not think of these contacts with women in terms of a relationship. They were temporary alliances, passing arrangements of mutual benefit. Essential to their pleasure, in Willem's mind, was the certainty that they would – sooner rather than later – end.

His current bed-fellow was a KLM air hostess, twenty years his junior and the model of colour-supplement perfection. Madam La Baroness adored her.

'Aren't men a complete bore when you're so beautiful?' she speculated. 'With the constitution of a horse, I tend to have been treated like one. Loyally, by and large.'

'I've done pretty well myself. All things considered,' Disja responded. 'Been the odd bastard. Always is, isn't there?'

'I wouldn't know. Low mileage. Single owner.'

'Haven't missed much, I can tell you.'

'How does Pekelvlees rate? Up to scratch?'

Disja blushed. 'He's sweet. A friend, more than anything else.'

For the housekeeper's sake, when Disja visited – sometimes with her eight-year-old son – she was put up in the main guest suite, across the passage from Willem's dressing room and bedroom. She always came to him, never the other way round. They seldom spent an entire night together, each needing a decent sleep to make the day worthwhile. Despite his high colouring and pock-marked cheeks, Willem's skin was soft, his touch – of fingers and lips – gently sensuous. Impotent since the break-up of his marriage, he made love to the bodies of women with compensatory invention, his joy in Disja's presence in his bed peculiarly thrilling, to them both.

Willem recognised his indebtedness to the succession of women who accepted, without argument, the limitations of such a friendship. He delighted in buying his women expensive clothes, and in surprising them not simply with his material generosity but with the thoughtfulness of his gifts. On returning from America Willem had arranged for Disja's son to have the piano lessons she regretted the family had been able to afford for her as a child. Before leaving in May for a conference in Japan, Willem presented Disja with a piano, delivered to her flat in Hilversum on the night of her birthday dinner.

After the disappointments of Lexington and Norfolk Willem approached international conferences warily, with – in the Japanese idiom – spit-moistened eyebrows. Paid for by men in authority, their purpose was to enhance the status quo, never challenge it.

In Japan too? Surely they know better?

The promise in the title – Tokyo War Crimes Trial: An International Symposium – turned to bile inside Willem when he realized, on arrival, that Sunshine City Hall, the conference venue, was raised on the rubble of the recently demolished Sugamo

Prison. The shock of discovering that Frank Lloyd Wright's Imperial Hotel had also been torn down finished him off. He fell physically ill, in a fit of volcanic eruptions, at front and rear. He was rushed to hospital, where the night-duty doctor diagnosed acute food poisoning. Confined to bed, where he received – courtesy of the state – high quality oriental care and attention, Willem missed the conference. All he managed in the cause of A9 was a hand-written note to the Buddhists of *Soka Gakkai*, at their headquarters on Shimano-machi, in Shinjuku-ku.

'Does there happen to be around any man of law of the type of the late Dr Takayanagi Kenzo?' he wrote. 'If so, please be so kind as to forward to him all the material I have sent you over the years.'

Two days later Willem flew back to Holland.

The 1980s were not totally devoid of success for Willem. Dr T P Amerasinghe of Kadawata in Sri Lanka, Editor-in-Chief of *Aizen World*, accepted his six hundred-word article 'Pondering the Future', prefaced by a quote from George Orwell's *Nineteen Eighty-Four* – the year of publication.

> Who controls the past controls the future:
> Who controls the present controls the past.

Then, from London, Dr Alex Poteliakhoff, Acting Secretary of the Medical Association for Prevention of War, wrote appreciatively of Willem's thesis and proposed that MAPW adopt the principle underlining Article Nine. At the group's next Annual General Meeting this proposal was criticized by several members as a pious hope. Willem learnt, from the fiery minutes of the meeting, that a certain Dr Arnold tabled a compromise amendment: 'That the AGM, having discussed the resolution on Article 9 proposed by Dr Poteliakhoff, is interested to pursue this important issue and recommends that it be widely discussed, that material be published and that a conference be held on the subject.' Carried by six votes to five with seven abstentions, this was celebrated by Willem, at lunch with Madam La Baroness at *De Drie Eiken*, as an historic breakthrough.

Nor did the affair end there. Willem's name appeared alongside Professor Ian Brownlie QC's, occupier of the Oxford Chair of Public International Law, on the brochure advertising a MAPW one-day conference on The "Right" to Wage War, at the Royal Society of Medicine on Saturday 11 May 1985. Willem, the last to speak, equited himself adequately – in his view – and was disappointed that *The Lancet* devoted a disproportionately small space to his speech in its report. Dr Ronald Britten, in *The Lancet's* account, gave the star performance, with his optimistic analysis that the hypertrophy of paranoid attitudes to outsiders characteristic of nationalist fanatics was a passing phase. Like children who after a spell of destructiveness turn to reconciliation, repair and healing, the world's warmongers were destined to make federalist peace.

In heaven, Willem presumed.

Returning by train with his bicycle from a day of secret drinking in Amsterdam, Willem rode over the edge of his local platform and knocked himself unconscious on the iron track. An ambulance was summoned. Badly concussed and with a deep gash above his left, the least blind eye, he was confined to Arnhem's ex-military hospital for several days. Routine tests revealed that the severity of his sickness in Japan was due to cancer of the bowels. Specialists were amazed at Willem's claim to have felt no pain in guts ravaged by the disease.

'He's brave,' the Baroness explained. 'That's all you can say.'

'Will he take to treatment?' the doctor wondered.

'What do you reckon?'

They looked down at Willem propped up in the hospital bed, his head bandaged, mouth open, fast asleep.

The doctor smiled. 'He'll survive.'

Madam La Baroness beamed.

'Of course he will.'

Willem returned to hospital for a third stomach operation, scheduled – by chance – for the day the last of Japan's wartime leaders, Emperor Hirohito, died. Of cancer, in the early morning hours of 7 January 1989.

Two days later the new emperor declared public allegiance to the 1947 Showa Constitution, and dedicated his reign to *Heisei* – the achievement of world peace. Willem registered this distant encouragement.

nine

David and Susan Golding heard nothing of Willem's illness. Nobody in London they knew knew him. And Willem himself held strictly to silence.

'I don't mind,' David said – his hurt plain to see. 'I just feel it's a pity for him. To cut off like that. Without a word of warmth.'

Susan seemed to agree. 'He enjoyed the children. I guess he enjoys most things.' She paused, for thought. 'You disappointed him. So he scuttles off. Very sensible.'

'Could have sent a Christmas card. Let us know he's alive.'

'We're not, though. Because he's cut off our heads. Killed us.'

'Don't be silly, darling. Willem's a pacifist. He doesn't go around liquidating people.'

Susan laughed – with pleasure at David's generosity. 'You're incorrigible. He's the most violent man I've ever met.'

David put his hands to his ears – with equal delight in his clever, complicated wife. 'I don't want to hear. If you believe Willem Boymans has devoted his life to making war illegal principally in order to suppress a fancy for mass murder … well, you're entitled to your opinion. So am I. Nonsense!'

'Not at all. I've never been afraid of Willem losing physical control. All I'm saying … and you know it, because you're one of his victims … is that he's ruthless about people's feelings. Willem commits violence on emotions, his own included, on a scale I'm surprised he has the strength to sustain. And remain human.'

'He's certainly that. It's why I miss him.'

'You do, I know. I don't.' Susan kissed David, full on the lips. 'Want some supper?'

In truth, Susan had no better than tolerated Willem's arbitrary descents on them in London. He possessed characteristics she admired: independence of spirit; general asceticism; a disarming sense of his own ridiculousness. Others which she loathed: his objectification of women; his Oxbridge snobbery; the dried spittle at the corners of his mouth. Susan found it impossible to forgive Willem his denial of responsibility for how anybody else felt. His unconcern for the effect on others of the decisions he made was not the product of thoughtlessness. It was deliberate. Willem knew what he was doing, acted as he did in absolute antagonism to personal feeling, while staking his life on the fight for the sovereign rights of the individual to feel safe from war. Willem's presence irritated Susan mainly because of his inability to acknowledge this conflict at the heart of his thinking. Conflict and contradiction were – in Susan's view – inevitable, even desirable. She did not expect Willem to resolve fundamental differences, merely to admit that they existed and face the issue openly. Adult self-deception appalled Susan.

Susan saw how Willem did himself harm by this cavalier attitude to feeling. She recollected a conversation in Victoria Park, resting in the shade of a surviving elm, their backs against its trunk – William asleep in the stroller at their side, Carol and Daniel playing hospitals beneath the adjacent tree.

'Madams mystify me,' Willem confessed.

'Oh?'

'The other day a madam I know. No spring chicken. Gave me a terrible dressing down. Over nothing. Assassinated our very satisfactory arrangement, for no good reason.'

'That you could see.'

'Precisely. That's why I'm relating the saga. So that Madam Golding will enlighten me on the ways of women.'

'I can speak only for myself. Not for your friend.'

'Here's the gist,' Willem explained. 'Every year I do the beach walk from Hoek van Holland up to Den Helde. It's a five-day affair. Excellently organised. Amenable crowd of regulars. Camping equipment goes on ahead by road. All that sort of thing.' He looked across the grass, off into the distance. Passed the back of his hand across his wet mouth. 'Anyhow. *Comme d'habitude*, I shared the tent of one of my walker madams. Never occ-u-u-rred to me to ask the other madam's permission … her fury! Well! Now, tell me. Isn't that fantastically childish? A woman of her age? I simply don't understand.'

It was clear he never would understand. It was too late.

Susan found herself thinking more fondly of Willem now she was no longer obliged to see him. Discounting obvious aberrations, his politics were akin to hers. Susan agreed, for example, with Willem's dismissal of the Falkland War as a British tiff, of nil significance on the global scale. Whereas for David this experience of the nation at war had marked his political awakening. All three – Susan, David and Willem – were united in horror at the misplaced pride of mothers in their sons' bravado on dockside partings. Horror at the heroism of young Englishmen on the barren heaths of unknown islands in the South Pacific. Horror at the shadow of empire.

Willem's Article Nine campaign was doomed to failure because of the way he went about it, Susan had decided. Shifts in world opinion occurred through the identification of common interests and concerns, not by emphasis on difference. Progress was piecemeal, a process of accommodation: of the good from the old with the brilliance of the new; of safety with risk. Solution of existing problems released different difficulties to resolve, some a greater threat to human life than anything known before to man. Peace on earth – meaning rest, rather than the absence of war – was an impossibility. Susan did not mind that this was so. She agreed with Willem that the status quo required perpetual challenge. There was no final goal, not for the individual, nor for society, nor for the planet. Susan celebrated change in every area of her life, even in those with which she felt comfortable: within marriage and motherhood. The gains, in her experience, eventually outweighed the losses. Susan was convinced that Willem was right in demanding, on behalf of everyone alive, the creation of supra-national institutions with the authority to enforce world law. Willem's ideas she honoured; his methods she abhorred.

Unlike David, who thinly sliced his attention for distribution between multiple demands, Susan made the time to read the text which years earlier had launched Willem on his quest: Justice Pal's Dissentient Judgement. Pal epitomized the quality in mankind Susan most cherished: a capacity to deal with life as experienced day by day. Susan aimed to make herself into a lawyer like Pal. She wanted to discipline her fears to allow herself to see what was actually there, untinted by hope. On the foundation of what is, Susan sought to construct what could be.

When she first came to live in England Susan had toyed with the idea of applying her organizational gifts to orchestral management, of the London Sinfonietta, the only group serious enough about the avant-garde music her father had taught her to adore. With this career half in mind, she had enroled at the London Business School, a postgraduate clone of Fontainebleau's INSEAD. Already six months pregnant when she gained her MBA, Susan had devoted the next five years to the production and nurture of three babies. By the time she was ready to think again about work, the parochialism of the British music scene, its smug unconcern for wider social and political discourse had so alienated her that she became involved instead in Greenpeace. By accident. Through a neighbour in Bethnal Green, with whom, for something to do with their same-age children, she went one afternoon to inspect the Sir William Hardy, a ramshackle trawler moored in the West India Docks, bought by Greenpeace in February 1978 with the aid of a £40,000 grant from the Dutch branch of the World Wildlife Fund. Teams of volunteers – mostly women – were renovating the ship. Susan was attracted by scraps of overheard conversation. Things mattered to them. Fifteen minutes from home, the next day she went back to lend a hand. And the next. Until, three months later, the renamed *Rainbow Warrior* set sail to end Icelandic whaling.

From the outset there were elements of the Greenpeace philosophy with which Susan quarrelled. On all sides of the political divide she hated dogmatism. Susan subscribed to the best account principle, whereby she strove to make sense of her life by searching for the best available explanation on which, in time, with further thought, to improve. The Greenpeace activists tended to be too certain of themselves for Susan's taste. Too similar in character to Willem, in fact. Her sympathy was roused by the quieter members. Men like Jim Bohler, a deep-sea diver and radar operator with the US Navy during the Second World War, stationed on Okinawa, from where the atomic bombers took off for Hiroshima and Nagasaki. In the mid-1960s, in part to assist in his stepson's evasion of the Vietnam draft, Bohler had emigrated to Canada. Where he co-founded Greenpeace with the personal aim of bearing witness, of going to the scene of an objectionable activity and registering passive opposition by his presence.

Inspired by the example of such men, Susan felt a growing need to demonstrate her individual commitment to the campaign. With the passing of the weeks this need acquired the weight of necessity, and she set about deciding what best to do. It was her team's transformation of the fish hold of the *Rainbow Warrior* into a lecture hall, a meeting place for environmental consciousness raising, which gave her the idea of organizing a sponsored concert. Not some prestigious recital – Beethoven's late quartets, high-table choice of discs for a desert island – but a musical event of contemporary distinction.

A friend from Boston, now working in London, the young

conductor Richard Bernas, pointed Susan in the direction she instantly recognized as appropriate.

'You can't. It'd be like playing inside a kettle. Why not do something in the open air? On deck?' He raised his eyebrows, the creases on his forehead rising through an already receding hairline. 'Stockhausen's *Sirius*. You didn't go to Aix-en-Provence this summer? No indeed, why should you have. It was unforgettable. His first performance of the completed version. Ninety minutes of sorcery.'

'Might he agree?'

'I can ask.'

'Would you?'

'Sure.'

It all worked out perfectly. Karlheinz Stockhausen's son Markus, the trumpet soloist in *Sirius*, took charge of the initial arrangements – including installation of the sound-projection system, operated on the night of the concert from the wheelhouse by the composer, who had descended on West India Docks in a creative whirlwind two days earlier.

Susan distrusted the label genius. It dehumanized artistic achievement, permitted audiences to slink from application to ordinary life of music's transforming beauty . A genius was a bit of a freak. A fright. Foreign geniuses were particularly dangerous, in the eyes and ears of the British, Susan gathered from the antagonism of her colleagues to the pace at which Stockhausen talked. About inhabited planets, wheels of eternity, synergetic time odysseys.

'The man's nuts,' they said.

'He's not, he's a genius,' Susan regretted feeling the need to claim.

In a spare moment, over ploughman's lunch at the Sun In Splendour, Stockhausen composed a welcoming cadenza for the ship's fog horn to play. By which he attracted the audience's attention, advising them – through a loud hailer – to lie on their backs and watch the stars move across the sky, in cosmic consonance with his music.

'Unbelievable. The happening of the decade. London's heard nothing to compare,' Bernas cooed.

'It was pretty amazing,' Susan agreed, her eyes ablaze.

'He must dream sound. What a world he inhabits.'

'His own universe.'

The concert was a financial success too. In her promotion of the event Susan had requested either gifts of actual art or money designated to a particular project. The planting, say, of a stated number of named trees at a specific site. She wanted wealthy institutions to think about the issues, not instruct their accountant to send a token cheque. Warburgs, where David was by then an associate director, paid ten thousand pounds towards the purchase of high speed powerboats. Susan was happiest with the gifts guests brought with them on the night: a Fabergé egg from the Regent Street dealer in *objets de vertu*, Kenneth Snowman; from David Sylvester, the art critic, a Magritte bottle of clouds. Their reward was to perform the listening part in Stockhausen's act of creation. Without an audience to retain it music became spent sound, reverted to silence.

Personally, Susan tended to treasure in her memory things additional to the music. She loved to uncover biographical cross-connections between musicians she admired. In search of extremes of electronic expansion of the twelve-tone scale Stockhausen had worked on *Sirius* with Peter Zinovieff, the London-based engineer on whom Birtwistle also relied for assistance with the taped element in some of his pieces. Quality attracted quality, and bred from it, this confirmed to Susan. In contradiction of the public's image of inaccessibility, Susan found Stockhausen as engaging and articulate as a Bethnal Green barrow boy. He talked to her of his joy in the musicality of his sons,

Markus and Simon, both of whose specialist interests – improvized jazz and synthesized sound – inspired him to map new aural territories. The three Stockhausens, the other musicians and their half dozen technical assistants co-operated on the terms of familial trust and interdependence which Susan aspired to in daily life. To which everybody might aspire, given the chance of love.

At lunch in the pub Stockhausen described the dreams which lay behind his four years' labour on *Sirius*, pushing him so hard to realize their inner sound that he at one stage collapsed. Spent a week in hospital. Where the dreams recurred in hypnotic glory. Susan knew she would never forget how the tips of the composer's ears vibrated with crimson colour as he spoke to her of his vision. In memory of his visit Greenpeace named their next campaign vessel, a forty-six metre ex-pilot ship, *Sirius*.

One of the benefits to Susan of the concert was its silencing of the question: what did she plan to do with her restless intelligence? Within herself, Susan had always known domesticity was an interlude, a passing phase. Although little was directly said, she saw the relief in the faces of friends and family when her involvement with Greenpeace turned professional. They claimed their delight was altruistic, a response to the pleasure they presumed she must feel to be active again in the legal field, defending protesters at Sellafield in their battle with British Nuclear Fuels. Although her friends believed they were speaking the truth, Susan knew they were not. For reasons she did not fully understand, Susan was aware she made people feel uneasy. Even her parents had taken to evading the eye of her attention, afraid of getting drawn into an argument, picked up, twirled around and abandoned in a heap in the wake of her intensity. Only David, it seemed, she did not frighten.

'Let them be. Relax. Let go of the bone,' he advised one night in bed – where most of their talks took place.

'Why can't they speak to me?' Susan wailed, tears of hurt and anger leaving pink trails across her translucent cheeks.

'They do. You don't listen.'

'I do.'

'Hardly. You correct them before they're aware of what they're about to say.'

'It's obvious.'

'To you.'

'Not to them? If I can work it out, why can't they?'

'Because they don't think. They rub along. Paddle in the shallows. You're not wrong about the conclusions they could draw if they did think. I'm not saying you aren't a decent judge of other people's predicaments. The mistake is in imagining they see themselves accurately. How could they? Since they'd rather not look.'

Susan plucked at the cuff of her nightdress. She felt like telling David he was too much of a pragmatist.

If these people are as he claims, what a dreary hypocrite he is. Being kind and nice and neighbourly. In reality, he despises them.

At least I'm honest!

'No way to live,' she muttered.

'They're no loss. You could never be friends with people like that, my love.'

'With whom can I, then?'

Susan answered for herself: with her colleagues at Greenpeace.

The deeper Susan immersed her public self in the nuclear issue, the broader and more detailed grew the rules of engagement she devised to protect her private space from damage by work. The list, written on a back page of her pocket diary, transferred in its increasing length from year to year, began with two categorical conditions: first, because of family responsibilities, her physical person was never to be placed in danger of injury or arrest; second, every Friday, Saturday and Sunday night were to be spent with her children. These conditions she made clear to Greenpeace before accepting the post of legal adviser.

On one of her regular visits to the Cumbrian coast Susan had discovered a cottage owned by the National Trust, alone beside a farm track in the upper valley of the Esk, twenty minutes drive inland from the nuclear reprocessing plant at Sellafield. Birdhow the shepherd's home was called, three small rooms above the shippon, a windowless winter shelter for sick animals, where the chemical toilet was now installed and wood kept dry for open fires in the slate hearth above. Primitive and isolated, it was cheap to rent. The children loved Birdhow, running wild all day. And David too enjoyed the freedom of the place on the many brief breaks they took there over the years, never tiring of his ritual first early morning walk up to the head of the valley to review the great crown of Scafell, Scafell Pike, Esk Pike, Bow Fell and Crinkle Crags. While Susan never ceased to be moved by sight of Birdhow itself, its stone walls rising sheer from the grass of a lambing field, clipped short by the sheep, approached across a slab bridge over a tiny stream. She needed to do no more than arrive to feel well.

In the spring of 1986 the Goldings spent longer than usual at Birdhow, renting the cottage for three consecutive weeks, to coincide with a sustained Greenpeace offensive against Sellafield's discharge of ten million litres of radioactive water each and every day into the Irish Sea. David was free only for the first nine days, at the end of which he was flying to Dubai, from Manchester, the closest international airport. To negotiate the multi-million dollar sale of the majority shareholding in a Scottish gas extraction company. To an Egyptian, already the owner of three Highland estates. Figures on a balance sheet, items in an equable capital investment portfolio. Not land, nor crofters' cottages, nor the wild birds and animals. Life measured by financial weight.

All three children were old enough now to climb Scafell via Mickledore and Lord's Rake. Eight-year-old William, the youngest, was in many ways the strongest, and the most difficult to shift once his mind set. Tutored by David – who was himself boy-like in the making of holiday plans – to give each day a theme and schedule, little William dismissed out of hand Susan's proposal to leave Scafell for their next visit.

'No way!' he exclaimed. 'We're all fired up. It's Dad's last day.'

'"A man may stand on the lofty ridge of Mickledore and witness the sublime architecture of buttresses and pinnacles tormented by writhing mists and, as in a great cathedral, lose all his conceit"', David read out loud from Wainwright. 'Won't see a thing.' He nodded at the window. 'Harter Fell's in cloud.'

'By the time we get to the top it could've cleared.'

'True.'

'It's raining. You won't enjoy it,' Susan said attempting to dissuade.

'I will. I promise.'

'You can't promise what you'll feel in the future,' Carol, the thirteen-year-old, said. 'What if you break a leg?'

'I'll enjoy being rescued.'

The girl made a face at her impossible brother.

'You needn't come, Mum. If you don't want,' William said.

'I can't. I'm busy.'

'Then what're you worrying about?'

'You!' Susan laughed, and kissed the top of his head, revelling in the touch of her child's curls, the wakened smell of him. 'Monkey!'

Their knapsacks packed, she accompanied her family along the banks of the Esk for fifty minutes, as far as Tongue Pot, a favourite pool for summer swimming. On the way back on her own Susan was free to do something she had always wanted: scramble up the scree to a solitary yew. Which turned out to be further, higher and bigger than she guessed from the valley floor. An ancient tree, with fissured trunk. Three, maybe four hundred-years-old, an exceptional survivor. She desired to bear a tiny piece of the tree home with her. With the aid of a stone Susan broke off a projecting knot near the base, and pocketed it.

At the time when Susan calculated her children would be negotiating the slippery rocks beside Cam Spout, drops of iced spray from the waterfall stinging their cheeks, she was climbing aboard *Sirius*, in dock at Barrow-in-Furness. The day before, on a trip along the Cumbrian coast, the crew had set free three thousand five hundred emblazoned balloons, witness to the perpetual airborne release of radioactive gases from the chimneys of Sellafield. Today – 1 April, designated by Greenpeace British Nuclear Fool's Day – they were to launch onto the polluted waves above the sea bed exit of the plant's waste pipe one thousand wooden triangles, detailing the global destructiveness of nuclear energy. Susan was in celebratory mood. This was her first visit to the Lake District since the High Court triumph of the previous autumn, when her painstaking pursuit of British Nuclear Fuels Limited had resulted in the court imposition of a £10,000 fine for their criminal discharge of a radioactive oil slick. Hans Guyt, a Dutchman, charismatic head of the long-running Sellafield campaign, placed his arm across her shoulders.

'Never give up, do you?' he said.

'Never pick an argument I can't win,' she replied.

He laughed. 'What about the injunction against our interfering with the pipeline? And the fifty grand sequestration?'

'BNFL brought those cases. Not me.'

'We lost.'

Susan freed herself from Guyt's condescending embrace. 'We were bound to. The law was clear. I told you. It's wrong to let moral right affect your assessment of any action's legality.'

'Worth it for the publicity.'

'Then don't pretend I was expected to get you off the hook.'

The blanket of cloud was lifting as they rounded the harbour wall and headed out to sea. Susan's thoughts turned to the children, in the mountains. It did not occur to her, at that optimistic moment, to worry for their safety. Her wishes for them transcended everyday concerns, stretched to hope for their sharing with their father an experience worthy of memory. For David's sake, mainly. Because she knew, through observing her own father, how great his future need would be – when the children grew up and away – to feel an unbreakable link to them. For mothers it was different. Susan was certain her connection to Carol, Daniel and William could never be threatened. However hard they might try.

Susan and Guyt resumed their argument over lunch in the galley. In two weeks time, to coincide with a meeting of the Scientific Committee of the Paris Commission, Greenpeace UK was due to launch its Shut It campaign, setting out a ten-point plan and two-year deadline for the closure of Sellafield. Guyt conceded that successful resistance by British Nuclear Fuels was inevitable.

'It's all a pretence, in that case.' Susan indicated a copy of their leaflet on the table, strident in design and rhetoric. 'Pseudo-plans, which don't need to work because they'll never be put to the test.'

'Right. A ploy. A move in the game.'

Susan registered the self-satisfied smirk in the Dutchman's eyes and felt disgusted with herself, for permitting so much as moment's physical attraction to his animal ease. She hated the gamesmanship of the left, the way they made themselves into the obverse of the conservative coin, inseparable from a way of being which they thus helped preserve, at best turnover, never replace.

It's all so traditional. So cosy. So western European.

Willem believes in what he says. He's an original. Hans is just a type.

Images of her summers at camp in the Adirondacks flooded Susan's mind. Automaton acts of numb discovery in the moonlight beneath the pines at the side of the lake. Trysts and tales. Relief when these summer rites were completed without mishap. Nothing much changed when she became a counsellor – sex was no more fun without a tooth brace. Until her final year at Camp Capsicum, when David rescued her, and she first made love lovingly.

On her return to Birdhow late in the afternoon, driving cautiously through the puddles in the lane, Susan was surprised not to see smoke rising from the chimney. She let herself in and lit the fire, laid by David before he left, with rolls of folded paper to draw the flames up through cross-hatched layers of kindling wood to the raw lumps of coal. Before snatching at the unexpected solitude to read, Susan made a large pot of tea and a plate of toasted muffins for the children. She secured her hair in an elastic band, and bent her head to the freshly published pages of a new novel. By a writer whose work had always spoken to her eloquently of the woman. Of her restraint, her control, her solitary self-protectiveness; of her restlessness of will; of her drive for perfection. Lacking in compassion? Yes, perhaps. Not in passion though.

By the time David and the children pushed raucously into Birdhow's tiny main room the muffins were cold, the tea stewed.

'Sorry we're late. Were you worried?'

Susan glanced at her watch. 'Goodness look at the time!' She smiled. 'No, I wasn't worried. Lost in a book,' she admitted. 'How was it? Did you enjoy yourselves?'

There was no need for anybody to reply, she could see the answer in all four pairs of eyes. Whatever had happened, Susan recognized, without envy, she could never accurately be told. The day had already entered their memory as myth, the collective essence of family.

Something significant had happened to her too, Susan came to acknowledge through the remaining days on her own with the children in their rural retreat. A shift in feeling – which must have taken place over many months – raised itself to consciousness. She did not know what to do about her new feelings. Felt in no hurry to decide.

Maybe no decision was required?

Merely a moving on. To wider concerns than preoccupied Greenpeace. To a wider band of thinking.

Patience. Be patient, Susan said to herself.

ten

The fuss the medics made over the speed of his recovery from the operations irritated Willem more than the invasive dangers of his illness. Cancer cells were impersonal. His doctors variously inquisitive, impertinent, insensitive, indiscreet, illogical, immoral, ignorant and incoherent.

'Bloated on respect. On milksop gratitude for deliverance from death,' Willem fumed. 'I saved myself. With some expert help. Who do they think paid for their training? Who provides the fabulous facilities and stimulating work? I do, damn it! It's they who should thank me.'

He was with Madam La Baroness on the verandah of his garden room, together counting – from their calls, and from the drumming of their beaks against the trees – the pairs of greater spotted woodpeckers in the spinney. Willem reclined on a beach-chair, a tartan rug covering his knees.

'Shhh! There's another.'

'No, I can't. I'm sorry. We've got to talk.'

'What about?'

Baroness van den Hoorn stood leaning over the balustrade, wearing a short-sleeve woollen dress, skin drooping at her elbows. She turned her head to gaze at Willem. She looked frail, exhausted.

'Us. Me. Living here,' Willem responded.

She said nothing. Which he took for permission to speak for them both.

'We're killing each other. Not a sensible thing for two exceptional friends to do. Is it? Let me go. Don't fight. We'll both lose. I appreciate all you've done. You're the only person from whom I've ever tolerated kindness.'

'Don't ...'

The Baroness tried to speak, but was halted by the despicable flutter of a sob in her throat. She clamped shut her teeth.

'There are places in The Hague I can buy into,' Willem continued. 'With recuperation rooms and medical staff. Where they provide evening meals. It's time to return to the centre of things. Give A9 a final fly before I drop off my perch.'

'You'll call,' Madam La Baroness requested, control regained. 'Keep me up to date with progress.'

Willem arranged to purchase the freehold of a flat in a retirement condominium overlooking the northern dunes of Scheveningen, near the Alexander Barracks, a fifteen-minute bus ride from the parliament buildings at the heart of The Hague. He was closer to a seat of greater potential power, Carnegie's Peace Palace and its International Court of Justice, a pleasant walk through urban woods and parks from his home-to-be, past the gates of the miniature village of Madurodam.

All so civilized and undistinguished Willem decided it was a mistake, and instructed his family's banker to cancel the contract.

'Your prerogative, Mr Boymans,' this phlegmatic man of money advised. 'Costly. There's a penalty clause. Multiple fees. The other party's on top of your own. Can you afford it?'

'Can I?' Willem asked.

The banker tapped his quarter-spectacles on the file on his desk. 'I've warned you before. The settlement on your wife was unnecessarily generous. Your assets are dwindling. You're seventy now? Depends how long you live. Frankly.'

In normal circumstances Willem utilized his periodic visits to Amro Bank's head office on *Kneuterdijk* to bate the establishment. 'It's a personal principle, to sign my name on cheques in Japanese. You don't object, do you? I don't do it very well, I'm afraid. Better give you several versions,' he had insisted on arrival from New Zealand. Today was different. Willem felt closer to despair than at his worst remembered moment.

He stood up and strode to the window, stared down at the

swans on the *Hof Vijver*. What he actually saw he could not say, would not name, not even to himself.

'If I stay, when I do go it'll be feet first,' Willem said. 'Kleykamp, Jan Muschlaan. My terminal paddock. It's enormous, you know.' He turned back to face the bank manager. 'Eighty old crows. A dozen in pairs. The rest of us alone. Mostly madams. Kleykamp was an art dealer, they tell me. Built himself a house on the dunes. Years ago. I'll be okay. First night nerves. All my stuff's there. I can't back out now.'

Willem signed the papers authorizing direct debit payment of Kleykamp's charges, left a selection of his latest A9 missives for the banker's perusal, and set off for a bar on Smidswater where he fancied the waitress. Halfway down the *Lange Voorhout* Willem became aware of the need to piss – the suddenness of attack no longer a shock, the standard reaction, he had learnt, to radiation. He unbuttoned, and relieved himself against a linden tree. The flow was prodigious, Willem's pleasure commensurable. A girl in the window of a furrier laughed. Dressed in corduroy plus-fours, mustard socks and a tweed Cumberland cape, hatless, Willem bowed to his audience. The girl waved. Willem marched on towards the bar.

The woman in a black pencil skirt, dyed blond hair tied up in a coloured handkerchief, was not there. Willem sank his Jonge Genever, and departed. It was the wrong place – they did not serve food, had never employed a waitress. Nor was anyone in the next bar prepared to listen to him. At a payphone on the wall by the door Willem dialled Saskia's number in Amsterdam, pocket address book in one hand, magnifying glass in the other, receiver clamped between chin and shoulder. An unfamiliar voice answered. Saskia had moved to London. Where she lived in a sugar warehouse, with a furniture maker from Perth, the father of her child. She left years ago, the voice informed.

Willem had not realized so much time had passed since last

speaking to his artist friend. He sighed, and replaced the receiver.

Returning late to Kleykamp he was unable to manage the entry system, and summoned the night porter. The corridors seemed intolerably bright, unnaturally wide, the floors highly polished. He clutched the handrail, to steady himself. A priest emerged from the lift door at the end, wearing slippers, his arthritic body bent double.

'Ahah! Enemy within the walls!' Willem called after the padre. 'Don't imagine you'll trap me, you old fox!'

For days Willem wandered around with tears streaming down his cheeks. He stopped eating, and was admitted to the sick room for observation. Here the care of the nurses – in sleek uniforms, their hair pinned out of sight beneath caps, necks bare – revived him. He began to recognize individual faces among the Kleykamp staff, learnt their names, noticed smiles of personal concern, sensed their satisfaction with his progress. Back in his own apartment, on the top floor, he discovered the balcony and the passage of the sun across the sky, the clear sea wind and the screech of the gulls.

'You're in better spirits, Mr Boymans,' the office secretary remarked. 'Forgiven us?'

'Do you know?' Willem confided. 'Mine must be the finest flat in The Hague. The air! The view!' He gesticulated extravagantly, his words booming down the corridor. 'What a fortunate fellow I am.'

This was sheer bravado. Willem had run out of dried fruit, carnamelk and cereal for his breakfast. And washing powder for his socks. And toothpaste. And apricot jam for tea. And salted peanuts. And bread. Everything, in fact. A return visit to the supermarket, three blocks away in a cute square, with a hairdresser, two cafés, bank and post office, could be postponed no longer.

Keep calm. Deep breaths. Come on now. In .... one, two, three, four. Hold it ... yes, slowly out ... one, two, three, four ... again ... that's right. Steady does it.

You can't see. Can't decipher the labels. Distinguish the shapes. Can't read the prices. You panic, forget what you came for. Shout at the staff. Blame the crush of customers. The strip lighting. Drop your keys.

Don't!

Don't worry, nobody minds you taking your time. Ask for help. Why not? They're used to old people, the place is full of them.

Brick by brick Willem built a redeeming routine. He found, in a junk shop, a pull-handle orange press and engaged the Kleykamp maintenance man to mount it on his draining board. Each day began at sunrise with the ritual pressing of a pint of fresh orange juice, and the taking of his first tumbler-full onto the balcony – where orange peel accumulated in a wire basket rescued from a skip. His head raised to greet the sun, Willem often spent an hour with this single glass of orange juice, in the quiet of the early morning, remembering Caldera – repeating identical thoughts, rerunning the same internal picture show. He was forced to buy a new bicycle, on discovery – to disbelief, and despondency – that he could no longer reach the pedals of his old machine. In the middle of most afternoons Willem cycled down past the fairytale tower of the water pump station to a nudist beach on the borough boundary between Wassenaar and 's-Gravenhage. He hung his clothes on the barbed wire fence which closed off the dunes for military exercises, and walked miles along the strand to dry after his swim, picking up and bearing home appealing pieces of driftwood.

One windy autumn afternoon Willem was confronted by a pair of madams out for a stroll along the wide wet sands, dressed in see-through pac-a-macs and rapeseed-yellow sou'westers.

They raised their fists at his ancient nakedness, threatened to summon the police if he did not immediately recover his clothes. Willem laughed loud into the sea wind. There were – at the most – thirty people in sight on the entire expanse of the northern strand, a mile from his barbed wire coat rack, more from the nearest telephone to call the law. He smacked his thighs in delight; and later rewarded himself with tea at the rest house in the woods of Meijendel, returning the long way round to Jan Muschlaan. Willem prized his daily bicycle ride. Although at times he fretted for his safety, terrified by the motor scooters with which he shared the cycle path, unable now properly to hear or see them in advance, their brushing by causing him to wobble, occasionally to fall. He pedalled leaning forward, his body rigid, on red alert for paths which might cross or merge, anticipating the crash of death with a careless youth.

In time, Willem located a divorcée to bed regularly. The manageress of a local dry cleaners, who shared her villa in nearby De Kievet with a Finnish au pair, charged with exercizing her dog while she was out at work – a Staffordshire bull-terrier which his lover enticed into the downstairs lavatory with a knuckle bone, and locked the door, before Willem was due to call. The dog, she warned, was jealous. And clever. Had recently learnt to raid the fridge.

The manageress adroitly enjoyed their rounds of limp sex, and Willem dared hope his troubles with women were over.

Around the corner from Kleykamp, off Ruychrocklaan, was the pedestrian back entrance to the park of Clingendael, a taste-monument to the picturesque. At the centre of the park the one-time palace was now a sister centre to the Royal Institute of International Affairs at Chatham House in London, the reactionary ethics of which Willem deplored. Keen to make use of their library and reading room, stocked with current and back issues of all the foreign journals he needed, Willem hid his antagonism when applying for a visitor's card. Cambridge graduate and war hero, a distant relative of the Rotterdam family of cultural philanthropists, he was welcomed into the fold. It amused him to compose his cryptic letters of war with the world, lounging at leisure in the power-brokers' own sanctuary. Willem was adopted by the female staff as their pet eccentric, a part he played handsomely, with his upright manner, wisps of grey-blond hair and coffee break gifts of chocolate éclairs. His correspondence with – among others – the Dutch Minister of Defence, Sir James Hammond of the British Special Forces Club and the Tokyo Chief of Police, Willem kept to himself. Copies of less contentious memorandums he distributed liberally on his near-daily visits.

WJB 90/12
Kleykamp
5 June 1990

The Irish Question
    Q: Why does six fear seven?
    A: Because seven ate nine!
    ... when and where:
    'Nine' stands for Article 9 in the 3 May 1947 Showa Constitution.
    'Seven' stands for the advent stated in The A9 Syllogism, postulate 23 December 1948: when on 23 December 1948 in the courtyard of Sugamo prison shortly after midnight ex-Premier Hideki Tojo and his six companions were hanged, and those seven implosions shattered the obsolete concept of state sovereignty.
    'Six' stands for the mob of Senile Imbecile Cretinous

Knavish Saboteurs ('SICKS') which now for full four
decades deliberately and successfully has obfuscated A9. Or
simply 'sick children' as too compassionately, maybe, they
have been referred to in the words:

> The woods of Arcady are dead,
> And over is their antique joy;
> Of old the world on dreaming fed;
> Grey truth is now her painted toy;
> Yet still she turns her restless head.
> But O, sick children of the world,
> Of all the many changing things,
> In dreary dancing past us whirled,
> To the cracked tune that Chronos sings,
> Words alone are certain good.
> Where are now the warring Kings?
> And idle world is now their glory,
> By the stammering schoolboy said,
> Reading some entangled story:
> The Kings of the old time are dead;
> The wandering earth herself may be
> Only a sudden flaming word,
> In clanging space a moment heard
> Troubling the endless reverie.

Note: The Irish poet W B Yeats wrote this at the time of
what used to be known as 'The Great War' of 1914–18. It is
featured on the closing page of WJB's unpublished 1964
typescript *The Pacific Path to Peace* which concludes with
the conjecture that by no means improbably:

Like babes-in-the-wood, the moon may say, gliding
through perpetual night, like babes-in-the-wood they died.
For they harkened to the word, as babes are taught to do,

and never even came in sight of thinking out for themselves what is right.

A pity it is, musingly the moon may say, a pity indeed of such a size as justifies its spilling about the Milky Way. The greatest pity ever, or so it seems to me, that the word was spoke so loudly that the song was never heard – the song which sighed so softly that:

The wandering earth herself may be
Only a sudden flaming word ...

END

On his way home to Kleykamp on the day of distribution of this particular leaflet Willem mistook Clingendael's algae-coated moat for a clipped-grass path he had failed to notice, jumped down the bank and plunged waist deep into stagnant water.

Unaccustomed to television, Willem watched with escalating fascination and unease the build-up to the Gulf War, communicated to him in fuzzy black and white images on a portable TV retrieved from the refuse bay at Kleykamp. For hours on end Willem lay without movement, stretched on his back on his bed by the window, a batwing aerial balanced on his chest, mesmerised by the pictures beamed from around the world onto the screen on a shelf on his bedroom wall in dune-side Scheveningen. Address after address to nation after nation by kings, prime ministers, presidents, dictators, warning 'my' people of the danger of civilized life's imminent collapse.

If an unelected autocrat loses his mini-throne in the Arabian desert and the price of oil rises, skateboarding ceases to be viable in Venice, California? Willem did not understand. And he wanted to. Hence this fixation on real-time TV news. The verbal audacity of Western leaders stunned him. He watched and thought and eventually made personal sense of it all.

Saturation television is proving most instructive! The cleverest politicians tell the truth, knowing they will never be believed. Knowing that a sanguine citizenry will assume they mean something else. That they're lying, in order to confuse the enemy.

Nobody in Britain believes John Major intends to pulverize the shattered populace of Iraq until they hand over their President to the Red Cross to stand trial for crimes against humanity. 'No, no, Mr Major's smarter than he looks,' the Brits mumble into their pints of Australian lager. 'It's a bargaining position. Got to be. War crimes, who cares? The *Belgrano* was well sunk. It's the frogs you want to watch. That Mitterand. With his weasel diplomacy. Banging on about a non-military resolution. What's he really up to? That's what I want to know.'

That's what the people are saying.

I was the same. I didn't take war seriously. Not until 1944, and we were there. Doing the unimaginable things it never crossed our minds they expected us to enact. On the ground. To other human beings.

On television on 23 January 1991 General Colin Powell, the youngest Chairman of the Joint Chiefs of Staff in American history, born and bred poor in the Bronx, the son of Jamaican immigrants, stated his case plainly: 'Our strategy for dealing with this army of occupation of three hundred and sixty thousand men is very, very simple. First we're going to cut it off. Then we're going to kill it.'

Willem heard the words, saw them form on the General's lips and still, despite all he had experienced, all he had read, all he had thought, did not believe Powell could mean what he clinically said.

'We are not, not not, not, not deliberately targeting civilian casualties, and we never will,' General Norman Schwarzkopf –

the commander of Operation Desert Storm – insisted at a press conference on 4 February. 'We are a moral and ethical people.'

A week later, on 12 February 1991, the former US Attorney General Ramsey Clark presented an alternative version of the events of war in his on-site report for United Nations:

> In all areas we visited and all other areas reported to us, municipal water processing plants, pumping stations and even reservoirs have been bombed. Electric generators have been destroyed. Refineries and oil and gasoline facilities and filling stations have been attacked. Telephone exchange buildings, TV and radio stations, and some relay towers, damaged or destroyed. Many highways, roads, bridges, bus stations, schools, mosques and churches, cultural sites and hospitals have been damaged ... We are raining death and destruction with our technology on the life of Iraq.

At 4.00 the next morning over a thousand civilians, the majority women and children, died in an air raid shelter in the Amiriya district of Baghdad, when an American F-117 Stealth Fighter dropped two 2000-lb delayed-fuse, laser-guided bombs down a ventilation shaft past the ten-foot thick concrete ceiling of their bunker. King Hussein of Jordan – British-educated, an old Harrovian, prize-winning cadet at Sandhurst Military Academy – declared a three-day period of national mourning for his Iraqi brethren. Willem conceded that the King had a point. Allied pilot shoot-ups of Jordanian truck-drivers plying their legitimate trade on the main road from Amman to Baghdad, eight hundred miles from the fraternal Arab quarrel in Kuwait, had to be illegal. 'The West aims to obliterate all the achievements of Iraq and return it to primitive life by using the latest technology of death,' His Royal Highness King Hussein ibn Talal pronounced. 'This is an assault against all Arabs and

Muslims, not only the Iraqis. The real purpose behind this war of offence is to destroy Iraq and rearrange the area, putting it under foreign hegemony.'

Sickened by the militarism of the President of Iraq, plain Saddam Hussein, Willem nevertheless found himself admiring his insight into the motives of the political elite:

Western Imperialism attended to its interests in oil when it established these dwarf states of Kuwait and the Emirates. Thus it prevented the majority of the sons of the people and the Arab nation from benefiting from their own wealth. As a result of the new wealth passing into the hands of the minority of the Arab nation to be exploited for the benefit of the foreigner and of the few new rulers, financial and social corruption spread in these mini-states ... Any Iraqi, Arab or Muslim taking part in a commando attack against the nations participating in the barbaric aggression against Iraq, will be considered a martyr in the Mother of Battles ... Victory is now and in the future, God willing. Shout for victory, O brothers. You are fighting thirty countries, and all the evil and the largest machine of war and destruction in the world.'

Stirring stuff, Willem muttered at the television. They'll never get rid of him.

'The free flow of oil is necessary to protect our jobs, our way of life, our own freedom and the freedom of friendly countries around the world,' argued the American President, George Herbert Walker Bush, a wildcat Texas oilman, co-founder in 1953 of the Zapata Petroleum Company, through which he acquired his private millions. 'American jobs, I'd say, come under the heading of the security of the world ... We're dealing with Hitler revisited, a totalitarianism and brutality that is naked and unprecedented in modern times. And it must not stand. At stake is not only some distant country called Kuwait, but the kind of world we'll inhabit.'

Dead right! A world dominated by trade, in arms and in oil, structured to keep secure the rich in their wealth.

> Hell no, we won't go
> We won't fight for Texaco

Willem clapped the film of the American dissidents all along the route of their protest march through the snowy streets of Washington.

War resolves nothing. Doesn't everyone on earth know this by now?

At the end of the forty-two days of Gulf War Willem threw his salvaged television set into the moat at Clingendael.

'Hypocrites! War-worshippers! Criminals!' he shouted at the emotionless windows – and stomped off for a walk in *Nieue Scheveningse Bosjes*.

As often happened, Willem lost his bearings and missed the part of the woods he was aiming for. Close by a different stretch of public land, he came across a house set back in seclusion from the street, which it struck him – without warning – would have been the perfect home for his mother. For him too. In a country where as a growing child, because his mother would have felt she belonged, he would also. Willem sat down on a log bench opposite the bright brick house.

He stared in not out. At himself. With unforgivingness at the infrequency with which he gave any kind of thought to his parents. Willem fought for honest recall of when a picture of his mother had last formed in his mind.

Years ago. How many?

Willem was unable to name the year she physically died. Because for him his mother was by then already dead.

Was she never alive to me? Or did I decide, one lonely afternoon of my childhood, mentally to kill her? I don't remember doing such a thing. Don't remember dreaming of doing it.

Sad. It's sad.

Willem surveyed his retrospective choice of family home. It was obvious, now that he properly looked, what had attracted his attention. The ochre brick, enlivened by string courses and window embrasures in rust and ash-grey, reminded him of his favourite building in The Hague: H P Berlage's Gemeentemuseum. Which must be in the vicinity, he thought, not entirely sure where his walk had ended up. The grounds were enclosed within a wall, of the same brick, integral in design to the house, with cut-out sections of modernist railings and a pair of matching iron gates to the crescent drive. The evergreen trees in the compact garden – a cedar of Lebanon, several scotch pine and two monkey puzzles – appeared perfectly placed, by man not nature, their branches casting protective shadows, barely moving in the breeze. In the far corner a tarmacadam tennis court made Willem grin, at the thought of surprising cousin Rupert with the sophistication of his top-spin serve, mastered in practice. His smile widened, recognising that if he had grown up in Holland, his East Anglian sort-of-cousins would have remained strangers. And boarding school a British joke, not a yoke around his neck.

Willem thought of Berlage as Frank Lloyd Wright's European delegate. A man of narrower ambition but broader intellect. An influential writer and teacher, and gentle moralist. Willem abruptly stood up and strode off into the woods, away from the house. He was furious. At the lazy escape he had permitted himself from difficult feelings about his parents into idle architectural chatter. Equally suddenly he stopped, lent back against the trunk of a silver birch and gazed up at the giant cauliflower clouds stacked one behind each other across the sky. He had no knowledge, he realized, of the histories which had formed his parents' personalities. Knew little to nothing about these two most important people in the world. Willem felt closer to Justice Pal, an Indian whom he had never met, than to his father, a distant stranger.

He pulled from the pocket of his waistcoat a watch and chain. It was two o'clock. At four Madam La Baroness was due for tea, her first visit to his flat. Willem listened out for the sound of traffic, aiming to catch a bus home to Kleykamp. Hearing nothing, he walked in the direction he happened to be facing, and reached the road in a couple of minutes.

'A peck on the cheek for old Boymans?' he asked of the nurse he met in the lift.

'Why on earth should I?'

'Because I need it.'

The young nurse held higher to her chest a metal tray of instruments. 'Mevrouw Verhoeven needs her injection.'

On the mat in front of the door to Willem's apartment lay a re-used manila envelope, bulging with papers. He picked it up. In letters large and black enough for him to decipher was written: 'Never again, I repeat never give me your idiot scribble to read. Falkenhagen.' Willem dropped the envelope into the bin on the landing, and turned the key in his door. The outrage of his fellow-resident was predictable. After several talks over sherry in Kleykamp's communal music room, Willem had presented Falkenhagen with a Xeroxed selection of pieces calculated to offend an ex-prisoner of the Japanese in Java.

He let himself in, and sat down to await his guest. A moment later he got up, to open a window. The room smelt rancid. He could never work out why. Unable to spot fruit rotting in the tier of raffia baskets slung from a hook in the ceiling. Or the ants marching in columns from scrap to scrap of food on his kitchen floor. Or the grease on his plates, the bits of orange stuck to tumblers, the mould in abandoned mugs of half-drunk milky tea, the dribbles of marmalade down the sides of jars, of spilt soup down the fronts of cupboards and drawers. The cloth with which Willem cleaned his dishes he had cut from the leg of a worn-out pair of trousers. Rust blotched the steel blades of his familial cutlery. The fridge door he plastered with labels soaked from wine bottles, misaligned and overlapping.

Willem lived like an impoverished student, his bookcase built of bricks and planks, and with three folding park-chairs in chipped paint placed around the white fibreglass table in the centre of the room. Wreaths of red ribbon were tied to the scissors, and to the key to the balcony door. To many things. Because he liked the colour, and did not want to mislay essentials. Papers everywhere. Folders in dog-eared piles in blue plastic baker's trays stacked against the wall. A row of Japanese paper sunflowers in bottles on the window sill. Debris collected from the beach drying in the sun. Beside the toilet a bucket of clean, cold water.

Willem passed the palm of his hand across the stubble on his chin. That morning he had neglected to shave. On purpose. For the pleasure of engaging Madam La Baroness's concern.

'Pekelvlees, you're not taking care of yourself,' he imagined her cheerily complain. 'Don't let things slide. Look at me. At ninety!'

The Baroness was too ill, Willem instantly saw, to wonder why he had not shaved. She had come to take her leave. Without speaking the words, his dear old friend was saying good bye.

'I'll drive back with you. In the car. Spend a few days in the country,' he responded.

'There's no need, you know.'

'I'd like to.'

Madam La Baroness's face opened into a smile of great beauty. 'Would you really?'

Willem did not reply, for he was already packing into a JAL shoulder bag his minimal necessities.

Three days later, in the early morning hours of birth and death, she stopped breathing, in her bed in the moonlight. Willem was there in the room, in a chair by the door. He neither saw nor heard life depart, but felt it. And stepped to her side, where he stood holding her abandoned hand until its warmth fled. Only then did Willem pick up the phone to call the doctor. Who arrived with the local undertaker, pronounced Baroness van den Hoorn officially deceased, and suggested to Willem that a glass of whisky in the drawing room might be appropriate. They had not quite finished their drinks when a creak on the stairs announced her presence, in a body bag, which the undertaker slid into the back of his station wagon. The doctor climbed in front for a lift to his home in the village. Willem stood at the top of the curved flight of steps, both hands resting on the balustrade, and watched her leave.

Willem did not return to the Veluwe for a couple of years, until September 1994, to take part in ceremonies at Commando Headquarters in Rozendall, commemorating the passage of fifty years since the Battle of Arnhem. Select veterans, Willem among them, were due to make a televised parachute drop onto the territory they had liberated from the occupying forces. Willem had twice been fielded in hostility, in Atjeh as well as on the Veluwe, with the Nr 2 (Dutch) Troop, Nr 10 (I A) Commando Unit. Useless without his spectacles, a sitting duck for German patrols, he had secreted spares into special pockets about his body, so that one pair at least would survive an awkward landing.

On the celebratory day low cloud forced the commanding officer to abort the parachute drop. To Willem's relief, for he regretted agreeing to be involved, unaware then of the intended media circus. A ground-based military tattoo went ahead, at which the dozen veterans jointly took the salute on the rostrum from their young compatriots marching past. Willem wore his green beret floppy and free, not flattened to his ear. Of the numerous medals he could have pinned to his lapel he chose, on its own, his crowned MWO, the highest Dutch wartime honour, awarded – the majority posthumously – for the most outrageous acts of bravery.

His comrades bored him with their nostalgia for the muddle and fudge of war, glorified in national memory. Willem hated this collective deceit. And said so to the serving officer detailed to attend to a regimental hero.

'Fills me with glo-o-o-m,' he boomed. 'What right have they to deny their fear? Their incompetence. Their anger and bewilderment. The luck of their survival. It's not fair on you fellows.'

'I agree,' Willem was surprised to hear. 'I can't tell you how pleased we all were the government stayed out of the Gulf War. I never want to kill anybody.'

The veterans assured each other they did not look a day older, reminisced about the brassiere size of a barmaid in Eastbourne, and railed against modern football hooliganism, against immigrant cooking smells and against spoilt, disrespectful, disillusioned grandchildren. They were all, Willem discovered, drawing service pensions.

'You should apply, sir,' his officer-attendant advised. 'We owe it you.'

'Oh. Why?' Willem wondered.

'For whatever you were forced to do to earn an MWO.'

On returning home to The Hague Willem did indeed enquire about his pension rights. A simple procedure to most was built by Willem into an assault course. He protested against the request to supply a curriculum vitae, arguing that anything of

concern to them was already on military record and that everything else was private. At a certain point during the months of
cold warfare with officialdom Willem asked who had recommended him for an MWO and what they said he had done to
deserve it.

'I'm afraid that's confidential.'

'Don't be absurd!' He laughed. 'I was there!'

'Citations are confidential, to encourage people to make
them,' the secretary explained.

Willem leapt on this. 'So! Anybody can recommend anyone
for an MWO? Alive or dead?'

'Yes.'

'I could?'

'If you wish.'

'Whom do I contact?'

'The Minister of Defence. He passes the name and action to
us. And we consider it.'

To the letter he hand-delivered the next day into the Defence
Ministry in the Kalvermarkt Willem attached a copy of a recent
memorandum outlining the circumstances of the removal of his
readership privileges at the library in Clingendael.

> To: HE, Minister of Defence
> NL 2596 GH
> The Hague
>
> Following an interview yesterday with the MWO Kapittel
> Secretary at Nassaulaan 18, WJB hereby takes leave to
> nominate for award of the Militarie Willems Orde the
> following four persons:
> A YAMASHITA, Tomoyuki. d. 23 February 1946
> B MACARTHUR, Douglas. d. 05 April 1964

C   REVES, Emery. d. ???
D   PAL, Radhabinod. d. 10 January 1967

Mutations

A   As is remarked in WJB's 1989 publication Limpid Lemma
    A9-s no. 3: '... by virtue of having been hanged on account
    of having omitted to do what he ought to have done, by
    this aspect of his death General Yamashita can claim
    importance far transcending his notable achievements
    when alive. The application of this awesome doctrine to
    Japan's most celebrated soldier, to the Tiger of Malaya no
    less, naturally motivated the profoundly rational response
    embodied in Article 9 engendered at precisely that same
    time. Ironically, however, the doctrine of criminal omis-
    sion can hugely help us to get rid of war only if it be
    broadly understood, only if its terrifying implications be
    appreciated widespread. Whereas on such understanding
    being confined to the power elite, then the doctrine's out-
    working is precisely contrary. Then it serves simply to
    maximize the chance of he/she being on the winning side.
    Then it fuels the arms race.'
B   For his 5 April 1946 address to the Allied Council for
    Japan. Transcript available from the distinguished secre-
    tary aforementioned.
C   For his book *The Anatomy of Peace* (N.Y. 1945)
D   For his November 1948 Dissentient Judgement at the
    International Military Tribunal for the Far East.

Remarks

a   Naturally your excellency will wish to have amplified
    these mutations when submitting these names to the
    Kapittel. Which next meets in September, thus leaving
    your excellency's relevant research section ample time.

b   WJB is in principle prepared to act as consultant. At, of course, a handsome fee.
c   Relevant to case C is why, precisely, has his book since years been out of print.
d   Relevant to case D is why, precisely, is his Judgement nowadays available to the public solely in a form that is both scarce and fraudulent.
    With compliments
    W J Boymans MWO
    Kleykamp, NL 2597 TV
    9 June 1995

WJB Memo 95/14
On Assault and Battery
23 May 1995

(A & B, in brief)

A
a   The attached WJB 10 May 1995 letter to the Chief Police Commissioner in The Hague indicates the A & B endured by WJB that afternoon in Institute Clingendael.
b   This memorandum conveying supplementary information is drafted specifically for the chancellor of the Netherlands Orders at Nassaulaan 18, for the better functioning of his office in ensuring that persons under its aegis be treated with proper respect (i.e. WJB)
c   In the Clingendael Library WJB had asked to be permitted sight of a certain book. The madam librarian (ML, in brief) brusquely reported that Clingendael neither holds that book nor is minded to obtain it for WJB.
d   Having cast on ML a probably baleful look WJB heard her

use the phone as he was leaving the room. As carefully WJB was descending the stair (his balance nowadays is a bit wobbly) WJB was met by ML's burly protector. Who after he had floored WJB rather grudgingly pronounced his name to be Van Der Velde.

This utterly disgraceful incident need not be further commented on here it being now in the capable hands of the police commissioner supported by the chancellor.

B

a   Item A above outlines what WJB experienced around 16.30 on Friday 19 May 1995 at The Hague's Clingendael Institute for International Relations. This item B indicates what WJB had experienced the previous day, 18 May 95, when attending the Symposium of the Royal Society for the Study of Military Science.

b   The symposium (from the Greek word for drinking together) being well stocked with Generals, WJB enquired of several: what precisely is 'military science'? From the diversity of replies WJB concluded that he might as well fall back on his favourite pearl of wisdom culled from his six army years, to wit: 'Time Spent on Reconnaissance is Seldom Wasted'.

c   That admirable adage, generally speaking just as applicable to waging war as to boating on Biscay Bay as to exploiting a double bed, seemed to WJB as the symposium proceeded to be less and less appropriate to that particular occasion.

d   Consequently WJB found himself wondering what other Military Maxim could better catch the spirit of what was then being enacted. After some pondering WJB concluded that what was most appropriate was what was destined to

become the title of the Commentary he was due to draft the
following day. This title being:
B.B.B.
Bullshit Baffles Brains
FIN

The same team of veteran Dutch commandos was invited – as
guests of Her Majesty's Government – to join the Remembrance
Sunday march to the Cenotaph on 12 November 1995, fifty
years after General MacArthur's occupation of Japan put an end
to the Second World War. British generosity did not run to air
fares. Willem and his colleagues were sent return day-boat tick-
ets from Hoek van Holland to Harwich, and on by train to Liv-
erpool Street Station, from where they disembarked in a convoy
of taxis for their official hotel, the Bonnington, in Holborn. By
which time Willem's store of social chatter was exhausted, and
he declined to accompany the gang on their Friday night out on
the town: a slap-up early dinner in the hotel carvery, followed by
the musical *Miss Saigon*, rounded off with beers and singsong on
a troop ship moored on the Thames, close to Blackfriars Bridge.

> I feel, oh! so lonely tonight, I feel all alone,
> I'm just starving for a sight of my old Kentucky home;
> I can see my mother old and gray, I can hear the
> whippoorwil;
> I can see the light for me in the window of the
> house upon the hill.

> I've seen wonderful sights, wand'ring on my way,
> But I've spent such lonesome nights, and been
> weary thro' the day;
> I'm just longing for a mother's love, and I know
> she longs for me,

Can't erase her loving face, it's the sight of all the
sights I want to see.

Willem considered giving David and Susan a ring, to meet and
bury the flag of enmity. First, though, he phoned Saskia. Who
sounded full of life, and invited him to attend an East End art
event the following afternoon.

On the Saturday morning he walked, on his own, down to
Fleet Street to see the Lord Mayor's procession of boys in bands,
floats set with historical tableaux, old Red Cross ambulances,
the guns of the amateur Honourable Artillery Company, a fleet
of National Trust Landrovers and countless other representatives of a nation at notional peace with itself, charity buckets on
the rattle. In the crush of the crowd and the clamour of competing noise, Willem understood the point of little of what he saw.
He regularly checked his watch, and at the approach of the
eleventh hour on this eleventh day of the eleventh month slipped
away to pace alone beneath the chestnut trees of Lincoln's Inn
Fields. He picked up a leaf and stripped, with the nail of his
thumb, the crinkly brown flesh of the fishbone spread of its tendrils, exactly as he used to as a child, laying the leaf skeletons in
line across the floor of a succession of tree huts. During his
minute's silence, timed on his father's pocket watch from the
beginning of Big Ben's distant chimes, Willem stopped, stood
still, and thought … of Dr Takayanagi, as it happened, not of the
attack on the bridge in the Veluwe. Thought of the lawyer's bow
ties, and of the US army lighter with which he used to ignite his
pipe. Thought of Takayanagi's disappointment at the West's cas-
tration of Article Nine.

Aspiring sincerely to an international peace based on justice
and order, the Japanese people forever renounce war as a

sovereign right of the nation and the threat or use of force as means of settling international disputes.

In order to accomplish the aim of the preceding paragraph, land, sea and air forces, as well as other war potential, will never be maintained. The right of belligerency of the state will not be recognised.

Willem recalled Takayanagi sharing, at lunch, a childhood memory. Of lying on his side in his mother's lap while she cleaned the wax from his ears with a bamboo probe, depositing the dry flakes on his outstretched hand. Takayanagi had spoken of the utter trust he felt in his mother in the execution of this delicate task; and of his triumph in producing more wax than his sister; and of the depth of his sorrow at his wife Fumi's childlessness.

'I wanted so much to witness the woman I love being a mother, nurturing life,' Willem remembered him saying. 'My job would have been to sharpen the children's pencils for school. With a penknife. I'd have liked that.'

Willem cried.

Dried his eyes and dropped in to the Sir John Soane Museum, at no. 13, in the centre of the northern terrace, on the opposite side of the square to the chestnut trees. He made straight for the breakfast room, looked up into the mirrored spandrels and miniature glazed baldacchino, and smiled in delight at the architect's inventiveness, at Soane's rampant individualism. Here, he was never betrayed.

Nor with Saskia. Willem had a wonderful time at The Hanging Picnic in Hoxton Square. Saskia introduced him as 'my old *Oom* (Uncle) Willem' – the 'w' pronounced 'v' – to friends gathered about the pierced drums of hot coals, sharing their delicious food.

From a dovecote high on the trunk of a plane tree emerged the quarrelsome calls of a pair of crows, the cycle of complaint silenced every seven minutes with a croaky 'Fuck You!' Willem joined others beneath the tree, heads bent back deciphering the distorted words of the tape. And laughing.

On the outside of the iron railings, facing the pavement, local artists hung their work for sale. Saskia's self-portrait, with her head stuck between the bars, mounted life-size at the spot where the photograph was taken, confused Willem.

'How did you do it?' he asked – when he had worked out what was real.

'Secret.'

'Seriously,' Willem asked again. 'I need to know.'

'Maybe I'll tell you. One day,' Saskia responded – and tucked her arm through Willem's as they strolled from pitch to pitch.

STILL ALIVE IN '95: a T-shirt trumpeted.

Around the square goose-stepped a column of school kids, the *Socialist Worker* placards which they carried over their shoulders, like rifles, printed with the single word ENJOY!

Willem stopped to talk to a man seated on a campaign stool beside rows of mounted and framed miniature relief models of combat aircraft, religiously accurate in shape and livery, each labelled with its wartime history. Within one large frame were models of all three hundred and fifty-two allied planes shot down by the Luftwaffe's ace Major Erich Hartmann, inscribed with the date, time and place of demise, and painted on the nose with the individual emblems of the defeated pilots. A ram, a scorpion, a pack of cards, a palm tree … and four blue porpoises. Flight-Lieutenant Webster, Willem learnt, four times survived destruction by Hartmann, to test-fly after the war jets for British European Airways.

'Who's the hero?' the artist challenged.

'You,' Willem decided.

At Factual Nonsense, a gallery in the street at the foot of the square, Saskia took Willem to see the group show 'Other Men's

Flowers' – a title from Montaigne: 'I have gathered a poesie of other men's flowers and nothing but the thread that binds them is my own' – in which she was exhibiting. All fifteen artists contributed text-based prints. Saskia linked the words adore and abhor, in flowing copper-plate, sloping in opposite directions. Willem liked this. He was moved, also, by the piece by Saskia's friend Tineke. A turquoise lithographed letter in the artist's distinctive hand, addressed to the creator of Factual Nonsense.

> Dear Joshua,
> When my Soul is crying – And everything I have
> been is unimportant – And every thing I can be
> is of no importance I am alone – Screaming -
> Turning myself inside out wishing to god just
> part of me felt Alive.
> Well – if it's any consolation – And it is –
> I'm so Happy – to have met you – You're
> strange – different.
> Almost wired in a way – And I
> like you very much.
>
>   Love
>   Tineke

They were so direct, these new communities of artists. In London. Amsterdam. Cologne. Everywhere aiming to make themselves clear to each other, trusting an unknown public to tunnel to empathy. Willem admired their faith in the life of art. Felt in their company less foolish to hold to hope for the next millennium.

> Don't you just hate all those theories, critics, books on post-this and -ism that? We need those who cannot only call a spade a spade but take that spade and ram it down on the neck

that supports: popular entertainment, artculture, American-
ization, kitsch, fascism, until the tendrils that hold them to the
betrayed people collapse and their polluted blood flows back
into the motherland.

Couldn't have put it better myself, Willem internally chuckled.
A man after my own heart.

Spending his Saturday afternoon with Saskia softened the
awfulness of Willem's Sunday morning march to the cenotaph.
The fury he felt remained inert, and he behaved himself. The
tears which poured down his face he made no attempt to hide
from the silent crowds lining the route. He was amazed he could
walk, so intense was his sense of physical hurt, maimed by the
loss of life at his side. Not only his men, theirs also. Theirs especially. His pain swelling year on year, for half a century.

The accident occurred on the march back from Whitehall to
their original assembly point in St James's Park. They were
standing to attention, waiting for a cavalry band to pass by on
their right flank, where Willem was placed at the head of the
dozen Dutch veterans. Their instruments at rest, the band
passed in silence, apart from the rattle of harnesses, the clip-clop
of hoofs and the beat of the kettle drums slung from the shoulders of a great black horse.

Willem saw it all happening split seconds in advance, felt his
balance go, knew he would be unable to prevent himself falling
… blank. Nothing.

epilogue

i

In her rented room above a public house in Mare Street, ten minutes walk from the family home on the rim of Victoria Park,
Susan watched two men prepare to paste a poster to a hoarding
at the side of a building site across the road. She was meant to be
at work, completing a report for the executive director of
Human Rights Watch, Arieh Neier, a friend of her father's. A
report around which she had been formulating ideas for a year.
Off and on. About the legal status of refugee safe houses. Susan
was bored, irritated by the games politicians played with international law. She felt manipulated like a drum majorette, forced
to make a spectacle of herself, showing off her thighs to the
crowd. It was the last report Susan intended to write.

The Maiden advertisement board was mounted high on the
blind wall of the office adjacent to the site. The men bedded the
feet of their three-tier ladder into the rubble and raised it to rest
the solid rubber wheels of the top section against the wall above
the left hand corner of a Smirnoff vodka poster. One of them
took out two of the new rolls from the back of the van, picked
up a bucket of paste and began to climb the ladder. His colleague lit a cigarette – standing on the bottom rung, his back to
the ladder – and relaxed. Up above, the man with the dented
bucket hung it from an upper rung, and with a long brush
spread paste across the mock sand dunes. The speed and easy
accuracy with which the rolls were unfurled and nudged into
place at the end of the brush impressed Susan – in two-by-four

separate manoeuvres, the men taking it in turns up the ladder, their skills matched. The first of them, Susan noticed, wore a hearing aid and appeared, from the way he looked beadily about, to be severely deaf. The other, younger man, his hair shaved above his ears, falling from the crown of his large head in a curtain of bunched ginger curls onto his shoulders, replied with a nod and a smile and the occasional gesture of a hand. They knew precisely how to act together, and were finished – it seemed to Susan – almost before they had begun. In a tail-spin of gravel they sped away to the next site. Leaving behind, in white on red:

Windows '95, '96, '97, '98, '99 ...

The Economist

Susan sat at her desk by the dormer window of her bed-sitting room, her mind drifting back over the years. She permitted herself no regrets. Sued for no reprieve. It had been a struggle. Still was.

What else could it be? Life is, in fact, a battle. Evil is insolent and strong, goodness very apt to be weak, imbeciles to be in great places, people of sense in small, and mankind generally unhappy. Yet the world as it stands is no illusion, no phantasm, no evil dream of night; we wake up to it again for ever and ever; we can neither forget it nor deny it nor dispense with it.

So said Henry James, her compatriot and fellow traveller to Europe, in escape – in Susan's case – from the pressure to conform. Escape from the national fate of being parcelled up and labelled for the set periods of life: goofy teenager, hippy sophomore, radical researcher, earth mother, chic executive, mellow ruralite. Divine dotage.

Susan recalled the sense of panic communicated by friends at Greenpeace when she held to her word and left.

'For nothing?'

They refused to understand, disdain replacing glimpses of concern.

'For space to think.'

'About what?' someone asked.

'If I stopped to think I'd go mad,' another of them said.

Susan agreed that thought on its own is useless, breeds illusion. Out of self-interest man develops economic and political theory which he attempts to pass off as a universal system; born and reared in insecurity he craves the absolute. We are human, she had tried to explain to Hans Guyt, but behave as if we are gods. We should think about where we are wrong, not parade our rich-boy 'rights' around a servant world.

Day by day at her desk Susan had given a great deal of thought to the Gulf War. Whichever way she looked, through the mushrooming clouds of burning oil, one thing remained clear: the United Nations' troops had committed outright crimes against humanity in their bombardment of civilian Iraq, killing – in direct death from the sky, and by the disease and starvation which followed – tens of thousands of women and children in their homes hundreds of peaceable miles from the invasion of Kuwait.

La Conférence Diplomatique sur Le Droit Humanitaire, 1974 to 1977: Geneva Convention, Additional Protocol 1 (1977): Article 51 para 2: 'Acts and threats of violence the primary purpose of which is to spread terror amongst the civilian population are prohibited.' (Signed in self-righteous indignation by every sovereign member of the convention – except Rumania.)

'We cannot seek to uphold international law here, and neglect it there,' President Mitterand of France advised in a speech on 12 October 1990, warning Western co-leaders of the illegality of a war of attrition against Saddam Hussein.

Susan wrestled for accommodation with the shadow cast by Sir Winston Churchill across twentieth century thought about war. To many middle-aged Americans, nurtured on newsreel and sound-bite, the image of Churchill chomping a nuclear cigar was the stuff of freedom, the democratic symbol of an indomitable will to win. Susan herself could not help admiring parts of this colossus. Part one: years before war was declared Churchill publicly demanded action to halt Nazi persecution of the Jews. Part two: already in 1938 he proposed the federal organisation of European defence, it being obvious to him that the League of Nations was worse than worthless, a pretence at security. Part three: he was the first leader to call, in 1943, for the trial and execution of anyone, of any nationality, soldier and general alike, found guilty of acts of obdurate aggression.

And yet, and yet ... Susan fought for the common ground, for a view of justice with which all sides might agree ... and yet in December 1942 this same Winston Churchill persuaded his chiefs of staff to punishment bomb civilian Berlin. 'Two or three heavy raids,' he is reported to have blustered. 'Warning the Germans that our attacks are reprisals for their treatment of the Poles and Jews.' He who also presided over the fire-bombing of Dresden, in which the buildings and inhabitants of this ancient town were obliterated in a single vindictive night, victory in the war in Europe already certain.

How did this large man calculate which city's populace to sacrifice in retribution for their government's depravity?

'The creation of an authoritative all-powerful world order is the ultimate end towards which we must strive,' Churchill said. 'Unless some effective world super-government can be set up and brought quickly into action, the prospects for peace and human progress are dark and doubtful.'

The resonance of his language worried Susan. Authoritative, he had said, with habitual conviction that his and the nation's interests were synonymous. Another powerful man mistaken in the belief that to him had been revealed the only way forward.

Susan swivelled in her chair to face the room, stacked floor to ceiling, wall to wall with books. Nothing much else. Bare linoleum, no rug. No telephone. The gas fire was alight. She glanced at the framed photographs of her family on the mantel-piece. Susan smiled. Always the children and often David – when not abroad, on business – to look forward to at the end of another day's work, waiting to welcome her home. No longer children. No longer all always there at night, only William left in school. Locally, of course. Educated by the state to take his place in the world at its widest. At ease with race and class. And with sex. They impressed her, her children. Whenever she found herself in a muddle Susan guessed what each of the three might differently say, and the knot in her mind usually untied itself.

They had recently heard – from David's brother in Suffolk – of Willem's Remembrance Day death, his skull smashed beneath the hoofs of a horse. Susan was disturbed by the effect on David of this news. His complaint of personal betrayal was unexpect-ed, forcing Susan to recognise how marginally anyone came to know anybody else. David, the central adult presence in her life, was in many respects alien, capable of this childish aberration. The experience made Susan extra-determined to explore in her work the common ground and establish areas of incontestable agreement. Clarity, harmony, her guiding words, her talismans.

To Susan the means and the end were a single thread. She agreed with Mao Tse-tung: 'War, that monster of fratricide, will be wiped out by man's social progress.' And disagreed with him too: 'But there is only one way to do it – war against war.' Dis-agreed if by that he meant the taking up of arms, instead of laws.

A dynamic pragmatist? Consensual revolutionary? Some-thing of the sort, she thought of herself.

In this respct Susan felt differently from Willem, who had

taken flight from co-operation all his life, to judge from his papers, passed from David's care to her's, the departure point on several mental journeys of recent years. Susan acknowledged that, despite other differences, she and Willem cared about the same thing, set on parallel paths of protest by their horror at public silencing. For Willem it was discovery of the Tokyo Trial of 1946 to 1948 and the hypocrisy of victor's justice, at which not even a dissenting judge was listened to, much less the prisoners. For Susan it was reading in the *New York Times* in February 1966 a transcript of the trial in Moscow of Andrei Sinyavsky and Yuri Daniel, two dissident writers. In particular the latter's concluding statement to court:

> In the final plea of my comrade Sinyavsky there was a note of despair about the impossibility of breaking through a blank wall of incomprehension and unwillingness to listen. I am not so pessimistic. I wish to go over the arguments of the prosecution and defence once again.
>
> Throughout the trial, I kept asking myself: what is the purpose of cross-questioning? The answer is obvious and simple: to hear our replies and then put the next question; to conduct the hearing in such a way as finally to arrive at the truth.
>
> This has not happened.
>
> I was asked all the time why I wrote my story 'This is Moscow Speaking'. Every time I replied: because I felt there was a real danger of a resurgence of the cult of personality.
>
> This was not denied. I was not told: you are lying, this is not true. My words were ignored, as though I had never said them.
>
> It was the same story with another of my works. Asked why I had written 'Atonement', I would explain: because I think that all members of society – each of us individually and collectively – are responsible for what happens. All the prosecution said is: this is a slander on the Soviet people and the Soviet intelligentsia. They did not argue with me, but simply paid no attention to what I was saying.

There was a chance, Susan felt, that on the millennial tide things necessary might be encouraged to happen within the relation-ships of states. Ideas to which no attention had been paid before dismemberment of the Union of Soviet Socialist Republics and the outbreak of war in Bosnia, the belly of Europe, were now at the forefront of political discourse. Susan sensed an impending global gleam. It was time to make a public difference. At fifty years and three months old she at last felt equipped to fulfil the promise of her brilliant youth.

'Aren't you afraid you may've left it a bit late?' Susan was asked by the head of the international law practice – American radicals, with an office in Gray's Inn – to which she applied for a partnership.

'Yes,' she admitted, 'I am.'

'Why risk it?'

'I haven't the will to refuse a challenge. Is it guilt? I don't know. What keeps you going?'

'Habit.'

Susan smiled, amused at his openness, unconventional for a lawyer, the clutter of his room proof of life beyond contractual control. She liked his line of concern.

'By whom has your thinking been influenced?' he enquired.

'In the law of war? Kenneth Waltz. He's my guide.'

'Rousseau-vian.'

'Basically, yes. War occurs because there's nothing to stop it. Among states as among men there's no automatic adjustment of interests. In the absence of a supreme authority, the constant possibility exists that conflicts will be settled by force.'

'Obviously.'

'Nothing is obvious,' Susan said.

'Except that enrichment by war is a delusion. War destroys, leads on all sides to varying degrees of defeat,' the lawyer responded. 'There's no reason for it.'

'War isn't rational. It's intrinsic. I'm surprised there aren't more calls to arm, actually,' Susan argued.

'And that people don't kill one another in their homes? In their pain? It's a mystery, I agree.'

'They do.'

'Relatively few. Given the levels of social injustice. In what category of case do you intend to specialize?'

'Crimes against peace. And against humanity,' she affirmed.

Susan accepted the offer of a junior partnership in Murdoch Lessing & Wolf without discussion of salary.

Birthdays were of no interest. The best present to give Susan was to forget about her birthday – as her children had learnt over the years to do, accepting with grace that their mother was incapable of ritual surprise at parcels piled high at her place at the breakfast table. She put on a show on their birthdays; and when they were younger used to pretend to pleasure at her own. It was a relief not to have to now, wonderful to be herself with her children. A cup of tea in bed on the morning of her fiftieth birthday was all she had wanted from Carol, with a biscuit and a chat.

'Are you really making it a normal day?' her daughter had asked, aged twenty-two, perched on the side of Susan's bed.

Susan had played with the fingers of Carol's hand where it lay on the puffed cream duvet. 'I like my days. I'm already doing what I wish. Why spoil it on my birthday?'

'To celebrate.'

'Being alive? I do. Intimately. All the time.'

'What about us?'

'I love it that you exist. You know that.'

'That's not what I mean. You deny us the chance to express how happy we are that you were born. So that we could become your children.'

Susan recollected how difficult it had been not to cry into her teacup. She also remembered why it had felt important to hold back the tears: to preserve the illusion of separation she had struggled to construct between herself and her eldest child, her only daughter. Without this protective hedge, which they both knew to be artificial, manufactured of thought not grown from feeling, neither would have survived in creative health. They were too alike, too attuned. Too content with each other's company to be bothered with anybody else. Until they quarrelled, and reopened the wounds of mutual disappointment.

'We'll celebrate David being fifty. He'll want a party.'

'Dad's not you.'

'What would you like to have done for me?'

Carol had stopped to think, tapping the point of her nose – like a piano key. 'Hire an airship and float above London in the silence of space, drinking champagne. Pick chanterelles in the Quantocks, make a clear birthday soup and freeze it, so you won't have to waste time on lunch for months. I'd fancy buying you a motorbike. And borrowing it!'

'Your father wouldn't let you.'

'None of his business. It's my birthday.'

'Oh? I thought it was mine.'

'Mum, please! Don't be pedantic!'

Susan took seriously her duty to organise a public celebration for David's fiftieth birthday, two years after hers had dissolved in private peace. It was important to get it right. Susan hated careless mistakes. At anything. At peeling potatoes and failing to cut out every ugly black eye. An imperfect potato for Sunday lunch did not, she acknowledged, in itself matter. What angered Susan was evidence of loss of concentration, a wandering of the mind beyond control of consciousness. Such lapses frightened her. Flight from rational thought and action was unproductive use of time; random access to the subconscious raised images which threatened her intellectual destruction; during split seconds of ontological absence accidents happened – the slip of a knife to slice off a finger, the turn of the wheel of a speeding coach into …

No, I won't. It's not necessary. Why retell myself things I already know? Things everybody knows.

I want to get on. Get moving. Get sorted: as Daniel says.

Susan enjoyed order. She was one of those curious people who never left a mess in her wake, who rinsed each cup and plate and placed it in the dishwasher after use, passing a cloth across the drops of splashed water in the sink. For such a woman the arrangement of a cricket match on David's birthday in June was chicken feed – despite the fact that she had refused, after a single pre-marital afternoon at a Lord's Test Match, ever again to attend to her husband's favourite game (revelation that Harold Pinter and Tom Stoppard played celebrity cricket had at this same period anaesthetized her interest in British theatre). It was a question of setting the appropriate targets, then hitting them. Between the teeth. Susan delegated formation of the teams and preparation of the pitch and kit to David's brother Ben, current occupant of the familial home in Leiston, her parents-in-law having retired to the house in the spinney. Strawberry teas in the village pavilion, dinner in a marquee in the garden, the place settings, engagement of a jazz band, information about local hotels and the printing and circulation of invitations were her responsibility, the aim to fix each detail of the day to David's satisfaction.

Instead of staying with Ben in the big house, on this special occasion Susan booked the Martello Tower at the end of the beach at Aldeburgh. At night by the lake in the Adirondacks, where they fell in love, plagued by mosquitos, Susan's vision of

David's England had been dominated by his return time and again in their exchange of confidences to stories of the Martello Tower. Tales of adventure: of clambering about the half-ruined walls and parapets, manned by his childhood friends in defence against invasion by Napoleon. David had told his wife-to-be how the form of this brick gun-tower – quatrefoil, entered across the dry moat by a drawbridge – resembled the grey and white *papier-mâché* of his toy fort. Peopled by lead figures, their paint rubbed through constant handling. Cowboys and grenadier guards and farmhands deployed alongside the original set of medieval knights against marauding hoards of Red Indians and Zulu warriors and German stormtroopers, the lines of natural alliance, of innocence versus guilt never questioned. In the early 1970s the Martello Tower had been bought and restored by the Landmark Trust, together with eight acres of saltings on Orford Ness, at the neck of which it stood, on the breakwater a few feet from the sea.

Within the body of the tower were four rooms, sleeping five, with teak floors and vaulted brick ceilings.

David was amazed. 'I've never been inside.' His eyes shone. 'It's even more like a crusader castle than I imagined.'

'Than you imagine crusader castles were like,' Carol corrected – a stickler for accuracy.

'I think it's closer to being in a submarine, in feeling,' William said. 'No windows. And the waves breaking outside.'

'A badger's lair. In the bank of a wooded cline. That's not the sound of the sea on the shingle. It's terriers yapping at the mouth of our burrow. Too scared, by our smell, to enter. Dream on, man! Dad's fifty! He needs inspiration, a leg up into new stories. We've heard it all before,' Daniel teased.

On the early morning walk he took on their first full day at the Martello Tower, David picked up along the farthest shore of the Ness a piece of amber and three bloodstones, bourne south millennia ago in the moraine of a Scandinavian glacier. He told only Susan of his find.

On their two free days before the cricket match and dinner they behaved like tourists, doing things David had been brought up to believe were vulgar. A round-trip to Lowestoft in a converted lobster boat. Candy floss at the fair in Southwold, gently spinning in the shell seats of a Ferris wheel.

'I thought you'd like this quiet time together, before the celebrations. The last holiday we'll have, just the five of us,' Susan said. 'They'll drift away now. Make their own homes.'

David did not reply. His head was turned away from her, towards the lights of a cargo ship at sea, halfway to the horizon.

'Is something wrong?' she asked.

'I hope not,' he replied.

'Only you can tell, my love.'

They swung through the sky in silence, down towards then away up from the bustle of the fairground. And down again. Then up again. Near the top of each turn of the wheel, for a string of moments it seemed possible to journey ever higher, never to descend. To at least hold still, at the apogee.

Susan knew what David thought the cause of his anxiety was: her job. Knew also what in truth lodged at the core of his unease: sight of his own death, suddenly, it seemed, so close. The fact that David felt threatened by the intensity of her interest in her legal work was understandable. This did not put her in the wrong, she persuaded herself. As he slowed down, pondered early retirement from the City, she speeded up.

Why not?, Susan asked herself. Let him adjust.

I do love him. Interminably. I never said I'd die for him!

The cricket match was a great success. Captain of the village for the day, when David had hit exactly fifty runs he declared the innings closed, at a respectable hundred and eighty-seven for six.

'Fifty not out! See?' he beamed, tremendously pleased with himself.

In the field he took an impressive catch to dismiss the visitors' opening batsman, diving to his right at deep mid-on.

'Don't clap. It's not funny,' Susan castigated William, thinking David had tripped, afraid he might have hurt himself.

With final arrangements for dinner to check, Susan left before the end of the match, and walked on her own across the common in the sun, towards pennants fluttering from the twin flagpoles of the marquee. Cricket underlined aspects of Englishness beyond the reach of her sympathy: an imperial appetite to ingest, masticate and recycle rival races into the white milk of respectability – total assimilation or complete estrangement, there seemed no in-between. Worse – in Susan's view – was the Englishman's habitual silence about feelings. David's family were as bad as the rest, maintaining the private as well as public pretence that his grandfather had been the model of moral rectitude. And then there was their refusal to talk about being, at one time, Jewish. For the Goldings came originally from Russia, where until the pogroms following the death of Tsar Alexander II in 1881 the family had for centuries thrived on their faith in difference. Only in England had the habit of conformity become ingrained, was individualism sieved and – by David's generation – eradicated. David believed that enlightened might was right, that the establishment knew best for the rest. If she had been aware of this at the time, she might never have married him, Susan told herself.

Willem Boymans' nephews – his brother Dirck's two sons, with their wives – were among the eighty guests at dinner, the high point of which was Daniel's speech, delivered standing on a chair, in a blue bow tie, fashionable wing collar and slicked-back black hair – De Niro-like, he liked to imagine. Daniel had found in the attic of the house in the spinney a tuck box stuffed with old school reports. Select readings from David's placed the now-eminent banker in his childhood context, to the amusement of influential guests. 'Golding Minor is afraid of mathematics. If he demonstrated a bit more guts, he could do quite well in this subject.' 'Housemaster's report. Summer term 1962. David is a nice boy, helpful to Matron. His untidiness will, it is to be hoped, fade with maturity.' 'Measles put pay to a promising start to the cricket season.' 'He played a reluctant Titania in the Dramatic Society's excellent production.' At the end of his speech Daniel said he wished to state that he respected and loved his father and that ... But his voice cracked with the emotion of it all, and he stepped down from his chair mid-sentence.

To loud applause.

Susan was happy with her middle son. With the whole event. Until tears – of frustration – fell during the last speech, by David's oldest friend, which went on and on and on.

'You promised you wouldn't do this, Stuart. You promised me,' she mouthed.

'At the risk of our dear Susan's wrath, I cannot with a clear conscience deny you just one more story. Of that famous occasion when David and I went sailing off Cape Cod with his father-in-law. Now David, as you may or may not know, is ...'

'No, I'm sorry,' she apologized to their friends. 'He's taking advantage of the situation to break an agreement. I'm not having it.'

They glared at each other across the heads of the guests. The bore turned to his audience for support. Receiving none, he wilted, and folded himself back into his seat, head lowered. Susan beckoned to three magicians waiting by the flaming torches at the entrance to the marquee. While coffee was served the jazz band softly made music, and the magicians moved from table to table playing their tricks. Jewels vanished before disbelieving eyes, to reappear in a packet of cigarettes in some stranger's pocket.

'It's not possible.'

'It is, it happened.'

'How does he do it?'

Daniel smiled. 'It's a skill anyone can acquire, if they dedicate the time.'

'You couldn't!'

'I certainly could. So could you. If the insiders shared with you their secret. They're old tricks. Which I've no desire to exploit. Have you? What for? They'll never get us anywhere.'

In Susan's opinion the most promising signs of political change in world affairs currently came from the Far East, from Japan, generated by a surge of popular pacifism at the expulsion of US military personnel from the base at Okinawa. For over fifty years the Americans had manipulated Japanese fears of nuclear holocaust. Release – by their own hand – revived in the people of Japan self-respect. The West's way of rape and denial, the way of the bully-boy, of selective justice, need no longer be tolerated. There were subtler ways of escape from war: ways of substance and culture; ways of moral practicability; ways of brilliance and simplicity. Progressive, adaptable. The way of the future.

If Susan's years of study could be said to have led to any conclusion, it was this: unless we insist that law is imagination and mind, then imagination and mind will become law, of a kind which sustains the state and kills the individual. Susan was no knitted peacenik, no new age positivist. Man, she knew, was imperfectable. Benedict de Spinoza came close to the truth years ago: 'By sovereign natural right every man judges what is good and what is bad, takes care of his own advantage according to his own disposition, avenges the wrongs done to him, and endeavours to preserve that which he loves and destroy that which he hates.'

Susan agreed. And judged the point of living within a community to be moderate this destructive nature of individual man. Sadly, states had also proved to be bloodthirsty. Susan despised mass destruction, wanted the means to kill in interstate hate to be withheld from sovereign political right. She was encouraged by the fact that at the close of this century of war the Japanese planned to reassert their constitutional faith in non-belligerence and to revitalize their intellectual will to protect the things they loved by means other than the threat of violence. It was understandable that Japan's wartime generation, witnesses to the might of Little Boy and Fat Man, had declared their intention never again to maintain armed forces. That the Jiyu Coalition should now reverse the intervening years of militarization and propose the supra-nationalization, under UN command, of the entire Japanese self-defence force and armaments industry was equally sensible, in Susan's professional judgement. A logical response to settlement by the Swiss of the Nazi bullion problem: by making available an interest-free loan of three hundred billion dollars to the International Committee of the Red Cross for the foundation of a global Peace-Keeping Force. The proposed arrangements fitted the traditional needs of both these nations. Not a gift, nor a sacrifice, but a deal to eradicate the instability of war from the world market place, in which the Japanese supplied the men and the machines to form the basis of a credible planetary defence force and the Swiss paid for it. Japan rid itself of a belligerent capacity which contravened the country's constitution and Switzerland of money which could not be used because nobody owned it.

Determined to push for parallel enhancement in the powers of the International Court of Justice, Susan was registered to attend the Third Hague International Peace Conference, due to be held in the Dutch administrative capital during the last summer of the twentieth century. Murdoch Lessing & Wolf's client in this venture was a remarkable woman, Kyoko Hamada, who by 1999 had become the friend of the mind of whom Susan used to dream.

Kyoko had lived in London since the early 1970s. Within months of her birth, in China in 1944, the second child of a Japanese adviser to the puppet state of Manchuria, Kyoko had returned with her mother to the family's home in Nagasaki, in flight from the war. When her father, who had expected to join them, was drafted into the army, he sent word for his family to be looked after by relatives in the countryside. Where they were saved from death – 'Near the centre of the explosion the blast was so strong that all living beings and objects had been turned to powder. There were no corpses to be seen.' (Jun Higashi) – from worse than death, saved from nuclear survival – 'I saw that the skin that had been exposed was a reddish-brown. The victims' faces were horribly inflamed. They brought to mind "watermelon ghosts". Even their eyes were burned. The backs of their eyelids were red and swollen as though they had been turned inside out, and the edges of their eyes were yellow like the fat of chicken.' (Yosuke Yamahata). That same morning – 9 August 1945 – Soviet troops invaded Manchuria, taking Kyoko's father captive. At the US Military Tribunal before which he was tried for war crimes, Eiji Hamada escaped execution, the fate of over nine hundred of his compatriots, and was sentenced instead to three years in prison. These events, although she had personally experienced none of them, changed the course of Kyoko's life, were the principal reason, she told Susan, for her being in Europe.

'I haven't escaped,' Kyoko said. 'The reverse. Like the blinded man Higashi and Yamahata saw ten hours after the bomb fell, running on feet without flesh, on bare bone towards the epi-centre of the blast, I too need to be where it's worst. Where at the beginning of my life, on the opposite side of the world, my annihilation was plotted. Where the balance of power still lies.'

Susan agreed. 'Where the powerful still lie.'

'If I allow them to,' Kyoko responded. 'It's for me to see that I'm not deceived. And to let them know this.'

Kyoko was rich and solitary. The buyer for a string of Japanese design corporations, she lived in Oliver's Wharf, with a view up river from her balcony to the turrets of Tower Bridge, in an apartment acquired soon after her arrival in London, when the docks were undeveloped and the smell of spice wafted across the water from a working mill, now a TV studio. Kyoko enjoyed her job, and the ease with which she earned a great deal of money. She lived, though, for more serious things: to support the aspirations of young artists; and for the battle to make war illegal.

It took time for Susan to understand Kyoko. Mystery surrounded her, an inaccessibility beyond divisions of culture and experience. Their differences – in the underlying assumptions about life with which they were born and in their subsequent methods of dealing with its challenges – they freely articulated, enjoying mutual illumination. Susan came to believe that she and Kyoko occupied the same ground. Not physically, but emotionally. When they shared ideas, confessing to the monumentality of their ambitions, Susan was convinced they were talking about the same thing, that they pictured a similar image. The colours were different, the shape the same. Faith in their developing friendship enabled Susan to accept areas of Kyoko's Japanese experience into which she might never gain entry. She accepted this restriction because what Kyoko permitted her to know was sufficient to appreciate the complex pattern of her friend's personality, stretching back beneath imprisoned secrets of the past. Susan knew she knew Kyoko; she did not need to possess her story.

'For twelve years I kept a hamster. Seven consecutive hamsters,' Kyoko told Susan one afternoon, over tea beneath the pointed arch of a river window. 'I bought the first in error. An Englishman in the flat below said the pet shop owner in Wapping High Street killed the hamsters he couldn't sell. Instead of caring for them. The thought haunted me, until I took one home. Then I felt content. Though my silly neighbour had been teasing me, it turned out. The males I called Haruo. Jim, in Japanese. Or John. A common name. The females Haruko. At night I let my hamster out to play. See?' She pointed to the frayed ends of her beautiful curtains, loose-woven from undyed wool. 'Five Haruos and two Harukos tore with their toes strands for their nests. As high as they could reach. My hamsters calmed me, during a period when anger almost drove me mad. A cat or a dog would have been wrong. Such animals react, regard you with a look it's too tempting, when you're alone, to interpret humanly. A hamster exists in a separate world. With recognition only of itself. Do you know, with all seven hamsters, when I cleaned the bottom of the cage and laid out fresh paper, on being placed back in they instantly peed! Each one, every time. Claimed its territory. A Haruko died young. It was playing with the hem of my dressing gown. I didn't see it. Stepped back from the stove, and squashed it beneath my heel. A Haruo I lost, and heard a day later in the cavity between the walls of my flat and the next, scratching. I made a hole where the plaster was thin at the floor, put my hand in, and clicked my tongue to call it. It came and lay on my hand, which I pulled back into the room, returning the hamster to its cage. At breakfast one morning I could see this same Haruo was agitated. I didn't know the cause. Nor what to do. I didn't understand why I felt something was required of me. In the past I'd let my hamsters sort their problems out themselves. This time was different. I lifted it from the cage. Sitting on the palm of my hand it became calm. I didn't move. Two minutes later it was dead. In my custom, I wrapped the corpse in silk, put it in a tea box and dropped it into the river from my balcony, five floors up. Haruo the last. I knew, when the coffin hit the water, I must play no further role in death. Mine, yes. Nobody else's.'

Susan could not imagine a hamster cage in Kyoko's minimalist apartment. The frayed ends to the curtains she had assumed were by design, like every other detail, not a single superfluous object in the cool spaces of this private sanctuary.

'It's by no means clear that the Jiyu Coalition will survive,' Kyoko said, on another occasion. 'If not, the transarmament plan will be shelved. The proposals are flawed at present, I admit. Discussed by the people the arguments crystalize, and the way of truth defines its own form. I hope this natural process won't be tampered with by our enemies.'

In the course of preparing her official presentation to the Third Hague International Peace Conference, Susan was introduced by Kyoko to several stimulating minds. Yasusaburo Hoshino, Professor of Politics at Rikkyo University, described the encouraging revival in activism among his students, from seeds of protest planted during the Gulf War, when young recruits were supported by their contemporaries at college in refusing to participate in the bloodshed. Susan also met the veteran politician Takako Doi, who shared her memories of the election at which Japanese women gained the vote, in 1946, when the shame of defeat bred Article Nine.

'The child of my political coming of age. Such a lazy girl. Didn't care how she looked. Who she messed around with. Too permissive, to my taste,' Ms Doi explained – in Japanese, which Kyoko interpreted. 'Grown up at last. As I fade, she blooms. I'm glad.'

'And a little bit worried?' Susan wondered.

'For my generation's baby? Born of war? Not at all. She's tough as hell.'

Susan never managed to work out through which network of internationalist influence Kyoko originally made contact with Imtiyaz Daroush, a joyous Palestinian born and brought up in upstate New York. Once married to a Cornishman, Imtiyaz now owned a turquoise house on the outskirts of Salt, where she spent most of her time, in active intrigue within palace circles – a bird of rare charm in the careworn Kingdom of Trans-Jordan. Susan loved Imtiyaz's vivacity. Although life had not been simple for her – single motherhood, a fitful career on the stage, disappointments in friendship – she never complained, remained generous and impulsive. Settling in Jordan had brought with it a sense of personal security previously unknown, she admitted to Susan. Imtiyaz was the youngest of these three women, though not by much, for she too had passed her fiftieth year. All three friends, Susan noted, had chosen to leave their countries of birth, believing in the primacy of an individual's right to self-determination above the nation's.

Imtiyaz first visited Jordan as a guest of the Crown Prince, King Hussein's youngest brother, whom she met when he was an Oxford undergraduate in the late sixties, through a mutual friend in the theatre. Imtiyaz's inattention to her family's origins began, years later, to prey on her mind. So she wrote to Prince Hassan, and he invited her to stay. It was fun, she told Susan, to hear her name called at the plane's approach to Amman, and to be the first to leave on landing, met by the salute of an army officer at the foot of the steps. With his staff car on the tarmac to carry her off at speed through machine gun-guarded gates. No customs. No passport control. To the Sheraton Hotel not the Royal Palace, she was disappointed to discover.

'What about my suitcase?'

'It will arrive,' the adjutant assured her.

While checking in at reception a red telephone rang. The hotel's manager bowed into the mouthpiece, and handed it to her.

A familiar voice boomed: 'Timmy, good that you're here. Can I pick you up? In half an hour? I'm with friends around the corner. We're having a splendid evening. You must join us.'

It was some time since anybody had called her by her college nickname. Hassan was shorter than she remembered, and harder. The lobby porters, in fake bedouin dress, lowered their heads to the ground as he passed. Imtiyaz kissed not the back of his proffered hand but his brown cheeks. He looked exceedingly pleased to see her.

'Tomorrow you'll come to stay with Sarvath and I. In our guest house. For as many nights as you wish,' Hassan said, on returning her to the hotel at the end of the evening. 'Hope you don't mind. You might have grown two heads since we last met!'

'And if I hadn't passed the test?'

'You'd've been very well looked after here at the Sheraton. Not by me. Affairs of state. He's awfully sorry. He trusts you appreciated the basalt desert. Isn't Jerash stunning? When's your London flight? Tuesday? I'm afraid His Royal Highness has an appointment with Dr Kissinger. In Cairo. He wishes you a pleasant journey.'

'Ruthless!'

'Necessary. I've private time only for reliable friends.'

Imtiyaz's house was his not hers, a loan, exquisitely simple, in a biblical village in the bare hills above the malachite green of the Jordan Valley. Kyoko, Imtiyaz and Susan argued about the arbitrary nature of national boundaries in the Middle East, map-drawn by the great powers, without knowledge of the land or respect for its peoples. Kyoko dreamed of the imposition of a five-year global moratorium on border quarrels, during which time all issues of potential contention would be arbitrated and the maps redrawn. And never again challenged, any incursion to be annulled by the new World Defence Force.

'I'd do the same with names,' Susan said.

'How?'

'From midnight on 1 January 2000, everybody holds to whatever surname they have. Forever. No name changing in marriage. Future children to take their matronym. No fuss. No paternity tests. Who could rationally object?'

These flights of fancy relieved the tension of fine-tuning arguments to place before the Peace Conference. They did not work alone. The United Nation's Law Commission itself recommended the foundation of a permanent International Criminal Court, with powers to arrest anybody accused of crimes against humanity, put them on trial and impose sentence. Any sentence – short of death. Ten years earlier, in the spring of 1989, the Security Council had adopted the Second Optional Protocol to the International Covenant on Civil and Political Rights, aiming at the total abolition of capital punishment. Support for an idea seldom extended to its implementation. From the beginning, after Max Huber's proposals of February 1945 were officially endorsed at the Geneva Convention of 1949, successive US and British governments had opposed the allocation of permanent powers to any international court. Fifty years on their tactics were unchanged: agreement in principle; antagonism in practice – on the magniloquent grounds of national sovereignty.

Their true reason?

Fear of victim's justice, Susan and Kyoko suspected. Fear of the prosecution of presidents and of prime ministers for crimes authorized by the victors in war, indentical to those for which defeated leaders hanged.

At the heart of the final draft of the paper which Susan delivered to the Third Hague International Peace Conference lay her demand for six basic tenets to the constitution of the new International Criminal Court: the majority of judges to be drawn from states uninvolved in the conflict under scrutiny; enshrinement in world law of the third Nuremberg Principle – 'The fact that a person who committed an act which constitutes a crime under international law acted as head of state or responsible government official does not relieve him from responsibility'; the court's authority to be backed by effective force, unchallengeable by national, regional, racial or religious factions; no place of sanctuary anywhere in the world for those summoned to trial; referendum approval by the international community of citizens for the principles of law administered by the court; noncapital sentences to be carried out with respect for the individual humanity of the convicted.

ii

Kyoko's two passionate concerns, the driving forces of her life, were entwined.

'They're bound to be,' she maintained. 'However many different people I feel I am, they've all had the same experiences. They are all me. My campaign to end war is inseparable from my commitment to contemporary artists.'

Susan was puzzled, and disturbed. Kyoko's voice sounded strange, her language strained, unconvincing, her comments obvious.

'I know.'

Kyoko's dark eyes watered. 'Do you also know what I'm really saying?'

They sat at dinner, at a table below the Oxo tower, looking down on to the almost completed new offices of the Arts Council, half submarine half spaceship, docked on the vacant Victorian piers of the Chatham and Dover railway bridge.

'That you're proud of Joshua?' Susan asked, guessing.

'Not proud. Pleased for him. That the quality of his concept has been recognised.'

'By the establishment. In the inner art world he's been admired for ages,' Susan protested.

'That's not enough. He wants art to be everyday. To alter the fabric of living.'

'It does. It always has. Eventually.'

'Eventually is too late.'

'For Joshua?'

Kyoko nodded.

'Are you concerned?' Susan wondered.

'A little.'

'We'll soon know. Whether or not he's pulled it off.'

'We'll be satisfied. Will he?'

Susan was reluctant to enter into detailed discussion about Kyoko's young friend Joshua Compston, co-curator of the Millennium Art Show. Joshua had the capacity, even in his absence, to take over. To monopolize. Not for his own ends. Not to persuade people to do what he wanted. On the contrary, he sought – desperately – to enable others to create what they wanted.

Susan resented Joshua's intrusion into her post-concert conversation with Kyoko – when they would by now normally be enjoying a two-way flow of insights and impressions. She loved their regular visits to South Bank Four, and these suppers afterwards, at which they gave personal shape to the electro-acoustic wizardry they had just heard. This evening she sensed Kyoko's indifference to the music, was aware of her friend's preoccupation.

'Joshua takes risks,' Susan decided to respond. 'Isn't he into fun more than satisfaction?'

'Factual Nonsense. The global conglomerate FN. No FuN without U! Yes, he likes to amuse.'

'Hundreds of thousands will join him at Bankside during the year. Millions more follow the shows on satellite. There'll be nothing, when it's over, between him and his vision.'

'I hope so,' Kyoko murmured.

Joshua was neither the problem nor the solution, but a clue, Susan concluded, crucial to continuous renewal of her own friendship with Kyoko.

'When I met him he was seventeen. The most isolated human soul I'd ever encountered. Untouchable,' Kyoko had once told her. 'At a family supper with English friends. In their kitchen, in Battersea. Joshua was at boarding school with the son. Who'd invited him home for half term.'

Susan remembered Kyoko describing the totality of Joshua's conviction that nothing he said would be comprehended by anybody. He sat wedged into a corner of the pine pew, attentive to every word, spoken and implied. Tousled blonde hair almost white, thick working-man's fingers, strong shoulders and mild grey eyes. Without warning he began to talk – about Percy Wyndham-Lewis, the vorticist, creator of the polemical magazine *Blast!*

'Blinded by neglect,' he raged. 'Laughed at and then ignored. The greatest British artist of the modern era. Painter, publisher, novelist. And you blather on about Lucien Freud!'

'Wyndham-Lewis learnt in Kyoto to cut wood-blocks,' Kyoko said. 'His work is as Japanese as Whistler's, in its way.'

Joshua's jaw dropped. He stared at Kyoko with the look of an astonished child. 'It is,' he breathed. 'I agree.'

A few weeks later Kyoko received through the post an invitation to Joshua's eighteenth birthday party, on 1 June 1988, at his parents' house by the Thames in Chiswick. Then aged forty-four, old enough to be his mother and an enemy, anyway, of previews and cocktails and dinners, she declined and invited him instead to tea some other day, down river, in Wapping.

Although Kyoko refused to show Susan the long first letter Joshua wrote to her after their talk together, she often spoke of it.

'Individual phrases. And the feelings which impelled them onto the page, I see projected in square red letters across his forehead. Even now. Till the end indelible.'

Joshua kept in contact with Kyoko, sharing with her his frustrations, and testing his plans: the switch from a foundation course at Camberwell Art School to an art history degree at the Courtauld; the opening, in Shoreditch, of Factual Nonsense, not a gallery but a synergetic enterprise intent on exploding the gap between art, advertising, entertainment and high street retail; the mounting of Kyoko's favourite FN exhibition, 'Other Men's Flowers', its title lifted from the letterpress cover of Field Marshal Viscount Wavell's anthology of poems, Joshua's copy of which had been given to his father at school in the 1950s by an affectionate housemaster. During his visit to China in the Gilbert and George entourage for their show in Beijing, Joshua made a pilgrimage by train to the place of Kyoko's diasporan birth. From where he returned with a present: eight leaves plucked from a wild gingko tree, pressed between the pages of his book of notes about the journey.

'Didn't you like the Grisey piece?' Susan asked.

'I did. He's clever. Makes communicable sense of experiment,' Kyoko replied.

'To himself. He makes sense to himself. And can express it artistically. Being clever's got nothing to do with it.' Susan's irritation at the shadow Joshua had cast over the evening she projected onto Kyoko. Aware of the unfairness of this, she instantly apologised. 'I'm sorry, you …'

Kyoko interrupted. 'I'll speak for me, thank you. All we have access to is fragments. The edges of which art illuminates. Along lines of fractured contact.'

Susan accepted Kyoko's tangential criticism. She looked out of the restaurant window, down onto the new bridge. And smiled.

'At least Harriet Walter is chair of the Arts Council. The Blair government's managed one progressive step.'

Amid the glitter of opening events in the Millennium Art Show, at the top of Susan's list was 'Serra The Maestro', commissioned by Joshua from the multi-media *exploriste* – as Josh had christened him – Heiner Goebbels: founder of The So-Called Left-wing Radical Wind Orchestra, leader of the experimental rock trio Cassiber, creator of dozens of film, theatre and ballet scores, and composer of sophisticated chamber music for the virtuosi of his home band in Frankfurt, the Ensemble Modern. None of this was known outside Germany. Goebbels' international reputation rested exclusively on sound and sight of his scenic concerts, two of which – 'The Liberation of Prometheus' and 'Or The Hapless Landing' – had impressed Susan in their London productions. She admired the passionate theatricality, the collaborative energy of Goebbels' work. Its own-ness, a quality Susan had defined in her mind.

'When I create a piece I consider myself an architect,' Goebbels had explained in a pre-performance talk. 'Making a space in which the audience can live, can contribute its imagination.'

'There's nobody like him,' Joshua claimed. 'Using the music of pillaged texts, spoken by an actor. A friend. A co-conspirator. In the brilliance of an explosion, fused with his personal vocabulary of sound.'

'Words. You put people off,' Susan teased.

'Serra The Maestro' was staged in the last of the historic city warehouses to be converted, Amazing Place, on the opposite side of the Thames to Bankside Power Station, in the central courtyard enclosed beneath seamless glass, surrounded by the audience stacked on sliding trays into upholstered capsules on the three interior sides of the six floors.

Lying alone in her seat, the music of instruments and voice – relayed through pin-head speakers concealed in the upholstery – enveloping her, her gaze drawn down onto the stage bathed in oceanic light, Susan cultivated the illusion that Goebbels and his friends performed only for her. She gave herself to Serra the sea-monster, the Maestro, a creature conjured from waves of imagination: the composer's, the musicians', the smoky-voiced actor's, and her own.

The man at the centre of the stage – the actor – wore a brown felt hat, broad-brimmed, placed squarely on his head. No rake. No dimple in the crown. He was sitting on a three-legged piano stool, from time to time twirling around, feet off the ground, the wings of his linen jacket billowing. Five more stools were placed at strategic points about the stage. The overture completed, the actor stood up. Then lay on the ground. Sat up and – after removing his hat – scratched his head.

'I looked about me and saw with a start, on the ground not far from the car, a large tangle of metal. The thought vaguely crossed my mind that I had caused this wreck, that I had perhaps been involved in some accident without knowing it. Rising to my feet – immediately several hands reached out to steady me – I moved towards the metal and saw that it was the remains of a bicycle. The metal was hopelessly contorted and, to my horror, I saw Brodsky in the midst of it.'

The actor's delivery of this speech was by its nature musical, the rhythms of meaning in which were explored by Goebbels in his accompanying score, played on guitar, flute, double-bass and amplified kobachi. Susan recognised the text: from towards the end of Kazuo Ishigura's masterpiece, *The Unconsoled*.

'I left Brodsky and went to the car.' The actor strode purposefully to the front of the stage. 'Opening the boot I found that Hoffmann had crammed it untidily with assorted items. There was a broken chair, a pair of rubber boots, a collection of plastic cartons. Then I found a torch, and when I shone it around the boot I discovered a small hacksaw lying in a corner. It looked a little oily, but when I ran a finger along the blade the teeth felt sharp enough. I closed the boot and made my way over to where the others were standing around the stove.'

He relaxed, sat down on the nearest piano stool and smiled at Goebbels, whose hands were poised above the keyboard of a synthesizer.

'One, two, three ...'

The actor crossed his legs, rested an elbow on his knee, his chin in the palm of his hand, and listened to the anarchic sounds.

He smiled again, and made sure they had finished the instrumental interlude before continuing his story, in a conversational tone. Goebbels and his musicians readjusted to the role of accompaniment.

'The orchestra finally settled and a spotlight fell on the area of the stage near the wings.' The actor lit a cigarette, and dragged smoke into his lungs. 'For another minute nothing happened, and then there came a thumping sound from off-stage. The noise grew louder until finally Brodsky stepped into the pool of light. He paused there, perhaps to allow the audience time to register his appearance.'

'Certainly many of those present would have had difficulty recognizing him. With his evening suit, brilliantly white dress shirt and coiffured hair, he was an impressive figure. There was no denying, however, that the shabby ironing board he was still using as a crutch undermined the effect somewhat. Moreover, as he began to make his way towards the conductor's podium –

the ironing board thumping with each step – I noticed the hand-iwork he had carried out on the empty trouser leg. His desire not to have the material flapping about was perfectly under-standable. But rather than knotting it at the stump, Brodsky had cut a wavy hemline an inch or two below the knee. An entirely elegant solution, I could see, was not possible, but this seemed to me far too ostentatious, likely to draw extra atten-tion to his injury.'

'And yet, as he continued to advance across the stage, it appeared I was quite mistaken on this point. For although I kept waiting for the crowd to gasp on discovering Brodsky's condi-tion, the moment never came. Indeed, as far as I could discern, the audience seemed not to notice the missing leg at all, and con-tinued simply to wait in hushed anticipation for Brodsky to reach the podium.'

A period of silence. Of speculation. The actor's expression changed. Not just on his face, in his whole body.

'Brodsky swung his baton in a large arc, almost simultane-ously punching the air with his other hand.' The actor's ges-tures were redundant: the flap of a penguin's wings. 'As he did so, he appeared to become unstuck. He ascended a few inches into the air then crashed down across the front of the stage, tak-ing the podium, the ironing board, the score, the music stand, all with him.'

The clatter of music subsided.

'I expected people to rush to his aid, but the cry that greeted his fall faded into an embarrassed silence.'

The actor abandoned the stage, head bowed. As he departed, the guitarist – a woman – took his place, bearing her daxophon. Which she played hauntingly, to the ballet-like accompaniment of shadowy images projected through the multiple apertures of three anthropomorphic movie machines. Up onto the walls of the auditorium. Onto the faces of the audience themselves, looking across at each other from their capsules. The old projectors whirred. One was mounted on a turntable, spinning the film of a boy roller-blading around the edge of the emptied courtyard of Amazing Place, his image circling the lower walls, followed on his shadow-journey by the actual noise of the wheels across the boards of the stage. An audible ghost.

The actor returned, wearing the same felt hat, his jacket replaced by an open waistcoat over a collarless white shirt with full sleeves. He opened his arms wide. And disappeared, the performing space transformed into impenetrable pitch-black. The musicians continued to play out of the darkness. The actor reappeared, his position and gesture unaltered, now contained – in hologram – within a wire cage shared by a sleeping coyote.

'The manner of meeting was important. I wanted to concentrate only on the coyote. I wanted to isolate myself, insulate myself, seeing nothing of America other than the coyote. First of all there was the felt that I brought in. Then there was the coyote's straw. These elements were immediately exchanged between us: he lay in my area and I in his. He used the felt and I used the straw. That's what I expected. I had a concept of how a coyote might behave. It could have been different. But it worked well. It seemed I had the right spiritual forces. I really made good contact with him.'

Words spoken by Joseph Beuys, Susan read in the programme, the numinous German artist of Dutch extraction, inventor of 'An Energy Plan for the Western Man', chancellor of the Free International School of Creativity and Interdisciplinary Research.

'I took part in the whole of the war, from 1941 to 1946. I was in Russia.'

'What did you see there?' Goebbels asked the actor, acting Beuys.

'Certainly not art! What can I say? I was a fighter pilot. I cannot talk about war. There were dead people lying around, everywhere.'

'Were you in Stalingrad?'

'No I was more to the south, in Ukraine. The Caucasus. The Black Sea.'

'And when the war ended?'

'During the last year of the war I was stranded in the Western front. There were no more planes, no more fuel. When peace was declared I became a British prisoner of war.'

'Can you explain how you look on death?'

'If I knock my head against a sharp edge, I wake up. In other words, death keeps me awake. Death belongs to life, you know. Now the earth is dead. How can this death be surpassed, how can it be renewed, or regenerated? This depends on humankind's responsibility. Only people can do it. Death is a reality. It is a reality. And every day, what the international power is producing is death. Again death. Even harder, even better death, even more pollution, even more destruction, you know. Therefore there exists only this one necessity. To see that everything depends on us, and that we can do it. Very easily we can do it. It's not so difficult to do. The whole power exists with the people.'

The actor, who was German, in his field also a distinguished artist, communicated Beuys's thoughts as if they were his own, in guttural English. The music of Goebbels supported him, sought to express the feelings behind the idea inside their deceased compatriot's art.

The mood changed, slipping east, musically and visually. Light flooded the stage, gaining in depth and density, until shapes formed: a lilac light-mountain submerged beneath the surface of an electric blue sea below a cobalt sky. From the distant interior of Amazing Place escaped the song of a soprano. The sound approached closer to the courtyard. A woman wearing a beaded headdress, a shawl with tassels thrown across her shoulders, floated across the light-sea. Her skirt and bodice assumed the shape of the Ark, which came to rest on the peak of Mount Ararat.

The Armenian folk-singer displayed her extraordinary voice in a song without words, which nevertheless told a story, once known to everyone who heard it. A story of battles of the heart, lost and won; of invasion and conquest; of love and sorrow and reunion. Its swooping quartertones were made to sound, in Goebbels' accompaniment, contemporary.

The flood receded, and from a cave in the belly of the mountain the actor emerged, dressed in a lounge suit.

Music.

'I believe a revolution must be dreamed quite as much as engineered.'

Music.

'I am trying to deepen what I do and think. It isn't always easy, and always requires more isolation. Perhaps I shall end my days in some cell, still trying to look behind the nonexistent mirror? To surprise reason?'

Music.

'I can't really see any point in going back to a lost paradise. For me there is no paradise and there is no loss, of any kind.'

Music.

'Pierre Boulez said these things. And I happen to agree with him,' the actor stated.

Music, to the close.

Susan descended from her capsule and drove home, without searching for Joshua to thank him for the complimentary ticket. The next morning she wrote him a postcard.

Of the two principal curators of the Millennium Art Show – MAS, for short – Susan felt she had more in common with Carl

Freedman than with Joshua. She liked the fluidity of Carl's self-belief, considered it safe to challenge his assumptions.

'Joshua seems so strong. Claims he's invincible,' Susan commented to Kyoko a few days later. 'He can't be. Nobody is. He's kidding himself.'

'And Carl?'

'He knows the dangers. With Joshua I'm afraid of falling through the ice.'

Kyoko giggled. 'He'd save you.'

Susan laughed too. They had been to a difficult meeting, with one of the British lawyers in the Bosnian war crimes trial. It was good to relax with her dearest friend.

'Carl's from Bradford?' she asked.

'Leeds,' Kyoko replied.

'Originally?'

'I've no idea. Does it matter? He's Yorkshire-born. And his father before him.'

'Not if it doesn't matter to him.'

'Why should it?'

'It shouldn't but it does to many. To identify.'

'Identity politics,' Kyoko fumed. 'A device for not listening to what people say. If you know where we "come from", our nature is fixed in your mind. Us Japs, yids, gays, krauts, commies, pre-defined out of individual existence.'

Susan reached across the table to touch Kyoko's arm. 'Not by me.'

Kyoko stroked the appeasing hand. 'I know. I know.'

Susan filled their cups with fresh tea. 'I like the speed at which Carl thinks,' she said. 'He's twice as fast as me at making connections.'

'The mental network. The streams and tributaries of a great river system. Different from Joshua. He's a rocket.'

'A shooting star?'

Kyoko frowned. 'Incandescent? Maybe you're right. That he burns too bright.'

'He'll survive,' Susan reassured. 'His generation has powers of self-renewal. Mythological powers, I sometimes feel. Then I think: no, I mustn't burden them with my hopes.'

'Not Joshua. The weight of responsibility he bears is of his own making. He neither credits nor blames anybody else. For anything.'

'He cares, though. What people think. A lot.'

'"Memories of entertaining the crowd by crushing toads with purple bricks."'

'Joshua's letter?'

'"Knowing that when I feel happy I actually am happy is a difficult concept to grasp. Misery and destruction seem to come more easily. Against my reason my will dictates that all of me should suffer."'

'Aged seventeen?'

'"Because of my tiresome ardour of spirit I find it difficult to rest. I always have to search."'

'And find. They do find things out,' Susan felt it necessary to insist. 'These restless creatures. To the benefit of us all. If we listen, and watch.'

'We do. We will. Tomorrow.'

The next morning Susan and Kyoko were due to meet Carl at Bankside, for a private view of 'Black Rose', the main MAS exhibition, five days before the official opening on 14 February, St Valentine's Day 2000.

Carl was there waiting for them at the riverside entrance to the Tate Gallery of Modern Art, regenerated by the Swiss partnership of Herzog & de Meuron from the carcass of the power station. This inaugural exhibition was Carl's creation, Joshua having elected to manage the performance events and to host the year-long Partarty, six nights a week, from ten until dawn. Susan had not seen Carl in a suit before. He looked younger, and frailer. Though at thirty-five he was no longer young, and had never been frail, physically or psychologically. He was small-boned, that was all, with a pale complexion, no flesh spare.

'Smart suit,' Susan stupidly said.

They mounted one of the asymmetrical trees of translucent escalators, up onto the suspended walkway running at three-quarter height down the trunk of the building. The cross-river view from the top astonished Susan, looking along the line of the pedestrian bridge which connected the two cathedrals, direct from the Tate's Multiples Shop to the Gift Arcade in the crypt of St Paul's.

'Can the work compete? With the building and view?' Kyoko wondered.

'If not, it's not by artists,' Carl replied.

The two women followed him across an open sculpture court to the entrance to the temporary exhibition halls. Susan dropped a couple of paces behind Kyoko and Carl, to study them, to see if she could read the physical signs of their feelings. She herself felt tense, fearful of not liking what she was about to be shown, of being unable to hide her disappointment – presumed inevitable in the wake of Carl's ambition to make art as moving as a movie, as memorable as victory in the World Cup. Carl and Kyoko appeared relaxed, shoulders loose, fingers unfurled. Susan envied them their faith.

'I want you to understand. My only desire is to put on an exhibition I privately wish to see,' Carl had turned to say on the escalator.

The press release, which he had at the same time handed to them, stated the public aim, concluding: '"Black Rose" is an antidote. Injected into the cultural body to restore equilibrium to the heart and mind, and to that place where emotion and intellect are undivided – the soul.'

Passing beneath the arch of a rose bower – cast in shiny black bronze, many times magnified, the branches as thick as a man's arm, with flowers the size of pillows and thorns like bayonets – they abandoned the light, white galleries of the permanent collection to enter Carl's abstract of the world. Down a wide corridor lined in silver foil, along one wall of which were displayed fifteen Andy Warhol *Disaster – Electric Chair* paintings. Single and multiple images, each spotlit to precise size, isolating in solitude the seat of death.

Susan overtook Carl and Kyoko, and was first of the three to step from this glistening passage of vacant paintings into the pitch-black void beyond, its proportions measureless, the air vibrating to an electronic drone, barely audible, transformed from sampled sounds into a single low note. Floating – it seemed – in space were three vast rectangular projection boxes, blown-up astrachromes of panels by Hieronymous Bosch, teeming with crazed life: from the *Millennium Triptych*, from *Disembodied Souls Suffering on Earth*, and from *The Fall of the Damned into Hell*. Susan wandered towards the lightbox on her right. She found herself smiling. At the giant dismembered ears glowing in the blood-orange light of background fires; and at the monumental scale of several musical instruments, a hurdy-gurdy, an organ, a bombardon, house-sized, in and out of which scuttled naked figures. A man blew notes from a recorder gripped between the lips of his arse. Another musician she spied crucified against the strings of his harp, beautifully drawn, accurate in technical detail. Out of the toad-mouth of the choirmaster, a gryphon, spewed bars of music, the transparent pages of the score spread across the buttocks of an upended chorister.

'Look,' she whispered to Kyoko, standing at her side. 'The

bent man on the path beyond the pond, balancing an egg on his back!'

'Instead of his head. The bearer of perfection.'

Susan frowned, in an attempt to emulate her friend's seriousness. Her smile again broke through. 'I can't help it. Such fun he's having. Bosch, I mean.'

She sobered up in the next room, naturally lit, where pain was portrayed as a matter of daily fact. In the self-portraits – drawn, and cut from wood-blocks – of Kathe Kollowitz; in John Altikowlski's *17.15*, photocopies of the timetables of the trains conveying Jews across Europe to the extermination camps, pasted like wallpaper around the entrance and exit to the gallery; in Leon Golub's *Mercenaries* series, his paint scraped to the thinnest skin with a meat cleaver, the canvas rubbed raw, its surface dry as bone; and in all eighty-five of Francisco de Goya's *Disasters of War* etchings, mounted close together, the titles scrawled in chalk across the wall above: 'the same', 'so much and even more', 'the same elsewhere', 'this is still worse', 'I saw this', 'and that too', 'nobody knows why', 'Truth is dead' …

Susan had seen the Golubs before, at the ICA in 1982. Without emotional effect. Commodification of war over the intervening years had altered her response, and she now felt as well as saw their point. The gap-toothed seeming-smiles of the hired soldiers she received as screams, the victors no less battered and brutalized than their victims. This time she understood that by choosing to be in a room with pictures such as these she was herself compromised. Contaminated. The artist too. And Carl, the curator. Even Kyoko, the purest person she knew. Susan glanced across at Goya's Napoleonic looters and torturers, then back at the modern mercenaries, and shook her head. The same old apocalypse. No let-up. Status and power fortified by violence, by generation after generation experienced and forgotten.

Her head full of her own thoughts, Susan walked slowly

through the next room, looking at without seeing the wall-sized Jackson Pollocks and accompanying text from J G Ballard's novel *Crash*. She walked inattentively on through the fourth 'Black Rose' gallery, presenting thirty Cindy Sherman photographs, hung in chronological sequence, charting the breakdown from concealed anxiety in the black and white film still enactments to her dishevelled and degraded fashion poses, in full colour, the artist eye to eye with the viewer in mutual collusion.

Confronted in the art-free grey hall beyond with a choice of directions to take, Susan sat down on a steel bench and waited for Kyoko and Carl to catch up.

'Which way?' she asked.

'Is it too much?' Carl wondered.

Susan adjusted an earring. 'A bit grim.'

'It's everywhere, sickness and despair. Don't we gain strength from recognizing difficult feelings?'

'If we're equipped to survive.'

Frown-lines disfigured Carl's pale forehead, his black hair shaved to stubble. 'Deny the darkness and how can we tell when it's light? How forgive the crime of existence?'

'Art helps,' Kyoko replied – on behalf of the three of them, Susan felt. 'Stops us eating our own tails, like wild animals in cages at the zoo. Artists can't remove horror. They may attempt, by examining the intolerable, to overcome it.'

Carl pointed to the open arch on the right. 'In there's a new piece I commissioned from Douglas Gordon. *12 Hour Blue Velvet in Three Parts*. His usual stuff. Brilliant. It needs time, though. You could return later for him, if you like? Through there,' he added, pointing at the second archway, 'is a Mat Collishaw installation. A revival of *Untitled*, in its original state. I wouldn't like you to miss that. Then, well ... .' Carl shrugged. 'The show continues, room by room. Till the end.'

Susan had never heard of Collishaw, and did not know what

to expect. She stood at the entrance to the small room, which at first sight appeared empty, and cautiously raised her eyes to the ceiling, afraid – for no discernible reason – of what she might find.

On closer inspection Susan realized that a pair of narrow vertical slits in the wall opposite, reaching from below the level of her knees to above her head, were windows. She walked over and peered at a scene of frozen dereliction – the vestiges of some catastrophe to come, it struck her; while in the same instant aware she was in fact looking at an unrestored internal flank of the power station, girders rusted, bricks mildewed, against which Collishaw projected three slides of a woman hanging by chains from her feet, her arms outstretched, the image inverted, in sisterhood with the prophet Jesus.

The return succession of 'Black Rose' galleries began with a library-like space dedicated to archival display of the American artist Chris Burden's work of the mid-1970s. Despite the sensational nature of his tests of self-inflicted endurance, the grainy grey snaps and home-typed texts drained the events of glamour. On the night of 12 September 1973, in *Through the Night Softly*, Burden had crawled, hands bound behind his back, wearing Y-front underpants, through fifty feet of broken glass strewn across Main Street, Los Angeles. A tape recorder on a table beside the photographs relayed the scratched sound of his heavy breath. 'There were few spectators,' the documents noted, 'most of them passers-by.' About the *Shoot* records – where a friend at five paces trained a rifle on the flesh at the side of the artist's left arm and pulled the trigger – Burden had written: 'It was strange to see a smoking hole in my arm and to feel no pain. The combination of dispassionate written statement with the still image, like a police file, is really important. I offer no explanation as to why these things happened, or what they meant.'

violins violence silence

These words of Bruce Nauman's, in pink and lime neon, the letters overlapping, were suspended halfway to the roof inside the entrance to the next room, otherwise occupied by the sculptor's *Rats and Bats (Learned Helplessness in Rats II)* of 1988, on loan to the Tate from the collection of Mr Gerald S Elliott in Chicago. Susan gazed at the yellow Plexiglass maze enclosed within a steel and glass cube, emptied of life, her eyes drawn to the alternating images screened on six obliquely placed monitors: film of a rat in a cage, and of a man beating with a baseball bat a sack. Susan flinched at the sight suddenly of herself, caught in the shifting beam of a closed circuit video camera and projected larger than life onto the gallery wall. 'PAY ATTENTION MOTHER FUCKER', she remembered Nauman exhorting her, in a lithograph, years ago, before marriage and England, during the Vietnam War, when he art-spoke for the nation's conscience. 'My work comes out of being frustrated about the human condition,' Susan recalled Nauman saying on television. 'And about how people refuse to understand other people. And about how people can be cruel to each other. It's not that I think I can change that, it's just such a frustrating part of human history.'

Making art, to Nauman, was a matter of life and death. Melodramatic yet true, for him.

There were neon signs in the next room too, more intimate in scale and content than Nauman's. *Kiss me – Kiss me – Cover my Body with Love*: the request of Tracey Emin, a close friend of Kyoko's.

'It's strange the way friendship with Tracey, her company for an hour, a day, a night, eases and comforts. While contact with her work is often painful,' Kyoko said. 'Strange, because there's no fabricated division. Tracey seeks all the time to tell her experience of truth, in life as in art.'

'She demands my attention, I feel,' Susan responded.

'Why shouldn't she? She gives it too. Flowingly. Isn't that how friendship grows roots, bears individual fruit? In intense attentiveness to each other's stories of feelings? When you hold Tracey's deep, bright-dark gaze you see her seeing simultaneously you and herself, while you see yourself as well as her.'

'Yes. With Tracey things are mutual or not at all,' Susan agreed.

At the perspex barrier, as instructed, she removed her shoes and carried them in her hand to stroll across Emin's new autobiographical piece, a felt blanket carpeting the entire gallery, with texts and images sewn into a many-layered collage, leading the viewer on complex journeys through the artist's life and dreams. Her map of the soul.

'Nearly through,' Carl murmured.

'You've managed it. An exhibition which touches me,' Susan said.

'Thanks. I'm glad it works.'

'What drew you?'

'To become a curator of art? I got here by accident. Which suits me fine.' He paused. 'I like art's questionable status, its tenuous chance of success.'

Susan put her shoes back on and walked through into a melancholic room of late Rothkos, among which she peacefully took breath for many minutes. Before moving on to the penultimate gallery's display: Gilbert and George's *Dusty Corners and Dark Shadows*, sepia photo-pieces of themselves in the desolate chambers of their Spitalfields home; four or five quietly desperate oil paintings by Luc Tuyman; Edward Hopper's *Nighthawks*, *Office in a Small City* and *Rooms by the Sea*; the *Crying* video of 1993, by Georgina Starr; and Damien Hirst's *The Acquired Inability to Escape*.

'Why this, not another Hirst?' Susan asked Carl – the three of them staring through seven-by-seven-foot steel-framed plate glass at an architect's adjustable chair squeezed against a basic table, on which lay an open packet of cigarettes and in-use ash-tray, the internal space hurtingly restricted and hollow.

'Personal connections. Do I have to explain? Because I like the title, if you need a reason.'

Susan thought she understood.

The final work of the show – on a plinth, off-centre, in a room too large for it – ridiculed suffering. The creation of Jake and Dinos Chapman: their re-enactment by toy soldiers of each of Goya's *Disasters of War*, placed side by side on a flat green plain. A miniature monster dog retched half-digested human limbs. A cart at the cemetery gates disgorged its load – as if a band of revellers returning drunk from market. Painted lead bodies piled high in a common grave cuddled each other. Model swords and rifle barrels gleamed in play pen make-believe.

Above the exit to 'Black Rose', applied in an italic hand direct to the wall, Susan read:

> *Characters of ordinary morality, under circumstances such as often occur, are so situated with regard to each other that their position compels them knowingly and with their eyes open to do each other the greatest injury without any one of them being entirely in the wrong. It shows the greatest misfortune, not as an exception, not as something occasioned by rare circumstances or monstrous characters, but as arising easily and of itself out of the actions and characters of men, indeed almost as essential to them, and thus brings it terribly near to us.*
>
> Arthur Schopenhauer

'I need a coffee,' Susan said.

'Have you been to the cafe on the bridge?', Carl asked.

The two women shook their heads.

'It's interesting.'

Kyoko smiled. 'To whom? Not to you!'

Carl grinned, exposing the gap between his front teeth. 'You know me too well.'

The porthole lights embedded in the metal treads of the bridge changed colour at the alteration of angle and distance of vision. Looking back, Susan saw that a light which had been lemon on approach was mauve in her wake, a decorative conceit which appealed to her. The cafeteria was slung below the rainbow arch of the walkway, its trusses, roof and body abstracted from the contours of a bat, sleeping out the day upside down beneath attic rafters; though in colour and character more like a dragonfly, or a humming bird, constructed of anodised steel and clear glass, the bright clothes of staff and tourists visible from the river bank.

They sat at a spindly table in one of the zigzag window bays, the Thames flowing far beneath the transparent panels at their feet.

'I feel I'm in a helicopter,' Susan remarked.

'In a film.'

'On set. In a performance.'

'The coffee's good.'

'I think I'd better have something to eat. Or I'll faint,' Susan said. 'Can I get anyone anything?'

Standing in the queue to pay, Susan decided she liked the theatricality of the place, the focus of attention down onto the tidal waters and the passage of pleasure boats, of police launches and of a flotilla of barges full of disfigured traffic cones. When she returned to the table Carl and Kyoko were discussing Joshua.

'We're not competing. Partarty is no more nor less significant, in our eyes, than 'Black Rose'. The division came naturally. An extension of our essential concerns.'

'"Large scale spinning, reliance on the conviction of pure feeling", in Joshua's case,' Kyoko quoted.

'His needs are different from mine. He wants all the time to be at the centre of events.'

'Does he go each night?'

'Without fail. Before the first party-goers arrive till after the last leave. Circus master. Genie of The Utopic Space.'

'An aircraft carrier, holding steady through the storm. From which artists take off. And return to, to refuel. His self-image already years ago,' Kyoko told them. 'Arrogant fantasy? I never thought so. Knowing him, it seemed perfectly real.'

Overcoming her initial scepticism, Susan had grown to trust Kyoko's faith in Joshua. And now, after all the words, he was living his dream. In an inflatable multi-coloured plastic play place, tethered for this millennial year beside the nation's citadel of contemporary art. A travelling exhibition and event hall, erected and dismantled in a day; spearhead of FN's assault on the laxity and ennui of current culture; brain-child of Joshua and his best pal, Gavin Turk, the Surrey dissident, father, mother and son to 'Gavin Turk' the sculptor. The ultimate, the ideal, The Utopic Space. Where better to Partarty?

Drop a flippin' stitch or two, pick up a piece and uplift your splendid souls: Strictly Gordo's Shoreditch chant of the early '90s, rewritten in neon across the Bankside sky.

The Utopic Space – opening a week late, on 7 January – made no promises as to which of the advertised acts were to be seen on a particular night, as to what from Joshua's elastic list of artwork was to be installed on wall, floor or ceiling. 'You're the party-artists,' Joshua encouraged the uninitiated. 'Don't contemplate. Gyrate. You get what you make. Parti-cipate. Throw a plate. Break with your state of angst. Parturiate. Give birth, mate.'

Between the acts music played, selected from juke boxes.

People danced. On the stage. Between the tables. On top of tables. Some performers required Joshua's guidance, unaccustomed to the anarchy of self-entertainment practiced by a hip gang of weekend regulars. Other artistes loved it, queueing to enter on subsequent nights in private with the crowd, at slack half hours giving unpaid performances in rival corners. Jaap Blonk, the Dutch voice-man, was a notable first-wave success. Famed for his revival of Kurt Schwitters' noise classics of the 1930s, Blonk surprised audiences with twenty-minute improvizations, largely wordless, with their wild leaps from facial clowning through soundscapes of tragic beauty to wicked political caricature. Actor? Poet? Musician? Artist, for sure. Of expressive distinction.

On big band nights Joshua decreed that The Utopic Space be cleared of chairs, tables, vending machines and extraneous art-works, anything impeding celebration. Funky night out for friend and foe alike: he used to publicize the happenings at Factual Nonsense, spilling out into the street, a canyon of polychrome brick furniture factories down which he and his artist friends drank and danced away the summer of '94, the year the FN myth took public hold in young heads high on J & B's free cases of Bombay Sapphire. Partarty was Joshua's chance to demonstrate FN's fun on the planetary scale of his ultimate design.

The Leningrad Cowboys – from Helsinki ('other bands ride limousines, we drive tractors') – were the first in his line-up of gala stars to mark each full moon of this opening year of the new millennium. In their unicorn hairdos, hand-painted suits, half-metre winklepickers and Ray Charles shades, fresh from a tour of Australasia, the ten Fins were as dedicated as Joshua to serious fun. The same with the composer, architect and double-bass virtuoso Barry Guy, founder of the London Jazz Composers Orchestra, the year's second new mooners. Featuring Witch

Gong Game 11/10, variably structured around sound characteristics – Fast Time, Walkdown, Quietest Ever – represented by symbols drawn from the work of Scottish painter Alan Davie, held up by conductor Guy on art cards to direct individual members of his orchestra down alternative paths in the score. A kaleidoscope of notes. Music making for the open-eyed.

Susan had no desire to hear any of this. She and Kyoko were awaiting the June night on which Carl's brother Adrian was due to play, and Yurabe to dance.

'How will they manage it? Fix the calm to concentrate?' Susan asked.

'In their usual way. Patiently,' Carl replied.

'Such a contrast to … to everything, really.'

'Joshua likes that. Surprising people. He hates uniformity.'

'Will the audience listen?'

'Watch? Feel? It's up to Adrian and Yurabe. To catch them in the web.'

Yurabe danced Butoh. To music composed and performed by Adrian, on *shakuhachi*, *biwa* and *koto*, live and on tape; sound-sculpted about the place of creation through speakers; lit by syncopated spots and by the projection of slides of historical art onto Yurabe's whitewashed body. When Susan first saw them perform, in an orchard in Hampshire, she recognized what she had sought through the years to experience in concerts of modern music. Had on occasion found, in disparate forms. In Crumb, in Ligeti, in Kagel, in Stockhausen, in Birtwistle, in Boulez, in Xenakis, in Berio, in Goebbels.

'Butoh is primitive and sophisticated. Appropriate to the time and place of its emergence, 1950s Japan,' Kyoko had explained to her in the orchard. 'An art born of the will to rebuild consciousness from torn fragments of the spirit and mind. The Butoh dancer plays with his body like an instrument. Like a child in paradise, seeking the self abandoned there.

Though the movements are slow, the oscillation of emotion is rapid. A vortex of feeling. When he dances Yurabe is uncertain, he says, whether he's a bird or the sky.'

Susan recalled the brushed silk slip in which Yurabe reappeared from sudden darkness, to muted calls from Adrian on the koto. A bald old lady, tossed across the waves of summer grass, he rose from the ground into the air. His tensed feet very very slowly ceased to touch earth, the tips of the fingers of one hand grasping the branch of an apple tree, into which he climbed. Susan reheard in her head the music Adrian made at this point in the performance, with bamboo sticks on a graduated row of pottery bowls, accompanying a tape rich with sampled sound of traditional Japanese instruments.

She was looking forward to seeing and hearing them again.

Unhappily, Yurabe never danced in The Utopic Space. Because Joshua Compston died, and the Partarty with him. In the early morning hours of 6 March, alone, on a mattress hidden away on top of his picture store at Factual Nonsense. There was blood, and bruising of his face from the violence of his physical resistance to death. By his own hand – by accident, some of his friends chose to believe. Inhaling halophane from a bottle scavenged one night at the semi-derelict German Hospital up the road in Dalston. In search of sleep, Joshua stilled the beat of his heart till it stopped. Haemorrhage – in protest: from nose and mouth and from the sockets of his eyes – failed to awake him from the depths of his desire for rest.

'I was amused by the way I toyed with my life,' Joshua had written to Kyoko when he was seventeen. 'I would inwardly chuckle at the thought of drinking my painting white spirit. Chuckle because I regretted I couldn't have some orange juice (there was none left in the house). True, I never actually tried with a hundred percent desire for death, but some of the actions I perpetuated could have gone wrong. Or right, as the case may be.'

'I can hear his voice,' his friend Tineke wrote in the *Big Issue* on the eve of his funeral. '"We're going to do this thing – yeah – and we're going to do it right". He had so much energy, so much enthusiasm for life. My main fear for Joshua was that he always seemed the perfect candidate for spontaneous combustion. Sometimes when he got really excited on one of his Factual Non-sense party rants, he would glow with a burning intensity. He went to extremes of generosity, and of bringing people together within the vision of art. That's why he was loved so much.'

Artists carried Joshua's body – in a Turk and Hume painted coffin – from the door of his gallery home in Charlotte Road to Christchurch, Spitalfields. The crowd was escorted by mounted police and TV news cameramen. Obituaries in the national press outnumbered the reviews of FN events while Joshua Compston lived.

iii

'He mightn't have made an error. It might have been right. For him. Who are we to say? Joshua's death was his own affair. The loss we feel isn't his responsibility. What was he supposed to do? Give us less, to protect us from missing him so much when he disappeared? Which he warned us, many times, might have to happen.'

Kyoko paused. Susan remained silent, seated behind the desk

in her office at Murdoch Lessing & Wolf, surprised at Joshua's intervention into their business discussion, six months after his burial.

'An Icarus, he dared fly too high,' Kyoko continued. 'The wax melted and his feathers fell off. He was bound to die, I now see. I'm reminded of the pilots who flew missions to Okinawa. Dropping sheer from the sky onto the decks of American warships. At Chiran, in southern Kyushu, a day's drive from my home in Nagasaki, there's a small airbase from which the planes took off. Now a museum. With relics of their beauty. Their brevity. Like cherry blossom. Photographs of boyish laughter. A pilot taking leave, on the tarmac, of his dog. There are the sashes they used to wear, embroidered by a thousand female hands, binding them to sacrificial courage. Hundreds of last letters. From a boy named Shigeru, I remember. "It is time to go now. The cherry blossoms boarding the sacred planes are in full bloom. I shall join them and bloom splendidly myself. Father, Mother, everyone, please don't worry about me. Take care. I just wish you all a happy life in this world." What I admired about Joshua was that he never gloried in his pain. Never made of the struggle a legend.'

'Others have. Sadly,' Susan said.

'Which is why we mustn't romanticize our work. We'll be extra vigorous now. Victim's justice isn't a slogan, a dream. It's reality.'

Susan agreed. After authorization at the Third Hague International Peace Conference of a new International Criminal Court, their campaign to bring to trial a Western leader for his country's war crimes gathered public force. Theory was nearing practice.

Allied conduct of the Gulf War continued to be the focus of Susan's legal investigations. From before the official offensive against Iraq till long after it was over, numerous crimes had been committed in the UN's name. Documentation had emerged of US deceit of the General Assembly itself, through falsification of satellite photographs of the build up of Iraqi troops on the Saudi Arabian border, exaggerating the threat by five times. President Mubarak's support for inter-Arab warfare was bought: by American liquidation of Egypt's $6.75 billion military debt. Bombing of Iraq's electricity generators had reduced output to four per cent of pre-war supply – ninety-six of every hundred light bulbs in hospitals, schools and apartment blocks ceased to shine, destroying civilian life.

Water, Susan decided, was the vital resource disruption in the supply of which constituted the most blatant war crime. Under Articles 51 to 58 of Additional Protocol 1, the only legal defence of the coalition's destruction of Iraq's urban drinking water system was to gain 'definitive military advantage in the circumstances ruling at the time'. On the face of it unsupported by the evidence. For Susan had obtained documentary proof that Western policy makers designed the bombing raids as punitive, not strategic. Victory, they calculated, at minimal loss of Allied life, would place them beyond reach of the law.

'In the past it always has,' their barrister advised. 'A fit of millennial prodigality?' He wobbled his chins. 'They've given this International Criminal Court teeth. Which could bite. In my opinion.'

'The plaintiff has to be "a specified entity"? That's to say a nation state, not an individual? While the accused must be a person, not the state?' Susan double-checked.

'Correct. Any signatory to the convention able to demonstrate the existence of direct injury to its citizens or territory resultant from an illegal act of war authorized by the indicted individual.'

'We've got a case. It's time to find a country prepared to bring it.'

'I thought we already had. Or don't you believe in Imtiyaz?' Kyoko asked. 'I do. What can we lose?'

'The advantage of surprise,' Susan replied. 'If the Jordanians refuse, they'll trade knowledge of our legal arguments for development aid.'

'Why tell them the details?' the barrister challenged. 'Stick to the principles. They're common knowledge. The judgements at Nuremberg and Tokyo are law. They have the power of the beaten path.'

'Which nobody walks down!'

'Show a leader who's lost in war the way. He'll take it,' Kyoko reasoned.

Susan remained unconvinced.

Imtiyaz's research in Amman settled the question. She discovered that two Jordanian nationals, irrigation engineers on intergovernmental exchange, had been killed at work on a reservoir on the outskirts of Baghdad, the non-military target of deliberate Anglo-American aerial attack. Imtiyaz interviewed the families. Obtained from them copies of the death certificates. The outrage of his subjects' fellow-feeling for the people of Iraq impressed the Crown Prince when Imtiyaz told him, in confidence, of the tenor of their statements. Memories of desert massacre were fresh, fuelled by the displaced presence in Jordan of a million Palestinians, refugees from defeat by Israel in 1967, forty thousand of whom had volunteered to join the Iraqi army to defend the disputed border with Kuwait. The Hashemite Royal Family's legal, moral and internal political obligations pointed in one direction. Their personal, cultural and international loyalties in another.

'You're asking us to indict an ex-Prime Minister of Britain for crimes against peace? Accuse John Major of butchering our brothers?' Prince Hassan shook his solid head. 'He did, it's true. By his aim to exterminate an Arab president.' His head continued to shake, in anger. 'A disgraced politician. Leave him be. My revenge is to forget the man existed.'

In London, Susan persisted in her quest. The legal arguments fell into place one by one , forming a line of logic it was impossible, she believed, to refute. She set about persuading the rulers of Jordan to fulfil the will of their people. To the benefit of everyone. Of Britain's citizens too, she argued.

Susan had refused, from the birth of this idea, to think of John Major as an adversary. The war system was her enemy, not the prime minister in person. A fighter plane dropped the bombs on the engineers at the reservoir, not Mr Major. He was neither more nor less guilty of the slaughter of men than those who elected him to govern in their name. No guiltier than anybody else who believed in the justice of the Western world going to war to protect oil supplies from the Persian Gulf. Except that Mr Major, the commander-in-chief of his nation's armed forces, knowingly broke international law. Acts of aggression for which – like the war criminals of Germany, Japan, Rwanda and the former Yugoslavia – natural justice demanded that he stand trial.

Susan fought to disembowel the myth of security by force of arms.

How?

In her office one afternoon, turning the knot of Esk yew over and over in her hand, Susan found herself drafting Major a letter. It felt necessary to set the words on the page at her desk in Gray's Inn with precision. As if she could write the world right.

Susan added and crossed out, adjusted the balance of her sentences until satisfied there was nothing left inside worth seeking to communicate.

Dear John Major,

I've given so much thought to the matter about which I'm writing to you, that it's hard to know where to start. At the end? Yes, at the final point of it all: the illegality of war.

War is illegal. By the Pact of Paris (Kellogg-Briand) of 1928 the nations who fought the First World War agreed never again to settle their disputes in battle. Printed and signed, in black and white. Henry Stimson, Secretary of State of the United States of America, knew what he was up to: 'War between nations was renounced by the signatories of the Pact of Paris. This means that it has become throughout practically the entire world an illegal thing. Hereafter, when nations engage in armed conflict, either one or both of them must be termed violators of this general treaty law. We denounce them as law breakers.' Despite similar promises after the Second World War, we've had to await the new millennium for mechanisms to be put in place for the enforcement of this law. It's happened. Sense has prevailed. The laws of war are to be arbitrated by the International Criminal Court, its judgements policed by the World Defence Force.

While commitment to peace by the global powers stands firm, this time we need a case to bring which establishes the integrity of universal justice.

Before you stop reading, convinced I'm a utopian dreamer, foolishly reliant on the rule only of law, be patient with me a little longer. I'm aware of the inevitability of judicial prejudice and error. All the same, I'd argue that a supra-national court of law with the power to enforce even its mistaken arbitrations is an improvement on leaving countries in dispute to fight it out. Not in all but in most cases, an imperfect solution imposed by judicial authority is preferable to anarchy. And yes, I'm also aware that political expediency has been a more effective peacekeeper than legal treaty. It is the politics of collective security which has so far prevented the world from sliding into a final catastrophic holocaust.

My point, though, is to extend to all individuals the safety organized for themselves by the dominant nation states. I want the hundreds of thousands of people who die each year in armed conflict to be saved. I'm afraid I care more about soldiers than generals. About Iraqi soldiers too. And Jordanian engineers.

I expect you're familiar with the opening proposition of the United Nations Charter of 1943: 'Since wars begin in the minds of men, it is in the minds of men that the defences of peace must be constructed.' Now I realize that my feeling – though we've never met – that I know you is false. I don't really know anything about you of personal substance. All I know is how you appear in the media. How they – are 'they' more powerful than you, Mr ex-Prime Minster? – choose to represent you to me. Perhaps you're not the decent chap you seem to be, a person of human dignity, in victory and defeat. All the same, in your mind I'd say you'd say that the international element of your career in politics was dedicated to the enhancement of peace. My hope is that you'll agree to prove this, beyond question.

I'm enclosing a selection of documents, together with analysis of their relevance. These you may wish to pass to the present occupant of no. 10 Downing Street, to discuss with him and with the government's lawyers the merits of our case. I assure you we bear you no personal animosity and are committed to non-adversarial principles of legal procedure, aimed at uncovering the truth, not at outmanoeuvring the defendant. You will be listened to, intently. All the mitigating circumstances – there are many: you've behaved no differently from centuries of European leaders – will be aired and considered, if not by your counsel then by ours. Almost forty years ago, when I began to study law, I was deeply affected by reading about the show trials of Russian dissidents. I felt pained, within myself, at the inhumanity of their treatment. Since then I've done my best to see that the stories of the accused are heard, are listened to till they are understood. You may be dismayed at the final judgement of

your war crimes trial. Or maybe I will. Either way, we will both have
received a fair hearing. This I guarantee.

Like others who've experienced the pressure of leadership in
modern warfare, you no doubt share the determination of your
predecessors to outlaw war. I'm thinking, in particular, of the last
clause of the Atlantic Charter, signed by Winston Churchill and
Franklin Roosevelt on 14 August 1941: 'Eighth. They believe that all
nations of the world, for realistic as well as spiritual reasons, must
come to the abandonment of the use of force. Since no future peace
can be maintained if land, sea and air armaments continue to be
employed by nations which threaten, or may threaten, aggression
outside of their frontiers, they believe, pending the establishment of a
wider permanent system of general security, that the disarmament of
such nations is essential. They will likewise aid and encourage all
other practicable measures which will lighten for peace-loving
peoples the crushing burden of armaments.'

By offering yourself for trial the arms race will be slowed and
international security enhanced. It's within your powers, Mr Major,
to make history.

The death penalty is disbarred from use by the International
Criminal Court. If found guilty of crimes against peace and against
humanity you will not hang. Your lawyer will argue that war is the
continuation of peace by stronger methods, the necessary
enforcement of natural order, without which the world cannot
survive. It's possible the judges may decide that actions against Iraq
conducted by the British forces under your command were legitimate
self-defence. Your attorney will cite the then-current United Kingdom
manual of military engagement: 'A belligerent is justified in applying
compulsion and force of any kind, to the extent necessary for the
realization of the purpose of the war, that is, the complete submission
of the enemy at the earliest opportunity with the least possible
expenditure of men, resources and money.' Our counsel is bound to
suggest that the expenditure of men – not excluding, it is to be

presumed, women – in the Gulf War was disproportionate to the military need. In retrospect I guess you yourself regret killing hundreds of thousands of ordinary Iraqis, without also ending the reign of Saddam Hussein.

Are you convinced the path you chose was right? It wasn't lawful: that's our contention.

I've been influenced in my thinking by the philosophy of an Indian judge at the last successful prosecution of an ex-Prime Minister for war crimes, at a trial which took place in Tokyo between 1946 and 1948. This judge's name was Radhabinod Pal. He believed that international law must recognise the individual as its ultimate subject and the maintenance of his rights as its ultimate aim. The individual human being's freedom, in all its complex manifestations, is the purpose, Pal argued, of the rule of law as an instrument of peace and progress. Those two Jordanian engineers, at work on purification of the water supply to the people of Baghdad, were denied the freedom to live. For no good reason. Were killed by you, in law. By mistake, you may claim. No excuse, according to the direct precedent of the Tokyo Judgement.

Our purpose is not punishment. My friends and I believe that prosecution of you for your conduct of the Gulf War will lead, eventually, to destruction of the war system. I echo words spoken by a Greek delegate at the Geneva Convention on Human Rights of 1949: 'We are conscious of the will of all those whose lives, either as hostages, deportees, or in the field of battle, were sacrificed to the madness of men. All these martyrs do not demand revenge but they cry out that their sacrifice shall not have been in vain. They ask to be the last victims of these theories according to which man exists for the State and not the State for the happiness of its citizens.' War is human loss, never victory. There are better ways of resolving our differences.

Yours sincerely,
Susan Golding

Susan took the draft letter home with her to show Daniel, who was coming to supper.

A smile spread across his face as he read it.

'You're not serious about sending this?' he checked.

Susan laughed. 'Of course not.'

Daniel handed the four double-spaced sheets back to his mother, and sat down at the kitchen table. Though only thirty, his hair was beginning to thin, like his father's. Unlike David, he did not seem to mind. About anything very much. A BBC news journalist, he was incredibly easy going. Susan adored him.

'How're you getting on?' Daniel enquired.

'Fine. They've approved nomination of the judges. Eleven on the bench. We're due in court in the spring.'

'Shouldn't Bush be on trial too? I thought he was the main man in the Gulf War?'

'Yes, if we can get him.'

'You'll be away a lot.'

'Not far. The Hague. I'll fly home every weekend.'

'Has Dad forgiven you?'

'My lack of dependence? I think so. I haven't recently asked. It's his problem. Isn't it?'

Daniel nodded. 'Fancy a quick drink before supper? At The Mitre?'

'Sure. I'll change. Won't be a minute.'

Upstairs, in the main bedroom overlooking Victoria Park, Susan slipped out of her office suit and into a pair of jeans. Her pleasure in Daniel was different from anything else she had ever experienced. Not long ago she had worked out why. When her middle son almost died, as a baby, of meningitis, all she had wished for was his survival. Susan's subsequent love for Daniel was unconditional. She felt happy simply that he existed. That he was alive.

iv

The trial opened on 3 May, in the assembly room of a disused military academy, expensively converted to its grave purpose. The modernist building was rectangular, on three floors, with a squat granite tower rising above the central entrance. The double-height assembly room measured approximately ninety by one hundred and fifty feet, fitted out in walnut-toned panelling, with imposing daises for judges and defendants, and convenient perches for movie cameramen. The long, highly-polished judicial bench dominated the left-hand side of the court (as seen from the spectator's balcony, for entry into which queues formed early on the overcast first morning). Below the judges sat the recorder and clerks, facing separate desks in the middle of the room for the main prosecutor and leading defence counsel. Behind them were their assistants, with access to the prisoners' dock, directly opposite – at a lower level – the president's throne at the centre of the judge's bench, backed by the flags of the participating nations. Beside the judicial podium was the witness box, and on a matching spot at the other side of the room the marshal of the court's stand. Beyond these, at the far end, were more desks for the administration of proceedings, and a corner reserved for the defendants' families. The court was ringed at its upper levels by sealed glass booths in which worked translators, commentators, stenographers: the men and women of the world's press. The film crew's klieg lights hung from the ceiling, contributing to the heat and drama.

A team of military police, wearing white gloves and helmets, fanned out across the room in a final security check. On completion of which the defendants were led up hidden stairs into the dock. A handbell rang, the massive wooden doors at the end of the court room swung shut, and the judges entered in single file from their chambers.

Captain van Meter, the court's red-haired marshal, banged his gavel down on the sloping top of his stand.

'The Tribunal is in session and is ready to hear any matter brought before it,' he announced.

The President rose to his feet.

'Before assembling here today, the members of the bench signed a joint affirmation to administer justice according to law, without fear, favour or affection. We fully appreciate the great responsibility resting upon us. There has been no more important criminal trial in all history.'